What others are saying

Award:
This book was Finalist in the Sixth International Literary Awards at Washington State College, 1986 (titled The Ingenuous Soldier).

"*Cherries* weds a matchless sense of dramatics with the ability to tell a marvelous story. You have staged excellent, realistic action with convincing effect. You paint your main characters and supporting characters with passionate realism. *Cherries* has a compelling magnetic quality. Parts of it are unforgettably conceived and written."
--Manuscripts International, 1987

"*Cherries* has received a favorable response from our readers' staff. John Podlaski has created a moving narrative that carries conviction in its sincerity and point of view; some are colorful and harrowing experiences. It is recommended for publication for its high-voltage narrative style, contemporary interest, and human drama."
--Carlton Press, Inc., 1985

"Once I started reading John's *Cherries*, I couldn't put it down - intense, provocative, mesmerizing, emotional, and heartfelt. In this tome, John brings you with him to the fields, rice paddies, and jungles of war-torn Vietnam; he actually makes you feel as if you were there with his platoon. You feel the fear, the awe, the drama, the bravery, the sorrow, and sometimes even the humor, of young men in battle. John, thank you for sharing your experiences in the field of battle with us. I feel it is a 'must read' for all Americans who want to know just what our young soldiers went through then, and also for a peek into the window of what they are now going though in today's battlefields all over the world. I think all of us need to read John's story, as we owe sharing our warriors' experiences as ardent repayment to them for their sacrifices made in defense of our treasured freedoms. Thank you, John, for sharing your soul and your sacrifice. There are many of us who do indeed appreciate all of our veterans and their efforts."
--Jerry Kunnath, friend and author

CHERRIES

A Vietnam War Novel

Paul,

To somebody special that I grew up with. You have been a friend to me longer than anybody else, and must remember when I was in Vietnam. I remember all those wonderful memories when growing up: George T. Bass, Balduck Park car toboggan run, jam sessions in my basement & many others I can't remember. It is my pleasure to know you Pablo!

Janek Podlaski
7/29/2010

CHERRIES

A Vietnam War Novel

By

John Podlaski

Wordclay
3750 Priority Way South Drive, Suite 114
Indianapolis, IN 46240
www.wordclay.com

ISBN: 978-1-6048-1736-2

Cover design © 2010
http://DigitalDonna.com

Edited by: Mrs. Nicole A. Patrick
Editorial Coordination by: Mrs. Janice J. Podlaski

Printed in the United States of America by Wordclay

Dedication

A special thank you to all who have encouraged me to proceed with this novel. I am especially indebted to my daughter, Nicole, and to my wife, Janice - without them this work would not exist. This book is dedicated to them and to all American Soldiers: past, present and future.

"There's many a boy here today that looks on war as all glory, but, boys, it is all hell."
--Gen. William T. Sherman, Address, 1880.

Chapter One

Many U.S. Army personnel began their journey to South Vietnam from the Overseas Processing Terminal in Oakland, California. Outside the compound, hundreds of hippies and former soldiers picketed against the war. They targeted those soldiers who were dropped off by cabs and heading toward the main gate. Dozens of Military Police officers (MP's) were holding the protesters at bay and created a clear path through the mob. The crowd tossed flowers at the passing soldiers and chanted loudly for peace. Some in the group pleaded with the new arrivals, trying to convince them to quit the military and refuse to fight in the war. Most of the soldiers passed through the gates without hesitation; however, this was where some have been known to stop and seriously reconsider their options.

John Kowalski had passed through the main gate earlier in the day and was wandering through the massive facility, a converted airplane hangar, in search of friends from his Advanced Infantry Training (AIT) Platoon at Fort Polk, Louisiana. The entire training Company had received orders for Vietnam and each person was to report there after a thirty-day leave.

The PFC was maneuvering his six-foot frame through a maze of cubicles. The rubber soles of his newly issued combat boots squeaked loudly while crossing through the quiet sections. The fresh coat of wax on the red tile floor looked slippery and John took each step cautiously as if walking on ice.

The twenty-foot by twenty-foot cubicles were formed with eight-foot high pieces of plywood, rising up toward the thirty-foot high ceiling. Each of these enclosures held a dozen bunk beds; many were filled with sleeping youths waiting their turn to fly off to war.

His efforts to find a familiar face within the maze were unsuccessful, so he started off on a quarter-mile hike to the other side of the building, which was set aside for recreation.

He found the area to be quite active and noisy compared to the morgue-like atmosphere that he had just left. Here, there were hundreds of highly enthused soldiers, all dressed in green jungle fatigues – the green machine! Scores of pool and ping-pong tables cluttered the area, but were barely visible through the crowd. It was quite obvious that many of the players were having difficulty with their games due to the close proximity of the many spectators inhibiting their movements.

John stood on the outskirts looking in. He removed his olive green baseball cap and ran his hand over the light brown stubble of his peach fuzz length hair. Satisfied that it was again growing, he replaced the cap and traced a line across the rough four-inch long scar on the left side of his neck; the consequence of a confrontation with some escaped felons during Basic Training. His hazel eyes continued to scan the many faces, hoping to spot someone he knew.

Just then, a player on a nearby ping-pong table backed up quickly to return a hard serve from his opponent. He tripped over a spectator, creating a domino effect on the group standing behind him. When it was over, a young soldier, looking as if he were only fifteen years old, found himself sprawled out on top of the adjacent pool table. The remaining balls were scattered, some falling to the floor, along with a stack of ten-dollar bills. All of this happened as an African-American soldier, twice the kid's size, was preparing to take an advantageous shot.

He became enraged. "You dumb motherfucker! I had the game in the bag."

"It wasn't my fault," the kid explained in a shaky voice, "I got pushed up here by those other guys."

"Pushed, my ass," the black soldier began, "you just cost me a hundred bucks. So pay me what I lost and we'll call it even."

"I don't have that kind of money," the skinny kid replied as he climbed down from the table.

"Let me see your wallet and I'll take what I think is fair," the behemoth threatened, reaching behind the skinny kid to snatch the wallet from his back pocket.

The kid pushed back into the crowd, attempting to escape the reach of the thoroughly pissed off Army private.

"It was an accident! You're not taking my wallet!"

The crowd grew tighter to watch this altercation. There was nowhere left for the skinny kid to go.

"Come on brothers, are you with me?" the soldier called out to a group of black comrades standing nearby. "This white boy owes me some money!"

They all wielded cue sticks and pool balls and moved toward the petrified youth.

The young kid was quickly engulfed by a group of white soldiers who ushered him behind the pack. One of them stated in a southern drawl, "Why don't you boys pick on somebody your own size?"

Upon hearing this, the leader of the black group turned to his followers and said giddily, "I guess we have to kick a lot of white ass to get my money back."

"Yeah, let's do it. We're with you!"

Individuals within the black group were now beating the palms of their hands with the thick end of the cue sticks and lofting pool balls lightly into the air. Two of them broke ranks and moved toward the white group.

Suddenly, a dozen MP's forced their way through the crowd and arrived just before either of the two groups could strike a blow.

"Let's break this shit up!" the MP Sergeant ordered.

"That skinny white boy owes me a hundred bucks!" the black private protested, while pointing him out. "All I want to do is to get my money back and these white boys want to come over and start some shit with us."

"That's bullshit, Sarge," the southern soldier responded. "There was an accident. The kid fell on the pool table and fucked up their game. He doesn't owe him shit."

"Is that correct, Private?" the MP Sergeant asks with a deep, piercing stare at the skinny kid.

"Yes, Sergeant," he replied in a trembling voice, "there was a lot of shuffling and pushing behind me a few seconds before I found myself sprawled out on top of the pool table. I couldn't stop in midair."

"That's a damn lie!" the black soldier protested. "I give a fuck about the game; I'm pissed because he pocketed my money during all the commotion."

"I don't think he has the balls to do something like that," the Sergeant replied after sizing him up and comparing him to the young soldier. "I'd be willing to forget this incident if everybody just walks away and returns to what they were doing earlier."

"What are you going to do if we don't? Send us to Vietnam?" somebody called out from the crowd.

This comment was enough to change the atmosphere of the group and some began to laugh and snicker.

"Yeah, you'll still go to Vietnam, but you may spend a few weeks in our stockade first," the Sergeant responded.

The crowd started to disperse and soldiers moved away to resume whatever activities were earlier interrupted.

The black soldier shifted back and forth from one foot to the other, his expression changing as he tried to compose himself.

The MP Sergeant looked at him. "Well, what's it going to be?"

"I'll let it go, man. I don't need any bad time on my record. I want to serve my year and go back home."

"Then do I have your word that you won't bother these other people anymore?"

"Yeah, man, you got my word." He turned and walked back to the pool table and waiting friends. The kid had just vanished and was nowhere to be seen.

Once everything was back to normal, John turned and moved toward yet another undiscovered part of the large building. After a few minutes, he heard a familiar voice call out, "Hey, Pollack!"

He stopped and looked around for the source.

"Hey, Pollack, over here!" A tall, lanky soldier with red hair, freckles, and buckteeth was pushing through the crowd and waving frantically.

John's face lit up in recognition and he returned the wave with a wild one of his own.

"Bill!" he called out loudly after seeing his friend from training.

When coming together, they embraced warmly like long-lost relatives seeing each other for the very first time.

"Pollack, you son of a bitch, am I ever glad to see you." Bill, who was built like a scarecrow, slapped John's back a few times.

"I am too, Bill. How have you been?"

"I'm good, when did you get here?"

"About four hours ago. What about you?"

"Yesterday."

"Why did you get here so early, Bill? Didn't they have a flight available when you needed it?"

"I didn't fly, I took the train instead."

"You rode a train all the way here? Are you joking?"

"No. I've never been on a plane in my whole life. I was so afraid at the thought of flying that I checked into the train schedule and found that I had to leave a couple of days earlier to get here on time."

"All the way from Tennessee?"

"Yep."

"How did you get home from Fort Polk?"

"Bus."

"Damn! You missed out on three days of your leave just because you're afraid of flying?"

"Yeah, I know, I know. Don't remind me."

"Now you don't have a choice. There aren't any trains or buses that go to Vietnam."

"I know and thought hard about that on the way here. So I decided that I'm going to have to get drunk and pass out. This way, somebody can carry me on board."

"Maybe they can give you a shot or something to relax."

"No thanks. I've had enough shots for now. Once I got here, they rushed me all around. It was worse than the physical I had to take when the Army called me up. Now in this place, they move you along like an assembly line."

"I know what you mean. I had some clerk stop me just as soon as I walked through the door. After I told him my name, he looked through a couple of boxes and then handed me a file with my name on it and ushered me to the first available desk. There, some guy rushed me through signing twenty-five or so forms and then quickly passed me off to another clerk."

Bill produced a wide smile, "Yeah, that part took me almost an hour."

John continued, "Then this guy escorts me into a room and tells me to strip down to my underwear and get in line with everyone else."

"What did you think when you saw the ten doctors on each side of the line giving everyone shots with those air-powered guns?"

"I didn't have time to think. I just blindly followed everyone else and hoped for the best."

"A guy in front of me moved his arm just as the doctor pulled the trigger," Bill commented. "When the blood squirted out, I almost shit myself."

"The shots weren't too bad and felt like a punch in the arm. But as I'm standing here now, they're starting to ache badly," John said.

"It'll feel better in a few hours. I feel fine today," Bill volunteered.

"The thing I didn't like was that we had to ship all our clothes and stuff home. The clothing line was just like Basic Training. First, they give you these jungle fatigues, then socks, shorts, boots and green t-shirts and then it's a free-for-all at the end when everyone is trying to dress and pack their duffel bag."

"Yeah, but don't we look good?" Bill asked, striking a pose.

"Smells like clean linen too," John added.

"Have you found a bunk yet?" Bill asked.

"Not yet."

"Great, then come with me, I have a cubicle all to myself."

"Lead the way."

John followed Bill for about ten minutes through the maze until they reached his cubicle of six bunk beds.

"Looks like it'll be nice and quiet in here."

"Shit, it is now. Yesterday, you couldn't hear yourself think."

"And why is that?" John inquired.

"I had to share this cube with ten other guys that have been together since Basic Training. All they did was party the whole night."

"What happened to them?"

"They left on the first flight this morning. So I guess it's just you and me until a new neighbor moves in."

"That's fine by me. Have you seen anyone else from our AIT Platoon yet?"

"Yeah, matter of fact, yesterday, I bumped into Joel McCray and Larry Nickels. Do you remember them?"

"I do. Where are they?"

"They left this morning with those other guys. And you'll never believe who else was with them."

"Who?"

"Sergeant Holmes."

"No shit? I thought he was returning to Fort Polk this week to start training a new Platoon of recruits."

"That was his original plan, but he had his orders changed during leave and volunteered for a second tour."

"Why did he do a fool thing like that?"

"He told me that he was fed up with the civilians and all the hippies. He said that while on leave, he was spit on and people were getting on his case because he was training soldiers to be baby killers and then sending them off to Vietnam. He said there wasn't a day that went by without somebody picking a fight with him. After the cops had jailed him for the second time for disorderly conduct, he went and signed the papers."

"The world is filled with jerks. Too bad he had to volunteer for Nam to get away from it all. Did you know he was wounded during his first tour?" John asked.

"Yeah, I remember him telling the story about that big Tet offensive in 1968. He got some shrapnel in his back from a mortar round. But he also mentioned yesterday, that the fighting is not at the same level as it was in 1968 or earlier, so we all have a good chance of making it home in one piece."

"I hope that's true."

Bill Sayers was raised in the back woods of Tennessee and spoke with a heavy southern drawl. He was the third eldest of nine children, who shared in everything from chores to clothes, while growing up on the family farm. He never experienced the feeling of trying on new clothes for himself. All he ever received was hand-me-downs from his older brothers. When the Army issued him the first five sets of new fatigues, he treated them like they were made of gold.

In the AIT Company, Bill was well liked and always had something good to say about everyone. He was easily amazed by the stories told about life in the big cities. It was difficult for him to imagine doing things that many city folks took for granted as a normal part of everyday life. He walked everywhere, including the three miles each way to school and back. The first time Bill had ridden a bike was in the Army.

Bill and John became very close while serving together in the Army. They had developed a close friendship that made it easy to confide in each other on sensitive issues. Prior to departing on this thirty-day leave, John had promised to visit Bill in the hills one day, but only if Bill agreed to visit him in Detroit. Bill couldn't wait and continued to remind John periodically of this agreement.

All the excitement of the day was beginning to take its toll. Both of them were tired, but wanted to keep talking to stay awake.

"I had it rough last night," John started, "my mother gave me a going away party yesterday. All of my close friends and relatives were there. After dinner, we all sat in the living room and talked while the news was on. Everyone quieted down when a bulletin came on the TV from Vietnam. It seems some outfit ran into an ambush. They showed helicopters burning, dead and wounded are being carried past the camera, and the commentator is talking very nervously. Now wouldn't you know it, all the women look over at me and start crying? Each of them got up and came over to hug me."

"Damn," Bill said with a bewildered look upon his face.

"Well you know me," John continued, "I put on the brave act and told them that nothing was going to happen to me while I was in Vietnam. I told them that we'd all be back in this same living room in a year to laugh off those worries."

"What happened then?"

"About that time, everyone started to leave for home before it got too emotional. I went up to my bedroom and tried to sleep, but I couldn't. I kept thinking about that news story and got all shaky and nervous as hell."

"Pollack, you aren't alone. I'm scared to death too." Both of them sat quietly for a few moments.

John lay back on the bunk and glanced at his watch. It's 3:30 in the morning. He thought about what had happened since leaving

Detroit only fifteen hours earlier. Everything could be summed up as "hurry-up and wait".

On the flight to California he had been the only soldier on board. The stewardesses and fellow passengers had made him feel special. When they heard that he was en route to Vietnam, they bought him drinks, offered him magazines and candy, and wished him luck on his tour. He was very proud and felt honored by the way he was treated. His fellow passengers respected him and not one person had treated him as Sergeant Holmes had been treated.

"Hey! Pollack, get your lazy ass out of that bunk!" Bill shook him a few times.

Startled, John jumped up from the bed quickly, only to bump his head on the frame of the upper bunk.

"Damn you, Bill, you scared the shit out of me," he protested, rubbing the top of his head. John looked at his watch and noted that it was 1330.

"Jesus, Bill, it's one-thirty, when did you get up?"

"About seven-thirty this morning."

"Why didn't you get me up sooner?"

"Hell, I'd have been wasting my time. I know you city boys like your sleep. You would sleep all day long if somebody let you. Besides, it wasn't necessary for both of us to check the shipping list for today."

"What did you find out?"

"Both of our names are listed on the manifest. We're leaving for Vietnam at ten o'clock tonight."

Chapter Two

"This is your Captain speaking," the voice on the public address system of the Pan American jet announced, "we will be landing in Bien Hoa, South Vietnam, in about forty minutes. They are reporting sunny skies, temperatures of 97 degrees with 100% humidity."

Whoops and cheers erupted from the military passengers. "Welcome to Hell," someone called out.

The Captain continued, "As you know, we've passed through several time zones since leaving California, so let me take this opportunity to get you all up to date. First, there is a time difference of thirty-one hours between Vietnam and the West Coast of the United States. For example, in Oakland where many of you started your journey, it's eight-thirty on Friday morning. And right now in Vietnam, it's Saturday, August seventh, and it's four-thirty in the afternoon."

Again some comments referring to a time machine and blasting into the future were heard from the rear seats.

"After we touch down, we're asking everyone to remain in their seats until the plane comes to a complete stop. There will be no need to panic and rush for the doors as this airport is in one of the more secure areas of South Vietnam. It's very safe and none of you will be shot at. So sit back, relax, and enjoy the scenery.

"On behalf of the crew, we hope you have enjoyed your flight. We do wish you the best of luck while you are here in Vietnam, and also wish you God's speed for a safe return home. Thank you for flying Pan American Airlines."

"Yeah right, like we had a choice," one of the soldiers stated loudly to his companion across the aisle.

John was looking at his watch and trying to do the math in his head. "Bill, did you know it took us almost twenty-six hours to get here?"

"It's hard to believe isn't it? You may also want to think about us being on the other side of the world from Tennessee. It just blows my mind."

"I thought China was on the other side. Didn't you ever hear people say that if you dug straight down in your backyard, you'd end up in China?"

"Who is going to do a damn fool thing like that?"

"Nobody is. It's just a saying that I grew up with."

"You city folk have some strange notions about things!" Bill returned to watching the scenery passing below the cabin window, hoping to soon see something more than just clouds and ocean.

Prior to leaving Oakland, an Army Doctor had given Bill some tranquilizers to take prior to departure. On the fist leg to Hawaii, he sat in a half-comatose state in the window seat next to John. The effects had worn off an hour before landing in Hawaii, and after fully regaining his senses, Bill found flying to be rather enjoyable. He would tell everyone that his favorite part of flying was the take off, and how he enjoyed the same sensation as the astronauts when they left for the moon.

During this long flight, he had spent most of the time looking out the window, enchanted by the view from that height. It was a new world to him and he savored every minute.

Bill grabbed John by the arm and pulled him toward the window. "Look, Pollack, you can see land," he said excitedly.

John leaned over Bill's legs to see for himself. The word spread quickly and everyone started crowding the windows for their first look at their final destination. After flying over water most of the time, it was a welcome pleasure to see land below.

From fifteen-thousand feet, Vietnam appeared as a vat of shimmering colors. Bright blue threads snaked through shades of green, brown and yellow colored earth. A large mountain chain could be seen in the distant northwest and seemed to cut the country in half. It was suddenly quiet throughout the cabin as the laughter, talking and singing suddenly came to an end. The steady roar of four jet engines continued but was unnoticed as every passenger fixated on the scenery unfolding below.

As the altitude of the plane gradually dropped, the vistas below changed in shape and color and became more recognizable the lower they got. Soon, the sprawling city of Saigon and its neighboring villages took shape and grew in size as the jet approached and flew overhead. Cars and trucks appeared as they inched along the roads. Then on the final approach for landing, the tiny ant-like moving dots took the shape of thousands of people moving about.

The plane landed smoothly and taxied toward the terminal. A few moments later, it stopped abruptly as the engines began their dying throes. There was an absolute hush on the plane and only the rapid heartbeats of two-hundred new arrivals could be heard echoing loudly through the silence.

Suddenly, a loud noise erupted in the front of the plane when the cabin door opened. Everyone on board was still sitting quietly but fidgeting about and trying to get a better look of what might be coming through the doorway.

An Air Force Major walked through the opening; he was dressed in his best Class-A uniform with several rows of battle ribbons proudly displayed over his left breast. Following him inside were two Army Captains, dressed in green jungle fatigues and baseball caps. The trio walked up the aisle, stopping at the forward stewardess station.

There they stood for a moment to survey the new arrivals. The Major stepped to the side, lifting the microphone from the mounting plate on the wall.

"My name is Major Brown and joining me are Captains Willis and Sharkey. We welcome you to Bien Hoa Air Force Base in the Republic of South Vietnam." All eyes were fixed upon the Major as they listened intently.

"Our job today is to get you men off this plane, clear through customs, and complete in-country processing in a safe and orderly manner. After disembarking the aircraft, I want everyone to join up and stand in four ranks out on the tarmac. Once everyone is together, we will then enter the civilian terminal and proceed to the baggage claim area. After securing your duffel bags, proceed to the area marked Customs. There, you will empty the contents of your bags onto counters and submit to search of your body. The MP's will be looking for drugs and any other illegal contraband that you may be trying to smuggle into the country."

At that moment, many soldiers exhibited some nervousness. Some frowned and rolled their eyes, others stirred anxiously in their seats with a panicked look on their faces.

The Major continued, "If anyone is concealing contraband, then I strongly suggest you drop it in your seats as you leave this aircraft. No questions will be asked and nobody will come looking for you afterwards. This is also your only warning. If caught outside, you will be immediately arrested and taken directly to LBJ – which is Long Binh Jail for all you Cherries on board – and I can guarantee that you'll serve time for your foolishness.

"When you clear Customs, you will exit the terminal and board the awaiting buses. They will transport you to the 90th Replacement Center in Long Binh, which is about a three-mile drive. There, you will begin final in-processing and be assigned and transported to your new in-country unit.

"At this time, I would ask that all officers aboard please stand up and begin to disembark at the front door."

As they moved up the aisle way, John and Bill noticed a few items that had been left behind on the seats. Bags of weed, pills, and other unidentifiable items lay openly or tucked between cushions.

Bill and John shuffled down the row toward the front of the plane. "Look at this stuff. Do you think these people carried it with them all the way from Oakland? I seem to recall that some of us were searched before getting on the plane."

"No, I don't think so, Bill, it would have been too risky in Oakland. I believe people bought this stuff during our three stops along the way. There were a lot of shady characters in those terminals and I remember seeing a lot of money being flashed around."

"You're right, now that you mention it. I can remember overhearing some guys on our stop over in Guam. They were talking about having a big party once they got settled in. But I didn't think it would be with grass and drugs."

"Shit, Bill, dope users are on the rise. This stuff is getting quite popular back home and more people than we know are turning to it. Just give me a beer or a mixed drink and my cigarettes and I'll be happy."

"I'm with you there, partner. I wonder if anybody is going to try and smuggle some dope into the country."

"Your guess is as good as mine."

As each person walked out of the air-conditioned plane, they hesitated on the top step of the boarding ramp as the full impact of hot and humid air engulfed them. For a moment, it was difficult to breathe. Some made a feeble attempt to re-enter the plane, only to be pushed back out by the on rush of exiting personnel.

There was a green hue outside as the rays of silvery sunlight reflected from everything colored olive drab green: helicopters, planes, gun emplacements, and buildings with sandbagged walls around them.

Dozens of helicopters lifted off and landed in areas adjacent to the runway. Small green, single-seat Piper Cub airplanes and larger Phantom Fighter Jets were also moving about and taxiing toward different areas of the airport to wait in line for their turn to takeoff.

Bill and John cleared Customs easily and walked out to the waiting buses. They were identical to those used during training on the American bases and were also painted olive green like everything else around, with one distinct difference - there were no glass windows. Instead, bars and sections of chicken wire covered each framed opening.

The two close friends took a seat in the first row behind the driver.

"Why is all this shit covering the windows instead of having glass?" John asked the driver.

"It's there to protect the passengers from grenades or any other foreign objects that could be thrown in from the side of the road," he answered.

"Protect the occupants? It gives me the feeling of being a criminal on the way to prison."

"We are in prison, my man," the person behind John said with a smile. "Think about it. We're all locked up in this country for the next year and there's nothing we can do about it but serve our time."

"Yeah, you right!" some of the other passengers agreed.

Once the buses loaded, the driver closed the door and started the engine.

Two MP jeeps pulled alongside, stopping next to the lead bus. Both had long fifteen-foot whip antennas swinging from the two rear corners and dual M-60 machine guns mounted to a cross bar behind the front seats. The soldier standing behind the guns was busy loading them and ensuring they were in proper working order while the man in the front passenger seat talked casually into the handset of the radio.

"Look at the Rat Patrol jeeps!" John exclaimed.

"What's a Rat Patrol jeep?" Bill asked.

"Don't you remember seeing them on TV when we were young? They were always kicking the shit out of the Germans in Africa during the Second World War."

"You know, I never had a TV," Bill stated innocently.

"Oh yeah, I forgot. But take my word for it, Bill: they were a badass outfit."

The procession of five buses began to move and the two gun jeeps raced to the head of the line to fall in. As the convoy picked up speed, red dust from the road swirled through the air, making it difficult to breathe. Everything was immediately coated with the horrible residue. As if on cue, the new arrivals began choking and gasping for clean air. Handkerchiefs and shirts were quickly pulled over noses and mouths in an attempt to filter some breathable air from the thick red fog.

The convoy appeared to be traveling through a corridor. Both sides of the road had ten-foot high barbed wire fences running alongside. Hundreds of straw roofed huts, about the size of a single room lakeside cabin in the states, stood as far back as you could see. The barbed wire fences made it appear as if the area was either a prison or a refugee center.

Every person seen was very old. Some were in front of their huts, sitting on the ground or cooking over open fires. Others simply stood near the fence and watched the parade of buses pass by; every one of them was chewing something and spitting a brown liquid onto the ground.

"Those people are all chewing tobacco!" Bill exclaimed.

"That's not tobacco," the driver volunteered, "it's the juice from betel and nuts."

"What the hell are betel and nuts?" John asked.

"The Areca nut grows wild in the husks of some trees around the country. These people cure the nut and slice it into sections. For chewing, a few slices are wrapped in a betel leaf along with lime, clove or anything else to improve the bitter taste. When taken like that, it's a stimulant that causes a hot sensation in the body and heightened alertness, although the results vary from person to person. However, most of them mix other shit with it to get high."

"You mean like dope?" Bill asked the driver.

"Yeah, just like dope. Most of these people are high all the time. They wouldn't be able to stand it otherwise."

"It's kind of funny though; just look at all those folks by the wire. They remind me of the cows back home, all of them standing along the fence and steady chewing their cud. Their heads turn as you pass and continue to watch until you are long gone."

The driver laughs, "Yep, now that's original."

The convoy approached a tight right turn and each bus slowed to complete the maneuver. Several groups of villagers were standing at the corner waiting for the traffic to clear. Just then, John grabbed Bill by the arm and pointed excitedly out the window. "Bill! Look!"

Neither of them was able to say a word and continued to stare at the sight greeting them.

A group of seven women, each appearing to be well over a hundred years old, was standing at the corner, waving to the buses as they passed. Their wrinkles were deep and wide, their skin shriveled like prunes. It appeared that most were heading home after working in the fields since they were carrying rakes, hoes, and shovels. Two of them balanced long poles on their shoulders with large bamboo baskets attached to each end. Their black nylon pants and oversized shirts were covered with dried mud and other noteworthy stains.

Everyone wore straw conical hats that helped to shield their faces from the strong rays of the sun and they were all smiling happily. Four of them were toothless and the remaining three had only a few teeth left in their mouths. All looked as if they had mouths filled with black licorice. Their lips, gums, teeth, and insides of their mouth looked like a poster advertisement from the Cancer Foundation, warning against the dangers of smoking.

"That's what happens when you chew those betel nuts all your life," the driver commented when seeing them.

Bill and John could only look at each other and shake their heads in disbelief.

"Daaaaaaaaaaaamnnnnn!" John finally said in one long drawn out breath.

Further up the road, young children were everywhere. Most were small boys of pre-school age.

"Hey GI, you souvenir me cigarettes, candy, you numba one," they called, running along the side of the road to keep up with the buses.

Some of the guys on the bus felt sorry for them and began flicking cigarettes through the chicken wire windows. This resulted in several scuffles as each group began to zero in on the tossed tobacco sticks, fighting each other to claim the prizes.

In the background, behind the packs of fighting youths, stood the little girls, not older than eight years or so. Some held half-naked babies in their arms and others shouted at the fighting youths. A few of them even entered the fracas and began to pull the boys apart, appearing to scold them.

"Why are all the little girls holding babies instead of playing like the boys?" John asked the driver.

"Those little girls help raise the family, cook, and clean around the hut while their parents work in the fields."

"What a shame."

Every human being passed so far on the convoy was either very old or very young. There were no teenage boys hanging around on the corners or middle-aged men walking around in the villages.

At another turn, the buses slowed down again. One corner had a small outpost shaped like a triangle. Large bunkers were at each corner of the complex; machine gun barrels poking through several of the gun slits. A twenty-foot high tower and spotlight was centered within the compound. The little base was encircled with loops of barbed wire and walls of sandbags. All in all, about twenty Vietnamese soldiers could be seen within the compound. It was also unlikely that any of them weighed in at more than a hundred pounds.

"Look at them guys, they're only kids."

"Shit, Bill, we're not much older ourselves."

"Yeah, but we can put in our year and go home. These poor guys probably live up the road apiece and will have to continue fighting this war long after we leave."

"I guess you're right, Bill. I just can't imagine having to fight a war in my own neighborhood back home. It's got to be hard to keep focused on a day-to-day basis when you don't know if your property is still there or if your family is okay after a firefight. What a life!"

Five minutes later, the bus made a left turn and slowed to a crawl as it approached a gate straddling the road, similar to Fort Apache in the western movies. A sign over the gate read: 'Welcome to the 90th Replacement Battalion – Long Binh'.

Chapter Three

As the buses unloaded, a trim and muscular Army Captain stood on a platform, patiently waiting for the group to get into some type of military formation. He continued to shift his weight from one foot to the other and appeared to be either impatient or nervous. His deep tan and unblemished complexion accented his straw colored hair and blue eyes. His green jungle fatigues were heavily starched and sharply creased – front and back – and fit as if he was poured into them. There wasn't an ounce of fat protruding from his rock-solid two-hundred pound frame. After five minutes, he turned on the microphone and began speaking.

"Good evening, gentlemen," he began. "I'm Captain Richards, and I'd like to welcome all of you to the 90th Replacement Battalion. As I call out your name from the roster, fall out into the building behind me. There, you will exchange your greenbacks for Military Payment Certificate (MPC), the military currency that is used in this country. Greenbacks are illegal here, and possession of any after you clear this area is a Court Martial offense. After you leave the building, find an empty bunk in one of these six barracks." He pointed out the buildings across the street and behind the formation.

"Tomorrow there will be shipping formations taking place at 0800, noon and 1600 hours. These readings are mandatory and everyone must be there. Those of you called out tomorrow will be transferred to your new units. The rest of you not leaving will be assigned to work details around the center. Until that time, you will be on your own and free to use all the facilities available to you in this center. Okay, now listen up for your name."

The 90th Replacement Center was a large camp, two miles long and one-half mile wide. Bunkers alternated with towers on the perimeter. To their front were varied configurations of razor sharp barbed wire, stretching out for at least five-hundred feet. The six-foot high protective barrier resembled spools of thread in a neglected sewing drawer. Flares with trip wires attached to their pins were mixed within the wires. When pulled out, the flare would illuminate the immediate area in the dark of night. Deadly Claymore mines were positioned randomly and could be detonated from within the bunker if the enemy was spotted in the wire. Small metal cans full of loose stones bobbed in the wind; a sudden pull on the wire caused the cans to clang a warning to the bunker guards.

The barracks were single-story, green buildings and closely resembled their cousin buildings in the states. There was, however, one exception – no glass windows - just like the buses. Instead, mosquito netting covered each opening. In the event of a rocket or mortar attack, these openings would provide additional exits for quickly vacating the building. The roof overhung sufficiently to keep rain from coming through the special windows.

John waited for Bill just outside of the money-changing building, standing in the shade of a palm tree. The late afternoon sun hung low in the royal blue sky but was still strong enough to make standing outside of a shaded area uncomfortable. When Bill finally exited, the two of them proceeded through the ninety-five degree heat toward the first of the barracks.

They entered and luckily located two beds, side by side, on the far end near the back door. Duffel bags were tossed onto the bare mattresses and both men flopped down beside them.

"Well, John, what are we going to do now?"

"Let's go for a walk and scout this place out."

"Lead the way." Bill worked his way out of the bed and onto the dirty plywood floor.

They exited the building and walked down the few steps leading to the road, stopping briefly to study the lay of the land.

"Let's try down there and see why all the people are hanging around in the street," John suggested, pointing in that direction.

They walked up the road only to come upon a large purple building. The sign on the door read, 'Alice's Restaurant'.

"Will you take look at this?" John asked excitedly. Latching onto Bill's arm, he pulled him toward the building. "It's a goddamn restaurant, right here in the middle of a war zone. Let's go inside to see what they have."

"Okay, I've got your back."

Once inside, they found the restaurant to be divided into three sections: a dining room, a game room, and a bar. They hesitated for a moment in the doorway taking it all in.

"How about getting something to eat?" Bill asked. Patting his stomach, he continued, "I'm starved!"

"Sounds like a plan. I'm kind of hungry too."

They sat at a table in the middle of the dining room and were quickly offered menus by a young Vietnamese girl. She was about four and a half feet tall, with long, flowing, silky black hair. She wore black silk pajama bottoms under a knee-length powder blue dress; slits extended on both sides from her hips down. She was tiny and it was impossible for her to weigh more than eighty pounds. She stood by the table with an order pad and pencil in hand, smiling politely, awaiting their order.

Both of them quickly scanned over the single page menu framed in black leather and covered with clear plastic. Several items were listed: hamburgers, hot dogs, fries, barbecued chicken, coleslaw, ice-cold soda and beer.

It only took a few seconds before they were ready to order.

"I'll have a hamburger and fries," Pollack said and handed the menu back to the waitress.

"I'll have the same," Bill chimed in.

"What do you want on your burgers? We have tomato, onion, ketchup, and mustard."

"Everything for me, please."

"Me too," Bill added.

"What would you like to drink?"

"What kind of beer do you have?"

"Falstaff and Black Label is all we have."

"Ewww!" the men responded with sour expressions on their faces.

The waitress sensed that neither of them was happy with the selections, so she apologized, "I'm sorry, but this is all we have."

John pondered over the choices. "I never tried Falstaff beer, so I guess I'll try one of them."

"A beer is a beer and you can't be fussy. Make it two of them there Falstaffs." Bill raised two fingers into the air.

"Okay. I'll be back in a minute with your beer, but the food will take a little longer." She left to take the order to the kitchen. Her waist-length hair waved at them with each step and swung gently from side to side.

"You should be ashamed of yourself, Bill."

"What did I do now?" Bill frowned and looked confused.

"Did you hear that chick talk? You were born and raised in the states and this Vietnamese girl speaks better American than you do."

"Shit, you call that American? I speak excellent American and her accent isn't anything close to mine." They both laughed.

The atmosphere in the restaurant was a refreshing change. It was so peaceful; a person would find it difficult to believe a war was even going on outside the perimeter.

As expected, the décor inside of Alice's Restaurant catered to the peace-loving hippy movement. Posters of rock stars and the concert at Woodstock hung from the dirty white pine walls. Black neon lights helped to enhance the psychedelic posters and made the bright colors stand out. Gold colored beads hung in the doorways and crackled like pebbles dropping onto the cement floor when someone passed through them. A strong smell of incense permeated the air; several trails of smoke could be seen reaching up to the dimly lit ceiling at various locations throughout the building. The aroma was somewhat pleasant and did an excellent job covering the stench of cigarette smoke and beer. The jukebox played a variety of music, changing periodically from hard rock to soul music and even an occasional country western song.

Suddenly, something interesting caught John's eye. "Bill, there's slot machines in the next room."

"Wow, I've never played one before."

"Me neither. Let's go and try one of them before the food gets here."

They jumped up and hurried over to the bank of nickel machines. Once there, they were stumped as to how to put their paper money into the one-armed bandit because all they could find was a coin slot. The new military payment certificates were all in paper, including the denominations less than a dollar.

One of the nearby players observed their dilemma and volunteered, "Go over to the cashier window. They'll change your monopoly money for tokens."

"Thanks!" both soldiers replied in unison and crossed the floor toward the cashier window.

They exchanged five dollars MPC for one-hundred nickel tokens and walked up to one of the ten machines. Playing three tokens a pull and winning a few here and there, they were only able to play on the machine seven minutes before losing all their coins. Disappointed, they returned to the restaurant table to find their food and beers waiting for them.

It was twilight outside when they exited the restaurant. However, the dim lights hanging from the front of each building enabled them to see in the fast approaching darkness.

Further up the road, the sound of music, cheering, and loud whistling made them curious enough to investigate. Once they were able to wade through the crowd, to their amazement, they found a seven-member band performing on a stage. Three female dancers were half naked and slowly removing the rest of their outfits. The surrounding bleachers overflowed with cheering soldiers; most were on their feet and roaring their approval.

"Oh my God!" Bill hollered above the noise. His mouth opened wide and his jaw dropped to his chest, exposing rows of pearl white filling-free teeth; his eyeballs bulged out and almost appeared as if they would pop out of his head. His mouth moved up and down, trying to speak words, but nothing came out. He then closed his mouth again and swallowed hard. "Come on, Pollack, let's go find us a seat," Bill finally managed to spit out in between his heavy breathing.

There were no seats available anywhere so the two of them migrated to the area between the stage and bleachers and joined other excited youths who were standing and packed tightly into the small area.

"Do you believe this?" Bill asked. "This is surely the first time I've ever seen anything like this."

"You mean seeing the almost naked women or the live band?"

"I've never seen a naked woman in person before."

"So what's the big deal? These Asian girls aren't shit. I've seen guys in Basic Training with bigger tits."

"I did too, but they didn't affect me the same way. How often will we be able to see something like this?"

"Now how in the fuck am I supposed to know that?"

Bill wasn't able to respond as he became hypnotized by the strip tease taking place upon the stage. The crowd in front of the stage tightened up and pulsated forward as additional men arrived and tried to force their way in to get a better view of the show.

Pandemonium broke out when one of the girls got completely naked. Those in the audience erupted in catcalls, whistling, pumping fists into the air, clapping hands and whooping it up, the bleachers sounding as if they were going to collapse from the impact of a hundred feet stomping loudly on the wood boards.

When the other two girls became naked, the three of them began to dance wildly, gyrating in different directions and moving from one side of the stage to the other. Each of them made obscene gestures and teased the audience. After a full minute of individual flaunting, they all returned to center stage, slowly arching backwards and began pumping their hips to the beat of the wild song. There was nothing left to the imagination now and many in the audience were freaking out; some men had to be restrained by their buddies in order to prevent them from rushing the stage and molesting the girls.

The band had written the wild song playing and none of the Americans had ever heard it before. The rhythm was contagious and sounded like something out of a King Kong movie, enabling the girls to gyrate and work themselves into a sexual frenzy. Most of the men in the audience were caught up in the sound and found it difficult to simply watch without gyrating to the beat themselves.

When the number finally ended, the girls quickly dashed off stage and entered into a portable dressing room. The musicians set their instruments to the side and also joined the ladies in the small room. The audience was still in a high state of excitement and now realizing that the concert was over, began to clap their hands and chant for an encore. Several minutes elapsed and not one person had left the area; the chanting and clapping continued in hopes of convincing the band to return for one last song.

The dressing room door opened and the musicians busted out, running across the stage to their instruments. Seconds later, the three girls exited and were then dressed in different colored silk robes; all had towels in hand and were wiping their wet foreheads and faces. The audience roared its appreciation.

The lead guitarist began plucking out soft notes to quiet the crowd. The center dancer of the three picked up a microphone and smiled at the crowd. "We are the Crescent from the Philippine Islands and want to thank all of you for attending our concert. This will be the final song of the evening and is dedicated to all of you. Be safe and good luck!"

Suddenly, the guitar tempo changed and the band joined in, the dancers beginning to sway and rock side to side. That song would be played a hundred more times during various in-country concerts in the many months to come. The crowd quieted and the girls began singing 'The Green, Green Grass of Home'. It was a sad song that stimulated memories of home and of those left behind. The rowdiness had ceased and the atmosphere took a complete one hundred eighty-degree turn. Many in the audience were singing along and swaying sideways to mimic the singers on stage.

Bill and John left before the end of the song in order to beat the rush back to the barracks.

When they get there, they found most everybody already sleeping, except for six guys down on the far end of the building. Two of them sat on John's bunk. When they approached the men, the talking stopped and the group looked up at the two new arrivals.

"How you guys doing? My name's John and this is Bill. Seeing you're sitting on my bunk, do you mind if we join you?"

One of them, who appeared to be the leader of the group, spoke up, "Hell no, we don't mind. Come on and have a seat. This is Dan, Billy, Paul, Mike, Joe, and I'm Steve," he said, pointing them all out as he said their names. "We're just shooting the shit."

That was the end of their second day at the Replacement Center, which meant that they should have had a pretty good idea where everything was. When interrupted, Paul had been in the middle of a story about the massage parlor on the next block. For the benefit of their new acquaintances, he started over from the beginning.

"It was a real bitch, man. They had twelve tables in this room. You strip in this little back closet, hang your clothes on a hook, and walk out with a towel wrapped around your waist. I got on the nearest table where this forever-smiling chick was waiting for me. There were at least nine other guys getting massages at the time. Man, that chick had magic fingers. In the fifteen minutes she worked on me, it felt so good that I almost fell asleep. She was just about finished working on my legs when, get this, she asks me if I want a hand job."

Everyone laughed.

"Go on, Paul, don't stop now," said one of the guys on the bunk.

"Well you know that sounded pretty good to me," Paul continued, "I never had a chick do that to me before, so I asked her how much and she tells me twelve bucks."

"Twelve bucks," Joe blurted out. "Shit, I'll beat you off for twelve bucks."

The laughter was so intense that it is difficult not to have tears in your eyes.

"Come on, guys," Paul pleaded. "Let me finish."

It took a few minutes before the group was able to stop. Finally Dan volunteered, "Go on, Paul. We'll try not to laugh anymore."

"Okay, well I told her that I only had five bucks in my wallet so I'd come back another day. Then she says, 'No sweat, GI, I do for five dorrers'. Shit, I thought that was a bargain, so I told her okay. Now, instead of taking me someplace else that was more private, she pulls my towel off right then and there and grabs a hold of me. That was the last thing in the world that I had expected to happen. I jumped right off that table, embarrassed as all hell, snatched back my towel and wrapped it around my waist. She had a confused look on her face and some of the other guys were also looking over at us. I caught my breath and told her calmly that there was no way in hell I was going to let her do this right here in front of everyone. She smiled – looked right into my eyes and asks me if I was a Cherry boy."

The small group couldn't take anymore and began to howl and roll around on the two beds. The racket began waking some sleeping soldiers; they bitched at the group and told them to keep it down. Nobody wanted to start any trouble so the group apologized and continued to converse in a lower tone.

"I don't believe it. Our own Paul chickened out. Poor thing couldn't handle the pressure," Dan said sarcastically.

Paul shot back coldly, "If you think you're such a badass, then why don't you go try it tomorrow?"

"That will be the day I pay some chick five bucks to beat my meat," Dan stated, nodding his head affirmatively and looking at the rest of the group for support.

"Yeah, you probably do it every night too, don't you?" Paul retorted.

Joe interceded, "God damn it, Paul. Don't get bent out of shape. You know we're just fucking with you."

Paul just sat there and fumed. It would take him a few moments to get composed and have the color return to his face.

The group quickly changed the subject and began to talk about other things for the next couple hours. At that point, they called it a night.

During one of the discussions, Dan had mentioned that there was a radiophone next to the PX, called a MARS station. There, a person could call home for a small fee. It wasn't a telephone and both parties had to use proper radio procedures and etiquette, like saying "over" when one party finished talking, which opened the channel for the other to reply. Bill and John agreed that they would give it a try the following day.

The next morning, all six soldiers that Bill and John spent the evening with had their names called out on the shipping manifest. They were all assigned to the 101st Airborne Division and would be going up north to a place called Phu Bai. Somebody in the crowd stated that the 101st was in dire need of replacements as the North Vietnamese Army (NVA) regulars were kicking their asses in a valley called the A Shau. Rumor had it that entire Platoons were wiped out in these hard-core firefights.

After all the names on the manifest were called, Bill and John left quickly to avoid any work details and headed straight for the MARS station to place calls home. Instead, they found a long line of expectant callers and observed several pages of names posted to the door; this was discovered to be the waiting list. Neither had any idea how long it would take to rotate through the list, but added their names in case they were still at the Replacement Center when their turn came.

Since there was nothing else to do until the next reading in a couple hours, both decided to walk around the center. They found an outdoor movie theater, another restaurant, a swimming pool, a post office, two basketball courts, a baseball diamond, and the notorious massage parlor. It was like visiting a recreation center or youth camp, with the only sign of war being the bunker line.

After the noon manifest reading, those who were not called were held back in the formation. Several Non-Commissioned Officers (NCO's) weaved through the formation, grabbing personnel for various details. Bill, John and a dozen other soldiers were selected for a painting detail by a buck Sergeant who didn't look older than any of them. This time nobody was able to escape.

John and Bill's group painted in the hot sun all afternoon. It was also ironic as they were painting the fence enclosing the Reception Center's swimming pool. The water teased and beckoned them all day. Finally, unable to control himself any longer, Bill dropped his brush, rushed through the gate, and jumped fully clothed into the refreshing and cool water.

Not expecting this to happen, the rest of the paint detail exchanged glances in stunned silence. Then, as if on cue, the rest of them dropped their brushes to follow Bill's lead. They splashed around in the water, unchallenged for several minutes, like a group of grade school children on a field trip. All at once, two service club attendants emerged and ordered them from the pool. Reluctantly, one by one, they emerged from the water and returned to their tedious detail.

Clothes dried quickly in the hot, blaring sunshine and soon they were all sweating again, contemplating a second dip in the pool. At five in the afternoon, the project only required another hour to finish, but they were all relieved and told to go to the mess hall for dinner.

After John and Bill ate dinner and cleaned up, they returned to Alice's Restaurant. This time, their attempt to win on the slot machine was successful when Bill hit the jackpot with the very first three tokens.

Bill stood there dumbfounded and watched the hundreds of coins drop into the tray below. Bells and sirens were sounding from the machine and a red strobe light above signaled to everyone that a jackpot had been won.

"Glory be, this sure is my lucky day! Just look at all these here coins," he cried out joyfully.

The noise and strobe quickly attracted other soldiers who collected around the machine to see what all the commotion was about. Everyone watched the payout window; numbers continued to climb and approach one-thousand. Falling tokens were already filling the tray below. Those standing around showed mixed support; some congratulated Bill and were happy for him, others simply looked on, saying nothing. One guy in particular appeared to be quite upset and turned to his buddy, protesting loudly, "Damn! I just left that machine. Had I stayed and played another coin that jackpot would have been mine!"

Someone turned and responded to him loudly, "Yeah, but you didn't and now it ain't. So get over it and give the guy a break!"

"Fuck it, don't mean nothin'," he mumbled and walked away.

Meanwhile, Bill frantically raked the tokens into old coffee cans and found it difficult to keep up with the machine payout. The counter was still rolling and had passed fourteen-hundred. Suddenly it stopped at fifteen-hundred and all at once it became quiet again.

Someone yelled out, "Way to go man, you just hit for seventy-five! Don't spend it in one place."

It took several more minutes for the two of them to transfer all the coins from the machine tray into empty coffee cans. When they finished, they muscled the five filled cans over to the cashier cage. The woman behind the counter congratulated them and paid Bill in military certificates.

"Come on, Pollack, it's time for us to drink a few beers and celebrate," Bill said proudly and guided John to a nearby table.

After a few hours of drinking beer, both were surprised to find that neither of them could stand without support.

"Oh shit, I can't see things clearly anymore," John stated, holding on tightly to the back of his chair.

"I can see okay, but everything is spinning like I'm on a merry-go-round," Bill responded.

"Are you gonna puke?"

"I don't think so right now, but we need to find the way back to our bunks."

"I do remember that we have to turn left and go to the last row of barracks on top of the hill."

"Let's get started before we pass out."

The two of them leaned onto each other, shuffled through the door and down the steps to the road. Some of the by-standers watched them closely, amused by their inebriated state. Once the two of them reached the road and turned left, they started singing marching tunes from Basic Training while weaving across the road. They were off tune and very loud, one trying to sing louder than the other. Angry voices echoed in the darkness from every building they passed:

"Hey, assholes pipe down!"

"Shut the fuck up out there!

"Sing another note and I'll personally come out and kick your ass!"

They disregarded all the threats and warnings, not stopping until they reached their destination. Once inside, they collapsed.

The inhabitants of the 90th Replacement Battalion were abruptly awakened at 0300 by the loud blast of air raid sirens.

Those who were drunk or stoned sobered up immediately. In the confusion, everyone scrambled around and bumped into each other, trying to vacate the building. Some of the fast thinking guys dove through the mosquito net covered windows and scurried into the nearest bunker between the barracks.

A voice on the public address system was yelling barely audible instructions above the shrill sirens. "Yellow alert, yellow alert – head for the nearest bunker and take cover immediately!"

Once inside the bunker, everyone sat nervously on the ground without a clue of what to do next.

Voices rang out from the total darkness within. "My heart is pounding so fast - it's going to explode."

"What in the hell is happening?"

"Are we getting hit?"

"Where are our weapons?"

"Yeah, how are we going to protect ourselves?"

"What in the fuck does a yellow alert mean?"

The sight within the bunker was bizarre as the twenty soldiers were all in different levels of dress. Some were sitting barefoot with nothing else on except their green boxer shorts – one of them even had a helmet on. A few were wearing trousers and boots, others wore shirts with their shorts, and three were completely dressed with helmets on their heads. One of them stood next to the entrance of the bunker and held a broom – the handle facing outward like a bayonet on a rifle.

About that time, a heavy set guy wearing a cook's hat and apron, leisurely strolled into the bunker and took a double glance at the guy standing guard with the broom.

Shaking his head side to side, he took in the curious picture. Of course, since he'd been at the Replacement Center for almost four months, similar scenes had played out repeatedly.

"Relax, guys, it's only a test," he said in a reassuring voice.

"What do you mean a test?" someone asked from the darkness.

"The camp officers fuck with us every other night and run this alert at different hours. It's supposed to remind us that we're still in a war zone. It doesn't bother me none because I'm in the kitchen all night long cooking. The sirens should stop and they'll give the all clear in a sec."

"What a bunch of lifer mother-fuckers," someone mumbled.

"At least they could have given us some warning. Now I've got to clean the shit out of my pants," said another.

Five minutes later, the "All Clear" sounded. Everyone began to file out of the bunker and return to the barracks, thankful, but nevertheless pissed off about the inconvenience. Most of them dropped onto their bunks, but were still too shaken by the experience to fall asleep. Most just lay in bed awake until dawn.

Bill Sayers and John Kowalski's names were called out at the first shipping formation of the day. Both were assigned to the 25th Infantry Division and would travel to a place called Cu Chi, about twenty miles northwest of Saigon. The convoy was leaving at 1000 hours.

"Thank you, sweet Jesus!" Bill said solemnly, "thank you for not sending us up to the 101st."

"Amen," John added.

Those called were beginning to arrive with their duffel bags and told to drop them onto piles identified by unit. Bill and John dropped theirs in the area designated for the 25th Division. With an hour remaining before departure, Bill and Pollack rushed over to the PX to purchase 'boony hats', which were similar to those worn by amateur fishermen. The soft green cloth-like material enabled a person to shape it into any configuration necessary to keep the sun out of their eyes and off the back of the neck. They were lighter and more practical than the traditional baseball caps the newly arrived recruits wore. Both waited for a seamstress to embroider their names on the brim of their hats. John scanned the counter full of division patches.

"Bill, let's get us a patch for the 25th Division and we can have it sewn onto the hat too," John suggested.

They scan the board behind the counter to see that the patch looked like a red strawberry, two inches wide by four inches long, with a yellow lightning bolt piercing it diagonally. They each purchased one and got them sewn in place.

John then moved to the next counter and spotted a large Bowie knife in the showcase.

"Check this out," he called over to Bill.

John had already purchased the knife, threaded his belt through the leather scabbard, and was in the process of tying the bottom leather lace around his right thigh.

"That looks cool as hell!" Bill said, admiring the new item.

"Makes me look kind of badass doesn't it?" John stated proudly.

"Yes it does. I think I'll buy one for myself," Bill said and placed his order with the salesperson.

Neither of them thought of the knife as being much more than a decoration. However, they would both find out later that it was the most valuable tool used while patrolling through the jungle.

At 0930 hours, five two-and-a-half ton trucks, commonly called deuce and a half, arrived. The bed of each truck was layered with sandbags to protect the occupants in case they ran over a mine in the road, and a soldier stood behind the cab manning the tripod mounted M-60 machine gun on the roof. The Rat Patrol jeeps also arrived to escort the Cherries to their next destination.

Bill and John were among the first twenty to board the trucks and were fortunate enough to get a seat on one of the two platforms running the length on each side of the vehicle. The other fifteen had to sit in discomfort on the hard sandbagged covered floor.

The convoy moved out precisely at 1000 hours. Once leaving the security of the 90th Replacement Battalion, a lone helicopter gunship joined the convoy and circled lazily overhead to provide additional security for the parade of five trucks.

They passed endless rice paddies where the Vietnamese people worked painstakingly in knee-deep water, harvesting their crops. Young boys rode on top of huge water buffaloes whacking the big brown animals on the behinds with a bamboo stick.

Whenever convoys passed each other in the opposite direction, everyone flashed peace signs to one another. Periodically, Armored Personnel Carries (APC's) could be seen hiding in the bushes on the side of the road. Their gunners would wave to the convoy from behind 50-caliber machine guns.

After traveling at speeds in excess of 40 mph, it took no time at all for the convoy to reach Cu Chi – home of the 25th Infantry Division.

Chapter Four

The Rat Patrol jeeps concluded their mission after leading the convoy deep inside of Cu Chi. All one-hundred twenty-six Cherries stood in the trucks, trying in vain to rid themselves of the clinging red dust.

Bill laughed when John removed his sunglasses.

"What's so funny?"

"You have white rings around your eyes."

"So what, that's funny?"

"Yeah, with all that red shit on your face you look like a fucking raccoon."

"At least you can see my eyes. Your whole head looks like it was dipped in shit."

"Go ahead and have your fun," Bill announced. He brushed himself feverishly in an attempt to get all the dust removed from his clothes. "Give me a hand wiping my back and I'll brush you off."

"Okay, just don't play with my ass when I turn around," John stated.

"You're all ass and I won't be able to avoid it."

"What, are you a comedian now?"

As they finished brushing each other's back, loud voices on the side of the trucks were barking commands to the group.

"All right, Cherries, un-ass my trucks!"

"Come on, come on, move it!"

"I mean now! Let's go, everyone!"

"I want four ranks starting right here," bellowed an impatient looking Puerto Rican Sergeant. He stood forty feet away and drew a long line across the ground with a large stick. "Let's go! Get on the line, I don't have all day!" he barked.

The Cherries leapt from the trucks and moved quickly to form four ranks, unsure if punishment was forth coming for not doing it fast enough.

"What the fuck, are we in basic training again?" John mumbled to Bill.

"I hope not. We're supposed to be all done with that. This is Vietnam, isn't it?"

The Sergeant paraded back and forth in front of the formation. He wore a black baseball cap with the word 'Cadre' stenciled on the front in large white letters. It was impossible to see the look in his eyes, as they were covered with mirrored aviator sunglasses. His abnormal sized beer belly spilled over the belt and buckle around his thirty-four inch waist and bounced with every step taken.

"Listen up, Cherries!" he shouted in an attempt to get the ranks to settle down. "You are here for a mandatory week-long course of in-country training. During this time, we will review your past training and teach you all about your enemy. Our first class will begin in fifteen minutes. When I give the word, grab your gear and store it in the hooches behind me, then return to the exact location you are standing in right now.

"You'll all have plenty of time to unpack and get squared away later. You have ten minutes, starting now. Move out!"

The ranks collapsed as men rushed into the various hooches. As soon as Bill and John came upon two empty adjacent cots in the third building, they threw the gear on top and moved back outside.

"What do you suppose this is going to be like?" Bill asked.

"Most likely a lot of classroom training, just like we did in Basic."

"Hell, I thought there's a war going on here. Why are we going to sit around in classrooms?" Bill complained.

"You heard the guy. He said that we were going to learn all about the enemy."

"What more do we have to learn? There's a little guy with a gun that's trying to shoot me and I shoot him first. It's that simple. We don't need to learn anything more."

The Puerto Rican Sergeant led the formation to a large shaded area not too far from the hooches. This was the first classroom of the day.

"Have a seat on the ground, gentlemen. If you have any smokes, feel free to light up."

He stood in front of the group, next to a large six-foot wide green chalkboard mounted between two trees. The name 'Sgt. Ramone' was written largely with white chalk.

"Don't be afraid to sit on the ground," he stated after observing the reluctance of some to do so. "You'll be mighty lucky if this is the dirtiest you get in this country. You ground pounders (infantry) will be living on the ground. So get used to it now while there's no pressure on you."

When the entire group was finally seated, he continued, "This area is where you will meet for most of the classes during this course. My name is Sergeant Ramone," he enunciated both syllables and then used the stick to point out his name on the board.

"I will be one of your instructors during this next week. Today, we'll review military maneuvers, different attack and defensive formations, the military Alphabet, coding, map reading, and the proper use of the PRC-25 field radio. Are there any questions before we begin?"

Nobody raised his hand.

"Good, let's get started."

Later that day, John and Bill unpacked their belongings in the single story screened building.

"Those classes we just finished weren't all that bad," John stated.

"Now I beg to differ with you. It was boring as hell to go over all that shit again. We've had enough of it shoved down our throats in the last six months."

"It may be boring, but look at it this way. It's one less day that we'll have to spend in the field."

Bill appeared to ponder the statement for several seconds, then replied, "I guess you're right."

John looked at his watch, surprised. "Damn, it's already ten-thirty. We'd better get some sleep. I have a feeling it's going to be another long day tomorrow."

Both lie down on the hard olive-colored canvas cots and quickly fell asleep.

The following morning, everyone was issued an M-16 rifle before heading out for the first class of the day.

"Good morning, gentlemen," the instructor began, after every person was seated in the outdoor classroom. "We will be spending the morning taking these weapons apart, cleaning them, and then putting them back together again."

Moans and objections echoed from the crowd.

"Aw, fuck!"

"We did all this shit hundreds of times already."

"What a fucking waste!"

The instructor, having heard enough, got everyone's undivided attention when he struck the chalkboard with a stick; it sounded like the sharp crack of a rifle.

"Knock off the bullshit!" he ordered. "This part of the class is so important; it may very well save your lives." He pushed both hands into his pants pockets and walked among the group. "It's true that you've done this a hundred times already, but how many of you can do it blindfolded? Do you know that most attacks and firefights occur in the dead of night when it's pitch black and you can't see shit? Now just suppose your weapon fails during one of these firefights and gooks are rushing over the wire and coming to kill you. Are you able to take it apart and fix it, in the dark, so you can protect yourself?"

He hesitated for a few seconds and then continued, "Before we break for lunch today, each of you will have the same opportunity to do just that. The circumstances will be different; it won't be pitch black, no gooks will be trying to kill you, but you will successfully demonstrate this ability while blindfolded."

Again, protests and moaning erupted from the group.

"This is bullshit!"

"Fuck this shit! I'm a cook and probably won't handle a rifle the whole time I'm here."

It seemed like the infantry guys took the advice to heart and began to disassemble and assemble their weapons. Each time, they were more proficient and confident. There was no need for blindfolds, because they were all able to demonstrate this task with their eyes closed.

After lunch, the group returned to the classroom with weapons in hand.

"I sure feel more confident being here with a rifle in my hand," Bill said.

"I know what you mean! We've been here almost a week and this is the first time I've actually had one in my hands."

"Isn't that odd too with everything we've heard about Vietnam during our training in the states?"

"You're right about that, Bill. I was expecting to get shot at when we walked off that plane."

"Me too. Now, if you think about the replacement center and now this place, aside from the convoys, I haven't seen anyone carrying a weapon or heard shots fired since we've been in this country."

"I don't know what to think. Maybe all that shit in training was just a bunch of brainwashing."

"Maybe, maybe not," Bill responded. "This is supposed to be a secure rear area, and maybe they killed all the gooks around here. I heard some of the guys talking earlier about fire bases out in the boonies. That's where the real shit hits the fan."

"I wish we could just stay here," John said sincerely.

"Me too, old buddy."

The class spent the afternoon on the firing range, where each soldier was able to test fire his weapon. Many of the targets got hit; bits and pieces of cardboard could be seen sailing through the air and then falling to the already littered ground. Puffs of dust rose up from the ground as bullets impacted and buried themselves into the ground near the targets on the hill beyond.

After each person had fired thirty rounds, they gathered up and began to walk back to the outdoor training classroom.

Sgt. Ramone waited there for everyone to complete the short walk back from the firing range. "Gentlemen, everybody enjoy target practice?"

"Yeah, it was great!"

"About time!"

"Good, I'm glad you enjoyed yourselves. We're done for the day except for cleaning the weapons. Nobody goes to chow until each weapon is spotless and returned to the armory. I'll be looking them over later this evening and God help the poor slob who didn't do a good enough job. After chow, you are on your own until the morning formation. Have a good evening!" Sergeant Ramone left the Cherries and headed toward the mess hall.

"Well, so much for our sense of security!" John stated.

"I know the feeling."

The following morning, the class returned to the firing range, where they found several different weapons laid out, both across a table and at different intervals across the range. Five additional Cadres were also present to assist the class.

Sgt. Ramone split the class into five groups so the weapons could be test fired and rotated between the groups, ensuring that every person had an opportunity to fire them all. The arsenal consisted of M-79 grenade launchers, 50- and 60-caliber machine guns, one sniper rifle with an attached scope, smoke grenades and a 60mm mortar tube and base plate. The Cadre would put on a demonstration and fire three rounds: white phosphorus, night flares, and high-explosive, for those soldiers seeing it for the first time. One person in each group would also have an opportunity to fire a LAW, a two-piece plastic disposable rocket launcher. When opened fully, it measured thirty inches long and looked similar to a shortened World War II bazooka.

After lunch, work details were assigned to pick-up the spent brass shell casings from the ground, to rebuild the practice bunker that had been destroyed by the LAW, and to clean the arsenal of fired weapons.

It was late in the evening when the last detail returned to the barracks.

On the fourth morning, John and Bill walked to the range with the rest of the class.

"What do you think they have in store for us today?" Bill asked.

"I don't have a clue, but it does seem odd that we're going without weapons."

"It sure does," Bill agreed.

Upon arriving, everyone took a seat on the ground; this was now an automatic reflex and nobody hesitated or complained.

A large, black Staff Sergeant, resembling a professional football player, was the instructor for the day. He held a short rifle in one hand; wood covered most of the barrel and stock. A half circle, twelve-inch black magazine protruded from it just in front of the trigger guard. At the end of the barrel was a two-foot long, finger thick, pointed silver rod.

"What kind of gun do you suppose that is?" Bill asked and motions toward the instructor.

"I've never seen anything like it before. Maybe it's a gook gun or something new we have to learn how to fire."

Bill simply shrugged, "Makes sense to me."

The six-foot, eight-inch, two-hundred and sixty pound instructor removed his black cap with his free arm and then used the sleeve to wipe sweat from his forehead. Moisture on his freshly shaven head glistened in the sunlight. After returning his cap, he smiled brightly to the class, exposing a gold cap on one front tooth.

"Gentlemen," he began, "let me introduce you to the Russian made AK-47 Assault Rifle. This little beauty is the primary weapon of your enemy."

He held the rifle high in the air for all to see.

"At times, it is more accurate, deadly and dependable than your own M-16. This banana clip holds thirty rounds to our twenty," he said, ejecting the magazine and holding it high in the air.

"You should also note that their bullets are larger." The instructor set the rifle on a table then pushed out one of the rounds from the magazine, before setting the clip down on the table. While he held up the gook bullet in the air, he withdrew an M-16 round from his pocket and also held it up for the class to see the difference.

"This 7.62mm round is the same used in our M-60 machine guns. There is a lot of power to this round and it will do some damage if you are hit. As you can see, our M-16 rounds are smaller, but they are also designed to tumble once they hit something. So a hit to the stomach may exit from the hip, tearing up everything in between."

He placed the two rounds in a pocket and picked the rifle up from the table. "And this is the bayonet," he continued, grabbing the silver steel appendage and unfolding it until it clicked and locked in a fully extended position.

"It is permanently fixed to the rifle and folds down when not in use. If Charlie sticks you with this, you'll be in a world of hurt."

He replaced the weapon on the table, then looked up to scan the many faces in the class; most showed concern.

"During the last six months of training, each of you has become accustomed to the sound your own rifle makes. Today, I will fire this rifle and some other enemy weapons to demonstrate the distinct sound each one will make. It's very important that you are able to recognize these different sounds because all rifles are not the same. This war in Vietnam is a guerilla war where the enemy is heard more than he is seen. If you are ambushed in the dense jungle, and somebody is shooting next to you, you must be able to determine immediately if it is a friend or foe. You're life and the life of your fellow soldiers will depend on it.

"I'm quite certain that all of you have always been on the sending end of a bullet since joining the military. How many of you know that every weapon makes a different sound when the bullet is flying toward you?"

The class shifted about nervously, and nobody raised their hand in acknowledgement to his question.

"Is this fucker going to shoot at us?" Bill whispered.

"Would it surprise you?"

The Sergeant continued, "Before this day is over, I will guarantee that each of you will be able to distinguish between the pop of this AK-47 and the sharp crack of your own M-16. So, let's get started." He picked up the rifle, reinserted the magazine and chambered a round. "Listen closely!" He fired ten single shots, spaced about three seconds apart, then switched to automatic and emptied the magazine in two short bursts. "Gentlemen, that was the sound of your enemy's weapon when firing away from you. Now you get an opportunity to hear the same weapon when it is firing at you."

He moved the class up the range, half way to the targets, and returned to the firing line. They were sitting on the ground, facing the targets. Some panicked when he fired a short burst from the AK-47 over their heads. They rose to their feet when the shooting stopped and quickly bolted toward the firing line, like fullbacks running for a touchdown. Yet others began crawling toward a nearby dried stream bed and lay prone on the ground.

Upon seeing this, the Staff Sergeant roared with laughter.

"Damn, you Cherries never cease to amaze me! Listen up," he was not trying to embarrass anyone, but could not get the words out and started to laugh some more. "Nobody is going to get shot on this range. I'm firing twenty feet over your goddamn heads, which is an extremely safe distance."

He turned and addressed the half-dozen soldiers standing on the firing line with him. "Get your asses back out on that firing range with the others."

They were reluctant to do so and one of them turned around and kicked at the dirt, in hopes of creating a dust cloud so the Sergeant couldn't see him. Finally after some coaxing and encouragement, they all walked back to mid range and lay in the creek bed with everyone else.

"Okay, let's try this again," the Sergeant yelled when they were all safely in place.

The group remained in that position for almost an hour as Staff Sergeant Jones fired the different enemy weapons. Aside from the AK-47, his arsenal also included an RPD Machine Gun, SKS Rifle, and a Chicom Pistol. When he was confident that his class had learned the lesson for the day, he called out, "The demonstration is over; everyone come back to the firing line."

The soldiers stood up and brushed themselves off before walking toward the awaiting Staff Sergeant.

Once they were all clear of the firing range, he gathered them together. "Okay men, are there any questions regarding the sounds that you've heard today?"

Nobody raised his hand.

"That's good, I must have been real convincing. Before we break for the day, I have one final demonstration for you." Staff Sergeant Jones walked over to his Jeep and emerged with another strange weapon.

"Gentlemen, this is a Rocket Propelled Grenade and launcher, it's called an RPG for short. It is very deadly and is most feared by the mechanized and aviation units, although, the gooks do use them in routine fire fights. It's just like our LAW and has the ability to penetrate seven inches of armor before exploding. This weapon is responsible for shooting down helicopters and destroying or disabling APC's and tanks as well. Unlike the LAW, it has no back blast so the shooter doesn't have to worry about a clear field of fire behind him. Now keep your eye on the practice bunker to your front."

The RPG resembled a four-foot long green pipe with a long, orange, pineapple shaped missile sticking out from the front. There were a couple of extra rounds lying on the ground. It appeared that the missile was attached to a stick that is loaded into the bore of the weapon.

Jones leveled the weapon, aimed through the sight, and fired. The missile and trailing exhaust could be followed through flight with the naked eye. The impact created a cloud of dust a microsecond before the entire structure exploded. The results were more devastating than that of the LAW demonstration the day before. Debris scattered further away; rebuilding would take twice as long.

"Holy shit," Bill exclaimed, "look at what that thing did."

"Wow, that is some awesome weapon," John added.

"How do you stop something like that?"

"By shooting the fucker before he fires that damn thing!"

"What if you don't see him first?"

"Then when you see it bearing down on you, either jump the fuck out of the way or take a second to kiss your ass goodbye."

The next few classes were the most intriguing of the entire week, as they revolved around enemy booby traps and how they are deployed.

Sergeants Jones and Ramone were the primary instructors.

"Most of the time, booby traps are so cleverly concealed, they remain undetected until it's too late," the black Sergeant stated. "In these classes, we will make you aware of the many different types of booby traps and how to avoid them. You must also take precautions against supplying Charlie in the field.

"Use extreme caution when using trails and roads, entering village huts and tunnels, uncovering caches, moving around on rice paddy dikes, and on frequently used landing zones. These are all coveted locations for booby traps.

"Most of these traps are intended to maim and not kill. Charlie uses them for two reasons: the first is to slow down a unit, and the second is the probability of shooting down the unarmed helicopter when it arrives to evacuate the wounded."

A few minutes passed and Sergeant Ramone stepped before the class. "Many booby traps used by the enemy are armed with pressure release devices. A person is safe when standing on one, but the second he steps off, the sudden drop in pressure will explode the charge. You could lose a foot, leg, or even die from shock.

"One of the most feared mines by the infantry is the Bouncing Betty. It's usually buried and has a tripping device sticking out of the ground. This mine has two charges: one will propel a balloon-shaped explosive charge upward, and the second will explode at waist level. Shrapnel is thrown into the stomach and groin areas. If you survive, chances are excellent that you'll go on without your manhood to start a family."

Many of the men reached down and checked their genitals as if they were doing so for the very last time. Each looked at his neighbor with pursed lips and wide eyes, shaking their heads in pity.

"Some of Charlie's booby traps include American issued items. At times, the infantry soldier is hot, tired, and gets lazy. The long patrols in this hot climate will force many to discard items to lighten the unbearable loads. They may throw away belts of ammunition, grenades, Claymore mines and M-79 rounds into the jungle.

"However, some of these items are also left behind quite by accident. After a break on the side of a trial, you may get up and unknowingly have an item fall off or out of your rucksack. Charlie makes it a point to search those trails thoroughly.

"He loves to find grenades, as they are the easiest to convert into a booby trap. All he has to do is to tie them to a tree and attach one end of a trip wire to the pin and run it across the trail. The thin fishing line is hard to see, but is strong enough to pull the pin from the grenade when somebody walks into it.

"Favorite scrounging areas for Charlie are those locations where either a re-supply had taken place or the site of a former night defensive position. GI's always have an abundance of supplies and seldom use all they get. Unwanted C-Rations, detonation cord, and personal effects are discarded throughout these areas. Some are buried, but most are not."

Sergeant Ramone broke in to continue on the topic, "A Claymore mine is an anti-personnel plastic mine, eight inches wide by five inches high, and one inch thick. It contains hundreds of one-quarter inch steel balls, which blow outward when it is detonated. It will cover an arc of one-hundred and thirty degrees and have a killing zone within thirty feet. Every soldier in the field carries at least two of them, which are set up during the night around defensive perimeters. Sometimes, they are left behind and forgotten.

"Heat tabs are another simple luxury soldiers can't live without in the field. They are used to heat water and food. Most of us hate C-Rations as it is, and eating them cold is out of the question. If you run out of the heat tabs, some soldiers will crack open the Claymore mines and remove the plastic C-4 explosive to heat their meals. If it isn't compressed, it burns like gasoline. The casing with the imbedded steel projectiles is discarded. And guess what Charlie does with them when he finds them?

"The United States Armed Forces has fired millions of artillery and mortar rounds since their arrival in this county, and occasionally, some are duds and don't explode. Charlie is very resourceful in finding them and converting them into booby traps. He will hang them in trees or lay them on the side of a trail. They are usually armed in one of two ways: either by trip wire or by a command detonation device. This kind of booby trap can waste an entire Platoon."

Jones cut back in, "We're all creatures of habit and many soldiers are injured because of them. At least one of every five soldiers will either pick up or kick a can if it is seen lying on a trail. Charlie is aware of this strange habit and will booby-trap anything that may appeal to the curiosity of young soldiers or fortune hunters looking for souvenirs.

"The punji pit is another type of booby trap. They vary in size from one foot to six feet deep. The bottom of the pit is lined with many pointed stakes that are roughly as round as a pencil. Most of the sharpened ends are dipped in shit and can be fatal if they break the skin. They look very natural in the middle of a path once twigs and leaves cover them.

"Many of them were dug during the 1950's when the French fought here, and over time, they have long since rotted. If a soldier were to step into one of these older pits, the stakes would crumble and the most he'll end up with is a sprained ankle or knee. The new ones are rare and were primarily used earlier in the war.

"Do not accept bottles of whiskey or soda from the villagers, as many of them are VC sympathizers. They have been known to grind up glass and put it into sealed bottles. The glass shards are so fine that they can't be seen by the naked eye. If you drink from these bottles, the slivers of glass will tear up your insides.

"For those of you heading out to the bush, let me leave you with a final thought. Burn or bury what you don't use. Never leave it behind for the gooks to find, because they'll find some way to use it against you.

"That concludes your in-country training. If you picked up on anything in this course that will save your life, then we have succeeded at what we were trying to accomplish. At this time, we'd like you to return to your hooches to retrieve your gear and then fall out into the assembly area. Once everyone is in formation, new orders will be distributed and transportation will be available to your new units. Good luck!"

"What outfit are you going to, Bill?" John asked.

"Alpha Company, 1st Battalion, 27th Infantry."

"Me too!"

"So far, so good. We've been together this long; it would be a shame to break us up now."

"Yeah, I'm happy too!"

They picked up their gear and moved toward one of the trucks.

"Where are you guys headed?" the driver called down from his cab.

"1st Battalion, 27th Infantry," they replied.

"Hey, that's the Wolfhounds, you guys really lucked out."

"Why is that?" John asked.

"Shit, you haven't heard? The Wolfhounds are the most ass-kicking outfit in this division. They're so bad that the gooks have hung wanted posters with large rewards all through their area of operations."

"No shit!" Bill and John responded in unison, excitement seen in their faces.

The driver announced, "Throw your shit in the back and jump on board, I'll run you guys up the road to their area."

"Thanks!" The two men got on board to join the other twenty.

The truck stopped at the 2nd Battalion, 27th Infantry Wolfhounds first, and twelve of the soldiers jumped off and started walking toward the orderly room. It was a coincidence that the remaining eight on board were all going to Alpha Company with the 1st Battalion.

When they arrived in the new area, the First Sergeant had been expecting them. He was waiting outside the orderly room and standing next to a large blue board, mounted on the front of the gray wooden building. 'Company A Body Count' is printed on top in tall white letters. Just below the heading, a human skull was secured to the board; two bones were painted and ran diagonally behind the skull. If the board were black it would have looked like a pirate flag. In any case, the purpose of the board was to represent death.

Each of the four Platoons was listed under the skull and crossbones. Body counts were posted in a column to the right. First Platoon had the highest number of kills with thirty-seven. Fourth Platoon only had twelve.

After the First Sergeant was certain that all the Cherries noticed the tote board, he introduced himself. "Gentlemen, my name's First Sergeant Johnson, but you can call me Top. I'd like to welcome you all to Alpha Company, 1st Battalion Wolfhounds. As you can see by the number of our combined kills, we are kicking ass out in the bush."

"How often do the numbers go back to zero?" someone asked.

"We go back to zero each quarter, so what you see listed today is from July first until now. If there are no more questions," he hesitated for a moment and not seeing any hands raised, he continued, "When I call out your name, raise your hand so I can see you and I'll assign you to one of the four Platoons."

Top called four names before calling Bill and then John immediately after him. Bill was assigned to the Third Platoon and John to the First.

"Way to go, buddy," John consoled.

"It was bound to happen sooner or later."

"Let's talk to Top after the formation and see if he'll put us together in the same Platoon."

"It's worth a try and we don't have anything to lose if he turns us down," Bill said.

"Tomorrow," Top continued after all the names were called, "you eight men will move out to our forward Fire Support Base Kien. You'll draw out weapons and all the other supplies needed right before leaving in the morning. Once we're done here, you can head over to the Platoon barracks and find an empty cot for the night. Signs on each building will let you know if you have the right one or not. I want everybody back here in formation again at 0800 hours. Until that time, you are all on your own and welcome to visit the Service Club or PX down the road. You're dismissed!"

Bill and John had no luck with the First Sergeant, who quickly shot down their request to be together. Disappointed, they departed in different directions, but agreed to meet again in front of the orderly room in fifteen minutes.

"Are you okay with checking out the sights in this camp?" John asked.

"I've been dying to see this place. Between those classes, eating, and sleeping, we haven't been able to do shit in the last week."

"Well, we better get started as we only have a half day to sight see."

Cu Chi was the main base camp for all units of the 25th Division, and it would take the rest of the day for them to tour the enormous base.

"These rear echelon troops really have it made here. It's like living in a big city," John stated matter-of-factly while observing the surroundings.

They found the PX to be similar to a large department store. A person could buy anything from newspapers to television sets. It even had a catalog department.

The Service Club had a library, writing rooms, a TV room, a small cafeteria, and individual recording rooms.

The recording rooms were a little larger than a telephone booth, but in it, a person could listen to his favorite record or tape, or just relax in privacy. It was said that many of the soldiers in Vietnam recorded letters to their families on cassette tapes and then sent them home. When one was received, they could return and play it back on the provided recorders.

Every night, the Red Cross female volunteers (Donut Dollies) conducted bingo games in the cafeteria. Since it was free, there was usually a large turnout. The prizes were small: usually a billfold wallet or a small transistor radio, and the games were not really important. The soldiers only went there to see the American female volunteers. Outside of the hospitals, this was the next best place to see "round-eyed" women.

Just down the street from the Service Club, they found an Olympic sized swimming pool with one and three-meter diving boards. Bathing suits were provided for those who wanted to take a dip. It too, was fairly crowded during the late afternoon.

Further down the road, stood an authentic Chinese restaurant. Rumors had it that the food was delicious, and was a welcome change from the Army chow or Service Club hamburgers.

During the tour, someone mentioned that the forward infantry companies were taken out of the field periodically and brought to Cu Chi for three days of rest and recuperation (R&R). He said that resting in the security of the base camp was a great way of relieving the built-up stress after grueling weeks or months in the bush.

John lay wide-awake on his cot. Thoughts of leaving for the firebase in the morning rambled through his head. He had no idea what it would be like and the uncertainty continued to feed his anxiety. He flashed back to an earlier conversation with Bill just prior to calling it a night. Bill was nervous too, and expressed how sad it was that they wouldn't have each other for close support any longer. However, Top assured them that their paths would cross on numerous occasions, not only in the field or the firebase, but also during R&R in Cu Chi. He said that they shouldn't take the separation as if they'd never see each other again.

John was a pessimist and thought that every time something was going to change, he worried that it would not be in his best interest. But in reality, nothing bad had happened to date. On the contrary, every change had turned out to be a good experience. Perhaps the odds would continue in his favor and the next day would be nothing to worry about. He felt somewhat relieved and eventually dozed off, alone in the First Platoon barracks.

The next morning, Top instructed the eight infantry Cherries to empty out the contents of their duffel bags onto the ground. All clothing was to be turned in and separated into piles in front of the row of soldiers. There was no need to take clothing out to the firebase; clean uniforms would be provided during each re-supply in the field. Of those personal items remaining, they were told to take what they want to carry on their back. Everything else was to be returned to the duffel bags, which would be secured and accessible to them whenever they returned to Cu Chi.

The Company clerk, PFC Jimmy Ray, led the line of men to drop off their duffel bags and to receive their weapons and a limited amount of gear. Each man received an M-16 rifle, a bandolier of two-hundred rounds of ammunition, twenty empty magazines, a steel helmet with liner, two canteens, a canteen cup and some web gear, which resembled a wide canvas belt, and a set of suspenders.

Top gave them an hour to get everything squared away. Each of them loaded their twenty magazines with ammo; ten were placed into pouches on the web gear belt and the rest stuffed into the empty bandolier, which could be hung over the shoulder. After they finished packing and gave their weapons a final inspection, they lined up at the portable water tank (water buffalo) to fill their canteens. The water was still cool from the lower night temperatures, but it would soon be warm and difficult to drink. Top wished them well and sent them on their way.

The Company clerk escorted the group to the landing pad near Battalion HQ, where three Huey Helicopters waited. Two were completely filled with clothing, mail, ammunition, and cases of C-Rations, beer, and ice. The eight new grunts were to load up in the remaining chopper.

John and Bill teamed up and headed towards their transportation. The insignia of the 25th Infantry was painted onto the nose of each helicopter.

"These are some bad ass looking guys," John stated.

The two door gunners wore flak jackets and sat one on each side of the helicopter. They were busy checking the M-60 Machine Guns mounted on a swivel to their front, the barrels pointed down and outward from each side. They each opened a can and extracted a belt of ammunition, placing one end into the loading mechanism ensuring the securing cover was locked into place. The other end of the belt was deep within the ammo can and would provide the gunners with a string of three-hundred continuous rounds.

The entire crew was dressed in green flight suits with dozens of zippered pockets, and olive green flight helmets with black sun shields. The helmets included internal speakers with a small microphone on a flexible metallic arm attached to the side of the helmet. They were used primarily for communication. A cord extended from the helmet to a jack in the wall. When they were all plugged in, the crew could communicate with each other through the internal intercom, as well as broadcast over the radio on many available frequencies. Both pilots wore a shoulder holster with 9mm pistols.

"They look cool as hell," John commented, taking a seat on the floor just behind the pilot. His legs stuck out of the helicopter and dangled toward the landing skids. Bill took a position in the doorway between John and the door gunner.

"Yep, sure does!" Bill agreed and looked for a way to hold on tight.

When the grunts were all on board, both door gunners leaned out to check the area around the aircraft. Announcing that the rotor was clear, a loud whining noise began as the turbine engines started. The overhead rotor blades began to turn and gain momentum with each rotation. The helicopter began to vibrate and shake wildly as if trying to break away from the invisible bonds securing it to the ground.

It lifted from the ground a few feet, slowly at first, throwing dirt and stones in every direction. When at a height of six feet, the chopper turned one-hundred eighty degrees, dipped its nose slightly, and then raced forward. The three-helicopter formation climbed into the sky, heading away from Cu Chi.

As the airships gained speed and altitude, the wind rushed in through the open side bay doors to catch the unsuspecting Cherries in what could be described as a mini-tornado or vortex inside.

"Hey, Pollack, hold on to me," Bill hollered in a panic above the noise of the engines and wind.

"Shit, you hold me. My ass is sliding toward the door and I don't know if I'm being sucked out or blown out." John yelled, hoping that his voice could carry over the loud noise level.

"Come on, Pollack, I'm not kidding!" Bill screamed, "I can't stop myself from sliding out the door."

"Use your right hand to hold onto the door gunner seat and then loop your other arm in mine. I'll use my left arm to push away on the wall next to the door."

That seemed to work as both felt like they stopped sliding. However, their faces paled and their eyes widened full of terror.

"Keep doing what you are, it seems to be working," John exclaimed, "because neither of us is getting out until this thing lands."

Once the flight left the populated areas around Cu Chi, the sights below became mostly thick jungle and small villages with surrounding rice paddies. Dirt trails snaked everywhere extending in many different directions. Suddenly, a large clearing came into view, and bunkers and barbed wire surrounded an area the size of a football field. Artillery guns and mortar pits were positioned near the center of this compound. There was movement below as many individuals could be seen walking about without shirts and gathering around the main gate.

The sliding sensation finally subsided as the helicopter slowed and dropped altitude. Bill and John puffed their cheeks out and breathed slowly from their pursed lips in an effort to catch their breath.

The flight took twenty minutes and prepared to land in an area by the front gate, just outside of Fire Base Kien.

Chapter Five

As the choppers hovered above the landing zone (LZ), once again a tremendous back-blast of wind from the horizontal blades sent anything not tied down sailing through the air.

Several soldiers waited nearby; each of them faced away from the landing formation, covering their eyes for protection against the flying debris.

When the three choppers finally touched down, the rotors never slowed, but continued turning at a high RPM. One of the nearby soldiers ran out toward the lead helicopter while the others converged upon the two re-supply helicopters.

"Okay, Cherries, it's safe to get off," yelled the lone soldier. "Put your shit over there by the first hooch inside of the gate," he instructed, pointing to a dilapidated square block of boxes and sandbags. "Then give us a hand unloading those two re-supply birds," he added before rushing off to the next bird in line.

A single long line led away from each of the two helicopters; crates and bags were passed to each other along the human conveyor line. After placing their gear near the hooch, the Cherries split up and joined their hosts at the end of each line, which now extended through the gate twenty feet. In five minutes, both birds were unloaded and the contents stacked into piles almost two-hundred feet away.

As the two lines of soldiers dissolved and moved away, the RPM on the choppers increased significantly. In turn, each of them lifted from the ground a couple feet, dipped the nose forward, and then dashed away into the cloudless blue sky. In less than a minute, the windstorm and loud whooping noises stopped.

Bill and John bumped into each other en route to the main gate. "Bill, that was tough as hell. I tried everything humanly possible to keep up and not drop anything."

"In my line, somebody did drop a box, but the line never stopped and stuff continued as if nothing happened. The guy wiped himself off and jumped back in without missing a beat."

"I never did anything like that before," John admitted. "Things were moving so fast that when I turned back around, the guy in front of me was already dropping his package; I caught a lot of them in midair."

The other six Cherries joined up with Bill and John and then headed over to where their equipment was stored.

"I think those other guys are trying to size us up," one in their group stated.

They stole a glance at the group from the firebase and found them to be watching the Cherries, making comments amongst themselves. There was pointing, snickering, and some of them were giving each other a high-five.

A distinct difference existed between the two groups. Dressed in brand new fatigues that still had creases, the Cherries looked as if they did not belong there. The sleeves of their shirts were neatly rolled up, just above the elbow; all but the upper most button secured, and the tops of green T-shirts peeked through from underneath. Hair was short, faces cleanly shaven, and the green canvas sides and black leather of their boots sparkled in the glaring sun.

The other group, however, was just the opposite and offered the Cherries a preview of how they would soon look. Many of them were shirtless with deep brown tans; their uniforms severely wrinkled, bleached by the sun and a thousand laundry washes, some sleeves cut off, and all appeared to be two sizes larger than needed. None wore belts and their boots were muddy brown and yellow, some not even laced up.

Three black soldiers stood out from the firebase crowd. Each was adorned with jewelry fashioned from black shoelaces. Braided necklaces hung from their necks, and four-inch wide braided bracelets were wrapped tightly around their wrists. One of the soldiers had a braided cross hanging from his necklace. This form of 'braiding' was the same taught in arts and crafts at summer youth camps. The square and round version was always popular when making lanyards or whips with the thin, flat, different colored lengths of plastic strip. In this case, shoelaces resulted in a much thicker and larger version. The jewelry was a fashion statement, signifying the Black Power movement, and many of the black enlisted men in country wore them.

Suddenly, two black Cherry soldiers left their group and walked over to the other three after immediately noticing them. They began a ritual handshake referred to as 'DAP'; hands moved up and down each other's arms, shoulders touched, fingers snapped, chests were beaten, palms slapped, fists bounced, finally ending in a traditional handshake. The last step in this process was for them to take their free hand and encapsulate the clenched hands. The greeting between the five of them lasted ten minutes.

One of the remaining Cherries remarked to the others, "Ain't this a bitch? I bet after all that, they still don't know each other's names."

The group chuckled and some began to give each other high fives.

One of the three original black soldiers, the shortest and possibly the youngest, left the group and approached the Cherries. He was lighter skinned than the others. Large dimples in his chubby cheeks were more noticeable than his missing earlobes. He walked with a slight limp trying to support his weight on the stronger left leg.

"Any of you Cherries from Detroit?" he asked, looking the group over.

John said excitedly, "Yeah, I am," and raised his right hand in acknowledgement.

"Where in Detroit are you from, Chuck?" he asked when John was within a couple of feet of him.

John stopped in his tracks and scrunched his face in disgust. Shaking his head from side to side, he replied, "First of all, my name's not Chuck. You can either call me by my name, which is John, or by my nickname, "Pollack". It's your choice. And yes, I'm from Detroit and live in the Harper-Van Dyke area."

The short black man began to laugh, reaching to his crotch and then turning to smirk at his buddies. "Don't you know that over her in the Nam all you pretty white boys are called Chuck?" he asked in a singsong style. "You've been born again and should start getting used to your new name."

"Aw, fuck off!" John responded. "I don't believe in all that Black Power shit. You guys think you own the fucking world? I've got many black friends back home and none give me any shit like you're trying to do."

John backed up a few paces so he could see both the smaller soldier and the four other black soldiers nearby. He didn't want any trouble, but if something were to start, he'd be ready. Looking the short soldier straight in the eye, John said, "Why don't you just go back to your 'bloods' and practice up on your DAP? You may get good at it someday! Or better yet, maybe I could teach you."

Immediately, the black soldiers in the other group started to howl and laugh. They gave each other high-fives and began swaying, leaning into each other as if they were all going to fall over. Then their catcalls began.

"Hoowee, I know I heard that."

"Damn, blood, I guess he told you."

"Be glad I'm not standing up there with you. I couldn't keep a straight face."

Upon hearing John and then the catcalls, the smaller soldier frowned and bowed his shaking head, not quite sure he heard John correctly, but nevertheless embarrassed in front of his peers.

"Hey, brother man, all white boys from Detroit like you?" one of the black soldiers with a small pick sticking out from his Afro hairstyle asked.

"I don't know what you mean, but in Detroit we all try to get along with each other. Besides, aren't all of us here on the same side?"

"Yeah, man, don't sweat it. It don't mean nothin', we just fuckin' with ya."

The short soldier raised his head and looked to John. "That was a good one, man, I didn't expect a comeback. What Platoon are you in?"

"First."

"Good for you!" he simply stated and walked over to rejoin his group.

After several moments, the veteran group walked over to merge in with the Cherries. They began questioning them about hometowns, Platoons they're assigned to, football teams, and that 'free love' they've been hearing so much about. The chatter gained momentum quickly and became more intense as the group evolved into several small discussion groups.

The soldier, who earlier challenged John, approached him slowly. He stood about four inches shorter and leaned in to his ear. "Hey man, relax," he whispered. "My name is Junior Brown. My folks live near Six Mile and Van Dyke, which isn't too far from where you live."

Caught off guard, John did not answer him immediately. Instead, he continued to stare at the shorter man, unsure of what may come next. Suddenly, Junior took him by the arm and gently led him away from the group to an area behind one of the mobile water tanks (water buffalos).

"Look here John, I'm sorry about that Chuck shit earlier. I'm really not like the rest of the brothers, but it's an image thing and something I have to do when not in the bush."

"What image?" John asked suspiciously.

"Well, you know, the brothers have been preaching that we are the minority over here and we need to stand together to protect ourselves. Ever since the riots in Detroit and Newark a couple of years ago, they say it looks bad for a black man to be friendly with a white person." Junior shuffled his feet and put his hands into his pants pockets. Both glanced over to the mixed group to see everyone talking to each other and being very cordial.

"That's a bunch of shit, Junior! If that were true, then why are you talking to me, and why are the other brothers now acting friendly with everyone else over there?"

"It's a family thing," Junior began. "See, as it turns out, all of us are in Alpha Company and many of us have now found that we are also in the same Platoons. This firebase supports the entire Battalion; guys are here from every Company, and family got to stay together."

"Aren't we all one big happy family here?"

"In a way. Consider Platoon members as brothers to each other and then think of those from other Platoons to be your cousins. So as a Company, we're one happy family. The other companies are like neighbors: you'll help them out and all, but you don't really want to get into their business. We watch over our own, regardless of color, both in the bush and here on the firebase. I didn't say it yet, but I'm from the First Platoon too. We have to watch each other's backs and have to depend upon one other. Can't let race fuck that up."

"So you're telling me that we're brothers now?"

"Yeah, isn't it a bitch? But I will tell you, my brother that you blew me away when you mentioned where you lived. In the four months that I've been here, every time I meet someone who says they are from the city, they end up living in Battle Creek, Port Huron, or Flint. When I heard you mention that you were from Detroit, I thought, oh no, here we go again. Then when it finally hit me that we were almost neighbors, it shook me up."

"We're actually a couple of miles apart from each other, but even so, I've never met anybody yet in the service that lives so close to me."

"Why don't you go and get your gear and I'll show you around and help you to get squared away? Then we can rap a little about home."

"Okay, but can you give me a few minutes first? I want to talk to my buddy and let him know what's going on. He's in the Third Platoon so I guess he's our cousin."

Both laughed.

John walked over to where Bill and the rest of the group were listening to one of the "brothers" speak.

"Damn, Pollack, I thought you and that guy were going to mix it up," Bill commented. "I did keep my eye on you just in case."

"Thanks, Bill! I thought it was going to come to that too, but it turns out that he isn't bad at all and is almost a neighbor of mine back home. He's from the First Platoon too and is going to help me get squared away."

"Well, I'll be damned!" Bill said, somewhat surprised. "You know that you're the only one out of this bunch that is not assigned to the Third Platoon? This guy here," Bill pointed out the person talking, "he's from the Third Platoon too and is telling us that they lost half of their men last week."

"How did they lose half of a Platoon?"

"Morris said that ten of them finished their tour and left for home and four others were hurt by a booby trap."

"Did they get hurt bad?"

"He said nobody died, but assured us they won't be back any time soon."

"Shit! Booby traps, just what we need." Both thought back to the final class of in-county training that they completed a few days ago.

"Bill," John said after regaining his composure, "I'd better be going. I'll look you up later if I get the chance."

"Oh, okay. Take care of yourself," Bill said. They clenched hands, not in a conventional handshake, but almost chest high. Palms were together and thumbs were intertwined. They pulled themselves together and patted each other on the back.

John gathered his gear and returned to where Junior waited. Together, they left and headed for one of the hooches.

"Hey, you and that other guy seem to be real tight," Junior stated. "Have you known each other very long?"

"Only since we've been in the service. His name is Bill. We went through Basic and AIT together and then met up again in Oakland."

"That's pretty cool! And now you both lucked out and got into the same Company over here." Junior held open the makeshift door of the hooch and walked inside after John.

"This is some weird shit," John stated, looking around. "I've never seen anything quite like this before."

"It sure beats sleeping under the stars. You'll do enough of that out in the bush."

This 'hooch' was as big as an average-sized bedroom back home. It was built from wooden artillery shell crates each measuring two-feet long by one-foot high and two-feet deep. They were filled with dirt and sand, stacked atop of one other; each wall measured roughly twelve feet across by seven feet high.

A picture collection, comprised of Playboy centerfolds, hung from the walls. Each picture was framed with wood and covered with clear plastic sheeting. The total display reflected the efforts of a professional. The newest picture was over a year old.

The ceiling had a base of flat steel plating that traversed the walls and was covered by a half-dozen layers of sandbags. Several four-inch thick wood beams were spaced evenly throughout the hooch to support the heavy roof. A hundred-bulb string of holiday tree lights hung overhead and was the only light source available.

The cool dampness was a relief from the muggy heat outside. No air circulation existed, but the sweet smell of incense burning in a corner was enough to cover the predominantly musty odor.

"Junior, just how strong is this thing?" John asked.

"I don't know. Never seen one destroyed. If you think about it, we're only forty feet from the perimeter wire so it has to be strong. They say that it'll take a direct hit from a mortar and stop bullets, but those 122mm rockets and RPG's bring hell to bunkers and hooches. I wouldn't want to be in here then."

"Did this place ever get hit?"

"Yeah it did; twice at the beginning of last month. Normally, there is an infantry Platoon here to provide security for the Artillery unit on the firebase. But on that first day, there was an entire Company here and they were packed in like sardines. During the night, the gooks put some Sappers in the wire. One of them was careless and hit a trip flare, which lit up the whole area. There was a mad minute when everyone just shot at shadows outside of the perimeter. They said the sight and sound of all that firepower was awesome. Blinding white when the Claymores and thrown grenades exploded, and there were also red strings of light ricocheting everywhere as hundreds of tracer rounds were fired. The next morning, they found six bodies in the wire and several blood trails leading away from the firebase. Then two nights later, after the Company had returned to the bush, the fire base was hit by twenty mortar rounds, but only a couple of guys got hurt."

"Where's the Company now?"

"They're in a place called the Hobo Woods. There are gooks and booby traps all over the place. In the two weeks they've been there, they've killed twelve gooks and found a couple of caches. But we lost a bunch of guys too; some of them should be back in a week or so."

"When do you think I'll be going out?"

"They were just re-supplied this morning, so you missed your opportunity. You'll most likely go out on the next one in a couple of days."

"Are you going to be going out too?"

"Not for a while. I caught some shrapnel in my leg last month." Junior lifted his pant leg to show John two raw and scabbed cuts on his calf. "I'm still restricted to light duty and pull bunker guard each night until I can walk without pain."

"Wow, how did that happen, Junior?"

"The gooks mortared us during one of our re-supplies."

"Did it scare you when you got hit?"

"Scare me? Hell yes, it scared me. Brother, I thought the bottom of my leg had been blown off." Junior hesitated for a moment as he replayed the incident in his mind. "I was happier than shit when I found out there were just two pieces of shrapnel, but they went right through the muscle. I had to learn how to walk again and it still hurts like hell."

There was an awkward silence for a moment and John cleared his throat to continue his questioning of Junior, who quickly offered, "I know you have a lot of questions. I did too when I first got here, but why don't you save some of them for later? We should go and see the Executive Office (XO). He'll want to meet you and know that you're here."

Junior led the way out of the hooch. The sudden brightness stopped John in his tracks. He quickly shielded his eyes and hoped it would not take too long to get his vision back.

"That's why you got to get some shades like me," Junior quipped. "Not only do they make you look good, but they help in times like this."

They began moving again. Junior reached into his pocket and pulled out some dirty and crumpled military bills. "Come on, John, I'll buy you a cold pop."

They stopped at a tent that was filled with cases of soda and beer. Near the entrance stood a fifty-five gallon drum, filled to the brim with cans of soda and smothered in quickly melting ice.

"Better get them now while they're cold," said a soldier in charge of the store.

"He's right," Junior stated, "enjoy it while you can. There is absolutely nothing cold to drink in the bush. Everything will be either piss warm or hot."

Junior paid for the two drinks. John quickly opened his can and took several long swallows.

"Whew! This hits the spot!" John proclaimed and then wiped his mouth with an arm sleeve.

"Not bad for a dime," Junior stated. "After you've been in the bush for a month, you'd gladly pay ten dollars for an ice cold pop."

They finished the drinks and threw the empties into the trash barrel. Junior then led them to a large bunker in the middle of the compound, which was the main communications bunker, where Battalion personnel constantly monitored all activity in the field. They walked down six steps and entered a large room. The walls were filled with maps outlining the Battalion's present area of operations. A small red 'X' pinpointed individual locations of each unit in the field; at least thirty of the marks were scattered around. Several PRC-25 radios lined one of the walls; each was monitored by one soldier, who appeared as if he had more important things to do. Whenever a new position was received, he would walk over to one of the maps and change the location with a grease pencil.

"Hey, L-T," Junior called out, "we have us a new Cherry in the First Platoon. Do you have time to meet him before I help him get squared away?"

"Just a second, Junior," a First Lieutenant mumbled from behind a handful of reports. The right side of his face was slightly disfigured, as if it was burned during his childhood. "I'll be right there."

The XO stood about six feet tall, and couldn't weigh more than a hundred-fifty pounds. His custom tailored uniform was starched and neat looking. The creases on his pants could cut paper. Even his boots were spit-shined and glowed in the room.

Until a few weeks prior, he had been the First Platoon's leader and had humped with them in the bush for nine months, which was three months longer than the normal duty for an officer. The Colonel had to force him out of the field to serve as the XO for the Company. He only had six weeks to go before he was homeward bound to the normal world. His job at the base was to coordinate efforts between the grunts (infantry) in the field and the rear, making sure they got everything they needed. Another part of his duty was to write letters home to the families of any soldiers killed in the Company.

He walked over to John and extended his hand. "Hi, I'm Lieutenant Dobry. Kowalski, isn't it?" John took his hand and shook it warmly.

"Yes, sir."

"Welcome to Firebase Kien. Pick Junior's brain and gather all the information you can from him. He's been here a while and knows many of the tricks used in the bush. Tonight, to get your feet wet, so to speak, I would like you to accompany Junior on bunker guard. This will give you an opportunity to learn a few things and to get your eyes accustomed to working in the darkness of night."

"Great, at least I'll have some Company for a change," Junior exclaimed.

"Then, tomorrow afternoon, you'll accompany a team going on road security. You'll be trucked about six clicks (kilometers) from here to a small knoll overlooking the main highway to Saigon. The team provides security for the passing convoys. They have been going to the same place for the last two weeks and nothing has happened up until now, so you might enjoy the experience. Your team leader will brief you before leaving right after lunch."

"When will I be going out to the field?" John asked.

"The day after tomorrow, when the Company receives their next re-supply."

After a brief moment of silence, Lt. Dobry asked, "Do you have anymore questions for me?"

"No, sir, I don't. But if I think of any, I'm certain that Junior will be nearby to answer them."

"That's good enough for me. Junior, would you take John over to supply and help him draw out the rest of the equipment he'll need for the bush?"

"No sweat, L-T."

"And be sure to give him a hand packing his ruck," the L-T added.

"Shit, sir, it was already on my list of things to do."

The Lieutenant looked at his watch and noted, "It's almost dinner time, so you two should head out and grab a quick bite first. Remember, you've only got a little more than an hour before you have to report to your bunker."

"Yeah, just can't work on an empty stomach," Junior stated, patting his stomach.

"I'll see you two later then, have a good night."

"Catch you later, L-T," Junior responded. John waved and nodded his head slightly in response.

"Junior, the L-T appears to be a real decent officer."

"That he is, and he doesn't act like the other lifers here. You'll find all the officers in the bush to be like him. You'll see what I mean when you get out there."

After dinner, they headed to supply and drew out the items that John would need for the field. It took the two of them to carry everything back to the hooch. Only fifteen minutes remained before they had to report for the night guard duty.

"We need to get your stuff together for tonight and head on out. It's almost time," Junior said, noting the time on his watch.

"What do I need?"

"Just take your air mattress, poncho liner, web belt, your 16, and throw the rest of your stuff on the cot."

They took what was needed and left the hooch.

The earth surrounding the firebase had been bulldozed to create a protective berm, four feet high and encircling the various hooches, tents and smaller bunkers within the compound. Twelve standard sized bunkers, eight feet cubed, were evenly spaced on the perimeter. Supplementary firing positions, consisting of nothing more than semi-circular metal culverts encapsulated with several layers of sand bags, stood in between each bunker.

To their front, rows of spiral barbed wire extended outward for fifty feet. Single strands of wire, pulled taut at ankle length, intermingled within the other coils.

Trip flares, hanging metal cans with stones, and Claymore mines completed the defensive perimeter. Hundreds of detonation wires that were attached to mines snaked along the ground through the sharp barbed wire and connected to triggering devices within each bunker.

A green rectangular box with a telephone receiver cradled on top was also standard equipment within each bunker. A wire attached to the landline phone connected each bunker to the Command Post (CP). During the night, each of the bunkers would be called periodically and asked for a situation report (sit rep). The phone could also be used to request illumination rounds from the mortar crew in the event someone saw or heard movement within the wire.

Junior showed John another standard piece of equipment, the Starlight Scope. It looked like a telescope, three inches in diameter and twelve inches long. An infrared light source within enabled the viewer to see in the dark when looking through it, although everything appeared in a green hue.

Their bunker number was five.

Junior walked to the small firing ports in the front of the bunker and pointed out into the wire. "The Claymores within our area of responsibility are spread out across our front and all point forward," he said, redirecting John's attention to several devices lying in a row across a sandbagged shelf, under the firing ports. "These are the detonators for each mine. If you notice, only the center ones are pointing straight ahead and those on either end are pointing in slight angles to either the right or left." Junior pointed them out to ensure John understood the difference. "These detonators point toward the mine in that direction. So if you see something in the wire, pick-up the right one, remove the safety and squeeze it."

John lifted one of them for a closer examination.

"As you can see," Junior continued, "the clackers are similar in design to the V-shaped exercise grips that a person might use to strengthen his hands and wrist. Except these offer very little resistance and only a little amount of pressure is needed to collapse them. We usually squeeze them two or three times in quick succession until the mines blow.

"This is your first night out here so don't panic and start blowing up the whole place just because you hear something. Wake me if you get spooked. And above all, don't fall asleep during your watch."

John acknowledged with a nod and then looked out into the wire, trying to familiarize himself with the scenery to his front by making a mental picture of what he saw. Of course, it would all look different to him when it was totally dark.

Meanwhile, Junior cranked the handle on the landline, waited a few seconds, then spoke into the mouthpiece, "This is number five, manned and secured for the night."

After Junior returned the handset, he looked over to John. "Another thing I forgot to tell you is to not smoke or light a match in the open. If you must have a smoke, then you have to cover up and light it like this."

Junior placed a cigarette in his mouth then covered himself with the poncho liner. When he emerged, the cigarette was lit.

"That's how you light it," he continued, "To smoke it, cup your hands over it with the filter sticking out between your thumbs like this."

The flaming portion of the cigarette was totally invisible in Junior's cupped hands; only the butt stuck out.

"You have to bend over low to the ground to take a drag. You'd be surprised how far a person can see a lit cigarette or flame at night. It makes a nice target of your head for a gook to shoot at."

John tried it.

"My man," Junior said, complimenting him after the demonstration. "You'll get better with practice." Junior looked at his watch and noted, "We'll take turns at watch tonight and split it up every two hours. This way, we can each get a little rest during the night. You can have the first one, and wake me in a couple of hours. You have any questions?"

"Not that I can think of."

"Okay. Don't fuck it up now."

Junior lay down on the air mattress and covered himself with his poncho liner. It was beginning to get chilly in the bunker, so John covered his back and shoulders with his own poncho liner and moved upstairs to the top of the bunker. Sitting with his feet dangling from the roof of the bunker, he quietly looked out into the wire.

It was dark enough for the shadows to begin playing tricks on his eyes; he became concerned and jumpy. As the shadows continued to move, John slowly lifted the Starlight Scope to his eyes, hoping any sudden movement would not cause a volley of bullets to be fired in his direction. He was momentarily relieved to see that his shadows were only the leaves of a distant tree shaking and not from some gook sneaking up on him.

At nine o'clock, John retreated to the inside of the bunker, and as he entered, the landline buzzed. This startled him, as he has already forgotten about the phone. Taking a few deep breaths, he walked over to the buzzing phone and lifted the handset to his ear.

"Hello," he said meekly.

"Number five, this is the CP. Give me your sit rep," ordered the voice on the other end of the line.

"This is number five, all clear," John reported.

"Roger, out."

He replaced the handset onto the cradle then turned to continue his vigilant observation into the blackness. At ten o'clock, he woke Junior and took his place on the air mattress.

"Everything go okay?" Junior asked.

"Except for that damn phone scaring the shit out of me, it wasn't too bad."

Junior smiled and moved to the front of the bunker.

"Get some rest and I'll wake you at midnight for your next shift."

After about a half hour, John had just dozed off, when the sound of a large explosion caused him to jump from the air mattress and move aimlessly through the bunker. "What's happening?" he hollered in a panic, "Are we getting hit?"

Junior reached out and grabbed John by the shoulder. "Damn, John, settle down. We're not being attacked."

John stopped, undecided upon what to do next.

"Sit your ass down and catch your breath," Junior ordered. "You just scared the fuck out of me by jumping up like that."

"I – I didn't mean it," John stammered.

"I know you didn't, but you sure got a lot to get used to before you go out into the bush."

John tried to catch his breath and heard voices from the center of the compound: "Adjust right one-five degrees, charge four, six rounds hotel echo, fire."

Then it dawned on him. The destructive rounds were outgoing and not incoming. "Those big guns are really loud this close up. Why are they firing?"

"The CP said that Charlie Company spotted flashlights about five-hundred meters from their location. They've asked to fire several 105mm rounds around the area and will send out a patrol in the morning to investigate."

Just then, a distant and deep thump, thump, thump could be heard as the artillery rounds impacted several miles away. A buzzing sound also came from the same direction, almost like a circular saw cutting across a wood board.

"What's that new sound?" John asked.

"It's probably a Cobra Gunship. We'll know for sure in a minute."

"Now how in the hell can you tell that from this distance, especially in the dark?"

"You're a question machine. Just keep facing in the direction that you heard the shells hit. If we're lucky... look, there, see it?" Junior asked, pointing to a long, thin red line in the sky; it extended from somewhere in the air to the ground.

"Get some Charlie Company!" Junior cheered.

After a second, the end of the red line raced to the ground and the distance went dark again. These 'lightening strikes' continued for a few moments and then stopped.

Every fifth round on a belt of ammunition was usually a 'tracer round', chemically treated to leave a gas vapor trail. When fired from the mini-guns of the Cobra, the rate of fire is so intense that those rounds appeared as a solid line to the target.

"Wow, that looks pretty," John volunteered.

"It is to us, but you can bet your ass the gooks don't think so. They say that when a Cobra flies over a football field firing that mini-gun, you'll find a bullet in every square foot of that field."

"Damn!" was all John could say.

After the show, things quieted down and John returned to the air mattress where he just lay there, wide-awake. The rest of the night continued without incident and John became accustomed to some of the nighttime sounds of war, which made it easier for him to relax.

The next morning at six o'clock, they were relieved from guard duty. Both decided against breakfast, and instead, headed straight to the hooch to get some sleep.

When John awoke at eleven, Junior was already gone, so John headed toward the mess tent to get a bite for lunch. He didn't have much time to spare, as the road security team would be leaving at noon.

In the mess tent, John was surprised to see Bill standing behind a serving table, dishing out mashed potatoes from a green insulated container.

"Hey, Bill, got stuck with KP, eh?" he ribbed.

"Yeah, but it ain't bad. It's just like slopping the hogs back home. All I gotta do is pass out this food. The cooks do all the pot and pan washing."

"That doesn't sound all that bad. Were you able to sleep last night with all that racket going on?"

"I slept for shit, John, and lost count of how many times I bounced into the air from my cot."

"You should have seen me. I was on bunker guard last night with that black guy, Junior. Talk about jumpy. It was a real bitch for me."

"What are you doing this afternoon?" Bill asked.

"I have to go out on road security detail in forty-five minutes. I understand we'll be back by seven, so maybe we can get together then, okay?"

"Sounds good, don't do anything stupid while you're out there. I'll look for you later."

The road security team was located on top of a small knoll, three miles from the nearest village. Using binoculars, the six men took turns at watching the road and the surrounding rice paddies. The view was so unobstructed that they could see for what seemed like five miles in either direction.

The entire time they were there, the soldiers were surrounded by at least thirty kids at any given time. Most of them were hustlers who tried to sell them anything from pop and whiskey, to women, chickens and dope. It was like a flea market with everybody making a sale pitch. The time passed quickly.

One of the guys, a pimple-faced blonde reading a comic book, looked up and commented to the group, "Be very glad that the kids are out here with us today."

"Why is that?"

He dropped his book and looked John in the face momentarily. "If they weren't around, then something would definitely happen out here. The villagers know when Charlie is around and are smart enough not let their kids be in the middle of a firefight," he remarked before returning to reading his Archie comic book.

The security team returned to the firebase at 1930. It was later than expected, but the cooks held back some food for the late arriving details. The small tent was crowded so John took his tray of food back to his hooch. When he walked in, Junior was waiting for him.

"Come on, man, I've got twenty-five minutes before guard duty, and we've got a lot of packing to do before then," Junior stated.

"I didn't have a chance to eat yet," John protested.

"That's too bad. I promised the L-T that I'd help you get ready for the bush. You're going out tomorrow and I won't have another chance before you leave."

"Oh, okay. Let's get this over with," John whined.

"First thing we have to do is fit this aluminum frame to your back. All your possessions will be carried on your back so you better make sure it's comfortable."

When the frame was fitted properly, Junior removed it and attached an empty ammo can to the bottom of the frame. "Put all your important shit it here, like your wallet, camera, radio, writing paper, and anything else that you want to keep dry and uncrushed."

Once the can was filled and the waterproof lid clamped into place, Junior attached John's rucksack to the top of the frame, allowing the bottom to rest on top of the ammo can.

"John, main thing to remember is to keep this thing balanced. Everything will have its own place. You'll have to get rid of this air mattress," Junior said, tossing it to the side. "It squeaks and makes too much noise in the bush."

"What will I have to sleep on?"

"Your poncho and the hard ground, just like everybody else."

"Aw, that sucks!"

"Hey, man, this isn't a Boy Scout outing," Junior scolded, "Now, go through this case of C-Rations and pick out the meals you want to eat for the next three days, but take just enough to get by. Don't take any breakfast meals; it'll cut down on the weight. All you'll really need in the morning is coffee or cocoa and they don't weigh shit."

John separated the meals and placed them on the bottom of the ruck. Next, they rolled up the poncho liner and stuffed it inside, covering the cans of food. There was barely enough room left to fit two Claymore mines, wires, and clackers into the pack. The flap was then pulled over the bulging ruck and secured tightly. The packets of cocoa powder, sugars, coffees, plastic utensils, heat tabs, and cigarettes were all placed into the pouches on the rear and sides of the ruck.

They added four one-quart canteens next, two placed on each side of the ruck for proper balance. Four smoke grenades and trip flares tied into the straps on the back of the ruck. The handles of six grenades could be slipped into the metal rings on the front of the web harness for easy access. The last thing they did was roll up the vinyl poncho and tie it to the underside of the ammo can with two shoelaces.

"Well, it's packed. Try it out," Junior suggested.

John put on his web harness, looped the bandolier of ammunition around his neck, and then tried to pick up his rucksack. Surprised, he was unable to lift it beyond his knees.

"Goddamn!" he exclaimed, actively struggling with the pack, trying to swing it onto his back.

Junior laughed. "My man, there's a trick to it," he said and reached to stop John so he wouldn't hurt himself. "Put it back on the ground, and sit down with your back against the frame."

John dropped the pack and sat on the hard packed ground. He slid backwards across the dirt, stopping when his back touched the frame.

"Place your arms through the straps and pull yourself up by grabbing hold of something. If you can't locate anything, then turn over onto your knees and try to get up that way."

John secured the frame to his back and managed to pull himself up, taking hold of a support beam next to him. Once on his feet, he weaved from side to side and almost toppled over before Junior reached out and grabbed him.

"It'll take some time to get the feel of it. Try walking around some more," Junior encouraged.

The longer he stayed on his feet, the easier it appeared. After a couple of minutes, John was certain he could manage without falling onto his face. He flashed a wide grin to Junior.

"How does it feel?"

"Not bad now. This sixty pounds doesn't seem all that heavy once you get used to it."

"Get used to it?" Junior laughed loudly. "Bro, listen up, I've been humping a ruck for four months, and I still ain't used to it yet. Wait till you start humping that thing out in the bush. You'll swear to God it weighs three-hundred pounds. It won't be long before you cut down to one meal a day and look for other ways to make the load lighter."

Junior looked at John with admiration at the way he tried to conceal his strain under the heavy load.

"Okay, now put the ruck down. Later, you can practice more. I only have a couple minutes left to finish up."

John dropped the ruck to the ground and looked at Junior in disbelief. "I thought we were all done."

"We're done with the ruck, but now we have to get you ready. Take off your shorts, socks, and belt, and get rid of them," Junior ordered.

"Get rid of them?" John asked. "Are you joking?"

"No joke, my man. Believe me when I tell you that they won't be needed in the bush. With all that humping and sweating out there, you'll rub your balls raw if you wear drawers. And without the belt, the ticks and leeches won't be able to get under your belt line and burrow into your skin. Socks will only give you problems in the bush. Without them, you're feet will stay drier and you won't have as many blisters. You can either take my word and do it now, or learn it the hard way."

John didn't want to argue with him any further, so he removed the items as Junior suggested. When he was finished, he reached for his tray of already cold food.

"Not yet, brother," Junior cautioned. "We still have one last item remaining on the checklist."

"Now what?"

"Take your shoelaces halfway out of your boots."

Without further question, John untied his first boot and looked up to Junior with a face of uncertainty. "Why am I doing this? I'm not interested in braiding my shoelaces. This silver chain around my neck is all the jewelry I need," he stated sarcastically.

"Would you just knock off the shit and do what I tell you? I'm already late for guard duty," Junior shot back.

"Okay, Junior, now what?" he asked when both boots were half laced.

"Take the dog tags from the chains around your neck and attach one to each shoelace. Then, retie your boots."

"Won't they get all muddy on my boots?"

"They'll get muddy, all right. But at least they won't rattle as they do now hanging from your neck. You'll find out how important noise discipline is in the bush."

John sat back and stared at Junior after tying both booths. "I'm afraid to ask, but are we finally through?"

"Yeah, man. Go ahead and eat your chow. Try and get some practice with that ruck tonight; it'll make it a little easier on you tomorrow."

"I'm sorry I was so impatient, Junior. But all bullshit aside, I really do appreciate all of your help. I couldn't have done it by myself."

"That's okay. What are neighbors for anyway? Some day, you'll be able to help out a Cherry and he'll thank you the same way. Like I told you yesterday, we have to take care of each other." Junior gathered his gear for guard duty and was about to rush out of the door when John intercepted him. "Junior," he called, placing his hand onto the black man's shoulder, "I'm starting to get a little worried. Will it be real bad out there?"

Junior stopped cold. "No sweat. You'll do just fine. Respect and listen to the old timers who've been here for a while, and do exactly what they tell you. Who knows, it might be weeks before you have your first fire fight, and then again, it may be tomorrow. Just don't go out there thinking you're John Wayne, because it'll get you killed. Get some rest tonight and don't worry about it. I gotta go. I'll see you in the morning before you leave." Junior turned, gear in hand, and quickly dashed out through the doorway.

In the morning, everyone struggled with their gear and stumbled out of the main gate toward the helipad. When the Cherries arrived, every one of them immediately fell to the ground, exhausted. Alpha Company wasn't in position yet to accept re-supply, so the group had to sit in the hot sun and wait for over an hour.

The engines started, thus signaling an end to the uncomfortable wait. The Cherries awkwardly got to their feet and quickly boarded the choppers to wait once again. John and Bill found themselves sitting in positions identical as those of their first helicopter flight. A look of dread and despair came over them.

"Maybe our rucksacks weigh enough to hold us in."

"Let's loop arms anyway. It seemed to work the first time."

"Okay, at least we know what to expect this time."

Through the whirlwind, Junior could be seen running toward John's chopper.

"Thought you'd leave without me saying bye?" he yelled over the noise of the engines.

John could only shake his head and try to force a smile.

"Good luck, John! I'll see you soon."

The door gunner motioned for Junior to back away. The RPM increased wildly and the chopper began to rise. In an instant, Junior was gone.

Chapter Six

The choppers flew at a high altitude over the deep green jungle and hills. Occasionally, a clearing was seen on the peak of a hill; they were either prior cutouts of landing zones or the devastating results of bombs and rockets during past encounters with the enemy.

On a sightseeing excursion of what could only be referred to as a tropical paradise, each Cherry sat nervously on the chopper with his weapon held tightly in his hands. Eyes displayed fear and cast frenzied glances throughout the aircraft, stopping in recognition when locking on each other. Most chewed gum and moved their jaws rapidly in anticipation of landing in the hostile bush for the first time. The speed of the chopper formation appeared slow because of the distance from the ground, but in reality, they flew over a hundred knots.

After twenty minutes in the air, yellow smoke rose from the corner of a small clearing ahead. The door gunners were alerted of the impending landing and moved into action. They raised the machine guns toward the surrounding jungle and peered over the top of them for any signs of the enemy.

The chopper banked slightly and began to drop into the smoke-filled clearing.

"Nice knowing you, Bill," John said and looked into Bill's sympathetic eyes.

"Likewise."

The only personnel visible in the waist-deep elephant grass were two soldiers standing in different locations on the LZ. Each of them held his rifle in both hands, high over his head, as a guide for the helicopter to land at his position. Once they touched down, groups of soldiers quickly materialized at the edge of the clearing and moved out toward the choppers.

"Get the fuck off the bird and hurry into the tree line," one of them hollered over the noise to the helicopter full of Cherries. He pointed toward a large bamboo thicket on the side of the clearing.

They quickly pulled themselves across the floor and leapt from the chopper, then ran as fast as they could into the protective cover of the jungle treeline. Once there, they stood in a group, unsure of what to do next. Watching the group of soldiers in fascination, the unloaded the re-supply choppers. They pushed and threw everything out of the doors and onto growing piles on the ground. It took thirty seconds to unload them, and then the lone soldier standing in front of each chopper dropped his arms to give a thumbs-up sign to the pilot. The turbines stepped up their whining pitch and the sounds of the rotors intensified; then quickly, each of the pilots jerked his bird back into the sky.

When they were gone, the unloading party picked up and began carrying boxes and sacks to different locations around the small clearing.

"Hey, guys, follow me," one of them said as he passed; he carried a case of C-Rations on each shoulder.

He led them through the brush to a spot where a group of ten men sat around, some of them conversing in a small circle.

"This is the Company Command Platoon (CP)," the stranger informed the Cherries. "Stay right here and somebody will help you in a minute." He continued to move across the area to deliver the supplies he was carrying.

The Captain was in conference with his four Lieutenants. Each of the men had a grid map spread out on the ground in front of him. Squiggles of red grease pencil lines and symbols were drawn on each. They discussed the routes of travel and individual responsibilities for the next three days. The other soldiers, outside of the circle, sat and lay casually on the ground in small groups. Their rucks and attached PRC-25 radios sat beside each of them; two have long, twenty-foot tall antennas. The phone operators continuously chatted on their handsets with the firebase and with Battalion HQ in Cu Chi.

When the staff meeting ended, the Captain was the first to see the new group of Cherries.

"Gentlemen," he said to his officers, "it appears that our new replacements have arrived."

- 80 -

They all turned and candidly glanced at the group. Then the Captain, a short man appearing to be no older than the Cherries themselves, stepped out of the circle and moved toward them.

Waving with his shorter, modified M-16 rifle, he quipped, "Welcome to the war. I'm Captain Fowler." He stopped, turning to face the four Second Lieutenants, who then slowly rose from the ground and folded their maps. He motioned with his right arm to the four men and turned his head to address the Cherries.

"These men are the officers of Alpha Company," he began, "Lieutenant Ramsey is from the First Platoon." A tall, blond haired man with wire rimmed glasses acknowledged the group with a smile. "Lieutenant Jones is from the Second." A light skinned, black man with the right brim of his boony hat folded up Aussie-style, raised his arm in greeting.

"What's happening, blood?" one of the black Cherries asked while raising a clenched fist in the air.

"At ease, troop!" replied Lt. Jones. His stare was glaring.

The Captain quickly glanced at the two men, wondering how far this would go. Satisfied, he continued, "This is Lieutenant Carlisle from the Third." He motioned to a slightly overweight and shortest of the four men, who smiled broadly.

"Most of you men are assigned to my Platoon," he volunteered cheerfully.

Captain Fowler smiled in acknowledgement. "And finally, we have Lieutenant Quincy from the Fourth Platoon." The partially bald man and oldest of the four, removed a corn-cob pipe from his mouth and smiled, exposing a mouthful of crooked yellow nicotine-stained teeth.

"We work as a team in the bush," the Captain continued. "Every one of us wants to get out of this alive and return to our families in one piece. So listen to your Squad leaders and follow their instructions.

"The Company will be leaving in two hours. You men know which Platoon you've been assigned to, so join up with your L-T and they'll show you where the rest of your Platoon is camped. So let's get this re-supply over with and get out of here." Captain Fowler was all business and didn't give any of them a chance to ask questions.

Upon seeing Lt. Ramsey gathering the rest of his gear, John quickly left the group of fellow Cherries and moved toward him.

"Excuse me, sir, my name is John Kowalski. It appears that I'm the only one going to the First Platoon."

The L-T picked up his rucksack with the left hand and swung it over his shoulder. He then offered John his right hand to shake. "Glad to meet you, John," he said, shaking the soldier's hand warmly. "Did you join this man's Army or were you drafted like most of us?"

"I was drafted, sir."

"You can dispense with the formalities out here in the bush. There's no need to call me "sir"; L-T will be fine."

"Yes, sir. I mean L-T," John replied.

Lt. Ramsey chuckled.

"Come on and follow me. I'll show you where our position is."

John followed Lt. Ramsey as he led him around the outskirts of the clearing to the other side of the LZ. En route, they passed various groups of soldiers lying about in the underbrush. They were writing letters, eating, sleeping, playing cards, or packing their rucks with new supplies. A few of them looked up as the two passed, offering a nod of encouragement. Others made comments from the shadows.

"Welcome to Hell, Cherry."

"Just look at this! Uncle Sam is robbing the cradle and sending them over right out of high school."

"Somebody throw this boy a towel so he can wipe behind his ears."

"Fuck him, he probably won't last the night."

There was laughter as the men began to congratulate each other for their ingenuity and quick wit.

"Don't pay any attention to them," the L-T offered, "it's kind of an initiation and we all go through it."

The two-man parade continued.

When they reached their destination, only a handful of guys were seen sitting in the shade around twice as many rucksacks.

"Just park it right here," Lt. Ramsey stated. "You'll be in Sixpack's Squad."

"Where are they now, L-T?"

"They're on Listening Post (LP) about two-hundred meters out, watching for Charlie in case he tries to surprise us during re-supply. I'll introduce you to them when they get back in." The L-T walked away.

John sat on the ground and leaned against one of the trees. He scanned the area and mentally compared it to the woods on Belle Isle back home.

Belle Isle was a small island in the middle of the Detroit River, between the shores of downtown Detroit and Windsor, Ontario, Canada. One obtained access to the island by crossing over a half-mile long bridge from the east shore of Detroit, unless of course, he had a boat. There were several marinas with docks in which to tie a boat. In 1926, it was from the same bridge that the famed magician, Houdini, attempted a dangerous water escape trick. It ultimately resulted in his death as he drowned in the murky waters below. The residents of Detroit would came to the island for relaxation and to escape from the everyday tensions and stress of big city living.

During a summer weekend, the beaches, picnic areas, athletic fields, zoo, aquarium, and flower gardens were always filled to capacity.

As an alternative to visiting the crowded public areas, many people simply drove around the island. The panorama of freshly manicured lawns, ornamental flowers growing on the sides of the road, and lovers paddling canoes through the many internal canals was enough to tranquilize the senses. When the canals froze over during the winter, most filled with ice skaters parading in circles and hockey players participating in pick-up games.

It was fairly common to see entire families either sitting on blankets at the shoreline or in cars parked on the side of the road. All watched in awe as the large lake freighters and pleasure boats passed in both directions.

The woods on the island were always dark and mysterious. Sometimes, while driving through the shadowy forest, occasional deer and other forms of wild life made their presence known to the few that ventured into their domain.

Vines and bushes surrounded the tall trees and grew wild, reaching up from the ground to choke them. The brush was so thick; it was near impossible to enter beyond twenty feet of the road.

Insects thrived both in the air and on the ground. It was usually considered safer to journey through these woods by car. Sometimes, high school students could be seen on foot as they moved through the mile-long section of the island during the night. They would do it on a dare and consider it more challenging than a haunted house. Tales of murderers, crooks, ghosts and deformed people lurking in the dark shadows compelled the jittery youths to bolt through the dark abyss.

Nevertheless, it was just as chilling of an experience to drive through them during the day and presented a great relief after exiting.

It was difficult to see the bright sun through the thick foliage; the jungle flourished with shadows that danced around and made it appear to be late in the afternoon. John was startled to glance at his watch and find that it wasn't yet noon. He thought to himself, 'this is impossible.

The damp ground and musty smell made him feel uncomfortable. When he looked into the clearing of the LZ, the bright sunlight affected his eyes the same way it did when exiting a movie theater in the middle of the day.

The radio operator nearby interrupted his observations, calling out, "L-T, both LP Squads are coming in."

"Thanks, Bob. Notify the rest of the perimeter," the L-T ordered, "No reason at all for an accident."

After five minutes, the first member of the Squad crashed through the brush, swinging a machete with purpose. He was drenched in sweat and moved toward the pile of rucksacks. Then, one by one, the other members exited through the same hole in the jungle. John's heart skipped a beat when he recognized Larry Nickels and Sergeant Holmes among those in the short column.

Even from a distance of fifty feet, John could make out the noticeable and jagged scar on Sgt. Holmes' face; it started just above his top lip and was concealed by a thick black mustache. It continued across the left side of his face, ending abruptly below the ear. His shaggy and curly black hair appeared longer than most, and was held out of his face by a green bandanna tied securely around his head. As six feet, six inches tall, he towered above the rest of the soldiers.

Larry carried an M-60 Machine Gun across his shoulder. An unbroken belt of ammunition wrapped around his body from his waist up to his chest. He was built similar to Sgt. Holmes, but stood almost a foot shorter. Somehow, he had managed to obtain a black beret, which covered the blond hair on his head. Larry wore a pair of oversized plastic-rimmed glasses, which, at first glance, appeared to be goggles. He was the first of them to spot John.

He pushed Sgt. Holmes to get his attention. "Hey, Sixpack, look, it's the Pollack," he hollered out in surprise.

"Well, I'll be damned!" Sgt. Holmes remarked when seeing John sitting there.

Both raced over to where John stood and wrapped their sweaty arms around him.

"Pollack, what a surprise," Larry exclaimed.

"Am I ever glad to see you guys."

"Me too," Sgt. Holmes added, "it's always good to see a friendly face."

"What Squad are you in?" Larry asked after releasing John from a bear hug.

"The L-T said that I was going to be in Sixpack's Squad. I'm waiting for him to show up."

"Look no more," Sgt. Holmes said, "you're looking at him."

"No shit?"

"No shit, Pollack."

"Why do they call you that?"

"I'll tell you later when there's more time."

"Hey, Sixpack," Larry interrupted, "we better get our supplies before they're all gone."

"You're right. Pollack, stay right here, and we'll be back in a short." Both grabbed their rucksacks and headed over to where the supplies for the First Platoon were held. A red nylon bag with 'U.S. MAIL' stenciled in bright white letters lay off to the side. Larry dropped two letters into the red bag and picked out a pair of washed fatigues from a pile of delivered clothes. Both he and Sixpack were in dire need of new fatigues, as theirs were torn and heavily soiled with sweat. While they changed, John noted that neither of them wore underwear or a belt.

"Junior wasn't bullshitting me," John stated to nobody in particular.

After the change, they quickly picked their supplies and began packing them into the deflated rucksacks. In ten minutes, both were done and returned to the area with bulging rucksacks.

"Pollack, come with me," Larry said upon reaching John, pulling him by the arm. "I'll introduce you to the rest of the Squad."

They walked over to the only remaining guys who were busy packing their own rucksacks.

"Hey, dudes, we have us a new member in the Squad. I want you all to meet Pollack. We go all the way back to Basic Training," Larry informed them, placing his arm across John's shoulders.

John smiled to each of them as Larry said their name and pointed them out. "This is Zeke, Wild Bill, Doc, Frenchie, Scout, and the gook is Nung."

They all acknowledged John with either a smile or a faint wave.

"I can see you're all busy, so we'll talk to you guys later." Larry then turned to leave with Pollack in tow.

"Why is there a gook with the Squad?" John asked.

"Nung is our Kit Carson scout. He used to be a gook, but changed sides after some renegade VC killed his family. He once fought against us in this very same area, so after his retraining in Saigon, he was assigned to us as a scout. Nung usually knows when something's not right. The other guys have said that his intuition has saved this Platoon many times already, and they have a lot of respect for him."

"Can he be trusted?" John asked.

"Hell yes, man. He's like one of the family."

After returning, they found Sixpack sitting on the ground, leaning against his rucksack and smoking a large cigar. Both sat down on the ground close to him.

"Hey, Sarge, how about telling me why they call you Sixpack now," John asked.

"I guess now is as good of a time as any," he replied after exhaling a puff of cigar smoke in John's direction. "I brought a six-pack of beer to Nam with me from Oakland. It's stored back in the rear with my personal belongings, and I plan to open and suck them dry in celebration on the flight home after my tour. The guys in Cu Chi were amused by this and began calling me Sixpack, so the name stuck."

"Did anybody else we know make it to the 25th with you?" Larry pushed his glasses up higher on the bridge of his nose.

"Only Bill Sayers that I know for sure. He went to the Third Platoon."

"No shit? Do you remember him, Sixpack?" Larry asked.

"Not really."

"Bill Sayers is that red-headed hillbilly who looks like Howdy Doody. We met up with him in Oakland?"

"Oh yeah, I remember him now. Everything fascinated him."

"That's the guy!"

The three of them collected their gear and then joined up with the rest of their Squad.

Before they had a chance to start any conversations, the L-T walked over. "I can see you found the right Squad," he said, looking directly at John. "The three of you act like old friends. Do you know each other from back in the world?"

Sixpack responded, "Pollack and Larry were both in my AIT Platoon back in Fort Polk."

"Pollack? Is that a new nickname that you just gave him?" asked the L-T.

"No, he got it in Basic. We've been calling him that since," Larry volunteered.

"That's great. Pollack it is! I do hate to break up this reunion," he said, turning to address the Squad as a whole. "The bird is on its way to pick up the mail and extra supplies. We'll be moving out as soon as it is airborne. Third Platoon will be on point, and we'll follow with the Company CP. Get your people ready, Sixpack." The L-T turned and walks back to join his RTO, Bob.

"Oh, just fucking great!" Zeke protested. "Those motherfuckers make one loud noise while they're with us, I'll shove those radios right up their asses."

"What's wrong with the CP?" Sixpack asked.

"Those guys don't know what it's like to be quiet. They're forever yakking on their radios, cussing and complaining during the humps, breaking branches, and always slowing things down."

"That's not fair, Zeke," Sixpack interrupted, "we need those guys and their radios in the bush."

"I know we need the radios, but I just don't care for the fuckers that carry them. They make me too nervous."

"Relax, Zeke, let's see how it plays out. Maybe there's been a change since you moved with them last."

"Okay, but if they..."

Zeke was cut off by the pop of a smoke grenade out on the LZ. The familiar whipping and chopping sound of an impending Huey helicopter echoed through the jungle, getting louder as it approached. It soon landed and picked up the unused supplies, airborne again within fifteen seconds.

After the sound of the chopper faded, the RTO called out, "Third Platoon is coming through and we're starting to move out."

Within a minute, two soldiers approached and headed toward the hole in the jungle, where the two Squads had come through earlier. The lead guy (point man) held a machete in his right hand and carried his M-16 by the handle in his left. The person directly behind him carried a shotgun and followed the point man closely. There was a twenty-foot gap, and then a line of soldiers began to pass.

As they went by, those who know each other exchanged words of encouragement.

Every one of them bent forward at a thirty-degree angle and tried desperately to manage the heavy loads they carried. They would be lighter the next day, as some of the food and water will have been consumed.

"Okay, saddle up! We're moving out right behind these guys," the L-T ordered.

As the First Platoon members struggled to stand and help one another get to their feet, the last person in the passing column, Bill Sayers, approached. His eyes were wide and a smile lit his face when he saw Pollack, Larry, and Sixpack standing together.

"Hey y'all!" he called. "Can I get a transfer to your Platoon?"

"Not right now, but hang in there and I'll see if I can pull some strings."

"I'll be counting on it, Sergeant Holmes."

"It's Sixpack to my friends."

Bill hesitated, "Okay, Sixpack."

As he passed, members of the First Platoon fell in to join the caravan. The heat was unbearable, feeling like two hundred degrees. Shirts were already soaking wet from sweat and they'd only been moving for ten minutes. Pollack continuously wiped sweat from his burning eyes with the sleeve of his shirt. Beads of sweat also ran down his back, collecting in an uncomfortable puddle where the rucksack frame rests on the small of his back. He tried to relieve the itching sensation but couldn't do so without removing the rucksack.

Zeke's helmet bobbed up and down in front of Pollack as they inched along. On one side of the cover, he had written, "Fighting for peace is like fucking for virginity," and on the other side he had simply written one word: "Short".

Zeke had only thirty days left before his yearlong tour would end. He had been with the same Squad the entire eleven months, and at twenty years old, was considered one of the "old timers" in the Platoon. The L-T occasionally called on him for advice before sending out patrols, and he was considered a valuable asset to the Platoon. In his time here, he had witnessed many situations that required a cool head; he had seen many of the gook tactics and could recognize potential ambush sites. His cool head and street-wise attitude helped him get through it so far without a scratch. He had already received two Bronze Stars for Valor when he saved two guys hit during a firefight and trapped by the enemy. He crawled through the gunfire and pulled them both to safety.

Pollack's steel helmet began to give him a stiff neck and the straps of the rucksack made his shoulders numb.

"I hope we'll be stopping soon for a breather. I can't go on any further," he uttered to himself.

He continued to absentmindedly follow Zeke for the next thousand steps. His only concern at that point in time was finding a way to manage the extreme weight on his back coupled with the hellish temperature. Finally, word passed back to take five. Pollack let the weight of his ruck pull him to the ground. Once he slipped out of the ruck straps, the circulation began to return to his numb shoulders, but the throbbing pain remained. He unhooked one of his canteens, drank three-quarters of the warm water, and then poured the rest of the contents over his head.

"Hey! Dumbass! Easy with the water," Zeke scolded in a hushed voice. "It has to last you two more days. You keep drinking like that and you'll be out of water in an hour, get all cramped up, and fall flat on your ass."

Pollack was embarrassed as he noticed everyone else taking very small sips of water; nobody poured any over themselves.

"Sorry, Zeke," Pollack whispered back humbly. "Thanks for the advice."

Two minutes passed and Pollack looked to Zeke, whispering, "Why does everyone have green towels hanging from their necks? Isn't it too hot for that?"

"The towel doesn't make a difference in this heat, but it is a great help when humping. It serves as a cushion under your shoulder straps and it comes in handy for wiping sweat from your eyes instead of using your shirt sleeve."

"Thanks, teach."

"Don't mention it."

Pollack quickly pulled his towel from his rucksack and draped it over his shoulders.

Up ahead, people began to move about and help each other stand up. The caravan was on the move once again.

This time, the towel helped in making it a little easier on Pollack. Later when the next break was called, he wasn't hurting quite as bad.

In the two hours of humping, the Company had only managed to travel one click (one thousand meters or one kilometer) through the impenetrable jungle. The column stopped and bunched up when the point man came upon a large, unmarked trail. It measured ten feet across and showed signs of recent activity. The Third Platoon sent out small recon patrols to investigate in both directions, while the rest of the Company dropped in place to takes a break. After a twenty-minute delay, the column began to move once again.

When Sixpack's Squad reached the trail, they crossed it one man at a time. As Pollack moved across, he noticed a few members of the Third Platoon crouched fifty feet away on both sides of the column. They were watching for gooks and providing security while the Company traversed the open ground.

After the last man in the Company had crossed the trail, the column halted once again. This time, however, it was to set up a Night Defensive Position (NDP) for the night.

Before individual positions could be assigned, each of the four Squads in the First Platoon was forced to give up two men who would combine to create two ambush teams. They would spend the night watching the trail from different locations. Zeke and Frenchie quickly volunteered from the First Squad.

"I want to be as far away from this CP as possible. With only thirty days left in this country, I don't want to get hit because of some noisy assed radio operators," Zeke declared.

"I don't blame you!" Frenchie added.

As the captain briefed the ambush teams, Sixpack assigned the rest of the First Squad sleeping positions around the First Platoon's sector of the perimeter.

They passed around the few available machetes among themselves to dig out sleeping areas. They hacked away at branches, roots, and stones, until they were sure that nothing protruded from the ground to poke at their sleeping bodies during the night.

When ponchos and liners were in place on the ground and the gear stored properly, only then were they able to prepare dinner. Everyone had his own recipe and special additives from home to make the C-Rations taste better. Heinz-57 sauce and Tabasco were two favorites; Squad members passed them around freely.

After dinner, Sixpack instructed his Squad as to the placement of Claymore mines and trip flares. The guard position had to be set up in a central location and accessible from every sleep position. Once the position was chosen, a clear path had to be made so very little noise was made during the night changing of guards.

It was still somewhat light in the jungle when all the duties were complete to fully secure the NDP. Each soldier took a few minutes to get familiar with the immediate surroundings. During the black of night, when it's impossible to see, it would be essential to know the routes of travel, as well as the sleeping positions of your guard duty replacement.

Sixpack assigned each member in the Squad an individual time for night watch. Pollack had the shift from five to six in the morning. Since it was the last watch, he also had the extra duty of waking everyone up at the end. He was ecstatic and lucky to be able to get a full night's sleep on his first night in the bush.

Pollack squeezed out some bug juice into the palm of his hand, wiped the liquid across his exposed skin, and lay on his makeshift bed. He was totally exhausted from the long hump that day.

Sixpack walked up to him. "Hey, Pollack, are you all squared away for the night?"

"As good as I'll ever be."

"Good. Later when you're on watch, the CP will be calling you on the radio for a situation report. Our call sign is Romeo-six. If everything is all right, you don't have to say anything, just push in on the call switch of the handset once. It's called keying the mike. Make sure the volume is turned down on the radio and hold the handset near your ear at all times. If you're called or if something happens, it has to be available quickly without stumbling around in the dark looking for it. If you get nervous, wake me and I'll keep you Company. I know the first night in the bush is a bitch and I can sympathize with you."

"Romeo-six, keying the mike, keep the volume of the radio turned down, check, I think I have it," Pollack recited.

"Hang in there," Sixpack replied, then turned and prepared to leave.

"Sixpack!" Pollack called. "How about answering a question before you leave?"

"Sure, what is it?"

"The night before last, when I was on guard duty at Firebase Kien, I saw a Cobra working out. Junior, the guy with me, said that Charlie Company saw something and had requested the artillery and gunships. Did they find anything?"

"Yeah, but it doesn't sound too good. The L-T told us earlier that it was more than they had bargained for."

"What do you mean by that?"

"They sent out two Squads on this routine patrol to check the area this morning and found six gook bodies. They began to celebrate and got careless, making too much noise on the return to their NDP. The gooks had heard them and hurriedly laid an ambush. When they were hit, half of them went down. The rest took off, shooting wildly toward the gooks as they ran. They were greatly outnumbered and left their dead and wounded buddies behind. When they returned within an hour in full force, all the bodies were gone."

"What will happen now?"

"They asked for Alpha Company's help. We'll link up with Charlie Company tomorrow and make a sweep of the area to see what we can find."

"You think we'll find the missing bodies?"

"I don't know. The gooks will probably be waiting for us. So we'll have to have our shit in order."

Pollack took a few deep breaths. "I sure hope there aren't going to be any gooks around."

"I'm not too fond of a firefight either, but don't lose any sleep over it. I'll see you in the morning."

Pollack lay back down and in the twilight tried to spot stars in the sky through the thick overhead jungle. He knew it was impossible to see the sun in the daytime, but just maybe it was different at night.

His astronomy search was cut short by something he hadn't noticed earlier. Only ten feet above his head were two large spiders. They were as big as pancakes and sat in the exact center of their circular webs. A chill ran down his spine and goose bumps broke out on his arms. He was scared to death of spiders and couldn't move to a new area, because it was already too late. And by no means was he going to knock them from their webs to crawl around on the ground with him.

Now that he was forced into an uncomfortable position, he hadn't any alternative but to keep an eye on them. He stared at them for ten minutes, just to make sure they didn't move around. As he did this, he noticed swarms of flying insects just above the webs. The larger dragonflies and horseflies dominated the airspace as they darted through swarms of buzzing mosquitoes. He hoped that a few of them would get caught in the webs so maybe the spiders would be kept busy for the rest of the night without contemplating dropping in on him while he slept.

Pollack covered up with the poncho liner and tucked it in over his head. It kept him from getting bit by the pesky swarms of flying insects, but the buzzing around his ears was unbearable.

"Hey, Pollack, get up, it's your watch," someone whispered in his ear.

He sat up trying to focus his eyes in the pitch-black darkness, believing he had been blinded while asleep.

"Who's that?" Pollack whispered.

"It's Scout," the same voice replied. "Take hold of my arm and I'll guide you to the watch area."

He picked up his rifle and ammo then snatched a handful of Scout's shirt allowing him to be led like a blind man. Pollack was totally unaware of his location, which caused a feeling of total helplessness.

"Are you going to be alright, Pollack?" Scout asked, sensing something was wrong.

"Scout, I think I'm blind. I can't see shit," Pollack whispered.

"Give it a couple of minutes. Just sit down and I'll stick around until your night vision comes to you."

Pollack sat quietly with Scout. After a few minutes, he could finally make out the shadows of a few bushes and trees to his front. When he turned to face Scout, he was able to see the profile of the Indian sitting next to him in the darkness.

"Okay, thanks, I can see you so I'll be fine now."

"I'm glad. It's always a bitch when you first wake up out here. It happens to everyone. Oh well, at least I still have forty-five minutes to get some sleep. Here's the radio handset," he said, holding it out and tapping him on the shoulder. "I'll see you later."

He vanished into the darkness, leaving Pollack alone at watch.

John sat perfectly still, straining to see. He held the handset to one ear and tried to listen in on eerie jungle sounds with the other.

"Thank God it'll be light in half an hour," he said to himself.

Just then, he heard a rush of static in the radio receiver and a voice whispering, "Romeo-six, this is Alpha-one, sit-rep, over."

Pollack squeezed the handset once, as Sgt. Holmes had instructed him earlier, which caused the noisy static to cease for an instant and then return after the button was released.

"Sierra-six, this is Alpha-one, sit-rep, over," the voice through the handset continued. A break in the static could be heard again. That continued for the next couple of minutes until all the elements of the Company had been contacted, including the ambush teams.

The jungle began to lighten up a little at a time toward the end of Pollack's shift. He watched as a fog begins materializing. The moist dew appeared to move as it saturated everything within four feet of the ground. When he felt his poncho liner and fatigues, he found they were already wet.

At six o'clock, he took his rifle and walked over to where Sixpack was sleeping. After Pollack gave him a couple of shakes, he opened his eyes.

"Morning, Sarge," Pollack said cheerfully. "It's time to get up."

Sixpack jumped to his feet and began to stretch.

"Thanks, Pollack," he said. "Start waking everyone else in the Squad. Tell them to hurry and eat breakfast. We have to be ready to leave on a patrol at seven."

"Will do." John left to wake the other five men, making sure he passed on the information Sixpack had instructed. As he was doing this, the two ambush teams had arrived at the NDP and individual members were moving through and returning to their designated squad locations. Sixpack caught both Zeke and Frenchie when they arrived and personally informed them of the upcoming patrol.

When Pollack returned to his sleep area to pack up his gear. He looked up to where the two spiders were last night, and found them still centered in the webs. Had they not been there, he would have scoured the ground looking for them before sitting down.

He pulled out a heat tab and began to heat some water for hot cocoa. It was ironic for a person in the country to be so hot during the day and so cold during the night.

Pollack added a packet of cocoa powder to his canteen cup of hot water, stirring the contents with a plastic spoon. Before taking a drink, he raised the cup as in a toast, and said, "I made it through my first day in the bush; only three hundred thirty-five more days to go."

Chapter Seven

When Sixpack called for a pre-patrol briefing, the Squad had not yet finished eating breakfast, as most of their time had been spent retrieving Claymore mines and trip flares from their hidden positions of the night before. They began to trickle over carrying their unfinished coffee, cocoa, or C-Rations to consume while they listened to the briefing.

Sixpack and Scout had extracted a brittle muffin from a vacuum-packed C-Ration tin and were spreading jelly over the top. Then with the painstaking care of a diamond cutter, they pecked at it gingerly so it didn't fall apart and crumble in their hands. Doc, Zeke, and Wild Bill took a seat on the ground and leaned back against a nearby tree with a two-foot diameter trunk. They each brought a can of semi-solid scrambled eggs to chew on while drinking cocoa. Pollack sat across from Sixpack and appeared very nervous; his canteen cup full of cocoa shook in his hand as he raised it to his lips. Larry arrived and continued brushing his teeth while looking for a suitable place to sit down. After finding one, he removed the toothbrush and spat the foamy liquid onto some nearby bushes. He then swirled around a mouthful of hot coffee and swallowed the sweetened liquid. Nung was next to Sixpack, quite content with his meal of cold spaghetti and meatballs.

"Listen up, guys," Sixpack began after taking a few sips of hot coffee from his canteen cup. "We have to check out the trail we crossed yesterday."

"How far down will we have to go?" the Cherokee Indian nicknamed Scout asked.

"I don't know. We have to be back in a couple of hours, so we'll play it by ear."

"What's happening in two hours?" Wild Bill asked. He scratched at some mosquito bites protruding from a large wild stallion tattoo on his forearm.

"We have to assist Charlie Company in a sweep of their area later and help them find their missing guys."

"That's going to be fun," Zeke said sarcastically.

"Okay, back to the patrol," Sixpack continued. "When we reach the trail, we'll go west for a while and scope it out. I don't want anybody walking on the trail itself. Stay off to the side and cut bush if you have to. Something this well used could either be booby trapped or watched by the gooks, and if we're spotted, we don't want to be caught out on the open trail. The order of the march will be Nung, Scout, Larry, then me, Pollack, and Doc. Frenchie, you and Zeke bring up the rear."

"What about me?" Wild Bill asked.

"I want you on our left flank. Stay within twenty feet of the column and keep us in sight at all times."

"Who's going to carry the radio?" Zeke inquired. He held a small metal tube and squeezed out a generous portion of white salve onto each of his red, swollen feet and then rubbed them vigorously to work the medicine in. His feet were infected with jungle rot, a fungus quite common to GI's in the wet jungle. The skin on his feet looked like prunes with some spots looking like layers of skin had already come off. The smell was nauseating and Zeke's attempt to disinfect the raw skin and wrap his feet with a roll of sterile gauze just didn't seem to be enough.

Doc glanced at Zeke's feet. "Looking much better, my man."

Zeke nodded his head in agreement.

"Bob, the L-T's RTO, will be going with us."

"What does the brass know about this trail?" Scout asked.

"Not a thing, so I'm going to sketch the trail on my map as we go along. I want everyone to bring a Claymore with them. Zeke, you and Frenchie grab enough supplies to build a Mechanical Ambush. We'll find a good spot and set it up before heading back. If we run into gooks, break contact, and work your way back down the trail to regroup. Remember, nobody leaves anyone behind if he's hit."

"How soon before we leave?" Pollack asked.

"In thirty minutes."

At seven sharp, the First Squad left the defensive perimeter and set out for the trail, walking along the same path created the day before. They were supposed to be spaced evenly apart, with at least ten feet separating each man in the column. But the dense, tangled jungle did not allow for it without each man losing sight of the person in front of him.

They were not humping rucks and were only wearing web gear and suspenders. Each had a canteen, ammo pouches, grenades, a Claymore, and smoke grenades secured to them. So without the added weight, the ten men were able to maneuver quickly through the tunnel of foliage and cover the two-hundred meters to the trail in thirty minutes.

"Look at the size of this thing!" Larry exclaimed. "I bet the gooks can drive a semi-truck through here."

"They can make it wider yet by cutting down this elephant grass," Wild Bill chimed in.

"Yeah, then it would be a three-lane highway," Zeke emphasized.

"It sure didn't look this big yesterday."

"Hell, we didn't have this much time to admire it."

Nung walked through the chest-high elephant grass then squatted near the trail. The dirt on the oversized trail was packed solid from heavy use and most likely continued into Cambodia.

"No wonder it isn't on the map," Wild Bill speculated, "There's no way a plane can spot it through these tall trees and heavy overhead cover."

"It's natural camouflage," Zeke added.

"I wonder if we're the first GI's to stumble across it," Larry remarked.

"I doubt it, but it has to have been some time ago," Sixpack replied.

"Sergeant, can I see you for a minute?" Nung called from a spot about thirty feet up the trail.

"What do you have?" Sixpack asked when reaching him.

"Look!" Nung parted some shrouds of elephant grass and held them apart so Sixpack could see the Ho Chi Minh sandal footprints along the trail. This style of footwear was most common to the Viet

Cong who produced them from old truck tires; the tread marks on the soles were plainly visible in the dirt of the trail.

"How old do you think they are?" Sixpack asked.

"They are fresh and only a few hours old." Nung felt along the impressions; the edges of the footprints collapsed when pushed down with his finger. Something left from yesterday would have been stiff and hard by now.

The two men rose to their feet and walked back toward the Squad.

"Listen up and keep the chatter down," Sixpack whispered upon joining the others. "Nung found some fresh prints in the elephant grass to the side of the trail about fifty feet up. We'll keep to this side of the trail and move through the elephant grass. Don't use machetes; this way the breeze will help cover any sound of our movements. Stay within sight of the person in front of you and keep your eyes and ears open."

Sixpack then faced Nung and patted him on the shoulder. "Nung, lead the way," he ordered in a hushed tone.

Nung moved through the now head-high elephant grass with his M-16 ready to fire. He was hunched over and stalking through the jungle with the agility of a cat. His head turned slowly from side to side with each step, making certain not to miss anything. Walking three feet behind him, Scout scanned the treetops and overhead cover for trail-watchers and snipers.

Larry had found two extra belts and fashioned a sling for his M-60 so it could hang from the shoulder. With this simple device, the gun now hung at hip level and he was able to pivot the heavy weapon from side to side and could now open fire instantly.

Sixpack stopped the column periodically to check his bearings and try to duplicate the trail on his map with a grease pencil.

Bob, the RTO followed closely on Sixpack's heels. The short whip antenna for the radio was folded and tucked into his ammo harness. In order to ensure noise discipline, Bob had the volume turned so low that it was necessary for him to hold the handset to his ear while moving.

Pollack tried to be as quiet as possible. He fumbled along, trying to place his feet into Bob's footsteps. His head constantly moved and his eyes looked in all directions for the enemy, which he suspected were hidden everywhere around him.

The Squad soon arrived at the location of Zeke's night ambush site. It was there that Nung decided to stop the column for a break. Each member stopped in his tracks and kneeled on the ground. Except for a few flattened areas in the elephant grass, there were no other signs of the ambush team having been there.

Pollack turned and looked at Doc, who was wiping sweat from his face with a towel hanging around his neck. When Doc saw him watching, he flashed a bright smile and gave a thumbs-up sign. Pollack silently returned the gesture.

Frenchie stood ten feet beyond Doc, aiming his M-79 Grenade Launcher at the trail while he watched the area behind the column. The weapon was loaded with a beehive round, a special shell that shot pellets, similar to a shotgun. Each of the rounds resembled an oversized bullet, one and a half inches round and three inches long. Frenchie's special vest was filled with beehive rounds, High Explosive rounds (like grenades), and White Phosphorus rounds.

Zeke was the last man in the column. He moved and sat in the high grass between the column and the main trail.

When the patrol resumed, they moved at a slower pace for thirty minutes before the column stopped again. Nung appeared excited as he moved up the column toward Sixpack.

"Sergeant, please come with me," he whispered after reaching him.

Sixpack turned to Pollack. "Stay put and pass it on," he whispered, before departing with Nung to the front of the column.

They returned in less than five minutes with Scout in tow. Sixpack circled his arm over his head, and then pointed toward the rear. The Squad performed an about-face and began moving in the opposite direction. After walking five-hundred steps, Sixpack halted the Squad and called them together.

"There's something big back there, but I don't know exactly what. It could be a base camp, but I'm not sure. There is a trail crossing ours. Nung and I followed it for about fifty feet and then stopped after hearing Vietnamese music and people talking. We spotted a gook lookout sitting on a platform up in a tree. It looked like he was watching for movement on the main trail. I don't know if he saw us, but we wouldn't have a chance against a place like that. I'm going to call the L-T, then request some artillery. Meanwhile, Zeke, you and Frenchie set up the mechanical on the trail right here.

Spread out five mines along the trail and place the tripwire in the center. Pollack, you can give them a hand and learn how to build one. Larry, take your gun to the side of the trail and blast anyone who comes walking this way. Scout, cover the other end of the trail. Zeke, you let us know when you're done."

As the Squad deployed, Sixpack called on the radio, "Romeo-one, this is Romeo-six, over."

"This is Romeo-one, go," the L-T replied.

"Romeo-one, be advised that we may have located a major base camp along the trail and I'd like permission to call in artillery on that position."

"Wait one."

While Sixpack spoke on the radio, Bob used the daily code sheet to cipher the coordinates so Sixpack could pass them over the radio without causing a delay.

"Romeo-six, Romeo-one," the L-T called after a few minutes.

"Go ahead, Romeo-one."

"Permission granted, over."

"Roger. I'll send the coordinates to Wolfpack and request the Fire mission. You can listen on their net to pick up my location."

"Wilco. Do you plan on leaving a Mechanical en route?"

"That's affirmative. We're working on it now."

"Roger. Keep me informed. This is Romeo-one, out."

Pollack assisted in placing a Claymore mine every ten feet along the trail and covering them with leaves and branches as instructed; the Mechanical Ambush covered seventy feet of the trail. Meanwhile, Frenchie unrolled detonation cord, cutting it into twelve-foot lengths. Zeke took them next, attaching blasting caps to both ends. After he completed two of them, he handed them to Pollack.

"Start connecting the mines," Zeke ordered.

"How?" John asked.

"Go to the furthest mine on the left and stick the blasting cap from one end of a detonation cord into the right side hole, and then take the other end and stick it into the left hole of the fourth mine. Do the same thing with the second cord and connect number four to number three."

Pollack connected the two mines and returned to where Zeke continued to work on the blasting caps. "Okay, I think I've got it now."

"Good," Zeke said, handing him two more cords, "Now connect number three to two and two to one with these pieces. What you're doing is called 'daisy chaining'. When you finish, cover all the white cord with grass and leaves. But make it look natural."

As Pollack worked, Frenchie removed two stakes from his sack and separated them. One had a generous amount of fishing line wrapped around the top of the sharpened stick; a plastic C-Ration knife was tied to the end. The other stick had two halves of a C-Ration can lid secured to the top with twine and rubber bands wrapped around the two pieces of metal to keep them together and touching.

Zeke took the stake with the metal lids attached and stuck it into the ground about two feet behind the center mine. Frenchie then handed Zeke the plastic knife from the other stake and backed away, unrolling the spool of fishing line as he crossed to the other side of the trail. Once in position, they took the slack out of the line and Frenchie drove the stake into the ground. Zeke inserted the knife in between the two metal lids on his stake and then pulled it free, repeating this process and making minor adjustments twice more until satisfied with the tension. It was strong enough to hold the knife in place during a sudden breeze or vibration, yet would pull out easy enough if somebody tripped over the line on the trail.

Scout returned and withdrew two fifty-foot lengths of brown electrical wire normally used to manually detonate Claymore mines. One end had an attached blasting cap and the other had a rubber plug that pushed into the firing mechanism or clacker. Two wires were sealed together into a single cord; a thin rubber membrane separating the two. He handed one of the cords to Pollack and said, "Take this and put the blasting cap into the empty hole on mine number five, then bring the rubber plug end of the wire back here."

Pollack headed toward the far left mine while Zeke and Frenchie worked together on the second pair of wires. The plug and blasting cap were cut off and the last inch of plastic covering stripped away, exposing the many thin copper wires on all four ends. Each was then twisted separately into a thick single strands.

A single hole pierced through the thin metal near the outer edge of both lids on the stake. Zeke inserted one of the twisted pieces of copper wire into the top piece of metal, twisting it around itself to secure it in place. He then repeated the process with the second wire on the other metal lid.

Pollack returned, handing the wire to Zeke, who quickly cut off the rubber plug, stripped the ends, and secured a wire to each of the two metal lids on the stake, like he did with the other cord. "Okay, we're all set. You two wait here and I'll double check everything."

First, Zeke pulled out the knife and reinserted it between the two lids for a last time before moving to check the five Claymore mines and camouflage. Satisfied, he walked out onto the trail, looking hard for any sign of the fishing line crossing the trail; it was well hidden and all but impossible to see.

Heading up the trail, Zeke called out to Scout, who was securing the area and hidden from sight, "Scout, we're good to go. Time to head back."

"I'm with ya, bud!" Scout replied. The two men hurried back through the elephant grass to Frenchie and Pollack, who had already unrolled the fifty feet of wire to its full length behind and perpendicular to the row of mines.

They dropped the end of the wire and the four men exited the jungle to join the rest of the Squad.

"It's ready to go, Sixpack. All we have to do is hook up the battery."

"Good job, Zeke! Take Pollack and Frenchie with you, connect the battery, and get back here on the double. We'll move back down the trail a ways and call in a fire mission on that base camp so we can get the hell out of here."

Frenchie produced a six-volt square battery and the three returned to where they'd left the end of the long wire. Once there, they lay prone on the ground while Frenchie secured each of the two wires to the battery posts. Both he and Zeke breathed a sigh of relief when no detonation occurred.

"It's ready to blow," he announced with a smile.

"How does this mechanical work?" Pollack asked.

"That's right. I forgot you're a Cherry and don't know shit yet." Zeke and Frenchie connected with a smile. "The fishing line running across the trail is pulled taut and only one end, the one with the plastic knife, will give if somebody trips through. Now the knife is keeping two pieces of metal from touching. As you know, the mines are daisy-chained so they'll blow after mine number five gets an electrical charge. To make that happen, you ran that last brown wire with a blasting cap to number five so it will be the first to blow and the others will follow in succession. I took the two ends of that cord and attached one wire to each lid. Then we took the two ends of this cord," Zeke shook it for Pollack to see, "and secured each wire to the same two metal lids like we did the first one. And just now, we've made this ambush live by hooking these two wires to the battery. So now there is an electrical charge running to both of the metal lids and the only thing keeping them apart is that plastic knife. So when it is pulled out, the two lids touch then BOOM." Pollack was startled. "The five mines explode in sequence and in five seconds, it's all over."

"We're a pretty good distance from the mines, so why did we have to lay on the ground to hook up the battery?"

"That's so a malfunction won't kill you. Some of these caps can be defective or the knife may have pulled out and you didn't know it. If the mines blow, you can still get hurt standing behind them, even from this distance."

"Has this ever happened before?"

"I've heard of it happening before, but I've never personally had it happen to me."

"Come on, guys, let's get the fuck out of here," Frenchie insisted, "We can play twenty questions later." They quickly got to their feed and allowed Frenchie to lead them back down the trail.

When they rejoined the balance of the Squad, Sixpack got onto the radio.

"Wolfpack-one, this is Romeo-six. I have a Fire mission at coordinates x-ray, papa, mike, Lima, Tango, Alpha."

"Roger, Romeo-six. What is your target?"

"This is Romeo-six. We have a suspected enemy base camp. Fire one round Willie Pete and wait for correction."

"Roger. We'll notify you when shot is out, over."

"Romeo-six, standing by."

After a moment of silence, a voice called out from the radio, "Romeo-six, this is Wolfpack-one. Shot is out."

The sound of the 105mm artillery gun firing from Firebase Kien reached the Squad a few seconds before the round whistled by overhead. They looked in the direction of the enemy base camp and watched for the White Phosphorus shell to explode in the air. If the calculations were correct, it should be seen three-hundred yards away.

A bursting white cloud was seen momentarily before the sound of the explosion reached the Squad. Sixpack checked his bearings, looked at the map again, and reported back to the artillery crew.

"Romeo-six, add two-hundred feet and fire six rounds of hotel echo (high explosive)."

Seconds later, Wolfpack-one responded, "Romeo-six, shot is out."

They heard the distant firing again, but this time, tremendous ear-shattering explosions shaking the ground followed the whistling overhead.

"This is Romeo-six, left two-hundred feet, and add one-hundred," Sixpack requested.

"Roger."

Fifteen seconds later, Wolfpack-one called, "Shot out."

This time the explosions triggered a secondary explosion.

"Goddamn!" Zeke exclaimed. "Sounds like we hit their ammo dump."

"Wolfpack-one, Romeo-six. We heard the report of a secondary explosion. Traverse the area and fire for effect," Sixpack continued.

He then tossed the handset to Bob. "Okay, let's get the fuck out of here."

They moved just short of a full sprint. Overhead, the rounds whistled as they continued toward the target. After fifteen minutes of continuous whistling and distant explosions, it suddenly quieted.

"Romeo-six, this is Wolfpack-one. Fire mission is complete," the voice over the radio relayed proudly. "Do you need anything else?"

"Negative, Wolfpack," Sixpack replied into the handset while running. "Nice shooting, and thanks for your help. We'll let you know what we find when we check it out. Romeo-six, out."

When the Squad arrived at the hacked out trail leading to the Company NDP, the sound of a loud ripple explosion from the trail stopped them cold.

"Hooweee!" Zeke cried out. "Sounds like those stupid fucks ran into our mechanical. I would sure like to know how many of them we killed."

"We'll find out as soon as we finish with Charlie Company," Sixpack replied. "But you can bet your ass, we won't check it out with any less than a full Company," he announced.

Bob called to the CP on the radio, "Alpha-one, this is Romeo-six, returning to NDP. ETA is five minutes."

"Roger, Romeo-six. Welcome back."

The First Squad had not been in the perimeter for more than thirty minutes before Sixpack gave the word to saddle up.

"Get your shit together," he ordered. "We have to hump to yesterday's re-supply LZ and catch choppers that will take us to join up with Charlie Company."

"How about giving us a break?" Larry moaned. "We haven't even caught our breath yet."

"I know, but the Captain says we have to link up and be on the move with Charlie Company by 1400 hours, so get the lead out. Let's go, let's go," he repeated.

Second Platoon had taken the point during the return procession, which took them across the same terrain they passed through yesterday.

The column humped the entire distance without a break. Once there, they were allowed to eat, as the birds would not arrive for another twenty-five minutes.

First and Second Platoons would be the first to be extracted. Each Platoon moved onto the extensive LZ, and then split into Squad-sized elements as they moved across the large, grassy meadow. When they were positioned for pickup, the locations of the eight Squads formed the letter "W".

"ETA of the birds is three minutes," yelled a radio operator from the CP.

When hearing that, each Squad leader turned to the north, split his team in half, and ordered them to each form thirty feet away on both sides of him. Using both arms, he then raised his rifle high over his head as a signal to the chopper pilot to land in front of him.

This would then allow the two groups of men to board from each side of the helicopter.

After several seconds, a green smoke grenade popped in the center of the LZ to signal the eight helicopters approaching in a similar formation to the men on the ground. As they began their descent, three Cobra Gunships arrived and circled overhead like mother hawks keeping an eye on their chicks. Once the choppers landed, the Squad leader joined the rest of his Squad in boarding them.

The flight to join Charlie Company only took ten minutes. However, without the air transport, it would have taken well over ten hours for the Company to cover the same distance on the ground.

Charlie Company's LZ could only accommodate two helicopters at the same time, forcing them to land quickly; both Platoons were on the ground within one minute of the first helicopter touching down.

The men moved into the tree line and waited for the rest of the Company to land. From the beginning, an animosity between the two groups could be sensed and it did not take long for the comments and innuendos to start.

"Look out, here comes badass Alpha to save the day."

"Yeah, that's right! If you sorry fuckers wouldn't have left your wounded behind, we wouldn't have had to come to bail your sorry asses out."

"Fuck you!"

"Fuck your mama."

"Leave mothers out of it."

"Why should I? It's her fault for raising an asshole."

Only a handful of individuals engaged in this banter and it appeared to be more of a personal vendetta between those few men. Different groups of Charlie Company soldiers lay in the shade of the jungle surrounding the LZ. One such bunch of men huddled together in the shadows of a large bamboo hedgerow. They were smoking cigarettes and paying little, if any, attention to what they saw or heard between the two groups. However, once the CP landed twenty minutes later, it all abruptly came to a halt.

One shirtless man with a green bandanna tied around his head and several necklaces of peace beads hanging from his neck approached the LZ, a radio operator following right on his heels. He rushed out to greet Alpha Company's leader.

"Morning, Joe, glad you've come."

"Hello, Henry, glad we're able to help." The two men shook hands and walked back into the thick vegetation.

Captain Joe must have known the Charlie Company Commander well, as he was not surprised or taken aback by the lack of professional appearance.

After reviewing the plan and coordinating the search, both companies moved out in separate columns to head deeper into the jungle.

The chopping noise heard overhead continued as two gunships kept pace with the moving search party. They would hover nearby and provide additional firepower in the event of an enemy attack. An Officer from Battalion HQ was also present during this search; his small Loach helicopter flew at treetop level. From above, he directed the two companies in their every move. The search turns out to be no more than an endless hump through the jungle as they continued to move deeper into the bush.

"I can't understand how we're supposed to sneak up on the enemy by making this much of a racket," Larry stated.

"It doesn't make sense to me either," Pollack added.

"At least they know we're coming. Maybe they'll run and hide."

"Don't you Cherries know anything?" Zeke spoke up. "We're going to be very lucky if the gooks don't ambush us."

"Give them a break," Scout suggested. "Don't you remember when you were a Cherry?"

"I do, but I wasn't as fucking ignorant."

"Yeah, so you say! But in reality none of us were any different when we first came here. We were all scared and full of questions."

Zeke did not respond and instead continued forward in silence.

At 1700 hours, the gunships left and both companies split up to find separate night defensive positions.

When they were five-hundred meters apart, Captain Joe stopped Alpha Company so they could set up a large perimeter.

Everyone in the First Squad was exhausted. Ponchos were just spread over the jungle floor without any concern for the condition of the ground underneath.

When Pollack applied some bug juice to his exposed skin, he winced in pain. After investigating, he found dozens of razor cuts on his face, neck, and arms. Surprised, he called for Doc.

"How did this happen?" he asked Doc.

"You most likely got the cuts from the elephant grass this morning. The edges are razor sharp and cut through skin unknowingly. It stings like hell when alcohol in the bug juice washes over them."

"Don't I know it?" John added.

Doc pulled a tube of ointment from his pack and squeezed a small dab of white cream onto his finger, wiping it across several of the small tears on Pollack's arms and face. "That should do it," Doc said after administering the first aid.

"Thanks, Doc."

"No sweat, my man. I have to go now. Just about everyone else is having the same problem so it'll be awhile before I can rest."

"Take it easy, Doc," John called to the departing black medic.

Soon, Larry and Wild Bill arrived at Pollack's position.

"What the fuck happened to you?" Larry asked.

"Doc said I was cut from the elephant grass this morning."

"Isn't it a bitch?" Wild Bill stated. "You don't know they're there until you use bug juice. Next time we're in the high grass, keep your sleeves rolled down. It'll be warmer, but you won't get cut."

"What kind of shit do you guys think we're going to get ourselves into tomorrow?" Larry asked.

"I can't begin to imagine," Pollack replied.

Chapter Eight

At 0900, Alpha Company arrived at the spot where Charlie Company had been ambushed. It was quite evident that a firefight had occurred, as the area was littered with brass casings from the weapons of both sides. They glistened in the sunlight like dropped gems as they lay along the narrow, bloody trail.

The captain halted the column and dispatched Third Platoon on a short patrol to recon the immediate area while everyone else took a break.

The sun blinded the men as it neared its apex in the hazy, blue sky. Most sought refuge from the hot burning rays; Pollack, Larry, and Wild Bill moved from the trail and took a seat in the shade of a small palm tree. A light, refreshing breeze blew steadily through the area. The long narrow palm leaves swayed gently and allowed tiny spots of sunlight to dance on the faces of the three young men.

"I can't begin to imagine what happened here three days ago," Pollack commented.

"I know what happened," Wild Bill began. "See those brass casings on the trail?"

"Yeah."

"Most of them are from AK-47s."

"So," Larry asserted, "Charlie Company was ambushed. There should be more rounds from the Russian-made weapons."

"That's not the point." Wild Bill searched for the right words. "Any time you are ambushed by the enemy, you try to break contact by returning more fire, then regroup to attack or withdraw. I could only spot a handful of M-16 casings, which means Charlie Company did very little firing after they were hit."

"But look at all the bloodstains on the trail and leaves; they can't all belong to the missing Squad."

"You'd be surprised at how much blood a body will lose," Wild Bill continued. "Two or three guys who are hit in the right places could have created all this mess."

The rest of the Squad, led by Sixpack, walked over to join the three men in the slowly disappearing shade.

"We're going out with a Squad from Second Platoon on a patrol," Sixpack informed them.

"What's the deal?" Zeke asked.

"The entire Company is splitting up to search a specific area within a grid. Our area is two-hundred yards up this trail. Once we get there, we'll fan out to the left of the trail and sweep the area on our way back. If any of you spot something, holler, and we'll check it out."

"Come on, let's get this over with," Zeke said, rising to his feet.

Fourth Platoon would stay behind to secure the equipment. They would remain on alert and ready to reinforce any of the small groups if they got into trouble.

After moving up the small trail for fifteen minutes, the two-Squad patrol made a turn to the left and had to cut their way trough the vegetation. After the last man had turned off the trail and entered onto the new footpath, he passed word forward that nobody was left on the main trail.

"Hold it up!" Sixpack raised his right arm to signify a halt when word reached him. Leaving his position in the column, he moved forward toward the point man. "Close it up some," he instructed, trying to get them on line for the sweep. "Keep about ten feet between yourselves. Come on, get this line evened out." Sixpack paced back and forth in front of the row of nineteen soldiers.

That part of the jungle was not very dense and consisted of knee-high elephant grass and small bushes as high as a person's shoulder. However, a hundred feet to their front, several thickets of bamboo rose up from the earth, appearing to be as large as houses; the green, thorny, and leafy hollow stems entwined tightly in the impassible clump of vegetation.

"Okay, let's move out," Sixpack ordered. The row of men began to move forward in a slow, controlled march.

As they advanced, they whipped at the grass with their legs and poked into the few bushes with rifles. Pollack was unsure of his duties as he moved forward at a leisurely pace.

"Hey, Zeke!" Pollack called to the soldier on his left.

Zeke broke formation and walked over to him. "Will you shut the fuck up?" He was pissed and his actions caught Pollack by surprise.

"Hey, I'm sorry. I thought with the flare and gunships that they knew we were coming anyway. Besides, I don't wanna pass over anything important."

"Aw, shit man," Zeke sighed, "just look for signs of somebody having been through here. See if you can spot any broken branches, blood splotches on leaves, or loose dirt on the ground."

"Why loose dirt?"

"It could be a tunnel entrance, shallow grave, or maybe a weapons cache. Just be careful not to touch anything," Zeke cautioned.

"Thanks, Zeke."

Zeke rendered an irritated expression before returning to his position in line.

Now aware of his task, Pollack continued the search, but spent most of his time looking down at the ground. The hordes of insects moving over everything mystified him. Several columns of large black ants moved in the same direction, carrying leaves, pebbles and twigs.

After following the caravan for thirty seconds, he came upon an area swarming with the small insects. It was not a social event for the many colonies of ants, but a war between the black ants he'd been following and thousands of vicious red fire ants. Reinforcements for both sides poured into the quagmire from all directions. It was a fierce battle. As fresh troops steadily arrived to join in the fight, others departed, carrying dead or wounded comrades in their jaws or on leaf stretchers.

When Pollack suddenly looked up, he found himself forty feet behind the row of soldiers. In a panic, he leapt through the battlefield like a young girl playing hopscotch.

No sooner had he returned to the line when he heard Sixpack holler from an unseen position to his left.

"Stop where you're at and work your way towards me. Somebody find the L-T."

Zeke sprinted toward the sound of Sixpack's voice. "What did you find?" he asked upon arriving.

"Looks like a cache."

Zeke and Sixpack began to work carefully. They gently probed for booby traps with knives before clearing away some underbrush and matted elephant grass from the side of a tree.

"Hot damn!" Zeke yelled.

"Careful," Sixpack cautioned, "let's wait until the L-T gets here."

Meanwhile, the line of soldiers had collapsed and gathered around the two men. Before any of them could ask questions, Lt. Ramsey arrived with the other two Squads and forced his way through the crowd.

"What is it, Sixpack?" he asked.

"Looks like a cache, L-T."

"Okay, give us some room and back away," he said to the surrounding mob. "Bob, get the Captain on the horn. Tell him we might have found a cache and I'll get back to him as soon as possible," Lt. Ramsey ordered his RTO.

While the three men further probed the entrance, the balance of the Platoon moved away to set up a small perimeter around them.

With the large hole in the ground exposed, Sixpack reached in and felt around.

"All clear, it's not booby trapped." He then pulled out a fifty-pound sack of rice from the hole.

"Shit, man, there's enough in here to supply an entire Platoon of gooks for a month," Zeke declared.

"What a find," the young lieutenant stated. "Let's empty this hole and see what it all amounts to."

"Pollack, Frenchie, Scout, Wild Bill, come here!" Sixpack called.

The four men left their positions on the small perimeter and moved toward the cache.

"What's up?" Scout was the first to ask when the men arrived.

"We've got to empty this out. Set up a line to my left. Zeke and I will pull everything out of the hole and pass it along, then stack it where the L-T tells you."

"How much is there?" Wild Bill asked.

"I don't know. We can't see the bottom," Zeke answered.

As the L-T supervised, the contents of the hole were passed along the human conveyor.

"Bob, call the captain and ask him what he wants to do with all this shit," Lt. Ramsey ordered. "Make sure you tell him there's enough to fill a chopper," he emphasized and then watched Wild Bill walk by with another large bag of rice in his arms.

Sixpack raised his head above the rim of the crater.

"Hey, L-T, there seems to be another cavern down there. Do you want me to check it out?"

"Go ahead, but be careful."

The eight-foot deep by six-foot wide pit looked like a miniature silo. Grooves had been chiseled into the rocky brown clay wall and resembled rungs of a ladder from top to bottom.

Sgt. Holmes cautiously made his descent back into the hole and once he reached the bottom, dropped to his hands and knees. First, he removed a thirty-eight caliber automatic pistol from a shoulder holster and unclasped the flashlight from his harness belt before removing it and leaving it behind. When the light was turned on, he moved forward on his forearms and knees into the four-foot by four-foot hole in the wall. He Held the flashlight as far to the side and away from him as possible in hopes that if a gook spotted the light and fired at it, he could return fire by aiming at the flash of the other weapon.

Sweat poured from him as he inched along the claustrophobic corridor. Twenty feet later, he came upon what he believed to be the end of the tunnel. Instead, he found that it continued after a ninety-degree turn. Sixpack held his breath, cautiously peering around the bend.

"Kiss my ass!" he uttered.

To his astonishment, there was a trap door in the wall with light emerging from its cracks. Curious, he moved slowly toward it. Once there, he placed the revolver on the ground and removed a Bowie Knife from the sheath, using it as an extension of his hand to probe around the wooden entrance.

After a painstaking inspection, he was confident that the door was not rigged with explosives. He sat back on his heels and took a few deep breaths, hoping to slow his rapid heartbeat.

After a minute, Sgt. Holmes regained his composure. Returning the large knife to the sheath, he picked up the pistol and took hold of the trap door.

"Here goes nothing," he said, pulling gently on the door. It made a loud squeak while opening, startling him enough to mutter, "Holy fuck!" He quietly closed the trap door and backed up several paces. Trying to turn himself around in the small confines of the tunnel, he found it to be impossible, so he quickly began to crawl backwards toward the silo.

"Zeke, there's one hell of a complex down here," Sixpack panted, standing and brushing the red mud from his clothes.

"Hey, L-T, Sixpack found an underground complex," Zeke called from his position at the top of the pit.

"Tell him to get the fuck out of there," Lt. Ramsey ordered. "We'll call for a tunnel team." The L-T rushed over to the rim of the hole and stood with Zeke.

After Sixpack reached the top rung of the earthen ladder, both Zeke and Lt. Ramsey took hold of an arm and pulled him from the shaft. His uniform and hair were drenched with sweat and coated with red mud from the nerve-wracking experience.

"Jesus Christ," Sixpack began, "I've never seen anything like it before." His heavy, labored breathing continued.

"Take your time, Sixpack," the L-T insisted. "After you catch your breath, you can tell us what you saw."

"Sir," he began, then stopped to take several more deep breaths, quivering as a slight and sudden breeze sent a chill down his wet spine. "I found a trap door at the end of the tunnel," he continued. "And after checking it for booby traps, I pulled it open."

Sixpack stopped again for a few more deep breaths of fresh air.

"Come on, Sixpack, the suspense is killing me," Zeke vocalized.

"Don't push him, Zeke," the L-T cautioned, "he'll tell us in a minute."

Sixpack smiled and continued, "When I looked through the door, there was a hallway large enough for me to walk down. It was all lit up and bright because of lights hanging on the walls. I can't believe something like that exists underground."

"Did you see anybody?"

"No, I didn't."

"Good. It'll be easier for the tunnel team when they arrive. "Nice work, Sixpack!"

"I was just doing my job."

"Nevertheless, it was a hell of a job," the L-T commended. "We need to comb the immediate area and look for breathing tubes in the ground, another entrance, or anything else suspicious."

"I'll get my men on that right away." He turned to the squad, "Zeke, gather everyone up and I'll join you in a few minutes."

"Will do!"

After the fruitless search, the Platoon gathered around the various piles of supplies.

"Don't touch anything," Lt. Ramsey cautioned. "Everything is listed on this paper," he said, waving it at the group. "Here's what we have so far: Six fifty-pound bags of rice, three cases of U.S. C-Rations, sixteen mortar rounds, five AK-47 assault rifles, two pistols, one RPD machine gun, five crates filled with thousands of rounds of ammunition, seventeen B-40 rockets, fifteen grenades, various medical supplies and uniforms, eight pairs of Ho Chi Minh sandals, four shovels, three picks, and five empty NVA rucksacks and web gear."

"Son of a bitch!" Zeke commented, his face showing concern. "What in the hell are NVA doing this far south?"

"I haven't the slightest idea."

"Zeke, what do you mean by NVA?"

"There are two kinds of gooks in the Nam, Larry. The Viet Cong, or VC, generally operate in this part of the country. They either snipe at us or spring a fast ambush before running away. Most of them are nearby villagers. The North Vietnamese Army, or NVA, on the other hand, are hardcore motherfuckers and go to army training like us. They don't run like the VC. Instead, they dig in and fight your ass, even if it means fighting to the last man."

"That doesn't sound good at all. Do you think this cache belongs to them?"

"You can bet your ass on that, Larry."

"What's going to happen now?" Pollack asked.

"I'm curious as hell to find out what else is down there," Zeke replied. "But we just have to wait patiently for the right people to do that job."

Suddenly, a Huey helicopter appeared overhead. The Brigade Commander had received word of the find and was circling for a bird's eye view.

"Look at that cocksucker flying around up there. Probably never had to hump the bush since he's been here," Zeke stated when he saw the C&C (Command & Control) Huey overhead.

"Hey, L-T," Bob called, "there's a bird on the way with a couple of teams and a tracker dog. They'll be here in ten minutes."

"Okay, people, you heard the man. Set up some kind of a perimeter. We don't want any dinks who don't know we're here to walk up on us," the L-T ordered.

When the team arrived, they went right to work. A dog handler and two other men descended into the silo, while the two intelligence officers who arrived with them remained above the ground. One of them took pictures of the cache from every angle as the other looked over the L-T's list of contents.

Along the hasty perimeter, the men took turns watching the two officers as they sifted through the treasure. They acted like a couple of kids locked up in a toy store. Both officers were frenzied, closely looking over each item before returning it to one of the piles. After forty-five minutes, one of the tunnel rats emerged from the hole.

"You guys really came onto something big," he stated to Lt. Ramsey, before turning to address one of the Captains from the intelligence team. "Sir, it appears that this is an underground staging area and hospital. We found two operating rooms, complete with enough medical equipment to perform major surgery. The place is loaded with documents and is unbelievably spotless."

Their faces lit up at the news. The same type of reaction would have been exhibited by the troops around the perimeter had they suddenly been informed that the war had just ended.

A One-Star General and his entourage finally arrived at the location. After a few words with the officer holding the camera, he headed to one of the piles of captured gook supplies. Placing a foot upon an ammo crate he picked up one of the AK-47's. After holding it proudly in front of him, he smiled so the photographer could take a couple pictures.

"Isn't this a crock of shit?" Zeke declared. "We find the fucking thing and the General gets his picture taken, just like he stumbled upon it himself."

"Why do you let shit like this get to you, Zeke? It isn't the first time and it won't be the last. If the Division General was around, his ass would be out here taking credit and posing too," Doc pointed out.

"Fuck those lifer motherfuckers!

"Lieutenant," a Major from the General's staff called to the First Platoon leader, "please get a Squad ready to go down into the tunnel with the demo team so they won't have watch over their shoulders while setting the charges."

"Fuck them!" Zeke blurted. "They took the credit for the find. Let them provide security and blow the bitch themselves."

Fortunately for Zeke, the General or his staff didn't hear his outburst, or if they did, chose to ignore it. Nevertheless, Sixpack strolled over and led the upset soldier away from the tunnel entrance. "Come on, Zeke, relax man. You're going home in three weeks and don't need to do anything stupid to blow it for you now. Just let him get his nut off."

"This is bullshit, Sixpack! It's been like this since I've been here. Every time something like this happens, the brass comes in and has their picture taken. We get dirty and they get to pose and smile. What's wrong with all of us posing with them? I wouldn't have a problem with that, but they've never even asked us."

"Zeke, I saw the same thing during my last tour. I guess it depends upon the individual. The Colonel we had used to involve everybody in the picture and then have articles written in the Stars and Stripes newspaper. They're not all the same. Just let it go. It don't mean nothin."

The two intelligence officers entered the hole to join the dog, his handler, and the two tunnel rats in the complex. They wanted to continue with their exploration to ensure nothing got missed.

Fifteen minutes later, the demo team touched down with the explosives. First Squad had drawn the shortest straw so they would escort the demo team and provide security underground. Three hundred pounds of plastic explosive, dozens of blasting caps, miles of detonation cord and several electronic gadgets needed to be moved into the complex.

Sixpack led his Squad of eight men down into the silo. Upon reaching the entrance, each man crawled into the tunnel and either pulled or pushed his cargo until exiting through the trap door and into the bright hallway of the underground complex. Everyone stood in awe, admiring the unbelievable sight before them; even Sixpack was taken back after already seeing this earlier.

"How in the hell does somebody dig something like this underground?"

"These people have been fighting wars in this country for decades. Since World War Two, it's been the Japanese, then the French, and now us. There is no telling how long this place has been here."

"I remember seeing old war movies that showed the POW's building tunnels from their barracks so they could escape. It seemed like it took them months to complete them," Larry chimed in.

"Yeah, but you got to remember that they had to scrounge for material. The gooks had supplies brought in by the truck full. Now, add a few hundred gooks to the plan and they can dig out complexes like this in no time."

"Good point, Doc!"

The walls were a little more than five feet high and so closely braced with wood planking that the dirt behind them hardly showed. As the Squad proceeded along the dirt floor of the corridor, they noticed a dozen or so portable lights hanging from the walls at ten-foot intervals. The Squad found several side rooms in the complex; most were small, measuring less than one-hundred fifty square feet. Four of them must have been for the recovering patients as they contained cots and storage cabinets in each of them. Two of the others were found to be medical operating rooms; they were the largest of all and twice the size of the single rooms. Those rooms had wooden floors and a bright reflective light hanging from the ceiling. Various trays of operating instruments rested upon rolling carts in a corner near small sterilizing units. The blood spatter on the floor, most likely from a recent surgery, stood out among the well-scrubbed and maintained walls.

The furthest room from the entrance had a small generator and an air pump supplying oxygen into the complex via bamboo tube ducting, which was why breathing tubes were not found on the surface.

Across from that room was an office and communication center. The two officers who had arrived from intelligence spent most of their time in there gathering various documents. Much of their findings consisted of patient files, medical supply request forms, and reconnaissance reports about nearby American and ARVN activity. A large map hung from the wall with arrows pointing in different directions, apparently signifying troop movements. Even the location of Firebase Kien and several other military compounds were circled and highlighted.

Earlier, the officers had found a PRC-25 radio, six extra batteries, and a couple of U.S. code books. The frequencies had been set to the same as Alpha Company, which accounted for their quick getaway. The gooks departed in such haste that they failed to take many important documents and supplies with them. To them, escaping with their very lives was more important.

When Doc, Zeke, and Frenchie entered one of the rooms, they found it empty and bare, which was unusual, as every other room had contained either equipment or supplies. Doc leaned against a wall and suddenly lost his balance as it gave way and swiveled inward.

"What the hell?" Zeke commented when he noticed the medic sprawled on the floor. "Doc, you okay?"

"The fucking wall moved." Doc was slow to rise, but managed to get to his feet when helped by Pollack and Larry.

Frenchie left to notify the others.

Zeke approached the small section of the wall and pushed it open. "Shit, this is nothing but wood and dry mud, and there's a stairway leading up."

Sixpack and the others entered the room after hearing of the new discovery.

"Wild Bill, go topside and let the L-T know we've found another exit. Tell him we're coming up, and for him to pass the word on to the rest of the Company so they don't shoot our asses up," Sixpack ordered.

When Wild Bill returned several minutes later, Sixpack and the others observed the dog and his handler cautiously ascending the steps and approaching the camouflaged exit, which was a small trap door, barely large enough for the handler and his charge to squeeze through. He returned after a few minutes.

JOHN PODLASKI

"You guys aren't going to believe this. Come take a look for yourself."

One by one, they climbed the stairway and exited the tunnel complex, only to find they were standing within a twenty-foot thick clump of bamboo with a small crawlspace cut through the thicket. Scout crawled first through the thorny vegetation and succeeded in dislodging the 'bamboo plug' used to camouflage the entrance.

"Wait until you guys see this," he announced from the other side.

Each of them made a similar statement upon exiting the thicket.

"Kiss my ass!"

"Holy shit!"

"Do you fucking believe this shit?"

An awkward and surprising sight greeted them. Members of the Fourth Platoon milled around the bamboo thicket with the rest of the Company's rucksacks, which still lay where they were dropped before the search began. In fact, the First Squad's rucksacks were only a few feet away from the camouflaged opening to the tunnel complex.

Both groups of men stood there, trying to process the fact that they had been sitting on top of the place for the last few hours and never had a clue that it was there.

"Now I know where the gooks took off to after their encounter with Charlie Company. They just slipped back into the ground like snakes."

"Your right, Zeke, but it doesn't look like they took the missing soldiers into the hole as we didn't see any evidence of them down below."

"They moved the bodies before Charlie Company came back to nose around the area. They needed to protect their complex and did what was necessary to not be discovered."

"It looks like they wasted their time, Sixpack, since we found it anyway."

"Yeah, but it looks like they expected us to find it. Otherwise they would have stuck around and put up a fight."

"If they left through this exit, shouldn't the Fourth Platoon have seen them?" Scout asked.

"Who said they left from this entrance? You saw how we stumbled upon it. Well actually, Doc did." Some laughter ensued.

"There are probably more hidden exits that we didn't find and most likely that's how they escaped."

"Anything's possible, Zeke. Maybe they just bugged out before we even got here," Sixpack replied.

"We'll never know the answer. It'll be buried with the rest of the complex and supplies."

It took almost two hours to set the charges in the complex. Zeke and Frenchie were the explosive experts in the Platoon, so they assisted the demo team with the setting and wiring of the explosives. After they finished, everyone returned topside.

The General was getting pissed because the complex was causing such a delay. He sensed the gooks were nearby, and the wasted time was depriving him of getting a body count.

While the Company awaited the word to move out, the Radio Telephone Operators (RTO's) in the CP started chattering excitedly amongst themselves. Bob left the group and hurried toward First Platoon.

"Charlie Company found their missing guys about a half a click away from here," he said excitedly. "They were all dead and found together in a shallow grave. Two bamboo poles marked the site; each had a severed head mounted on top. Now get this, there was a sign hanging from one of them that said, 'Wolfhounds leave Vietnam, or you will end up like your comrades'."

"Holy Jesus!" Larry was truly shaken by the news and wondered how something so cruel could happen.

"Bitch!" was all that Zeke could muster.

"Rotten motherfuckers," Wild Bill added.

"Wait, there's more," Bob interrupted. "They were naked and each of the bodies was missing their dicks."

A highly agitated Sixpack began to pace. He seemed to be muttering to himself while kicking at the dirt. "Now, see what happens when you leave somebody behind? I'd bet that only a couple of them were dead. The gooks probably enjoyed torturing the rest of them before they finally died." He bowed his head to disguise his weeping. "If we are ever on patrol and I get hit, so help me God as my witness, I'll blow away the first of you that turns tail and runs."

"That goes double for me." Frenchie also shed some tears as evidenced by the streaks running down his dirty face.

"Sixpack, I hate to interrupt, but we gotta get moving, and get as far away from here as possible before it gets dark!" Zeke exclaimed, bringing everyone back to reality. "You had better let the L-T know the complex is ready to blow. You may also want to ask him to check with the General, to see if he wants to personally push the plunger. If so, make sure he brings his cameraman."

"Too late, they already bugged out. Probably got too hot for them out here in the bush," Wild Bill volunteered.

All but Sixpack laughed at the comment.

After returning from his conference with the L-T, Sixpack informed the soldiers, "The Company is moving out, and we're staying back to provide security until the complex is blown. Then we'll escort the demo team to a nearby LZ where the rest of the Company will be waiting for us."

"This will make a very loud noise and will feel like an earthquake," Frenchie stated.

"I agree," Sixpack said, "Zeke, Frenchie, Scout, and Nung, you guys stick close to the demo guys. The rest of us will take your gear and wait for you down the trail."

The two groups then split up. The demolition team moved toward the silo while the remaining men headed in the opposite direction carrying a rucksack on each shoulder. The packs were very light, as most of the food and water had been consumed. However, everything would be replenished when the Company returned to the firebase the next day.

Sixpack's group paced five-hundred feet down the trail, stopping to wait for the expected explosion.

Meanwhile, the demolition team made their final preparations. The chief demo specialist took a roll of wire, splicing both ends onto the two wires leading up from the hole.

"Come on, guys, let's unreel this and move back to where it will be safer."

Nung took the point and led the group toward the trail that they would soon be traveling. Frenchie and Zeke followed them, staying about thirty feet back to ensure nobody snuck up on them or cut the wire.

"I think this is far enough," the leader announced, dropping to one knee. "Give me the plunger."

He unscrewed the two nuts on the poles of the small black box and wrapped a wire around each one. After reattaching the nuts securely, he pulled the plunger up until he heard a click.

"It's ready to go."

Scout removed the metal cap from the top of a twelve-inch long by one-inch round cylinder, fitting it over the metal on the opposite end. He held the cylinder tightly in his left hand and pointed it into the air, quickly raising his right arm to strike the cap underneath with the heel of his hand. There was a loud popping sound as a star cluster flare shot into the sky like a Fourth of July rocket.

Upon seeing the signal, RTO's began relaying the warning over their radios: "Fire in the hole!"

The demo team leader counted off, "One, two, three, ready, now!" He instantly twisted the handle on the black detonator box to fire the charge.

The ground erupted with such force that it lifted everyone within close proximity into the air. The tremendous explosion temporarily deafened them. Stones, dirt, and vegetation rained from the sky as the entire area became engulfed in a giant dust cloud.

Fifteen minutes later, the Platoon was back together and moving toward the LZ with the demolition team.

"That fucking place isn't going to hide any more gooks," Frenchie informed those around him. "All that's left of that complex is a huge hole in the ground."

"What happened to all the stuff we took out of that place?" Pollack asked.

"Fourth Platoon loaded most of it on choppers while we were wiring the place. The rest was burned," Sixpack replied.

"One of those pistols is mine," Frenchie said proudly.

"How do you figure that?" Zeke asked.

"The L-T had me tag it with my name and send it back to the rear on one of the birds."

"Shit, Frenchie, that gun is already tucked away in somebody's personal belongings back in Cu Chi. That tag is probably sitting at the bottom of a shit can in one of the latrines on the base," Zeke blurted.

"If it's not there when we get to Cu Chi and I find out who has it, they'll learn that they stole from the wrong grunt."

"Now you're catching on," Zeke admitted. "All those rear echelon motherfuckers are the same. They give a fuck less what we have to hump on our backs, or what kind of hills we have to climb to get there. They're happy as long as they don't miss the happy hour in their favorite Saigon bar at five o'clock."

Doc looked over at Pollack who was trying to absorb the information. "Don't pay him any attention. Zeke was never like this. He's just getting nervous because he's going home soon. They say that you can be as fearless as a lion after your first month in country, but then feel like a Cherry again during that last month. I'd probably feel the same way if I'd been through the shit he has in his eleven months in this hellhole."

"When are you going home, Doc?"

"I hope to board that Freedom Bird in six months."

"By that time, Larry and I will be the only ones left from this group today. We'll be the 'old men' in the Squad."

"Maybe not. Haven't you been reading the papers?"

"Not really."

"They are writing articles about Nixon wanting to pull the GIs out of Nam and send them all home. You might not even have to spend a whole year in this god awful war."

"That would be great! This whole place just scares the fuck out of me. I'm ready to go home right now."

"Aren't we all?"

At 1700 hours, the Company arrived at the same LZ where they had landed the previous day. They would bush there for the night and be transported by choppers to Cu Chi in the morning.

Pollack moved to join Larry and Wild Bill.

"I'm fucking exhausted," he said after arriving at their position.

"Me too," Larry added.

"Look at it this way. At least we did something different today. We didn't have to hump our asses off all day long in this jungle paradise," Wild Bill offered.

"That was the good part of it, but I've been thinking about what Zeke had said about the NVA."

"Yeah, it's unusual for them for be in this part of the country."

"It's not only that. Larry, you remember during training, they were always telling us that the gooks were smart and sneaky, but as a fighting unit, they were backwards and poorly supplied?"

Larry nodded.

"Shit, Pollack, you've been listening to the wrong people. Did you take a good look at that complex today? You would think they have it better than we do. We hump our ass off to find them and all they have to do sit and wait for us. It's no different than fighting in your own neighborhood: you know where all the safe hiding places are. It was highly impossible that a backward group of people built that place. I sure couldn't have," Wild Bill said.

"That's what I mean," Pollack admitted.

"That place showed class and ingenuity. If Sixpack hadn't stumbled across that cache, we would have walked right over them. You had better change your attitude about the gooks right now. If you don't respect them and continue to underestimate them, you'll never make it home alive."

Pollack pondered the thought before conceding, "I guess you're right."

"I know I'm right," Wild Bill concluded.

"Look at the bright side," Larry broke in. "Tomorrow we can get some rest and party in the rear."

"You're right! At least we can forget about gooks for a couple of days."

"I can't wait to drink something cold."

"At least I can agree on that."

Pollack thought back to Junior's remark on the firebase. He was right about a person being willing to pay ten dollars for an ice-cold pop or even a piece of ice in the bush; they had been drinking lukewarm water for three days. Suddenly, ten dollars seemed a cheap price to pay for the privilege of swirling an ice-cold liquid around in your mouth. They couldn't wait until tomorrow.

Chapter Nine

At daybreak, the activity inside the NDP was frenzied as everyone prepared for his return to Cu Chi.

"Who wants to trade a can of fruit cocktail for some pound cake?" Frenchie asked.

"I will!" Doc replied. The two men tossed cans through the air to one another.

"Does anyone need extra water?" Wild Bill held two full canteens in the air.

"You guys can have all my shit!" Zeke emptied the contents of his rucksack onto the ground. Several eight-ounce green cans of fruit cocktail, peaches, pound cake, and some smaller tins of peanut butter, crackers, and cheese, fell in a heap.

"Why are you doing this?" Scout asked from his position a short distance away.

"I won't need them anymore."

"What do you mean?" We're only staying in the rear for three days. Those cans are a grunt's most prized possessions. You'll be sorry, Zeke."

"You're wrong, Doc. My infantry days are over. Sixpack informed me last night that the Colonel had honored my request to be the mail clerk for my last three weeks in country. From now on, I'll be sleeping on soft mattresses in Cu Chi. No more humping for this kid."

"Congratulations!" Doc announced.

"I'm happy for you too, Zeke," Frenchie added.

"What luck!" Larry joined the others in snapping up Zeke's discarded treasures.

"You bet your ass it's luck," Zeke declared. "In my eleven months here, I've been sniped at, ambushed, pinned down, and overrun by gooks. And it is pure luck that I survived. Now, all I have to do is lounge around in the security of Cu Chi for three more weeks and I'm out of here on that Freedom Bird home."

"I'm sorry," Larry mumbled, "I didn't mean it to sound like that."

"Forget it, Larry," Zeke replied. "If you're lucky enough to survive as long as I have, then maybe a break will come your way too."

"What's your plan once you get home?" Doc asked.

"The first thing I'm going to do is to sit on a real toilet and flush it a hundred times." Everyone laughed. "Then I'll go to a fancy restaurant and order the biggest steak on the menu."

"Are your folks planning a welcome home party?" Wild Bill asked.

"Maybe. My mom said in her last letter that she was considering one, but would like to combine it with my twentieth birthday party, which is only two weeks later."

"Twenty years old! I thought you were much older than that."

"This war makes us all appear much older than we actually are."

"I'll second that."

John selected a can of fruit cocktail from the dwindling pile in front of Zeke, then moved over by Doc and took a seat on the ground next to him.

"I can't believe Zeke is only nineteen," Pollack said to the black medic.

"I'm just as surprised as you are."

"He might be young, but he sure knows his shit." "He sure does! Zeke is the only old-timer left in this Platoon. Our old L-T, who is now the XO, used to call on him for advice all the time. He's learned most of the gook tactics, and could sometimes spot an ambush before the Platoon walked into it. Now everybody looks up to your buddy, Sixpack, for his advice."

"Does Zeke have a sixth sense?"

"No. It's just a skill that he developed over time. Do you know that he was awarded a Silver Star for Valor a few months back?"

"No, I didn't. What did he do?"

"It happened back in May when our Company was in Cambodia. Second Platoon was ambushed and pinned down. When we arrived to help them, Zeke took it upon himself to single-handedly take out two of the gook machine gun bunkers. Then he ran through the hail of gunfire and pulled two wounded men to safety."

"Well, I'll be! Did he get hit?"

"No, he didn't, but it had to be a miracle."

"Why do you say that?"

"When I saw him later, his rifle had been shattered by bullets, his helmet had three creases in it, both his canteens had holes in them, and the heel of his right boot had been shot off."

"No shit? Somebody must have been watching over him."

"Amen to that."

"We still have some time before leaving, so I'd better take this opportunity to write my folks."

"Good move, Pollack. There won't be any time for writing in Cu Chi."

"What do you mean? I thought we were going to have three days of rest and relaxation."

"Call it what you like. Now let me enlighten you, my brother. Cu Chi is the next best thing to being back in the world. Hell, with all the beer parties, barbecues, movies, Service Club, and swimming pools, you won't have the time to do anything else."

"Well then, I'd better get started right now."

"Do you need paper or anything?"

"No thanks, Doc, I'm all set."

"Say hello for me."

"Will do." Pollack walked away.

"Where's Sixpack?" Wild Bill asked.

"He and the L-T are over in the Company CP area," Larry replied. "They're probably making arrangements for our pickup on the LZ."

"I don't know," Frenchie emphasized. "They usually don't spend this much time planning a pickup."

"What else can it be? We've been out in the bush twice as long as the other Companies in this Battalion. Alpha's R&R is overdue!"

"Maybe the brass has canceled the R&R."

"Why would they do that, Zeke?"

"I don't know, but I feel like there's something in the wind."

"I hope you're wrong."

"Here he comes now," Larry pointed towards the tall soldier heading their way.

"Good, now we can find out for sure."

"He doesn't look too happy!"

Sixpack inhaled deeply on a cigarette, threw it hard to the ground, and then drove the heel of his boot into the stick of smoking tobacco, grinding it into mush.

"Oh shit," Wild Bill uttered, "looks like bad news."

"Okay guys, come on and gather up," Sixpack waved for them to join him. "I know this is going to break your hearts, but we're not going to Cu Chi today."

Pollack dropped his pen before he was even able to write a first word.

"I knew it!" Zeke blurted.

"Why are they changing the plan?" Wild Bill was the first to ask.

"Battalion wants us to hump back to the trail we found a couple of days ago. They're curious about that base camp, and they want Alpha Company to go and check it out."

"Why do we have to hump?" Frenchie asked.

"The brass feels that since we left in choppers, we could surprise the gooks if we return there on foot."

"That's bullshit!"

"I know, but we have to follow orders. As soon as we're near enough to the camp, the artillery crews on Firebase Kien will fire it up again. All we have to do is go in and count the bodies. The whole mission shouldn't last more than a day or two."

"I'll still be able to go in today, right?" a hopeful Zeke asked.

"I'm sorry, Zeke, but the Colonel has canceled all returns to the rear until after this mission is over."

With his dreams now shattered, Zeke leaned back against the narrow trunk of a tree, feigned a weak smile, and laughed hysterically. Each member in the Squad glanced over at him, offering a silent look of sympathy.

"Fuck it! It's only two days. Don't you guys worry about me," Zeke hollered, donning his warrior face.

"How far is it to the trail?"

"On the map, it looks like about seven clicks, but the terrain is hilly and the jungle is thick. So it'll be a long, hard hump. We'll be lucky to get there by noon tomorrow."

"Are we getting re-supplied before we leave?" Doc asked. "I do need a few supplies for my medical bag."

"Yes, we are. In fact," Sixpack looked at his watch, "the birds will be here in half an hour. Only take enough supplies for two days and be ready to move out by nine."

When the re-supply chopper landed, a soldier jumped from the doorway to the ground.

"Junior!" somebody called from the vicinity of Third Squad.

Pollack turned toward the noisy helicopter and recognized the black PFC as he waved warmly to shadows in the bush. Pollack dropped his gear and moved quickly to intercept him.

"Hey, stranger," Pollack called when he was within earshot. Junior turned his head to see Pollack exiting from a clump of bushes.

"Pollack! I see you're still with us."

"My luck has been holding up. What brings you out to the bush?"

"The lead medic on Kien said that my leg is strong enough to hump. So here I am."

"I bet you couldn't wait."

"To be honest, Pollack, I missed the bush. Bunker guard was getting to be old hat. Besides, I have to get rid of these extra pounds," Junior rubbed his belly with both hands.

Pollack and Junior both laughed deeply.

"You have a long way to go before getting fat." Pollack pushed a finger into Junior's stomach.

"I hear we're moving out shortly, so I'd better be going. Let's get together when we have a little more time, Pollack."

"Okay, bro, take care of yourself."

"You too!"

Pollack slapped the palm of Junior's outstretched hand and the two men parted company.

Alpha Company was on the move by nine. They hadn't yet moved one-hundred yards before some of them began to voice their disapproval.

"Why didn't they let us walk part way before getting re-supplied?"

"All they think about is body counts."

"It doesn't make sense to me."

"Don't these people in the rear know what it's like to hump in the bush?"

"They're assholes!"

Pollack followed Zeke once again in the column. He found the camouflage cover on Zeke's helmet to be intriguing. The word "Short" was written on one side in large block letters, colored in with magic marker. He couldn't make out the saying written on the opposite side. Pollack quickened his pace and closed the wide gap between himself and Zeke as he tried to make out the evasive words. When he was only a step away, Pollack tripped and plunged headfirst into a bush. When he looked up, Zeke's eyes glared at him.

"Do you have a problem?"

"No, no problem, Zeke. I just tripped, that's all."

"Be more careful. The gooks can hear that kind of shit." Zeke offered John his hand and pulled him to his feet.

"Are you okay?"

"I'll be fine."

"Check the ground quickly to make sure nothing dropped from your ruck and then hurry and catch up."

As Zeke turned to resume humping, John caught a glimpse of the phrase on Zeke's helmet. 'Fighting for peace is like fucking for virginity,' John read quietly. 'That's heavy,' he uttered to himself after repeating the saying again.

After the column had moved two-thousand meters, the soldiers halted for a break. Pollack moved to the side of the trail and sat next to Doc.

"This is a bitch!"

"It'll get worse."

"I can't keep my pack in a comfortable position. Just when I think everything is okay, a vine snags onto my pack and stops me cold. How many times did you have to unhook me, Doc?"

"I can remember at least a dozen. But don't let those wait-a-minute vines get you down."

Pollack laughed. "What did you call them?"

"Wait-a-minute vines. Haven't you ever heard of them before?"

"Shit, no, this is the first time."

"Every grunt who has ever humped in the bush has heard of them. The name's catchy, don't you think?"

"Yeah," Pollack giggled. "What else do I have to look forward to?"

"Wait until we hit some bamboo thickets. We'll have to remove our packs and push them in front of us while crawling on our bellies."

"You're shitting me. Wouldn't it just be easier to go around them?"

"Sometimes we do, but most of the time they're so wide, we don't have a choice. I'm not bullshitting, you'll see," Doc promised.

"I hope you're wrong."

Suddenly there was a snapping of fingers and Zeke said, "Let's go!"

The men before him were already on their feet and moving forward. Doc and Pollack helped each other up to join the procession.

In the next four hours, the Company was only able to move a thousand meters through the thick, musty jungle. The point man had come across a shallow, ten-foot wide stream with slow-moving green and brown water. Captain Fowler decided to have his Company follow the stream in an effort to make up some lost time.

Pollack later felt a stinging sensation on both his neck and waist while standing in the ankle-deep water during the next break. He passed it off as perspiration irritating the small cuts caused by the jungle vegetation. When he reached up to check, another hand grabbed him by the wrist.

"Wait a minute, Pollack. You have a couple of leeches on your neck," Zeke announced.

He panicked and tried to grab at them to pull them off.

"Hold on! Don't do that. Let me squirt some bug juice on them. It'll make them fall off." Pollack winced in pain as the bug juice soaked into his open, sweaty pores.

After the second leech bloated up and fell from his neck, Zeke said, "All set. Check me over will you, Pollack?"

"I don't see any on you, Zeke," Pollack stated, taking a quick look up and down Zeke's backside. "How in the hell did they get on me? Did they crawl up my pants from the water?"

"These are land leeches. You probably picked them up before we even entered the stream. Don't let them scare you. They're more of a nuisance than anything else. If you want to stop any more of them from hitching rides, cover your exposed skin with more bug juice."

At 1100 hours the next morning, First Squad huddled together, chatting nervously about the anticipated mission. Zeke, however, had not joined them. He sat alone in the shadows of a bush, whittling on a small tree branch with his Bowie knife. Tan and green shavings collected around his feet as each stroke of the silver blade sent another into the air. The ground surrounding Zeke took on the appearance of a hamster cage, but nobody in the Squad made an attempt to stop him.

"Zeke sure is depressed," Frenchie noted, stealing a glance in his direction.

"I don't blame him. You saw him yesterday morning. Happy as hell, until Sixpack dropped the bomb on him."

"Why wouldn't they let him go in on the re-supply?" Larry asked.

Doc said, "Beats me. If it was my decision, he would have gone in."

"One man isn't going to make a difference on this mission!"

"I don't think that's the reason," Scout pointed out.

"What do you think it is?"

"Captain Fowler knows the mechanical on the trail was Zeke's. Maybe he thinks he's doing Zeke a favor by keeping him out here one more day, so he can see the results of his work."

"Do you think he really cares? Zeke is so short he's become paranoid. All he wants to do is get out of the bush. If the Captain thought of this gesture as a favor to Zeke, then he should see how happy Zeke is."

"Like the man said yesterday, he's okay and still has his shit together. If we hit anything on that trail, he'll be the first to react."

"I think he will too, Doc."

Sixpack approached the group. "Okay, saddle up! We're moving out in five minutes."

"Is there anything we should know before leaving?" Scout asked, rising to his feet.

"Just one thing. The firebase will start firing artillery in a few minutes. So don't dive for cover and start yelling 'incoming'." The group laughed nervously.

"They'll continue to lay it on while we move forward. Then when the rounds stop, a Squadron of Cobra helicopters will move in to cover us from the air while we sweep through it."

Zeke still hadn't joined the group. Sgt. Holmes frowned after looking in his direction.

"Hey, Zeke!" the sergeant called. "Are you okay?"

There was no answer. Zeke continued to stare at the ground, drawing circles in the soft dirt with the sharply pointed stick.

Sixpack walked over to him and patted him on the shoulder. "What's bugging you?"

"Don't you know?"

"Don't tell me you're still pissed about not going to the rear yesterday."

"You got it."

"What's the big deal? It's only one more day."

"That's not the point. If any other lifer or officer were in my place, the Colonel would have made a special trip in a Loach to pull him out of the field. They give a shit less about me. A Specialist Fourth Class doesn't rate any special attention. So why should they care?"

"You're making too big an issue out of this. There's nothing to worry about. Nobody in that base camp will survive the bombardment that's coming. After we count the bodies, we'll be in Cu Chi in time for dinner."

"Do you honestly believe in what you're telling me?" Zeke questioned. "Sixpack, you've already spent a tour of duty here. Have you ever swept through a base camp after artillery dropped a ton of munitions on it?"

"I know what you're getting at."

"Damn right you know what I'm getting at. Not once have I just been able to go in and count bodies. Those slant-eyed bastards wait for us. Every time we do it, the gooks put us in a world of hurt. What makes you think it'll be any different this time?"

"I don't. But I'm not going to let that stop me from doing my job. If it means a firefight, then by God it'll be a firefight. We have all had the proper training and experience to deal with this kind of situation. Just do what your instincts tell you and you'll be fine."

"Bullshit! Training and experience don't mean shit in the Nam. It's all luck. And today I don't feel like I have any left."

"You'll be okay, Zeke. Just keep your cool and don't try anything foolish. I need you. The rest of the guys are counting on you. Sixpack waved toward the rest of the Squad.

"Yeah, come on, Zeke. You can do it!"

"What's six more hours compared to forty-nine weeks?"

"We need you, Zeke!"

Zeke blushed after hearing the words of encouragement. He smiled nervously, placed the rifle across his shoulder, and moved to join the rest of the men.

"What the hell? I can't let my brothers down. If you need me that much, I'm yours."

Upon reaching the point in the trail where the mechanical ambush had exploded, Lt. Ramsey ordered the First Squad to check the vicinity.

"Look under rocks if you have to. I want this area thoroughly searched. We'll secure both ends of the trail so you won't have to keep looking over your shoulder."

"You got it, L-T." Sixpack turned to the others. "Let's get this done!"

He led the men through the ruined area. One-hundred feet of leveled vegetation were all that remained of the area in front of where the Claymore mines had been placed. Several nearby larger trees on the other side of the trail were also pocked from the small steel balls in the mines; white sap still leaked from the incisions. Five craters along the trail showed where the mines had been positioned; they were large enough to bury basketballs. The green vegetation on the other side of the trail was coated with a mixture of brown and red dirt.

"Sarge, I found something," Wild Bill said, looking at the ground on the other side of the trail.

"Looks like wheel impressions from a cart," Sixpack guessed after seeing the ruts in the ground.

"There's two sets," Wild Bill pointed out. "One is coming from the base camp, and the other, which is sunk deeper into the trail, appears to be returning."

"Looks like the dinks came out and picked up the pieces," Zeke declared upon reaching the two men.

"There are puddles of dried blood all over the place. It looks like we did some real damage here."

"Hey, guys! Come and take a look at this."

The balance of the Squad rushed over to see what Larry had found. Pollack was the first to arrive. "That's gross!"

"What do you make of it, Doc?"

"I need a closer look." Doc moved forward and had to swing his arms wildly to bat away swarms of flies that had gathered on that portion of the tree. "It's definitely human bone and tissue. There's more over here!" He pointed to several more small pieces that are strewn about the area. "The largest piece I can see is about as big as a cigarette lighter."

"Thanks, Doc. Let's all get back onto the trail and try to figure this out."

"How many gooks do you think the ambush caught?" Larry followed Sixpack and was pinching his nose with two fingers to escape the stench; this caused his voice to sound an octave or two higher.

"We might have caught a Squad or maybe two." Sixpack hesitated and then turned to see why Larry's voice had changed. "Why in the fuck are you holding your nose?"

"I can't stand the smell. It's like walking through a butcher shop full of spoiled meat."

"It is dead meat. You'll get used to it in time."

"The fuck I will."

"I don't like this one bit. There's not one body to be found, yet the evidence is overwhelming that the mechanical blew a bunch of them away."

"That's because there's a lot more gooks left and they came out and picked up the pieces, Sixpack. Remember that mechanical blew during the artillery barrage, so there were survivors, and they're probably waiting for us in the bunkers."

"The artillery in Kien just spent fifteen minutes dropping more rounds on that base camp. They couldn't have survived a second barrage."

"They survived the first time and because of that, they survived this time too."

"Nobody really knows for sure, Zeke. We'll have to take our chances."

"Don't say I didn't warn you."

"Let's get back to the rest of the Platoon," Sixpack suggested, ignoring Zeke's remark.

"What did you find, Sergeant?" Lt. Ramsey asked upon their return.

"The whole area is wasted. We found evidence of death, but couldn't find any bodies."

"That's good news!"

"We also found signs of a cart having been on the trail."

"Did you see anyone?"

"No, sir. But there are two sets of tracks. One of them is sunk much deeper into the trail, as if a great deal of weight was being moved."

"Thank you, Sergeant. I'll pass that onto the CP. Right now, we better get a move on. The rest of the Company is in position to sweep the base camp."

The Platoon had moved up the main trail, veering onto the smaller path that led into the encampment. Nung called to Sixpack, "Sergeant, look!" He pointed toward the upper half of a tree on the right side of the trail.

The platform in the tree, where Sixpack and Nung had spotted an enemy lookout perched a couple days ago, was still in place and unscathed by the many artillery rounds.

"I don't believe it," Sixpack shook his head in disbelief.

When they reached the outer perimeter of the base camp, the rest of the Company was already sweeping toward them through the massive area.

The full barrage of artillery had hit here. All in all, First Platoon counted seventeen bunkers; none of them intact. And unlike the underground complex, they did not find any tunnels, caches, or important documents lying around. A strong odor of burnt wood and musty soil hung in the air.

"See how those gooks screw with our heads?" Frenchie remarked. "I know we should have had a big body count here, but like always, they just take their dead away and leave us to guess at what happened here."

"I'm with you on that! At least we give them the satisfaction of knowing they hurt us after a fight. All they have to do is count the number of Medivacs that come in to pick up our dead and wounded."

"Let's do some grave hunting!"

"No fucking way, Frenchie," Sixpack replied. "We sit tight until the L-T returns. Maybe we'll get lucky and be able to move out toward the LZ."

"I'll buy that," Pollack remarked.

Lt. Ramsey returned ten minutes later. "There's nothing here so go ahead and break for lunch. Afterwards, we'll head north and cut a trail through the jungle to our new LZ. With luck, we'll be in the rear before nightfall."

"All right!" the Squad cheered unanimously.

Even Zeke allowed himself to smile as he sat down and prepared to eat his final meal of C-Rations.

The Company had split into Platoon-sized elements headed in the same direction; two hundred feet separated each of the four columns.

First Platoon had only moved five hundred feet when they came upon another large, well-used trail. Lt. Ramsey dispatched a Squad to investigate while everyone else took a short break.

"Lieutenant, you aren't going to believe this," the Squad leader informed him upon their return.

"What is it, Hawkins?"

"This is the same trail we've originally been following. It winds around the base camp and moves back in this direction."

The L-T removed a map from his pants pocket and studied it. "This part of the trail isn't on the map, either," he informed the young buck sergeant.

"We'd better be careful, sir!"

"Fuck this trail. Let's just get to our LZ." Lt. Ramsey returned the map to his pocket. "Hawkins, have your point men stay on a heading of thirty degrees. The LZ should only be three clicks away."

"Roger that." The black sergeant turned and headed back toward the front of the thirty-five-man column.

The men in the column moved along at a leisurely pace when the sudden sound of erupting gunfire and explosions to their right flank forced each man to the ground in search of protective cover.

First Platoon was momentarily stunned as they all hunkered down on the ground to await further instructions. The source of the gunfire was unclear, but it sounded like all AK-47 fire, and it was escalating. Seconds later came the distinct sounds of M-16 and M-60 machine guns returning fire - exploding M79 rounds and grenades added to the already dangerous noise levels.

Word passed along the line for each man to keep his head down, as Second Platoon was ambushed after stumbling onto yet another bunker complex. The fight was taking place about two-hundred feet to their right flank. Lt. Ramsey continued to relay information as he received sit reps from the engaging Platoon. The Captain communicated initial strategy to support Second Platoon.

As it turned out, First Platoon was the column farthest to the left and needed to protect Second Platoon's left flank. Third and Fourth Platoons would do the same on the right side of the battle. When the Captain gave the word, each flank was to squeeze toward the center and overpower the ambushers. Sixpack was already crouched and moving down the line of men, stopping at each prone soldier to organize and coordinate individual positions. He intended to create a small horseshoe configuration in order to cover their forward, right and left flanks. Even at that distance, bullets popped overhead and tore apart anything in their paths. Many impacted the ground nearby.

Pollack sprawled on the ground, unable to move. His mind told the body to go, but it would not cooperate.

Suddenly, numerous dry branches cracked and bushes rustled to their left flank.

Zeke rose to his feet. "Gooks!" he yelled, firing from the hip in that direction on full automatic.

Screams of both surprise and pain came from the unseen invaders, who quickly retaliated by sending a barrage of hot lead in the direction of Zeke and the First Platoon. Rounds flew overhead in both directions and dirt showered over the men as bullets impacted near them. The noise was deafening and made it impossible to communicate verbally.

On instinct, First Platoon reacted quickly. The machine gunners began firing in a wide arc at knee-high level. Others quickly joined in and fired in the direction of the unseen but advancing enemy. Frenchie fired beehive rounds from his M-79 grenade launcher, Scout tossed grenades, and Sixpack took well-aimed shots at shadows from behind a large tree. Nung and Wild Bill lay prone on the ground, firing their rifles at arm's length above them. Larry still tried to maneuver into position not yet firing his machine gun.

Pollack made his move to what he thought was a more secure position. Rising to his knees, he dove into a clump of bushes behind an old tree trunk to face the oncoming threat. In his haste, the barrel of his M-16 became buried in the soft earth and lodged under some protruding roots. He made an effort to free the weapon, but found that when he raised the rifle butt into the air, bullets began to fly in his direction, impacting near him and ricocheting from the tree trunk. Without access to his weapon, Pollack buried his face into the ground and urinated on himself. He lay motionless and afraid until the incoming fire subsided.

Larry's machine gun finally joined the fight. He fired five-second bursts into the jungle to his front, attempting to cover an arc of about forty-five degrees. It was only then that the enemy firing subsided enough for Pollack to free his rifle from the tangle of roots. However, the barrel was packed with dirt and mud. He knocked it against the side of the tree a few times, but only a few grains fell out.

He wondered to himself if the weapon would blow up in his face if he tried to fire it, but decided that he had no alternative. He took a couple of deep breaths, positioned the rifle on the far side of the tree, lowered his head to the ground, and then pulled the trigger.

The rifle recoiled, almost falling from his hands. Pollack examined the barrel and found the plug gone. He pointed the rifle in the general direction of the enemy and fired three-round bursts from overhead, emptying his first magazine in a matter of seconds.

Red smoke from several exploding canisters around them fogged the area. Snaking lazily through the air, it served to identify the friendly positions for Cobra helicopters, which had arrived and were circling above the firefight.

The ground shook, sending debris raining down upon them as the gunships launched rockets into the area where the enemy fire originated.

Incoming fire at the First Platoon stopped suddenly when the first of many rockets exploded.

"Hold your fire! Hold your fire!" the Squad leaders yelled repeatedly along the line until the last of the Americans stopped firing his weapon.

First Platoon's fight was over as their enemies had either been killed or forced out of the area. However, the rest of the Company was still engaged, but only small exchanges of gunfire continued with a concealed enemy.

Sixpack yelled, "Sound off! Anybody hit?"

"I don't know, I can't see anybody else this low to the ground, but I'm okay." Larry responded.

Sixpack conducted a roll call of his Squad. All of them answered but one, there was no reply from Zeke.

"Somebody find Zeke and see if he's hit!"

"Last time I saw him, Sixpack, he was just ahead of me. I'll take a look," Scout offered.

After a few minutes passed, Scout called out from an area twenty feet away, "I found him, but it's not good. He bought the farm."

"Can you pull him back to us?"

"I could with some help. His body is wedged in between some bushes."

"Pollack, Frenchie, and Doc, grab a poncho and go give Scout a hand!"

The three men low crawled to where Scout waited.

When Pollack reached the location, he took one look at Zeke's body and vomited uncontrollably. The other three men tugged and pulled at the body, trying to free Zeke from the jungle's grasp and place him on the poncho.

"Come on, Pollack, we don't have time for this!" Frenchie scolded.

"He doesn't have a face left," Pollack managed to blurt out.

"I'm sorry about that too, but there's still gooks around. So quit looking at him and help us. We've got to get the fuck out of here and back to the others."

"You're cold-hearted, Scout!" John said, taking hold of a corner of the poncho.

"No, I'm not," Scout retorted. "When you've seen as many dead bodies as we have, it doesn't affect you anymore."

When Zeke's body was lifted from his deathbed, Scout called to Sixpack, "We have a sick Pollack, but we're on our way."

"Move slowly and stay low. We'll cover for you!"

Some of the Platoon fired into the jungle behind the men in order to protect the slow moving group from being sniped during their retreat.

When the four reached the sergeant, he looked down at Zeke's limp body deep within the poncho and bowed his head. "Sorry, Zeke," he said quietly before acknowledging Scout. "The Company medics have formed up just outside of the base camp that we left from earlier today. They're treating the wounded there and setting up a staging area for the Medivacs, which have been called and are already on the way. The rest of us will meet up with you in just a bit."

The men started for the LZ. En route, they noticed other members of the Company carrying soldiers in various fashions. Some of the wounded had their arms draped over a fellow soldier for support and hopped along on one leg. Others walked on their own unassisted with gauze bandages tied or taped to different areas of their bodies. Several more four-man teams could also be seen carrying someone on a poncho. The parade of casualties continued to pour out of the jungle and move toward the same location.

The earlier artillery barrages had devastated the original base camp and nearby surrounding area, thus, creating an area large enough for the Medivac choppers to land.

The immediate area next to the LZ had taken on the appearance of an open-air aid station. Medics scurried about, using whatever supplies available to treat the many wounded. Some of the casualties were still bleeding through their bandages as they relaxed, smoking cigarettes and talking to friends who offered moral support. Others babbled to themselves or lay in a semi-comatose state. The corpses lay unattended and covered with ponchos in an area out of everyone's way.

The earlier smell of burnt wood had been replaced by the scent of sterile bandages, iodine, dried blood, and dismembered bodies.

Pollack bent over in a clump of bushes and vomited again.

"It gets easier as time goes on," Sixpack assured him after finding him. The Sergeant slapped Pollack on the back a few times in an attempt to console him.

"Medivacs will start landing in a minute or two. I want you to go and lend a hand in the loading of the wounded."

"I can't."

"What do you mean you can't?"

"I'm just not able to. The sight of the wounded and the smell in the air is making me sick to my stomach."

"This isn't going to be the first time something like this happens. You should be thankful that you're not one of the casualties. Go on now and help them, it's for your own good," Sixpack gave Pollack an encouraging look and pushed him forward.

Pollack resisted and looked up, tears running down his cheeks. "Sixpack, I'm hurting bad. I can't believe Zeke is dead."

"We're all hurting and feel the same way." The Sergeant draped his arm over Pollack's shoulders and guided him toward the waiting casualties. "I know you'll never forget him, but you'll get over the hurt soon. Now go and give those guys a hand. They need you right now."

Pollack used his shirtsleeves to wipe away the tears, but ended up smearing the liquid all over his dirt-encrusted face. It would be impossible to disguise the fact that he had been crying. Moving toward the injured men, he saw others with the same telltale signs of grief, so he was not at all embarrassed.

Four helicopters were en route to extract Alpha Company from the field and transport them to Cu Chi for three days of rest and relaxation. Each of the Squads of the First Platoon were in position for pickup; the LZ and the Squad leaders waited to raise their weapons and guide in the birds.

Fourth Platoon would leave on the last sortie and would stay positioned between the bunker complex and the LZ to provide security during the withdrawal of the other three Platoons. Artillery guns from Kien had been shooting rounds into the complex and surrounding area for at least thirty minutes. The intent was to inflict as much damage as possible before their replacements arrived and swept through that area.

"On a scale of one to ten, I have to rate this fire fight an eight," Scout volunteered.

"It was indeed a bitch," Wild Bill agreed. "I would have bet we were shooting at each other for over two hours, but I heard somebody say it lasted only thirty minutes."

"How bad did we get hit, Doc?"

"From what I've heard, the Company suffered nine killed and Medivaced twenty wounded. Except for Zeke, First Platoon didn't suffer any other injuries."

"How many did we get?"

"Nobody knows yet. Bravo and Charlie Companies are on their way to relieve us. They're going to sweep through the area and get a body count."

"I hope they have better luck than we did."

"Does anybody know just exactly what went down back there?"

"I don't know for sure, Larry, but I did overhear the officers earlier. It appears that the first base camp we found and destroyed with artillery was only an extension of the main complex, which we walked into today. The gooks were waiting for us, just as Zeke had said they would be. I heard that most of the casualties came from the Second Platoon as they triggered the ambush; and the rest were from Third and Fourth Platoon who came in to reinforce them so we could all pull back. Those in the Second who survived are lucky to have made it out of there."

"Luck? That's what Zeke used to call survival," Larry added matter-of-factly.

Nobody responded.

The artillery barrage ceased momentarily as the choppers approached the LZ.

When the birds touched down, members of Bravo Company jumped off and began running for the tree line.

"Get some payback for us, Bravo."

"Good luck guys!"

Some of the Alpha Company grunts just stared at the helicopters and didn't even acknowledge their friends from the

Sister Company when they passed. The look in their eyes is a faraway look – one of disbelief, sorrow, exhaustion and relief all rolled into one.

A three-day stand down in Cu Chi did not seem like a big deal anymore. After all, who could party after what had just happened? Maybe there would not be a party, but there should be plenty of alcohol, which was the perfect medicine to help one forget.

Chapter Ten

The Battalion area in Cu Chi was filled with enthusiastic cooks, clerks, and supply personnel, making preparations to host those companies returning from the field. Some busied themselves by erecting tents and cots; others separated clean fatigues and miscellaneous equipment onto long eight-foot tables. The cooks, adorned in white aprons and chef hats, tended to hundreds of rib eye steaks; barbecuing on open grills throughout the area. Blue smoke rose into the orange-red evening sky from each of them, and the scent of barbecue sauce temporarily camouflaged the real stench of Vietnam.

Tents had been set up across from the Company orderly room. There were no walls, but the large canvas roofs provided sufficient protection from either the rain or the sun.

Each of the five temporary shelters had twenty-four canvas cots arranged neatly in two rows.

Three fifty-five gallon drums were positioned just inside of each tent; two black barrels were completely filled with soda, beer, and ice. The sides of the drums sweated profusely in the heat; each bead of moisture raced down the side and collected in a puddle of tepid water. The other was empty and would be used to collect garbage.

Several wooden tables were set up in a row adjacent to the shower building; two of the closest held a hundred bars of green soap and clean towels. The remaining housed piles of clean fatigues and dozens of small Army issue cans of foot powder.

Choppers began to land in an open field a quarter-mile away. The First Platoon of Alpha Company disembarked and the men followed the road toward the Battalion area. Their appearance was

149

'unmilitary' by stateside standards. Fatigues were covered with mud, sweat, and dried blood. Most trousers were ripped and torn; some so severely that genitals were exposed. One could use hair length to distinguish between lifers, Cherries, and those who had been in the field the longest. Nonetheless, all their hair and faces were heavily matted and coated with layers of mud, salt, and red dirt.

The sight and smell of the infantry soldiers overwhelmed the rear echelon personnel, who tried to put as much distance between the two groups as possible.

Frenchie raised his head and sniffed the air like an animal in the wilderness.

"Steaks are on!" He pointed out the blue barbecue smoke rising into the air.

"It looks like they are planning to throw a party for us!"

Scout, Frenchie, and Wild Bill gave a war hoop, and then joined the others in a race for the showers. Rucksacks were dropped in mid-stride and tattered fatigues were peeled from filthy bodies. Naked men, with backs and buttocks covered by an assortment of mud, blisters, rashes, and jungle rot, quickly converged on the small building.

"What the hell is going on?" Pollack asked Larry.

"It looks like everyone wants to shower. Shit, you'd think somebody was giving away a million dollars."

"I smell food cooking, so why don't they eat first?"

"Those guys have been in the bush for two months without bathing. Wouldn't you like to clean up before eating something that smells this good?"

"I guess so."

"Well, what are we waiting for?"

"We're going to wait for the showers." Pollack pointed to the long line that had formed outside of the building.

In the morning, several pocket transistor radios tuned in to the American channel. The sounds of rock and roll vibrated and echoed throughout the area as the Rolling Stones poured it on.

The loud stereophonic music woke Scout first. He sat up on the cot, rubbed both eyes, and then buried his head in the palms of both hands.

Then Wild Bill and Frenchie, who had been sleeping on the hard ground during the night, rose to their feet and stretched.

"That was the best I've slept in the last two months," Wild Bill said proudly. "No bugs, guard duty, or going to sleep at seven. Shit, I feel great!"

"Me too!"

"Why do you guys do that?" Doc asked. He sat on the edge of his cot, lacing a boot. "Every time we're in the rear, you both sleep on the ground. What's wrong with these cots?"

"The ground is better," Wild Bill stated. Frenchie nodded in agreement.

"The first time I tried to sleep on one of those, I was awake all night. Those fucking wood frames come alive at night and poke the shit out of you. Every bone and muscle in my body hurt the next morning. No thanks, Doc, you can keep them."

"Would you guys please try to keep it down?" Scout pleaded from the side of his cot.

"What's the matter? Poor baby drink too much last night?"

"I don't think so," Scout replied. "It must be that cheap beer."

"What's wrong with cheap beer that's free?"

"Nothing, it's just that I haven't had any for a while and it sort of hit me all of the sudden."

"Guys," Doc interrupted, "it was cheap beer, but we didn't let that stop us. In fact, I think we outdid ourselves last night!" He kicked an empty beer can across the ground.

The four men surveyed the area. Paper plates with half-eaten steaks shared the cot with Frenchie, and at least a hundred empty beer cans lay in piles where they had been tossed.

"It sure was a good time," Scout managed to utter.

"I'll say," Wild Bill added. "Look at Pollack and Larry," he suggested, pointing to their cots. "Aren't they a pitiful sight? They were the first to pass out and they're still unconscious." They laughed.

"Let's wake them," Frenchie suggested.

"No, let them sleep it off. I don't think either of them has ever drank this much beer before."

"Look around. Are you blind?" Scout asked. "I don't think any of us has ever put away this much brew."

"Speak for yourself. Last night wasn't any different than a normal Saturday night back in the world," Wild Bill broke in.

"That's because cowboys can't drink and drive during the week," Frenchie mused.

"Wrong!" Wild Bill shot back. "We ride! Besides, if we did get really fucked up, the horses know the way home. All we have to do is hang on. I bet you can't say that about your cars in the big cities."

"I can," Frenchie blurted. "There were times when I was so drunk, I couldn't have made it home without my car knowing the way."

"Wild Bill does have a point. I don't ever recall reading about a four-horse pile up involving a drunken rider," Doc announced.

"You guys are all full of shit!" Wild Bill exclaimed, embarrassed by the laughter.

"Come on, guys, let's get this place cleaned up," Frenchie suggested.

"Why? Are we having Company?" Scout continued to rub at his forehead in an attempt to increase the blood circulation.

"We might," Frenchie surmised. "You know those public relations people always come looking for the Cherries whenever we're in the rear after a firefight."

"So what? Our Cherries won't be going anywhere," Wild Bill replied.

"That's true. And even if they could, Pollack and Larry wouldn't feel like answering questions," Doc added.

"Fuck the Cherries, and fuck the visitors," Frenchie declared. "This place looks like shit and I can't stand looking at it anymore. Are you going to help me or not?" He began to gather empty beer cans and throw them into the large trashcan.

"Yes, mother Frenchie!"

Later that Sunday morning, the Company assembled for a multi-denominational religious service near a portable stage where a traveling Filipino band had performed the night before.

Chaplain Dunkirk waited patiently behind a podium in the middle of the stage while soldiers begin filtering into the benches and bleachers. He paged through a Bible, inserting pieces of paper to mark certain passages that he intended to read during the service.

In front of the stage stood nine inverted M-16 rifles, their attached bayonets driven into the ground up to the hilt. A helmet perched atop the stock of each weapon and a pair of jungle boots, facing forward, sat poised to the front of every barrel. Each of them represented the Company's fallen comrades in arms.

Some soldiers teared up as they remembered fond memories of those friendships that were now lost forever. Others stole a solemn glance at the symbols and offered silent testimonials to those killed, whether or not they knew the fallen personally.

When everybody was in place, Chaplain Dunkirk, an older and balding Major, cleared his throat and spoke to the congregation.

"Good morning! I have stood before you as a spokesman of God on many occasions. And together, we have not only prayed for His protection and guidance during this war, but also to celebrate with Him on those joyous and festive occasions. Today, we are all here to pray for our deceased friends and fellow soldiers, who have entered into the kingdom of Heaven to join God by His side.

"The death of a close friend is God's way of testing us. It is very difficult to accept that our God is good and all giving, when he takes away someone close to us. It is on occasions like this that we must re-affirm our belief and faith in Him.

"We are all part of God's master plan, and each of us has a role during this lifetime. Once that role has been played out, God recalls us to his side for all eternity.

"I'm sure that we'd all like to live until we're eighty years old. But we don't know what our role is or how we are to play it out. So you see, it is impossible for us to determine when our time will come. It could be today, tomorrow, ten years from now, or even on our ninetieth birthday. Only God knows for sure. We must continue to have faith, not only in our God, but also in ourselves, in one another, and in our country. Without this faith, we are nothing.

"I'll talk more on faith later in the service. Right now, let's bow our heads and pray for our deceased friends." He read the name and rank of each of the nine dead soldiers. The men were only known by their first name or nicknames, so when their real name was spoken aloud for the first time, some in the congregation were unable to put the two together.

Fifty minutes later, the chaplain offered a final blessing. "The service has concluded. However, Captain Fowler would like to say a few words before you all leave." He waved a farewell to the men, retrieved his Bible from the podium, and walked over to the right side of the stage, taking a seat on a nearby chair.

After climbing the six steps to the stage, Alpha Company's commanding officer moved toward the podium.

Snickers were heard throughout the crowd as the Captain placed a few notes on the podium and stepped behind it. The officer stood five feet, six inches tall with only the top of his head visible to those men sitting on the low benches to his front. The microphone on the flexible holder would not bend low enough for him to speak on the public address system. He continued his struggle to manipulate the silver mechanism, which only invited more chuckles from the crowd.

Sensing embarrassment, he finally removed the microphone from its base and stepped out to the front of the blonde wood piece of furniture.

"I've decided to stand out in front of this speaker's box to address you men, but only as a courtesy to those of you who want to read my lips."

He succeeded with this icebreaker and the men laughed loudly.

"Now, if I can get serious for a moment, I have a great deal of admiration for you men, and I commend you on your performances during our ambush the other day.

"As you know, we were caught by surprise and suffered dearly as a result of it. These nine men paid the ultimate price." He motioned to the rifles below him.

"Later that day after we were withdrawn, our Sister Companies in the Battalion swept through the ambush sight without having to fire a shot.

"There were many caches and hundreds of documents uncovered. It appears that we had stumbled into the Division Headquarters for the VC Seventh Regiment. We're not sure as to the strength of the enemy we encountered during the battle, but the sweep confirmed eighty-seven dead bodies."

A cheer rose from the crowd as the young soldiers congratulated each other.

"Furthermore, there were immense trails of blood leading away from this complex in all directions. So both companies will continue their patrols through the area and try to hunt them down.

"Now, for the bad news, this battle has reduced our strength to a level that Battalion doesn't feel is effective. So, and I know this is going to break your hearts, Battalion is recommending that Alpha Company not return to the bush tomorrow."

The crowd was ecstatic. Boony hats flew into the air and cries of joy drowned out the captain's pleading voice. It took several minutes for the crowd to settle down before Captain Fowler could continue.

"Gentlemen! There must be a misunderstanding! I didn't say we weren't going to the field."

The joyous celebration ceased as the men looked to one another, and asking if they had heard him correctly.

"That's right! We will be going out into the field tomorrow, but we won't have to hump on patrols for awhile."

Inquisitive looks from the crowd prompted him to explain in further detail.

"Tomorrow, Alpha Company will depart for the Iron Triangle."

A look of anxiety spread across the faces of the old-timers in the group who knew of this evil place.

"As many of you already know, the triangle has a reputation of being the most hostile of all areas within the Division's area of operations. Every time our units patrol through this vicinity, heavy opposition meets them. Delta Company and the Corps of Engineers have spent the last week clearing out a large area in the center of it all. We will be joining them tomorrow and help to build a new firebase. The brass has already named it Lynch.

"This firebase is very important, as it will provide added security and firepower to those forces patrolling through the Triangle. We won't have to hump, but after a couple days of digging and filling sandbags, you'll all wish you were back in the bush again.

"Choppers will pick us up at eight in the morning. Enjoy your last day of leisure. That's all I have."

Most of First Platoon cleaned rifles in the tent and prepared equipment for the following day's move.

"That must have been one hell of a mess. Can you imagine piling up eighty-seven dead bodies?"

"Who knows for sure how many bodies there actually were Larry," Doc answered. "And certainly if they are following Battalion protocol."

"What are you saying?"

"It's not a secret that the gooks carry their dead away with them after a firefight."

"I've been a witness to that myself."

"The policy is something like this. If we find a puddle of blood measuring more than four inches in diameter, it is considered a kill. If we find a weapon by itself lying in the jungle, it too, is counted as one kill. And of course, a body always counts."

"Damn, I didn't know that," Pollack confessed. "I always thought a body had to be present."

"As you can see, it's not always that way."

"If that's true, why didn't we get credit for all the blood and body parts from our mechanical ambush?"

"I don't know, Pollack. We didn't stick around long enough to measure and count all the dried blood and body parts. Besides, it was a couple of days after the fact anyway."

"Those fucking lifers are the only ones worried about a body count in this goddamn war anyway," Scout volunteered. "Did any of you see the Company tote board today?"

"What about it?" Wild Bill asked.

"Major Stone was having the Battalion clerk add to the figures while he stood there and verified the numbers."

"So what's the big deal? That's just normal lifer bullshit."

"He was doing this during the church service," Scout replied.

"I still don't see your point."

"The clerk was next to me during the service and we were talking about Zeke, when that lifer motherfucking Major came over and yanked him away."

"Are you joking?"

"Wild Bill, I wouldn't joke about something like that. The poor kid didn't even have a chance to ask him if he could wait until after the service."

"What a sorry fucking thing to do."

"I'll say," Doc added. "That shit could have waited."

"That's not all of it," Scout interrupted.

"You mean there's more?" Larry asked.

"Yeah. It wasn't five minutes after the clerk had finished that some General showed up. As soon as he stepped out of the jeep, Major Stone guided him to the tote board. The General's face lit up when he saw the figures. He smiled broadly, and shook the major's hand vigorously. Then as they were walking into the building, the General slaps Major Stone's back a few times as if he was single-handedly responsible for killing those gooks."

"I'd like to know what kind of story he told the General." Wild Bill frowned deeply. "All he did during the ambush was to fly around overhead in that helicopter of his and watch the fireworks below. What a jerk! Did your clerk buddy have anything to say after returning?"

"He never did. I did catch a glimpse of him while the captain was talking to us; he was carrying coffee and cake to the Major's office." The men could only shake their heads in disbelief.

Just then, a stranger walked into the tent and approached those nearest the entrance.

"Excuse me, I'm looking for PFC's John Kowalski and Larry Nickels."

"It's time to write up the Cherries," Wild Bill announced.

"I'm Kowalski," Pollack raised his hand.

"And I'm Nickels," Larry added from the cot behind Pollack.

"Great! I'd like to take a few minutes of your time to ask some questions."

"Why and who are you?" Larry asked.

"I'm a reporter and the information will be used for an article in your hometown newspapers."

"Why? What did we do?" Pollack asked.

"You both earned the Combat Infantry Badge during that last firefight. You're heroes and we'd like the people back in your home town to know it."

"I'm not a fucking hero," Pollack quickly protested. "I was scared to death during that ambush and pissed myself. Then, I spent the rest of the day puking my guts out. That doesn't sound like something a hero does."

"Relax, Pollack," Doc interrupted. "It's just a formality. We all had similar experiences during our first firefight, but you'll get stronger as time goes on. This is a way of letting the people back home know that you are surviving and doing your best over here.

It'll also make your family proud to see an article about you busting your cherry."

The group laughed.

"What is this article going to say?"

"Before I answer that, are you aware that the Combat Infantry Badge is the most coveted of all awards eligible to an infantry soldier? Some lifers in the rear areas would do anything to get one."

"He's telling the truth," Wild Bill affirmed.

"Many soldiers in Vietnam won't even get one," the reporter continued. "You have to earn it through combat. And regardless of what you did, or how you felt during the fight, you're still entitled to this award. The article will let the people know who you are, where you're from, what school you attended, the year you graduated, who your parents are, and where you're stationed in country. The rest of the article will tell a little about the award itself, and how it originated. It is good publicity and the article will make your family proud. The format is the same for everybody, so all we have to do is to fill in the blanks."

"What the hell," Pollack conceded, "I'll answer your questions."

"Good! Let's get started."

Wild Bill stopped the PR man before he could leave.

"How about writing a story about our sorry-assed Major Stone and the stunt he pulled today?"

"Why? What happened?"

Wild Bill and Scout related the earlier incident for him, making sure not to leave out any of the details. After several minutes of listening, the reporter closed his notebook and returns it to his shirt pocket.

"I'm sorry, guys, but I can't write a story like that. I can sympathize with you, but we don't have all the facts and know what really happened."

"What if I can get them for you?"

"Don't waste your time. Even if I wrote it, the editors would shit-can the article. They would tell me that it's written in bad taste, and is bad for the morale. Besides, that type of behavior has always existed throughout the military as well as in civilian life. There are always a few assholes that ruin it for the rest of the decent people.

Just chalk it up to experience and let go of it. Dwell on the good and forget the bad."

"What good can come out of war?" Doc asked the confident reporter.

"Friendship and camaraderie."

"I agree that there is a bond that develops, but it's more of a dependency on each other for moral support and strength than anything else. It's the only way any of us will survive this insane war."

"That's the point I'm trying to make. You have all shared your inner feelings with each other at one time or another. I'd even bet that you have built such a trust between yourselves, that you could confide in each other and tell tales that you wouldn't dream of telling anyone else. And you really haven't known each other that long."

"The man has a point," Scout broke in. "I grew up with a couple of guys who are still back in the world. I thought we were the closest of friends. But when I think about it now, you guys know more about me than they do."

"I agree," Doc added. "You know I would do anything for you guys. Hell, even Pollack and Larry have become part of my life."

"You might not see each other after Vietnam, but I can guarantee you that each of you will remember this bond. So cherish it while you can." The reporter looked at his watch. "I have to go. You guys take care of yourselves."

"You too!"

He turned and walked out of the tent.

Doc stood up and headed to where the other four men sat on two adjacent cots. He extended both arms outward, balled his hands into fists, and positioned one of them in front of each group.

"Gentlemen," he said, "in the words of a famous singing group, we are fa-mi-ly."

All reached up and hit Doc's fists with one of their own.

"We are, indeed!"

That afternoon, Bill Sayers, Pollack and Larry managed to finally hook up. They spent the next couple hours drinking cold sodas and telling each other about the things they had experienced during the last month with the Company. When finally running out of words, they decided to walk over to the stage where a movie, Butch Cassidy and the Sundance Kid, was about to start. It was a western starring Robert Redford and Paul Newman, who played outlaws that get chased around the country and finally end up in South America. It was actually quite funny and all enjoyed it. After it ended, they said their goodbyes to each other and returned to their individual tents.

Pollack and Larry found that most everyone in the tent was either sleeping or writing letters. A card game was not even taking place. To them, it was just too early to sleep, so they dug out their supplies and joined in on the community letter writing exercise.

Both men were excited about the article that would soon be printed in the local newspaper back home, so they wanted to give their family some forewarning to watch for it. Pollack had kept all his letters simple since arriving in country and had never written about close calls or other dangerous activities. He always wrote about the weather and answered questions about topics seen on TV or heard from other sources about Vietnam. One particular question a few weeks ago was upsetting, as his mother had wanted to know if he was killing innocent women and children. He was so taken back by the inquiry, he was afraid to ask any of his fellow soldiers, in fear of being berated by the group. He simply responded that he'd never seen the enemy and seriously doubted that any were innocent woman or children.

Pollack bit the bullet and wrote that he had been in his first battle, which would now result in a newspaper article. He wanted to seriously play it down, so he wrote that the event was a normal occurrence and every infantry soldier received the award during his tour of duty. However, he knew that the news article would generate a deluge of questions in future letters from home.

When Pollack finished and packed everything away, he lay on the cot and prepared himself for day number fifty-two in Vietnam.

Chapter Eleven

At three in the morning, the Division helipad bustled with activity. Battalion Supply needed to have all the equipment and supplies ready for transport prior to the infantry's 0800 departure. However, their only lift truck was broken, so the supplies had to be moved around by hand. Large nets blanketed the pad and trucks full of supplies sat idly to the side, lighting the area with their headlamps. Pandemonium reigned as rear echelon personnel moved around in mass confusion; crates were carried on shoulders with nobody seeming to know where they went. Supply Sergeants and officers ran around with clipboards, trying desperately to organize the quagmire and meet their schedule.

Only a portion of the overall supplies were loaded by eight o'clock. The grunts were ready to leave Cu Chi and became impatient by this delay.

"What's the deal, Sixpack?" Wild Bill asked.

"It looks like we'll be here awhile, so make yourselves comfortable."

"Why do we have to wait until the supplies are loaded?" Scout whined.

"Because we're flying in Chinooks, and the brass wants to limit the trips."

"Isn't this just like the Army?" Doc commented. "It's always been hurry up and wait."

"You got that right," Scout agreed. "Only I wish we could do our waiting in the shade. This hot sun is a bitch."

"Go to sleep and it won't feel so bad."

"That's a great idea, Wild Bill, I can use a couple more hours of sleep."

"Wake us when they're ready to go." Scout and Larry lay on the grass, using their rucksack as a pillow.

"Don't worry about us waking you up. You'll know when the birds arrive," Sixpack smiled and continued to pace on the grass.

The rest of the Squad followed suit and tried to get in a few extra winks.

Three hours later, Sixpack strode to each man, kicking him on the sole of his boot. "Come on, you deadbeats, wake up! Birds are on their way."

"What the fuck?" Scout sat up quickly, unsure of his whereabouts.

"There's nothing like getting a suntan while fully clothed." Wild Bill fanned his damp fatigue shirt in an attempt to cool off his sweaty body.

"I know the feeling. Look at me! I'm soaked to the bone." Scout mimicked Wild Bill in his cooling off dance.

Others, who had removed their shirts earlier, scratched each other's back to relieve the itching caused by lying bareback on the grass.

After a few minutes, the men in the First Platoon gathered their rucksacks and moved toward one of the large piles of supplies on the tarmac. Progressively, louder chopping sounds from beyond alerted them of the quickly approaching helicopters.

The five giant birds, each looking twice the size of a city bus, had two large rotors overhead to carry the ship; they created such a whirlwind during final approach that it temporarily blinded everyone near the landing zone. Of course, the supply personnel were all wearing goggles and seemed immune to the onslaught of debris. Once the birds were down, a large hydraulic ramp on the rear of each helicopter lowered to the ground, enabling each platoon member access to their respective transports. It was still terribly windy and dusty, but the level of visibility was sufficient for the men to move through the dust storm and get on board. They sat on long fold down planks running the length of the aircraft; their backs leaning into netting that lined the fuselage - both rows of soldiers faced one another.

In the meantime, the supply personnel were gathering corners of nets and securing them to a towing hook on the bottom of each monster machine. The Chinooks would rise straight into the air at a very slow pace until the sling holding the net became taut and the bundle of supplies lifted into the air. The pilots would review their control panel gages to confirm that the total cargo weight was acceptable and safe to fly with before tilting the rotors slightly and flying away.

The formation of Chinooks circled over a large, round clearing surrounded by dense jungle. Green heavy-duty construction equipment sat unattended throughout the brown and red dirt-filled clearing. The large helicopters turned into the wind and began their descent. Several piles of debris burned in the northern sector of the clearing and thick black clouds of smoke rose up toward the airborne formation.

"Look at all that smoke! You can see it for miles." Pollack sat near the rear of the aircraft where much of the First Squad could see through the open ramp.

"It's a good beacon for the gooks to follow, too," Wild Bill pointed out.

"Just like sending out smoke signals and offering a personal invitation to come and visit us," Scout added.

"What the fuck are we getting ourselves into?" Larry wondered aloud.

Delta Company soldiers were spread out around the clearing, manning temporary guard positions near the tree line. Several massive bulldozers and graders from the Engineering Battalion had created the opening in the heavy jungle. In size, it equaled six combined football fields. The Chinooks first dropped their cargo in the center of it all, and then landed nearby to discharge the human cargo.

Red wooden stakes were placed into the ground at fifteen-foot intervals to create a smaller circle within the huge clearing which would be the actual perimeter of the firebase.

Captain Fowler called the Alpha Company Lieutenants together in a wet and muddy section of the clearing. He did not have a choice, as most of the clearing was the same. Boots quickly sank into the mush; deep sucking sounds were heard as the soldiers struggled to walk through this clearing.

"This isn't going to be a picnic out here. Many of you already know about the Triangle: it's filled with plenty of booby traps, caches and gooks. Most of the gook supplies and reinforcements from Cambodia must pass through this area. Military intelligence refers to this area as the Ho Chi Minh Trail of the South.

"The gooks are already aware of our presence here and what we're trying to accomplish. They have mortared the clearing twice in the last week and have caught some of Delta Company's patrols in ambushes. The Engineers also believe that the enemy is slipping into the clearing during the night, because they are finding mines, which weren't there the day before.

"If they decide to hit this firebase before it's finished, it could be a bloodbath. Therefore, we need an all-out effort from each of you in preparing this location before nightfall. So work hard for all our sakes."

Each Platoon was assigned the arduous task of building four-man bunkers along a portion of the perimeter. First and Second Squads of First Platoon busied themselves with the actual building, while the other two Squads began working on the area to the front of where the bunker line would be. Barbed Concertina wire were unrolled and staked in place. The men placed trip flares, Claymore mines, and other early-warning devices in strategic locations.

Wild Bill and Pollack painstakingly worked as a team in building one of the bunkers. Bill dug while Pollack filled sandbags and stacked them to the side. Both of their backs were deeply reddened by the sun, but they continued to sweat and tackle the backbreaking chore.

"Goddamn clay!" Wild Bill shrieked from the depths of a four-foot hole. "Why couldn't they have chosen an area with sand?"

"And make it easier for us? They probably set this up intentionally as a method of cleaning our bodies of all that cheap beer we drank in Cu Chi."

"I'd give anything to be out in the bush right now."

"That was quick. The Captain said we wouldn't feel that way for another couple of days."

"Fuck the Captain, fuck the Army, and fuck Vietnam." The chant came from deep in the ground, and started over again after a shovel full of dirt was tossed topside.

At 1900, Pollack and Wild Bill completed their fighting position and stepped away to admire their work from a distance.

"Looks great, doesn't it?"

"Not bad. But you have to admit, it was the hardest eight hours that we've ever put in."

"I know what you mean. I'm even too exhausted to eat."

"Just hope we're not picked for an ambush patrol tonight."

"Ambush patrol? Why would they send any of us out ambush teams? We've been working our asses off all day."

"Look around," Wild Bill suggested. "There are too many people in this perimeter and not enough bunkers to protect them."

"I see your point. One mortar round in the right place will wipe out a bunch of people."

Both men walked out to the barbed wire, turned around, and then looked over their portion of the perimeter. Scout and Larry were to their left, still working feverishly on their bunker. On the right, both Doc and Frenchie were also admiring their completed work. The two groups waved to one another.

"Not bad for a bunch of rookies!" Frenchie threw a softball-sized rock at their bunker.

"Hey, hey, don't try to knock it down just yet. Let us get at least one night of sleep in it first."

The men laughed.

"They may not be perfect but at least they'll be better cover than bushes and trees."

"Very true, Doc. I can't wait until tomorrow when we can use our new natural air conditioner. It's at least twenty degrees cooler down in the hole right now."

"Wild Bill, next you're going to tell us that room service is available."

The group shared another laugh.

Sixpack returned from the Lieutenant's bunker in the center of the firebase and called out to his Squad when close enough, "Come on, guys, we have to talk." Sixpack waved for the men to join him.

"Oh shit," Wild Bill mumbled, "looks like it's time to fuck with the First Squad again." He pulled at the barbwire, letting it snap like a slingshot. "Come on, Pollack!"

The two men left the barbed wire and merged with the other two-man groups as they converged upon Sixpack's position.

"Don't look so worried," he announced after seeing the forlorn looks upon their faces. "Delta Company is going out on ambush tonight."

The men exhaled deeply and cheered with delight.

"Personally, I would have preferred the ambush. Now, we have to fill in the gaps on the perimeter, which will be vacated by the ambush teams. Our Squad will take over the bunkers which you've just finished, but only two men will be in each. I know you're all tired, but the firebase will be on fifty percent alert tonight, so one of you will have to be awake at all times."

The men mumbled their disapproval.

"The Mortar Platoon will be firing illumination flares into the sky at fifteen minute intervals. So keep your heads down, and don't make yourself a target for a sniper. I don't want any unnecessary firing, unless you can actually see movement to your front. If we do get hit, watch the wire closely for sappers. If they get through, we can be in a world of hurt. The password for tonight will be 'Champion'. Are there any questions?? He paused.

"Okay, let's get ready for the night."

Wild Bill and Pollack sat outside their bunker, leaning against the soft sandbags. Pollack's appetite had returned, but he was too tired to heat a meal. Instead, he opened a can of cold beans and franks and nibbled from his spoon full of nourishment. Wild Bill placed a heat tab into an empty C-Ration can and punched several holes into it. After igniting it, he placed a canteen cup full of water on the makeshift stove.

Both of them quietly admired the sun as it set over the jungle.

"You know, this country has its pretty moments. Just look at that orange sun behind the palm trees. If I didn't know better, I'd think we were in paradise." Wild Bill sighed.

"It is like paradise. If you listen closely, you can even hear the birds and monkeys calling to us from the jungle. I don't recall it ever being this quiet in Cu Chi."

"Maybe it's the calm before the storm!" Wild Bill took a drink from his steaming cup of hot cocoa. "You'll think of this place differently in a couple more hours."

The two men continued to eat and drink in silence for several minutes. Finally, John turned to face his partner for the night.

"Why do the guys call you Wild Bill?"

"You know how it is. Everyone here has either done something to earn a nickname, or arrived with one like you did. In my case, the guys started calling me Wild Bill after seeing this picture of me from back home."

He withdrew a wallet from the rubber pouch in his rucksack, extracted a photograph, and handed it to Pollack.

"See what I mean?"

The picture showed a cowboy standing next to a brown and white Appaloosa horse. In the background was a snow-capped mountain range and wild sagebrush; both silhouetted by a royal blue, cloudless sky. Shoulder-length brown hair hung from under a black cowboy hat with a silver band. He sported a six-inch long but neatly trimmed dark brown beard that hung over the front of an unbuttoned tan buckskin jacket. A black leather ammo belt was wrapped around his waist. The white pearl handles of a revolver reflected the sunshine as it cradled in a black holster strapped tightly to his thigh.

"This is you?"

"Yeah, but you wouldn't think so."

"Shit, no. You look like an old west outlaw and twenty years older. Where was this picture taken?"

"In El Paso, Texas, when I worked on a ranch before I was drafted. Man, I can't wait to get back."

"Me neither." Pollack thought about that for a few seconds. "What's your real name?"

"Bill Hickock."

"Get the fuck out of here!"

"That's why they call me Wild Bill."

He placed the picture back into his wallet and returned it to the protective rubber bag inside of his rucksack. Then he leaned back against the bunker and lit a cigarette. Wild Bill drew deeply from the filterless stick of tobacco, exhaling the smoke slowly through the wide gap between his two front teeth.

"God, I sure do miss the circuit."

"What circuit?"

"I used to travel on the rodeo circuit all through the western part of the country."

"What are rodeos like?"

"Haven't you ever been to one?"

"Nope. Detroit isn't the kind of place to have a rodeo."

"You don't know what you've been missing. Shit, back home, everyone planned their weekends around the local rodeos."

"We didn't have that luxury."

"I understand. They're not as popular where you come from. You know I made half my earnings every year from the circuit."

"What were you selling?"

"I wasn't selling anything; I was a participant."

"You mean roping horses and shit?"

"Yeah. And bronco busting, cattle wrestling, and steer roping to name a few others."

"Were you good?"

"I have trophies and newspaper articles that say I am."

"Damn! I'm sharing a bunker with a real celebrity."

"Aw, knock off that bullshit, Pollack."

"No, seriously, I'm intrigued. Tell me some more."

"I'd like to, but it's getting dark. We'd better get ready for our watches."

"How do you want to work it?"

"Let's see," Wild Bill looked at the luminous dial on his watch, "it's almost seven-thirty. Why don't we each take a two-hour shift and then one shift three hours long? This way we can both get some sleep."

"Sounds good to me, I'll take the first watch."

"You got it."

First Squad's turn on patrol came the following morning. They were to move toward a trail junction a kilometer to the west of the firebase and set up a day ambush site.

After leaving the wire, they followed a large hard-packed road toward their destination. It wasn't twenty minutes before an APC patrol forced them from the road. The four Armored Personnel Carriers passed noisily, each carrying a Squad of men on top.

"Ahoy, Matey!" a few of the soldiers called from one of the steel monsters.

All wore strange hats with brims folded up high on one side.

"Who are those guys?"

"They're Aussies and have a base nearby."

"Australian? I didn't know they were here," Larry stated.

"Shit, yes," Frenchie broke in. "We're not the only people fighting the gooks in this country. I read about it once. The article had stated that fifteen countries were involved in this war, but I've only seen Koreans, Thais, and Aussies."

"You learn more about this place every day."

"Yeah, and just when you think you know it all, Larry, it's time to go home," Doc added.

"Now that's the way to go out on patrols." Pollack jerked his head in the direction of the departing dust-covered soldiers. "No more humping. Just put your shit inside and ride out your tour."

"Those are iron coffins," Sixpack said matter-of-factly. "Every gook within a mile can hear you coming. All they have to do is mine the approach and wait for your APC to blow its track. Then he'll finish you off with either a B-40 rocket or RPG. I've seen what they can do to those armored tracks. Everything inside gets cut to ribbons. It might look appealing, but you can have them."

As the patrol continued westward, the jungle surrounding them became withered and sparse.

"What happened to this part of the jungle?" Pollack asked. "It looks like somebody sprayed weed killer over it."

"It is weed killer," Sixpack replied. "Special planes used to fly all through this country to spray defoliant on the jungle."

"Why did they spray the countryside?"

"To eliminate and uncover all the gook hiding places. They had names for the operation and for the shit that was sprayed, but I can't remember what they were called. Hell, during my last tour, I can remember them spraying while we were patrolling through the jungle below. The shit came down like a monsoon rain and smelled terrible. We used to get skin rashes that itched like hell and breathing problems from inhaling the stuff."

"Was it dangerous?"

"Other than the rashes and stuff, everybody told us the stuff is not dangerous and not to worry about it."

"This area smells like shit, too!" Scout added.

"Must be the decomposition," Doc reported.

"Dead gooks have smelled better."

The Squad arrived at the junction and moved into the decayed underbrush to set up an ambush on line with the trail.

All the porous tree stumps were havens for red ants, spiders, horseflies, and other crawling insects, which feasted on the rotting vegetation. Most of the Squad was preoccupied with taking defensive measures against the small insects instead of focusing on the trail. Red ants stung unmercifully; horseflies left welts after biting their victims; and hundreds of spiders sent a chill down the spines of the young men.

Every insect spray bottle was emptied during the first hour; the precious liquid was used as a first line of defense. It seemed as though the insects were immune to the bug spray. Upon reaching the liquid line on the ground, they only hesitated briefly before moving through it and toward their human prey.

At 1700 hours, the ambush terminated. Everyone wiped hundreds of dead insects from their fatigues before standing up and gathering their gear to leave.

On the return to the firebase, the men gently caressed welts, rashes, bruises, and mosquito bites, while keeping their eyes on the surrounding jungle for the enemy.

When they arrived, they noticed two new semi-luxuries that were not there when leaving this morning: a shower and a toilet. The shower was erected in the middle of the compound and soldiers were already using it. Two fifty-five gallon drums hung suspended six and a half feet above a platform, which straddled a drainage ditch. Each barrel had a shower head attached to the underside, helping to uniformly distribute water, which is manually poured into the barrel by a 'buddy'. Sadly, the showerhead did not turn off so there was no way to collect water in the barrel. Whatever went in came right back out, but at a slower rate; the system worked more efficiently with a helper. Both men would fill several buckets full of water and then while one showered; the other would slowly empty a bucket into the overhead reservoir.

A crowd had already gathered around the shower. Some waited their turn with the cold, refreshing liquid, while others stood only to watch and pass the time of day. No curtains or walls enclosed the structure, so modesty was not an option.

Two outhouses had also been erected during the day. But, those too, had been constructed without the privacy offered by walls or curtains. Three fifty-five gallon drums, cut in half, sat under a twenty-inch deep by ten-foot wide long wooden plank. Three oblong holes were cut in the wood board and sanded smoothly where they'd been cut. One size fit all.

During the initial stages of building up the firebase, the outhouses caused many problems. The main concern was the location, which sat on the edge of the perimeter next to the barbed wire. When somebody had to use the facilities, his back was exposed to the jungle. This made it difficult to concentrate on the duties at hand, as the men continuously turned to keep an eye on the tree line.

Humility was the other concern when trying to take care of business in plain view of everyone in the firebase. It was much different than taking a shower in front of people, because taking a dump was considered to be very private and sacred. Not even a married couple wants to peek at one another during this normal bodily function.

Many of the young men developed painful hemorrhoids from not letting nature take its course. They would purposely try to hold their bowel movements until nightfall, when the cover of darkness allowed them to relax in a more private manner.

A few weeks later, First Squad took a break during one of their many patrols.

"These daily patrols are getting to me," Larry admitted.

"Look at the bright side. At least we're excused from all the bullshit details on the firebase."

"Yeah, like burning shit," Scout chimed in.

"What's that?"

"It's the worst detail in this whole stinking country."

"You only have to watch somebody do it once to know it," Doc added. The men snickered.

"What do you have to do?" Larry asked.

"When we return to the firebase every night, haven't you ever seen those smoking barrels over by the shitters?"

"That's just trash burning, isn't it?"

"Yeah, Larry, it is trash, but it's trash from your ass." The others laughed again while Larry and Pollack looked at them curiously.

"That's the shit detail. It starts early in the morning, right after breakfast. Sometimes, there's two guys assigned to the detail, but most of the time there's only one. When I had to do it, I was alone." Scout shuddered at the thought.

"It is a motherfucker," Wild Bill emphasized.

"Yes, it is," Doc agreed.

"As I was saying, the first thing on the agenda is to get the barrels out from under the planks. Sometimes, they're almost filled to the top." Pollack and Larry looked at Scout as if the top of his head just exploded.

"Especially if the mess hall serves beans the day before," Wild Bill smirked as he watched the two Cherries squirm and turn pale.

"Anyway, they don't give you any gloves or breathing devices. So dragging those cans some forty feet to be burned can be a disaster. You can always hold your breath, so you don't have to smell the stuff. But no matter how careful you are in moving them, there's no way of stopping the semi-solid contents from splashing onto you. Once that happens, you just don't give a fuck anymore."

"It's a real bitch too, especially if you aren't able to come up with a clean set of fatigues," Sixpack chimed in.

"I had to take a shower in mine, but the smell is still there," Wild Bill said, enjoying the show.

Larry and Pollack looked to each other, a repulsed expression on their faces.

Scout continued, "Once you have managed to pull and tug the cans away, you add a ten-gallon combination of diesel fuel and gasoline to them, provided there's enough room. Sometimes, you have to transfer some of it out from one can to another with a bucket to make room. Once that's done, you just throw in a lit match, and move back."

"Is that all you have to do?" Larry asked.

"No, you have to stir it too," John said jokingly.

"Give that man a cigar," Scout announced.

Pollack stopped laughing and flashed an inquisitive look.

"That's right, Pollack, you have to sit and watch the shit burn all day long. You stir it up every half hour or the fire will go out."

"How do you know when you're done?"

"When there isn't shit left in the can." A chuckle erupted from the men.

"That was good one, Scout!" Sixpack announced.

"It usually takes until seven in the evening to burn everything up."

"That's one detail I hope to never pull."

"Don't bet anyone on that, Pollack. Everyone does it at least once. And when our Squad's turn comes up, guess whose names will be on the list."

"Aw, fuck!" The realization hit Larry.

The day ambush positioned itself near the bend of a well-used trail. The area hadn't been sprayed, so the dense jungle offered good concealment and protection for the men in the First Squad.

Scout and Wild Bill stood on opposite sides of the single line ambush. Both men watched the trail intently while the rest of the Squad in between them relaxed and daydreamed. Larry wrote a letter to his folks; Sixpack spread a towel out in front of him and used it as a table to play a card game of Solitaire; Frenchie monitored the radio; Pollack and Doc shared the same tree trunk to catch a few minutes of sleep.

Suddenly, Scout bolted upright. "Movement, coming this way," he whispered.

The men quietly picked up their weapons and readied themselves for what might be coming.

"No firing until I open up," Sixpack instructed the team.

Five minutes later, a lone Vietnamese came into view walking on the trail. He wore black nylon pants, a blue denim shirt, Ho Chi Minh sandals, and a U.S. boony hat. He pointed his AK-47 up the trail as he proceeded cautiously.

The VC was almost in front of Nung's position, when he stopped suddenly after hearing some rustling in the bush. He raised an arm, looked behind him, and then moved toward the side of the trail, where the ambush team lay in wait.

The men froze in position as the young teenager tried to find the source of the noise. Nervous beads of perspiration ran down the faces of each man; fingers tightened their grips on triggers, and all breathing momentarily stopped. He didn't venture from the trail to make a visual reconnaissance. After a few sweeps of the jungle, he turned his right ear toward the ambush team and lowered his head in an effort to enhance his hearing. Maybe he could hear what he was unable to see. Finally, having satisfied his curiosity, he returned to the center of the trail and waved for others to follow.

He waited a few minutes before three similar clad youths came into view from around the bend. They wore conical hats, and carried rucksacks and weapons as well.

When the four men were within the killing zone, Sixpack fired his M-16; that was the signal for the rest of the Squad to open fire. The eruption of American firepower could be heard as far away as the firebase. The four VC dropped in their tracks after the ambush was executed. Larry swept the entire trail with the M-60; Scout and Wild Bill tossed grenades; Doc, Sixpack, Pollack and Nung continued to fire on automatic in the direction of the enemy. When no return fire occurred, Sixpack yelled, "Hold your fire, hold your fire!"

Scout and Nung jumped from their concealed positions and raced to the bend in the trail. They watched for any enemy reinforcements that might be on their way. Wild Bill and Doc did the same at the opposite end of the trail. Sixpack, Larry, and Pollack arose from the smoky underbrush and moved out toward the corpses on the trail.

The gooks weren't able to return fire during the ambush. It was so well executed that they didn't have a chance to escape. All four enemy soldiers collapsed instantly as their lives were taken from them. Even a contortionist could not assume their present positions. Blood continued to run from dozens of holes in their bodies and collected momentarily in small puddles, before being absorbed by the red earth.

Sixpack quickly moved to check the bodies for any signs of life. He found the last VC in a depression on the far side of the trail.

"We have a live one!" Sixpack announced. "Frenchie, get me a Medivac, and notify the Company that we have a POW."

"Roger." Frenchie returned to retrieve his radio.

"Pollack, keep an eye on him while I go through their gear."

He hovered over the wounded and unconscious soldier, making certain that his weapon stayed pointed at the man's head.

"If he makes a move to hurt you, waste him," Sixpack emphasized.

"I won't give him the chance."

Frenchie returned to the trail. "Hey, Sixpack! The Captain said we're to remain here after the Medivac leaves because a team from Intelligence is coming out."

"Why? We can strip the bodies," Sixpack protested.

"I told him, but he said they would take care of it, so we wouldn't have to carry the stuff back to the firebase."

"Now that's the wisest idea that man has had since I've been in this Company."

"I'm crazy about it too."

It took another month and a half to complete Firebase Lynch. By that time, Squad-sized bunkers had replaced the small emplacements; permanent and enclosed structures had been built for the showers and outhouses. The officers also saw to it that facilities for 'Officers Only' had been erected. A battery of 105mm Howitzers was now housed next to the two mortar pits.

Reinforcements had been arriving periodically to beef up Alpha Company's strength. Billie Joe Johnson, from Alabama, replaced Zeke in the First Squad. The men quickly nicknamed him 'BJ' and assigned him to Larry as an ammo bearer for the machine gun.

The new Cherry sat restlessly near one of the bunkers. His expression was one of awe and his head jerked every which way so as not to miss anything around the firebase.

"What's it like in the field?" he finally asked.

"You'll love it," Larry replied. "All we do is go out on daily ambushes and wait for Charlie to come by."

"Yeah, and we've been lucky too," Pollack added. "We must have killed at least thirty gooks since coming here, and haven't lost any of our own people."

The young hillbilly's eyes widened as he heard this report.

"Just be glad that you weren't sent to Delta Company," Scout announced.

"Why?" the tall, wiry kid asked.

"Because they're not as lucky or as good as we are."

The Cherry appeared confused and cast an imploring look to Larry.

"What Scout is saying, BJ is that Delta Company has only killed a couple of gooks while losing a bunch of their own to ambushes and booby traps."

"Wow!" the youngest soldier commented. "You guys must be good."

"We do have our moments," Scout replied.

"How much longer will we be here?"

"Just a couple more days. We're leaving on Thursday for the Michelin Rubber Plantation."

"To do what?" he asked in a strong southern accent.

"We're going to kill gooks! Jesus, man, you think we're going there to make tires? Don't be such an ignorant motherfucker!"

Doc interrupted, "Don't be so hard on the man, Scout. He just arrived and doesn't know what the Nam is about yet."

"It sure won't take him long," Larry pointed out.

"Who will take over the firebase when we leave?"

"See what I mean? All Cherries ever do is ask questions."

"Don't worry about it, Scout." Doc directed his attention to the newest man in the Squad. "Son, the higher brass has determined that this area is too difficult to patrol on foot. Shit, most of the jungle is rotting away around this firebase, so they're replacing us with the Fifth Mechanized Battalion. Their APC's will patrol through this area without a problem. Besides, in the last seven weeks, I haven't felt as comfortable here as I do at Firebase Kien. It'll be a pleasure to go back."

"Why is the jungle rotting?"

"That's a long story for another day!"

"How far away is Firebase Kien?"

Doc shook his head then smiles broadly. "Damn, BJ, I don't know myself. All I can tell you is that it's near the Black Virgin Mountain and in between Tay Ninh and the Parrot's Beak."

"Where is that?"

"I give up!" Doc threw his hands into the air and walked away.

Pollack leaned back against the bunker and smiled, recalling his first few days in the country. Watching and listening to Billie Joe was like a mirrored image of himself just two and a half months earlier.

"Don't worry about the bush, you'll do just fine."

"I have a few more questions; will you answer them for me?"

Pollack thought back to a remark Junior had made on Firebase Kien the night before he left for his first day in the bush: 'Someday you'll be able to help out a Cherry and he'll be grateful and thank you for your help and understanding.'

Pollack sat upright then called to the new Cherry, "Come over here and sit down. I'll try to answer your questions and help you get organized."

Chapter Twelve

The Michelin Rubber Plantation wasn't too far from the Black Virgin Mountains, which the Vietnamese called Nui Ba Dinh. From a distance of several miles, the mountain appeared to be black and laced with white crevices and tears, taking on a marble-like appearance. No other hills or mountains stood between the plantation and Nui Ba Dinh; it towered, tall and alone in the distance and could be seen for miles around.

Stories circulated about that mountain. It was said that the Americans had a base at the top of it, which could only be accessed by helicopter. They maintained a radio relay station on the top to boost communications between the military officials in Saigon and the rest of the country. The Army of the Republic of Vietnam (ARVN) had a large compound at the base of the same mountain. They were allies to the Americans, but they were content staying within the bases instead of patrolling out in the jungles. In between the two, the VC supposedly had an intricate tunnel system, which encompassed the entire mountain, top to bottom. It was surmised that the tunnel was so porous that if a couple of thousand-pound bombs were to fall on it, the entire mountain would collapse into a pile of dirt and stones.

The First Platoon operated on the outskirts of the plantation where several small villages lined the length of the dirt road. The area was sparsely populated and not considered a "Free Fire Zone." However, they maintained a curfew and anyone out in the open after dusk or before sunrise was considered the enemy and subjected to be fired upon.

They shared the road with shuffling villagers who made their way to and from the rubber plantation. Carts pulled by large water buffalo were filled with pails of dark liquid collected from the trees.

Other adults moved about in a very quick step balancing a long, bent bamboo pole on their shoulder with a filled pail attached to each end. All but the children wore straw colored conical hats with traditional black nylon pants and varied colored working shirts.

In the passing villages, children ran about chasing small pigs, chickens and barking dogs. They laughed and had fun, too caught up in what they were doing to notice the line of American soldiers passing by.

"This is just too weird! I would never have imagined that I would be walking on a trail in Vietnam alongside gooks." Larry transferred his machine gun to the opposite shoulder so one of the buffalos didn't snatch it from him.

"Last time we worked this plantation, we were on the western side of it and there were very few people around."

"Scout, how do we know which of these people are VC or not?"

"If we had that answer, the war would have been over long ago."

"I don't understand."

"One way, Pollack, is to ask them for their ID. Everyone has to have one to show they are honest citizens. But, that is also the easiest piece of ID to buy on the black market. So the VC also carry them and that's why it's so confusing during the day. Everybody is a farmer and villager during the day; some are VC at night."

"I agree with you, Scout, but carrying cards after curfew doesn't mean squat. If we spot anybody moving around after dark, then there's a very high probability they are VC. So we can shoot first and don't have to worry about checking ID because he looks suspicious."

"You got that right, Sarge. That's why I'd prefer the free-fire zones. Then we don't have to deal with this bullshit."

"You know these villagers in the boonies are mostly honest, hard working people who are trying to make a living. Most of the 'imposters' usually are found in the villages outside of the major base camps and usually have a job on the base. During my last tour, a Sapper Squad hit our base camp during the night. They created all kind of havoc, but the next morning, we found one of the base barbers dead in the wire with others from his Squad."

"Shit, it's like you can't trust anyone," BJ stated after hearing Sixpack tell the story.

"No you can't, so don't let your guard down, even in areas like this. It only takes guts for one of them to reach down into a bush and come out firing an AK-47 on full automatic at us. How many of us do you think he can take out?"

"Say no more, Sixpack. We get the message!" The Squad members adjusted their rifles to a more defensive posture. Some had been carrying their weapons either by a sling hanging over their shoulder, or by holding them on the handle and swinging the rifle at arms length along their sides with each step.

The parade continued with the Americans showing more curiosity than the villagers.

Sixpack led the column into one of the villages to look for things that may be out of place.

"This is the first time I've been in one of these villages. It's really a lot different than I remember seeing when riding on a bus or truck during my first week in country."

Old people still squatted in front of their straw huts, chewing betel nuts, and occasionally smiling as the Americans passed. Others sneered at them for the interruption and spit on the ground at their feet.

Dogs barked uncontrollably and chickens scurried about, pecking at the dirt with every other step.

"These are the sorriest excuse for chickens that I've ever seen in my life. Just look at them! They're nothing but skin and bones."

"BJ, they probably eat more than the villagers and are only good for giving taste to a pot of water."

"They're mean little fuckers though. This one almost bit my finger off when I reached for it."

Some of the nearby villagers covered their mouths with a hand and chuckled after seeing Larry jump into the air and back away from the small, snapping three-pound bird.

Young boys led the huge water buffalos around, prodding and beating at them with long, thin bamboo sticks. They showed no fear of these massive animals; nonetheless, the Americans gave them a wide berth.

Small children began tagging along and followed the soldiers through the village as if they were Pied Pipers. The little kids were about five years old and cute, with too-big pajama bottoms that they continuously tugged and pulled at while struggling to keep up.

"GI souvenir me chop-chop? Cigarettes?" The kids begged for handouts.

BJ handed one of them some of the red licorice that he'd been carrying. All at once, the kids converged on him.

"Hold on now, I don't have anymore to share." BJ held the licorice high into the air as the kids tried to climb up his body and pull down his arm.

"You're fucked now. Give them the whole package before they knock your ass over and take it from you anyway." The sight reminded Scout of what life was like on the reservation, as most of the Indians lived in poverty and did the same thing.

BJ quickly tossed the package off to the side and watched the pack of youths dive toward it in a free for all. This kept them busy for the next five minutes.

No child under two years old wore clothes. Most were naked and either sitting on the ground in front of their huts or is being carried in the arms of an older sister.

"Those little girls are awfully young to be baby sitters," Pollack stated after seeing dozens of girls carrying babies in their arms throughout the village.

"That's their life," Doc responded. They are only about eight years old and do all the housework, cooking and babysitting, while their parents are away at work in the fields or plantations."

"That sucks! My little sister is still playing with dolls."

"That's how it should be!"

Some twelve year-old boys wheeled up on their bikes next to the column of soldiers. They had Styrofoam coolers strapped to back of each bike that were filled with ice-cold Cokes.

"GI want buy cold Coke? Only one dollar?" They parked their vehicles and set up shop right on the side of the road.

Some of the soldiers stepped out of line and approached the young hawkers with dollar bills in hand. The bottles were so cold that condensation dripped from them.

"What do you think Larry, should we get one? I remember them telling us in training when we got here that we shouldn't because they may be poisoned or have glass in them."

"It doesn't seem to be affecting those guys that have already finished their bottles."

"Aw, what the fuck? They really look nice and cold. I'd probably pay ten dollars if that was the asking price." Pollack thought back again to the junior's words of wisdom back at Kien.

The two of them purchased the last two bottles of Coke.

"This is fucking great!" Pollack tilted his head back and allowed the rest of the cool, refreshing soda to run down his throat without swallowing.

"Yes it is!" Larry agreed.

By mid-afternoon, Alpha Company entered the Michelin Rubber Plantation, which was the largest in all of Vietnam. Each rubber tree was spaced evenly twenty feet apart and no matter in which direction you looked, the trees stood in a perfect row for miles.

Vegetation between trees was thin and sparse, rising no more than two feet above the ground. Each tree contained a pail that collected the slowly oozing sap.

Twenty minutes later, after moving easily through the plantation, the column stopped as a farmer approached them with his buffalo-drawn cart of pails. The animal sensed something whenever Americans were around and the old man had trouble controlling the huge beast. It wheezed and stomped its feet, then dug in and tried to pull free from the villager. Finally, the old man raised a stick and swiftly whipped it twice across the animal's snout. This had little effect. The Sergeant scanning the villager's ID was apprehensive about the beast breaking away and injuring him or his fellow soldiers, so he quickly returned it and directed the villager to move on. When the beast distanced itself from the soldiers, it relaxed and settled down to a more docile state.

"I gotta hand it to that old man, all eighty pounds of him. He handled that water buffalo like I used to break them wild horses back home," Wild Bill said in admiration.

"There is no way I'd try that. Goddamn thing would have stomped me to death."

"Yeah, Pollack, it would have been all over for you especially if you would have whipped his snout like the old man did."

"Wild Bill is probably the only person in this entire column who would have taken on the beast. Everyone else would have been long gone if he had broken free."

"There is no doubt about that, Frenchie, and I'd be at the front of that pack and leading everybody else." Doc continued to steal glances at the departing animal in order to convince himself that the threat of danger had passed.

First Platoon broke off from the main column and veered to the left on an angle of forty-five degrees from the column. They had planned to walk through the plantation for another half hour and then try to find a good spot for an NDP.

As they moved along, Pollack suddenly became startled by what he saw in the air. "Hey guys, you better take a look up above."

"Holy shit!" Larry stopped abruptly and scrunched his shoulders as a chill ran down his spine.

"They're all over!" BJ looked upward and walked right into Larry.

The largest spiders that most of the men had ever seen were suspended just above their heads. Their bodies were thin and oblong, measuring about five inches in length, but when you considered the legs, the arachnids were probably over a foot long. Perfectly round webs were spun and suspended between two rubber trees. Most were high in the air while others almost touched the ground. The size and colors of the spiders fascinated the soldiers; candy apple shades of green, red and yellow reflected in the light of the setting sun.

One of the guys pulled and snapped on a web to get a reaction from the spider. However, did not intimidate the creature, which stayed fixed in the exact center of its home.

"Do they bite?" BJ asked.

"Everything bites," Scout responded.

"Are they poisonous?"

"Not a clue. Care to find out?"

"No way!"

No suitable spots existed for a good night defensive perimeter anywhere within the plantation. Lt. Ramsey picked an area with a little more underbrush than he'd seen so far and decided to set up for the night. The L-T arranged the perimeter in the shape of a square and assigned each Squad a point on the compass so they could defend themselves on all four sides.

Sixpack's Squad set up on the north side of the perimeter. The open area did not provide any protection for the men in the event of a fire fight, but at least the low underbrush would afford some concealment from prying eyes, unless somebody stood erect or walked around. It would be another night of moving around on hands and knees.

Most of the interior of the perimeter was bare and the soft brown earth made sleeping easier for the men. They spread ponchos on the ground and covered themselves with the thin but soft green liner to create a sleeping position. Pillows consisted of nothing more than towels and balled up shirts. Most soldiers placed their rucksacks and extra supplies on the outside perimeter side of their makeshift beds in hopes of providing some protection if attacked.

Mechanical ambushes were set up to cover nearby trails, while trip flares and manually detonated Claymore mines were positioned for the night before anyone could relax or eat dinner. Everything had to be dismantled and secured before sunrise each morning so innocent villagers were not hurt after the curfew ended.

"You guys have to be careful and not hurt these rubber trees. We don't want to have to pay the tire Company for any damage," Sixpack announced.

"You've got to be joking," Larry said.

"Nope, it's true. This rule even goes back to when the French fought here. The deal is that if any unit is forced into combat within the plantation, the government at fault has to reimburse the rubber Company for any damages to its trees."

"That's a stupid fucking rule. We're in a war, how can they justify that?"

"Stupid or not, we have to follow it."

"This is unreal and gets more insane every day!"

First Platoon stayed within the plantation for the next several days. Squad sized patrols were dispatched daily to check the ID's of nearby workers and to investigate any trails that looked suspicious. Then, every afternoon about 1500 hours, the Platoon packed it up and moved to a different but similar site within the trees. The deployment of defensive measures after sunset and securing them before daybreak became routine.

During the fourth night, they heard odd noises around their perimeter. You could hear the distinct sound of leaves stirring, twigs breaking, and unfamiliar grunting sounds. Sixpack would scan the surrounding area with a Starlight scope, only to see the trees standing silently and nothing else. Most of the soldiers were spooked by this ongoing disruption and remained awake and on ready alert through the night.

The next evening offered a change of pace when the guy on watch spotted flashlights out in the field at about ten o'clock at night. The guard woke Lt. Ramsey, and then moved to Sixpack and shook him out of his slumber. "L-T needs you over by the CP." Sixpack grabbed his weapon and moved over to join the Lieutenant.

"What's up, L-T?" Sixpack rubbed the sleep from his eyes and waited for his vision to adjust.

"Night guard spotted flashlights in the fields outside of the plantation. Can't see much, but if you look closely," he placed a hand on the Sergeant's shoulder and pointed out toward the dancing lights, "I make out at least six of them."

"I see them, L-T, and don't remember a village in that particular area. But I do recall that field; heavy jungle borders it on the left and at the far end."

"I'll call in a fire mission and we can check it out in the morning." The two men referenced the map and both agreed on the coordinates for the first salvo.

Lt. Ramsey called Battalion HQ and waited almost a half hour to obtain clearance for the fire mission. By that time, the lights had disappeared, but he still requested the artillery barrage anyway.

Many of the sleeping men had been awakened by the commotion around the CP, so when the explosions occurred in the clearing about five hundred yards away, few of them were surprised. The L-T called for ten rounds to impact within that general vicinity.

Two hours later, some of the men heard the sound of a motorcycle moving across the open and toward the same area where the flashlights had been seen earlier. The sound was deceiving and it was very difficult to pinpoint the exact location as it echoed through the trees. The remainder of the night was quiet and uneventful.

In the morning, Captain Fowler ordered the First Platoon to move out of the plantation and investigate the area that exhibited all the activity during the night.

When the Platoon reached the clearing, the men formed up into two columns while crossing the open area.

"It looks like we're walking through an old rice paddy."

"How can you tell?"

Scout pointed to the right and left, and said, "Look over there, do you see the raised ground? Those are old paddy dikes that kept the water in and allowed the villagers to move through the fields."

"Why do you think it's not being used anymore?"

"Look around, BJ, do you see anybody around?"

"I haven't seen anybody since leaving the plantation. In fact, I don't even see any villages nearby."

"This is real old. If there was a village around here, they packed it up and moved out a long time ago."

"This is still a no-fire zone so keep on your toes."

The men soon reached the area where the artillery barrage had hit during the night. Here, the L-T had the Platoon form into a single line so they could sweep through the area and look for signs of the enemy having been there.

The ten small artillery craters were confined to an area one-half the size of a football field. Fresh, black dirt had rained over the area and now coated the ground and nearby vegetation. No trees stood nearby, but much of the vegetation surrounding each crater had been shredded by hundreds of flying hot steel projectiles. The grunts collected several pieces of jagged steel, no larger than a pack of cigarettes, as souvenirs.

"Man, if there was somebody out here last night, you'd think they couldn't have survived. Just look at all this devastation." Pollack raised his arm straight out and even with his shoulders then pointed in a half-circle.

"It's too weird. I haven't seen any flashlights on the ground or traces of blood anywhere in over an hour that we've been looking."

"If we haven't seen anything yet, then it's unlikely we'll find anything at all, Pollack. It's hard to judge distance at night and I can't guarantee this is exactly where the L-T and I saw the flashlights."

"Yeah, Sixpack, but didn't you say earlier that the lights were long gone before the fire mission? They probably weren't anywhere near this area when the rounds came in."

"That's what I think too, but we had to try anyway."

"We're not too far from the edge of the jungle over there," Larry pointed out to the dense vegetation only two-hundred feet away. "Maybe we should just keep walking until we reach it and poke around over there."

"I don't know. I'm already nervous about being out in the open so close to that tree line; it's the perfect spot for an ambush. Just hang loose and keep looking around here, and I'll check with the L-T to see what his plans are." Sixpack turned and walked over to where Lt. Ramsey was standing with his RTO, Bob.

"What are your thoughts about that tree line, L-T?"

"I've been tossing that around myself, Sixpack. We've got most of the day left to patrol the area and find a place for the night. Might as well get out of this sun and go take a look."

"When do you want to leave?"

"Instead of all of us going together, I want your Squad to recon the area first. Once you've got it secured, the rest of us will come up and join you."

"Sounds like a plan. I'll gather them up and we'll leave in five."

"Good luck!"

The Platoon was secured for the night in their defensive perimeter just inside the jungle and next to a well-used trail; Sixpack's Squad had come upon it during their recon of the area. The six-foot wide trail skirted alongside the jungle and continued westerly into the dense jungle, away from the rubber plantation.

The hard packed surface, with its recent activity, intrigued Lt. Ramsey especially in an area where nobody had been seen the entire day. The Captain agreed and ordered the L-T to set up an ambush on the trail.

Two mechanicals had been placed across the trail, one further west of their position and the other to the east. Trip flares and Claymore mines were in place, guard rotation was organized, and the stage was set for the night.

BJ had been assigned the last watch of the night and was ordered to wake everyone at 0545 so the mechanicals could be dismantled and brought back into the perimeter before the end of curfew at 0600.

The Army had issued a prime directive that no mechanical ambushes or trip mechanisms were to be left in place outside of curfew hours in those designated no-fire zones. Failure to abide could result in court martial.

In the morning, the Platoon was awakened, not by BJ, but by a large explosion and dirt raining down on many of the sleeping soldiers. The time was 0630 hours.

"You dumb motherfucker, you fell asleep!" Sixpack was heard scolding the new recruit.

BJ was disorientated and didn't know what to do or what to say. He leaned back against a tree, still holding the handset of the radio in his right hand.

"Our shit's in the wind now!" Sixpack looked out to the trail. "Scout, Frenchie and Nung, get out there and check that eastern ambush." He then looked to BJ. "Pray to God that some poor villager didn't stumble into it."

The Colonel was already on the radio scolding the Captain because he didn't have an answer regarding the explosion from the vicinity of his First Platoon's NDP.

Lt. Ramsey switched to the Company radio frequency and called the Captain to inform him of their predicament. He was just about to inform him that the last man on watch had fallen asleep when he was interrupted by sudden outbursts of gunfire; rounds ricocheted through the perimeter and everyone dove for cover.

Suddenly, the three men came crashing back into the perimeter, guns still smoking from their firing on the run.

"There's gooks on the trail!" Scout hollered. "Don't know how many, but the mechanical didn't get them all. They started shooting at us before we even saw them."

Not another word had to be said. The grunts lying closest to the trail began firing out to their front and along the trail to their right. Two Claymore mines were also activated, exploding near the aggressive enemy.

The remaining Squads on the other side of the perimeter hunkered down and held their fire until a clear target could be identified.

After just a few moments, the return fire became sporadic, then finally stopped. Sixpack was already on his feet gathering his Squad to go and investigate. The Third Squad moved further east through the dense bush with plans of exiting onto the trail just above the ambush site.

Scout and Nung led the way with Frenchie following close behind. They cautiously stepped out onto the trail and found themselves about seventy-five feet from the blown ambush site.

"Remember, we still have a live mechanical on the trail behind us. Should we disarm it before moving up to check out the other one?"

"No, leave it be, Wild Bill. If gooks got caught in this one while moving west, it may protect us if reinforcements try to come out of the jungle from that direction. We'll get to it later."

The eight men crouched down and ran in single file across the trail, moving further into the elephant grass and away from the jungle. When they were parallel to the ambush site, the grunts spread out and tried to keep five feet between themselves as they proceeded on line toward the trail.

The smell greeted them even before they saw the seven bodies spread along the trail. The first two in the column, having taken the full blast of the single mine ambush, were missing appendages and their torsos had been cut to shreds. The other five lay in contorted poses; blood still leaking from bullet holes in their bodies.

Each of the seven corpses was dressed alike and all had been carrying a rucksack, ammo pouch, and AK-47 rifle. Steel pith helmets with a single red star were strewn about the area. The rucksacks were full and bulging. A mortar tube and base plate lay in the middle of the line of dead enemy soldiers.

"Oh man, these are hardcore NVA soldiers. No wonder they held their ground and shot back at us," Frenchie said while scanning the corpses, his face showing deep concern.

"Looks like they were part of a supply train," Scout volunteered.

"Pollack go back and let the L-T know what we found. Then bring him and the others back here with you." Sixpack prodded at the bodies with his boot, watching for a reaction.

"I'm sure the L-T will be relieved," Scout mentioned.

"No doubt about it. Now all he has to do is to convince the Colonel that this was planned so BJ doesn't have to go to the stockade."

Right about then, the Third Squad stepped out of the jungle and approached the ambush site from the east.

"Looks like we just hit the jackpot," the black Squad leader announced when spotting the corpses on the trail.

"Yeah, but those are NVA dudes," a tall, blond ex-surfer from California stated. "I hope none of their buddies are hanging out nearby."

"Me too!" Frenchie continued to watch the open field with Wild Bill while the others searched over the bodies.

A rustling from the jungle momentarily startled the Third Squad members before they saw Pollack exit with the L-T and the Second Squad. They all gathered along the trail and then crowded around the corpses for a closer look. Some exhibited relief; some became sick to their stomachs and moved to the side of the trail to vomit, while others, mostly the old timers, showed concern.

"Sixpack, let's get some people out on security. We don't need anybody walking up on us while we're all together on this trail celebrating," Lt. Ramsey ordered.

Sgt. Holmes conferred with the other Squad leaders and they dispatched ten men into various directions away from them. Each of the two-man observation posts (OP's) would set up about two-hundred feet away to monitor the approaches into the area.

After the L-T reported to both the Captain and the Colonel, the radio traffic on the Battalion net became a chatterbox. Calls went out to anyone who needed to know about the ambush. After several minutes, the Colonel ordered the L-T to strip the bodies and inventory everything they found. A helicopter and two intelligence experts would be dropping into their location within the next two hours.

"These rucks weigh about a hundred and fifty pounds each. I'm curious as hell to see what's inside of them."

"Unbelievable! How can somebody who weighs so little carry so much weight?"

"No telling how far they had to come, but there's enough stuff here to keep them supplied for several weeks."

Rucks were emptied on the ground and the contents organized into small groups to the side of the trail. Most of them were packed with the same ammunition, food, medical supplies, and some varying personal effects.

Scout found a map and some official paperwork written in Vietnamese. He handed them to Nung who began to read the special orders.

After scanning through the documents, Nung and Scout approached the L-T with the find. "NVA are on re-supply mission and come from area in Cambodia. They travel over twenty-five kilometers and are supposed to deliver all supplies not far away from here."

"They would have made it if not for BJ," Frenchie exclaimed.

"Good point. If we would have pulled in the mechanical before six in the morning, they would have walked right past us while we were cooking breakfast."

"Yeah, but these guys would have lit us up if they smelled food cooking. They wouldn't have taken off like the VC might have."

"That's just too much for me to believe," somebody in the other Squad debated. "I'm thinking that they would have been bopping down this trail and chattering up a storm as they humped along. We would have heard them coming and set up a quick ambush."

"I don't think the results would have been the same, and there would have been a good chance that some of us would have gotten hurt." Frenchie replied, not as confident as his brother from the Third Squad.

"We'll never know will we?"

The seven soldiers had carried the mortar tube, base plate, ten mortar rounds, five-thousand rounds of 7.62mm rounds for the AK-47's, bags of rice, tins of fish and chicken, personal effects, cigarettes, official documents, letters and a map.

The helicopter and intelligence team hadn't spent more than fifteen minutes on the ground. The two men reviewed the bodies and took a few pictures with a camera before gathering up all the supplies, loading the chopper, and taking off.

After conferring with Nung about the papers he looked over and their map, the L-T dispatched a patrol to follow the trail into the jungle for five hundred meters or so. Sixpack assigned the task to Pollack, Scout, Wild Bill, and Nung.

The four men retrieved web gear, grenades, water, and extra ammo, and readied themselves to leave the security of the NDP. Sixpack stepped in their path. "Now don't get cute or try any hero shit out there. Just follow the trail like you're supposed to and take notes about what you see. Don't go any further than you have to. I know that I don't have to tell you that there are only four of you so avoid any contact at all costs. Nung, take point and try to get close to where these gooks were supposed to be heading. And stay sharp!"

"We'll be cool, and definitely in no hurry," Scout replied as they exited the NDP and stepped onto the trail only a few yards from where the dead gooks lay. It had been several hours since the mechanical went off and the bodies were already beginning to bloat up and attract swarms of flies. The scent was indescribable.

The four-man patrol followed the trail alongside the thick vegetation for twenty minutes when it suddenly turned and led into the dense jungle. Once inside, they found it cooler being out of the sun and under the triple canopy jungle. All of them were sweating profusely as they nervously moved forward along the trail. Nobody had said a word since leaving the NDP.

About two-hundred meters into the jungle, they came upon a fork in the trail. Nung held his arm up with a clenched fist; the signal to stay put, and moved up the right branch toward a small stream. He only walked about thirty feet and bent over on the side of the trail to have a closer look at whatever attracted his attention. Nung returned and motioned the group together.

"No can go this way. Beaucoup danger," he whispered.

"What did you see, Nung?"

"Come, I show."

Together, they walked the thirty feet to where Nung had spotted the warning. Something was wrong with the scene and definitely out of place in the middle of a jungle. Seven bricks lay on the ground to the side of the trail. Four of them were stacked neatly in one row, and the remaining three were butted up behind them. The space created by the missing brick in the second row formed a "V" whose point faced up that trail.

"See. Is sign for booby traps! Better we no go. We go try other trail for ti-ti (Vietnamese slang for a little bit)."

They quietly returned to the fork and Nung led them up the left trail. The discovery of the booby trap warning heightened their awareness another notch or two. They had slowed their approach in order to watch both the jungle for movement and the trail for trip wires. The slow pace continued for another two-hundred meters when a large, cleared area opened up to their front. All the ground vegetation had been cleared to the left of the trail in an area measuring about fifty feet square. On the other side, the trail could be seen re-entering the jungle and continuing onward. They were halfway across the clearing when they came upon another strange sight. Nung called for them to stop again.

To their right was something that resembled a hitching post for horses in the old western movies. Two poles, three feet high and ten feet apart, stuck up from the ground. A third and longer pole straddled the two and was thoroughly secured with vines.

The four men gathered around and glanced at each another with inquisitive looks upon their faces. They shrugged their shoulders and shook their heads to show that none had the slightest idea as to what it was used for or what it represented. The ground nearby was hard and smooth and there were no horseshoe or hoof prints imbedded into the earth.

"Let's head back," Scout whispered. "I'll take point. Nung, watch our backs."

Scout moved down the trail and the other three men followed. The small patrol moved slightly faster than they did coming up the trail, but they were still able to be very quiet in their movements.

All breathed a sigh of relief when exiting the jungle and returning to the open trail. Now the pace was even faster.

When the patrol returned to the NDP, there was only enough time left to report in with the L-T and grab a quick meal before nightfall.

They would all spend the night in the same place and send a couple of Squads onto the trail in the morning to further investigate what the small patrol had uncovered.

During the night, Larry got very sick. He developed a high fever and Doc recommended that he be dusted off in the morning. Everyone suspected he came down with malaria, but something else ailed him too; Doc couldn't put his finger on it.

The next morning before Larry was Medivaced, Sixpack ordered him and Pollack to switch weapons and ammo. Larry would take the M-16 with him to the hospital and Pollack would now carry the machine gun. John was really excited about the M-60 and knew that carrying it would be more work, but his reward was not having to go out on small patrols anymore.

Third and Fourth Squads departed on their patrol shortly after the Medivac helicopter left with Larry. Lieutenant Ramsey's curiosity piqued and he accompanied them to further investigate the trails in the jungle.

Pollack and BJ took this opportunity to tear down the gun to give it a good cleaning and oiling. When the task was finished, they lay out the belts of ammo, cleaned all the dirt from them, and then saturated each with oil. After a half hour, they were pleased enough with the results to pack away the cleaning supplies.

The patrol was gone for only an hour when the sound of an erupting firefight reached the NDP. It came from the same direction as the trails, which meant that the two-Squad patrol had made contact. The sound of AK-47 and M-16 fire grew louder and escalated to a frenzied pitch. The loud single explosions of grenades and M-79 launcher rounds punctuated the rifle fire. Seconds later, the telltale sound of two M-60 machine guns could be heard when they joined in the fray. Without a radio, those remaining behind did not have a clue about what was going on. However, it was clear that they must leave to reinforce their brothers.

"Grab your shit," Sixpack ordered the two remaining Squads, "We move out in thirty seconds."

Sergeant Holmes led the reinforcements up the trail at a fast trot. They were within a hundred feet of turning into the jungle when the other two Squads emerged with the L-T. They were also on the run and the L-T motioned for them to turn around and head in the other direction. It didn't take much effort to convince the others to do so. Lt. Ramsey halted them halfway back to the NDP and had them move into the high elephant grass to set up a small defensive perimeter in the event they were being pursued.

"What happened on the trail, L-T?" Sixpack inhaled deeply, trying to catch his breath.

"The gooks were set up at the fork of the trail and waited for us to get close. We weren't quite in the kill zone yet, but they opened up on us anyway."

"How many gooks were there?"

"I'm not sure, but I would venture to guess they had just as many men as we did."

"Why didn't they wait for you to get closer?"

"I think some of the gooks fucked it up, because we heard some misfires before the shooting started. That gave us all that split second we needed to jump off the trail, find some cover, and return fire. When they broke off the ambush, we kept firing and backing away, then took off at a run when we were able to."

"Anybody get hurt?"

"It is truly a miracle, but everybody made it out okay."

"So what do you want to do now?"

"First thing we need to do is to get some artillery fire going into that area."

"Good idea. I'll send out a couple of OP's between us and the jungle trail to give us some warning in case they decide to come after us."

The request for artillery was denied because of the close proximity to some of the villages in the line of fire. A short round could land in one of them and kill innocent bystanders.

Sixpack returned and could see that the L-T was pissed.

"They won't give us permission to fire artillery."

"Why the fuck not?"

"Villages are in the line of fire."

"We haven't seen one village anywhere near us! This is bullshit!"

"I know."

"What about gunships?"

"I'll try them next."

Fifteen minutes later, two Cobra gunships arrived and circled over the jungle in close proximity to where the ambush occurred.

The pilots switched to the Company net in order to speak directly with Lt. Ramsey about the fire mission. They informed him that they were unable to see through the triple canopy so they were reluctant to shoot unless a target area was first identified with smoke.

This disappointed both Sixpack and the L-T. He informed the pilots if that were the case, he would have to send his Platoon back into the jungle, after a recon by fire, to see if they could identify viable targets. Both pilots agreed to remain on station and support the Platoon until they were no longer needed.

First Platoon cautiously filtered back into the jungle and stayed low while moving up the trail. After a hand signal, the men quickly stepped off to the left and sought suitable cover. Nobody could predict if there would be return fire or not, so it was best to be prepared and ensure that your position could be well defended.

A star cluster flare was fired through the triple canopy to show the two Cobra pilots the location of the friendly forces below. It was also the signal for the men to open fire. The four machine guns, equally spaced through the column, were the first to open fire. The gunners traversed the area and fired hundreds of rounds at the invisible enemy. Those with M-16's fired off a couple of magazines into the vicinity of the ambush. When the L-T was satisfied with the recon by fire, he called for an end to the shooting.

BJ and Pollack smiled proudly to one other as their gun was the only one of four that kept firing without jamming.

Lt. Ramsey sent the pilots a sit rep and informed them that they were now entering the ambush site.

The Platoon began a sweep of the area, checking for any signs of the enemy. They found blood splattering just beyond the fork and all through the brush in between the two trails. Several blood trails were also discovered leading deeper into the jungle and those were only on the left path, which wasn't supposed to be booby-trapped. They continued searching the area for another forty-five minutes, but as always after an ambush, found no bodies left behind.

The L-T called the Cobra pilots to terminate the mission and to thank them for their support. He was also anxious to further discuss the area with the Captain and gave the order for the Platoon to return to the NDP.

When they arrived, the soldiers moved to their respective areas within the perimeter. It was Third Squad's turn to provide volunteers for the two-man OP's. They organized three teams and moved out within ten minutes.

During this downtime, and especially after a firefight, the weapons should be cleaned and oiled. Each Squad took a turn in completing this task while the other three remained on guard and defended the perimeter. It would otherwise be disastrous for the Platoon if some gooks happened upon the NDP and caught the entire Platoon with their weapons apart.

Some of the men took the opportunity to write home; letters were collected and taken to the rear during every re-supply twice a week. Postage stamps were not needed, as the soldiers in Vietnam only had to write the word "FREE" in the top right corner where a stamp was normally attached. It was said that if someone were to write a note on the side of a C-Ration box, it would be delivered as long as the piece of cardboard was properly addressed with the word "FREE" on it.

Yet others lay on the ground with their backs against rucks, reading books or listening to transistor radios with earpieces. Everyone was packed up, weapons were cleaned, and they were ready to move out on a moment's notice.

Lt. Ramsey had a map spread out on the ground and was in the process of making small marks with his grease pencil while listening to the Captain on the radio handset. He didn't look too happy and had been trying to make a point to the Captain, but he only succeeded in getting out two or three words before he was shushed and forced back into a listening mode. When he attempted this a second time, the results were the same. Finally, he threw his grease pencil down onto the map and tossed the radio receiver to Bob, who was sitting close by.

"Squad leaders on me!" Sixpack and the other three Sergeants dropped what they were doing and immediately moved over to join the L-T.

"The Captain wants us to stay in this same position again tonight and to dispatch two ambush teams after nightfall to cover the trail near its entry into the jungle."

"L-T, I don't mind the ambushes, but staying here for a third consecutive night isn't too smart."

"I agree, Sixpack, but there was nothing I could do to change his mind."

"Sir, some of the men are already complaining about the smell coming from the trail."

"Sorry, Rock, but there's nothing I can do about that."

"Have your men break the filters off from their cigarettes and give them to Nung. He's got some special liquid to put a drop onto each one. Then your people can put them up their noses. It's worked well for our Squad."

"Thanks for the suggestion, Sixpack."

"Which Squads are going to pull the ambush tonight?"

"Sixpack, I want your Squad to team up with Rock's Second Squad. We'll finalize our plans later this afternoon. Plan on leaving about 2100 hrs; it'll be dark enough by then."

"Hey, Scout, you know I would have volunteered for the ambush if we hadn't been picked ourselves."

"I would have been right behind you, Wild Bill. I'm not too fond of staying in the same place for three nights in a row. This is plain stupid!"

"That will be for the other two Squads to worry about."

"Doesn't it strike anybody as being odd that nobody is coming through here to investigate the explosions and shooting? After all, this is supposed to be a populated, no fire zone."

"I thought about that myself, Pollack, especially with these villages nearby. You'd think somebody would have showed up by now."

"This reminds me of something a guy told me when I was on road security when I first got in country. The guy told me to be happy when villagers were around, because they know when Charlie is in the area and don't want to be caught in the middle when there's going to be a fight. So, this must mean that gooks are out and about."

"That's why I don't like being in the same place all this time. If the gooks are around, they know we're here."

The two ambush Squads made final preparations for the night. Poncho liners were rolled and tied to the rear of ammo belts. There was no need for ponchos, as they would make too much noise; it was also highly doubtful that any of them would be lying on the ground anyway. Each of the men would most likely spend the night sitting wide awake against one of the many trees, wrapped up in a camouflaged poncho liner, staring into the black night.

It would be too dark for them to set up mechanical ambushes, but they did plan on taking along extra Claymore's and clackers to cover their small perimeter.

The men shared canteens and filled them to prevent water from sloshing around inside while moving. They also used black electrical tape to secure anything that could rattle or come into contact with anything else. Noise discipline was crucial in the dead of night, and the slightest sound could be carried through the air, thus alerting others of your presence.

The NDP would not set up any mechanicals that night either so they could keep the trails open in the event either ambush team were to get into trouble. This would allow reinforcements to quickly move in support of them or in the event the teams needed to make a hasty retreat. At least then nobody would have to worry about booby traps.

Squad members finished dinner and had last cigarettes before heading out within the next hour.

Pollack ate beans and franks from a C-Ration can when he suddenly dropped the can and started to shake like he had just walked into an icy cold freezer.

"What's up, Pollack?"

"I was just thinking back to the four of us on that trail less than twelve hours ago. We walked way beyond that fork in the trail."

"Are you wondering why we weren't shot at?"

"Yeah, Scout. You have to wonder if they saw us and just let us go, hoping that a larger group would follow afterwards."

"We'll never know and you can't spend time thinking about those kinds of things. It'll drive you crazy!"

"It's weird though. Did you ever almost get into a car accident and then later when you think about what might have happened, you get all shaky and shit? It's uncontrollable and you can't stop?"

"Adrenaline does that to you. It's kind of like getting into a situation where you have to make a decision to either fight or run. Your body sends this blast of energy to help you through this panic and if it isn't used, it's got to go someplace. So it starts to bleed out and give you those kinds of reactions. That's most likely what is happening to you right now. It happens to everyone and I wouldn't get concerned about it."

"Maybe it was just luck, huh?"

"It's very possible and no different than those seven gooks laying out on the trail. If we had done our job, they would have been lucky on that day too. Unfortunately, their ticket was pulled and it was time to go."

The two Squads quietly departed under the cover of darkness and moved along the trail toward their designated ambush sites, which should be east of the trail and just inside the jungle.

Pollack thought to himself that it was surely the spookiest thing he'd ever done in his whole life. Pitch black, the light of the partial moon offered little comfort as it rose into the night sky.

At the point, Frenchie used a Starlight scope and stopped periodically to get his bearings. The rest of the grunts in the single file held onto the shoulder strap of the man to his immediate front. It worked well when leading a group of blind men through the pitch-black terrain.

They slowly grew accustomed to the darkness and could see somewhat in the shadowy environment. Nobody spoke; communicating was done by the pushing and pulling of shoulder straps. Even so, they could travel at a satisfactory pace. However, once they turned and entered into the triple canopy, they lost it all again.

It was nerve wracking and Pollack thought to himself again, comparing the hump to walking through a Halloween haunted house, where you felt your way along, waiting for something to jump out and surprise you. To get surprised then and there could very likely result in death.

Once they reached their destination, the men stepped off the trail and into the thick underbrush. Claymore mines were immediately positioned next to the trail and the ambushers backed away to a safe distance while unwinding the spool of electrical wire. They remained within an arm's length of each other and tried to sit on the ground as quietly as possible. Both Squads would remain in that pose until sunrise.

Every chirp, crack, and croak solicited a reaction from the stealthy soldiers, but as nervous and jumpy as they were, they still maintained noise discipline and didn't overreact. Besides, they were fully aware that if a firefight was to develop and it became necessary for the teams to retreat, it could be disastrous.

The next morning, everyone breathed a sigh of relief, thankful that nothing had happened during the night. They waited until seven before starting back to rejoin the balance of the Platoon.

As they stepped back onto the trail and begin walking toward the doorway of the jungle, Nung stopped suddenly and motioned for everyone to get down. There was a hint of wood burning in the air and the sound of laughter and chattering to their left. Nung raised his right hand with two fingers, forming the 'Victory sign'. He pointed to his own eyes, and then extended his arm to point into the bush and raised four fingers. Sixpack was already moving toward the front of the column to where Nung squatted. After hearing the explanation, Sixpack rose up to his knees and peered through the brush toward the small stream. There, he could clearly see four gooks, sitting around a small fire on the bank, and two AK-47 rifles leaning against a nearby tree.

The Americans were already in a column on the trail; Sixpack used hand signals to organize them into a firing line. Meanwhile, the RTO quietly informed the rest of the Platoon that they had gooks spotted and would be engaging. On Sixpack's signal, everyone started firing toward the shadows near the stream.

A flurry of activity and flashes of movement were seen around the campsite. No one returned fire, and the Squads seemed to enjoy being the aggressors for a change. Now it was just a matter of sweeping through the area and counting the bodies.

Suddenly, several gooks with AK-47's opened fire on the Americans from their left flank and were dug in near the fork of the trail. The last two soldiers, closest to the gooks, were immediately hit and fell to the ground. No longer sensing a threat to their front, the grunts jumped into the brush and began returning fire. This threat lasted no longer than one minute and the firing stopped just as abruptly as it had begun. It was so frenzied that the RTO didn't even have a chance to inform the L-T of the ambush. But there was no mistaking that something was terribly wrong when the sound of AK fire erupted.

The two wounded forward soldiers started crawling along the edge of the trail to increase their distance from the gooks. When the firing stopped, the two men were quickly lifted up and carried away as they all retreated from the jungle.

Lt. Ramsey was the first to bump into the retreating men out on the main trail. A defensive perimeter had been hastily organized, a Medivac chopper requested, and the L-T was already outlining the next plan of action with his Squad leaders. The others kept an eye on the jungle.

One of the wounded had been shot in the left arm and the other was hit in the back. Their wounds were not life threatening and both men would return to Cu Chi after a short hospital stay.

The plan was to repeat exactly what the Platoon did a few days ago. Cobra support helicopters would come on station; the grunts would fire several hundred rounds into the jungle and then move in to sweep the area again.

They found blood all around the campfire, and the two weapons still leaned against the tree unscathed. Frenchie and Scout picked them up and slung the rifles over their shoulders. The First Squad continued its sweep and began to follow the small stream into the jungle. They moved against the flow and began to notice a red tint in the water.

"Blood in the water," Scout pointed out in a whisper while leading the Squad upstream. Those following acknowledged him with a quick nod.

The stream was shallow and less than six inches deep. The bottom was littered with small stones, leaves and twigs from the surrounding trees. Small minnows scurried through the clear liquid and water spiders darted across the top, trying to keep out of the way of the advancing soldiers.

"Looks like someone was dragged through here," Frenchie noted, pointing out the disruption on the streambed. Three and sometimes four parallel troughs, two inches wide, were dug through the stones and leaves at different intervals along the fifteen-foot wide stream.

Scout raised his right arm to stop the column. "Sixpack, we've got bodies up ahead."

Sixpack moved forward to join Scout. "We'll check them out; the rest of you fan out and keep an eye out for Charlie."

"There's two here and another one about twenty feet forward."

"Looks like these bodies were hit multiple times. There's no way they made it this far alone."

"That would account for the skid marks along the bottom of the stream. They were being helped or dragged deeper into the jungle."

"I wonder why they left them here when they were carried this far?"

"Could be that when the Platoon opened up before entering the jungle again, they probably needed to get away quickly to save their own asses. Did you also note that there are no weapons lying near the bodies?"

"Could be the same bunch that we opened up on around the campfire; we've got two of their weapons."

"Yeah, but somebody took whatever that third gook was carrying."

"I agree."

"That means there are more of them around here someplace."

After searching the bodies and taking everything of importance with them, the Squad followed some new blood trails along the side of the stream. They led away from the stream and finally ended after one-hundred feet.

"So where did he go?" Pollack asked.

"It looks like he just disappeared."

"That's what's so frustrating about this place. It's just like the earth swallows them up."

"You've probably hit it right on the head," Sixpack said, scanning the nearby area. "Remember that underground tunnel complex and hospital we found earlier? I would not be surprised if there's another one somewhere around here."

The Squad concluded the search of the area and formed back up with the rest of the Platoon at the fork in the trail.

When everyone was finally together, Lt. Ramsey gave the order for the Platoon to return to the NDP. They would remain there, once again for the night, and get resupplied first thing in the morning. They were running low on ammunition so the L-T didn't want to get caught up in a prolonged firefight and end up running out. After the re-supply, the Platoon would come back and create a new NDP, which would be closer to where all the ambushes had taken place.

First Platoon was told to carry enough rations for at least the next five days. The Captain wanted to minimize their exposure so they could work effectively in the jungle for the next several days. The gooks were very aware of the protocol for re-supply and knew that if a unit were in the area, helicopters would be landing every three days. The men hoped that that the gooks would get over-confident and come out into the open when they thought no Americans were around.

Everyday, they moved deeper into the jungle and followed the stream in its westward tract. Nightly NDP's were set up near the stream and ambush teams were dispatched to watch nearby trails or open areas.

Following a stream provided the men with an ample supply of drinking water, thus cutting down on the weight they must carry during the humps. The water looked clear, but upon closer investigation, small, barely visible creatures swam in it. Every canteen full had to be treated with two iodine tablets, which killed all the bacteria in the unsanitary water. It left a bitter taste, but there was no choice unless you wanted to die of thirst or develop hepatitis. Some of the luckier warriors had pre-sweetened Kool-Aid sent to them from home, which made for a flavorful thirst quencher. Nobody hoarded the treasure and drinks from Kool Aid canteens were openly shared with fellow soldiers.

After five days, not another human being had been seen during that time. The routine of moving daily and sending out ambushes at night without contact became boring. Some soldiers began to get over-confident and cocky, letting weapons hang to the side during humps and even talking louder than they should.

A re-supply had been scheduled for the following day, but the Colonel asked if the unit could get by for at least one more day, possibly two. He truly believed that the strategy would work and result in some enemy kills.

Sixpack and the other Squad leaders checked with their men on food status and found that they could squeak by for another couple of days. When Lt. Ramsey informed the Colonel, he was very pleased with the feedback.

The next two days proved uneventful for the Platoon, just like it had been since they started following the stream. It was obvious that either the gooks were well aware of their presence and were staying underground, or they'd vacated the area all together.

Arrangements were made for the Platoon to return to the LZ near their original NDP early in the morning. Then after a re-supply of hot food, clean clothes, ammo, mail, and other supplies, First Platoon would be airlifted to a new Area of Operations (AO), where the Colonel felt would provide promising results.

The Platoon left early in the morning and began to march back to their first night's NDP. The men moved at a swift pace with empty rucks and canteens. However, it still took them three hours to exit the jungle.

It wasn't long before the column had to pass the seven gook corpses on the trail for the last time. Not everyone felt the need to look at them; only the Cherries were fascinated and curious enough to do so. Most of them gagged and some had to step off the trail to vomit. Maggots, flies, and ants were still hard at work trying to devour the decaying bodies; only a small amount of flesh and hair on the bleached white bones remained. The smell wasn't quite as obnoxious as it was the week before; nevertheless, it was still rancid. The clothed skeletons still lay just as they fell, meaning that none of their comrades had been by to bury them yet. That was a good sign!

The men showed no remorse; only satisfaction in knowing that these were the remains of gooks that at one time had the capability of doing the same thing to them.

When the re-supply choppers left on the LZ, everyone was busy packing supplies for the new mission. Doc was busier than most as he treated everyone for one ailment or another. He administered creams and ointment to fight ringworm, jungle rot, cuts, and bruises.

The L-T walked around the perimeter congratulating everyone for a job well done. He told them that First Platoon had received credit for twelve enemy soldiers killed, while only suffering two wounded and one person sick. Battalion was ecstatic.

First Platoon had been lucky so far, and many of them wondered how long it would last.

Chapter Thirteen

The six Hueys circled above a small clearing, which appeared to have been cut out of the jungle some time ago. Looking down from the choppers, members of the First Platoon could see a small Loach helicopter flying low around the outskirts of the LZ. It attempted to draw enemy fire from the surrounding tree line before the troops landed.

"You know those guys have balls as big as watermelons, doing shit like that," Frenchie yelled above the noise of the engines.

"You ain't shitting. I'd never fly around like that just waiting to see if somebody will shoot at me."

"Yeah, but you'll walk along the trail and do the same thing. Those air jockeys think that grunts have big balls. Wild Bill, please show us yours!"

He was stunned by Frenchie's comment and couldn't even respond. Pollack, BJ, and some of the others began to laugh, momentarily relieved from their anxiety. However, it was short-lived and the laughter stopped abruptly when they saw green tracer rounds flying through the air. A stream of rounds from the tree line trailed the small Loach as the pilot took evasive action to get away. Several new streams of green reached up to them from yet another location in the same part of the jungle.

"Shit! This mother's hot," Wild Bill cried, quickly turning to face Pollack and BJ. "When the birds land, jump off and get away from them as quick as you can. The door gunner will be shooting at the tree line so don't run in front of him. When they lift off, start firing your gun into that same tree line. Okay?"

Both of them nodded.

The tiny Loach trailed smoke but managed to stay airborne. He dropped a red smoke grenade into the tree line, darted back up into

207

the sky, and then passed on final instructions to the Cobra gunships before limping back to base.

Two of the deadly birds dropped out of the sky and made a first pass; one followed closely behind the first and both fired mini-guns and rockets in the vicinity of the rising red smoke. Debris from the jungle rained onto the LZ as rockets exploded on their targets. Meanwhile, the Hueys had maneuvered into position so their glide path for the insertion was parallel to that of the supporting Cobras.

The formation was on its final approach, flying only fifty feet above the jungle when the two Cobras launched a second assault upon the tree line.

As the gunships kept the enemy's head down, the six slicks formed a straight line on final approach into the hot LZ; door gunners on the enemy side of the aircraft fired into the tree line as they neared the ground. Once they touched down, the birds emptied in seconds; soldiers quickly moved away, dropped to the ground, and began firing their own weapons into the same portion of the tree line.

Pollack and BJ felt as if they were running in slow motion. Belts of machine gun ammo, about five hundred rounds each, wrapped them from their chest to their hips. Once clear of the rotors, both dove for the ground. The weight of full rucks, combined with both the machine gun and ammo, nearly knocked the wind out of Pollack. He lay there with heart and lungs pounding wildly. BJ lay next to him with a look of absolute terror on his face.

The pilots knew that they were considered sitting ducks in a hot LZ, so they wasted no time leaving. One even took off too soon, eager to get back into the air, which forced the last of the troops to jump six feet to the ground. Luckily, nobody got hurt.

Pollack extended two bi-fold legs near the end of the barrel to support the weapon and started to fire machine gun into the jungle to his front. While firing, BJ, his assistant gunner and ammo bearer, linked the individual belts of ammo together to keep the weapon firing.

The second sortie landed with the next group of Alpha Company grunts. Soldiers jumped off and joined those already on the ground.

All at once, a large explosion was heard behind the grunts, causing them to momentarily stop firing and take notice. A helicopter from the sortie was ablaze; shrill alarms sounded as the bird twirled slowly toward the ground. When it crashed into the jungle at the edge of the LZ, a second explosion was followed by a mushroom cloud of yellow and red flame rising into the sky, finally ending in a fog of thick, dark black smoke. One could not see the small pieces of fiery steel and aluminum flying across the LZ. Screams of pain and calls for medics cried out near the crash site and in the area where Third Squad had taken refuge.

Two RPG rounds had hit the chopper and the crash killed everyone on board instantly. Upon seeing the crash, the Cobras were quick to respond and launch an assault into the new target area. Artillery rounds also began to fall into the jungle on the western side of the LZ.

The ground shook violently as each rocket and artillery round impacted. Three quarters of Alpha Company soldiers lay on the ground of the open LZ, firing their weapons at the invisible enemy within the jungle. The noise was unbearable and the concussions made the men bounce lightly as if resting on a trampoline.

While the battle continued, the last of Alpha Company landed, along with the CP, on the last and final sortie. Every time the birds had come in, the door gunner's machine gun barrels glowed from extensive firing so it was a wonder that they still functioned.

Once the entire Company was on the ground, the grunts spread out and moved into the jungle on the eastern side of the LZ. Security was in place, so word was passed down for everyone to sit tight as the fast movers (jets) were on their way to drop some bombs.

The Gunships left the area and returned to Cu Chi for rearming; they would return if needed. It was too late to warn anyone that the jets were already on station and had begun their runs. A loud 'vroom' noise echoed and an ear-shattering explosion sounded before anyone even noticed the jets. They climbed straight up, the sun reflecting from their wings like dancing mirrors. Their drops were right on target and the entire western tree line was set ablaze. The two Crusaders made two more passes and dropped each load deeper into the jungle.

The departing sound of the jet engines could still be heard when the Captain jumped to his feet, rallying the Company to cross the LZ and sweep through the smoking jungle on the other side.

He organized the men into a horseshoe formation, with Second and Third Platoons on the two sides, and Fourth Platoon at the base. First Platoon would stay behind to provide security for the CP, and to also take care of loading the dead and wounded onto the Medivac choppers when they arrived.

The three Platoons moved quickly toward the tree line in hopes of catching any gooks that may have been shocked and wandering around disoriented. There hadn't been a sound from the tree line since the fast movers had dropped their payloads; that served as a confidence booster to those conducting the sweep.

A team from the helicopter Squadron prepared to land and investigate the crash site. The bodies had already been pulled from the wreckage and added to those from Alpha Company. Not much remained for salvaging from the chopper as most of the cargo had been destroyed beyond recognition.

Lt. Ramsey greeted the Squadron members upon landing and offered his regrets. After briefing them about the battle, he pointed out the location of the crash site.

The men stopped for a moment at the bodies of their dead team members to offer a quick prayer before being escorted to the crash site by Sixpack and four other soldiers.

First Platoon was the first on the ground and therefore suffered most of the casualties there were also some from the other three Platoons. Not counting the four crewmen killed on the helicopter, Alpha Company suffered eight killed and fifteen wounded; less than half were from bullet wounds, shrapnel from the crash injured the rest. Some of the more seriously wounded men had pieces of metal protruding from their bodies. The medics did not dare remove any for fear of internal bleeding. Instead, they did their best to pack the wound, stop the bleeding and make the soldiers as comfortable as possible.

Pollack, Wild Bill, and Frenchie walked through the temporary aid station to survey the casualties. They were surprised to come upon Bob, the L-T's RTO.

"Bob, what happened to you?"

He winced in pain, wheezing and breathing heavy, upon hearing his name called. Large gauze bandages had been applied to his back and tied off across his chest. "That radio saved my life," Bob said and pointed to the side.

The PRC-25 radio lay on the ground and looked like somebody shot a few rounds of buckshot into it. Bob's rucksack also took a beating.

"Holy shit! Is all that from the crashed chopper?"

Bob nodded his head.

"What the fuck? Were you right next to it?"

"Naw, we were about thirty feet away when it crashed. The L-T and I were close to where the Third Squad had touched down and it seems like most everybody around me got hit except for the L-T who was standing in front of me."

"The man owes you his life!" Wild Bill exclaimed.

"Seems that way. He's already stopped by and thanked me ten times," he tried to laugh but could only smile slightly, wincing in pain once again.

"What are they telling you about your back?" Pollack asked.

"Doc thinks my lung is nicked and that's why it's so hard for me to breathe. But other than that, I'll get stitched up and have some R&R at the 93rd Evac (Evacuation Hospital in Long Binh)."

The four of them shook hands. "Good luck to you, Bob, and we'll see you when you get back!" The three men continued on.

Pollack did not know any of the wounded; however, Frenchie and Wild Bill recognized a couple men and stopped to chat. The visits were quick and they continued on and toward the line of bodies covered with ponchos.

It was then that the first Medivac chopper touched down to pick up the four seriously wounded soldiers. Just as soon as it lifted off, a second Medivac chopper landed to transport the next five wounded soldiers out of the field and to the hospital. The rest of the wounded and dead would have to wait for the two helicopters to return.

The windy chopper landings had blown the ponchos from the dead soldiers to leave the bodies exposed. Pollack and Frenchie ran to gather them and returned with an armful each.

They began draping the corpses and reached the center of the row when Pollack stopped suddenly. He dropped the ponchos on the ground, took in a deep breath and stared unbelievably at the corpse lying at his feet.

"Pollack, what's up? You know this guy?" Wild Bill asked.

A single tear dropped from his right eye, leaving a trail on his dirt-encrusted face for others to follow.

"Goddammit!" Pollack finally mumbled.

"Who is he?" Frenchie asked.

Pollack shook his head and wiped the tears from his face with a shirtsleeve. "Yeah, I knew him. His name is Junior and he didn't live too far away from me back in the world. When I got to Kien, he took me under his wing and got me ready to come out into the bush. I spent my first night there, together with him on bunker guard duty. He taught me a lot and without him, I would have been in a world of hurt."

"Sorry, Pollack!" Wild Bill and Frenchie left to cover the remaining four bodies.

Junior's head was almost severed from his body and he lay at an awkward angle, with his left cheek resting on his left shoulder. His fatigue jacket had been completely saturated with blood, most of which was still wet. Had the helicopter not crashed, he would still be alive and sitting here with the rest of First Platoon.

Frenchie and Wild Bill held the extended poncho and moved closer to Junior's corpse. "Hey man, sorry, but he's got to be covered up," Frenchie offered solemnly.

"I'm all right, go ahead," Pollack said in a shaky voice, backing away to give them room.

After the last chopper left with the corpses, the First Squad members headed back to the tree line, where the company CP and remaining soldiers were located. Most just sat on the ground and relaxed against trees. The air was filled with feelings of sorrow over the deaths of friends and relief that those contemplating were not among the injured. It was very quiet with the only sound being the squelch from the radios.

The rest of the Company returned from their sweep after two hours. All they found was spent ammunition. No bodies, blood trails, or bunkers, provided any evidence of the enemy. Once again, the gooks vanished into thin air!

The Company remained in its present location until the crash site could be vacated and everyone had an opportunity to eat lunch. Many of the soldiers were relieved to be back in a 'free-fire zone'; at least now they could fire at suspected enemy shadows without having to worry about innocent bystanders or getting clearance to fire.

"This shit ain't right! Those fucking gooks pop off some rounds, eliminate half of a Platoon, shoot down a chopper, and then di-di (Vietnamese slang for run away) out of the area before the heavy shit comes in."

"I know, Doc, it's like they're psychic and always keep a step ahead of us. It burns my ass!"

"What happened to that small Loach that got hit?"

"Not a clue, Pollack. I was so worried and focused on that hot LZ, that all I was thinking about was how to save my own ass."

"You and everybody else, Scout!"

"I didn't have time to think. I was so scared that my mind went blank and everything was happening in slow motion."

"Did you leave some turds on the chopper?" Wild Bill kidded the Pollack.

"I may have, but don't know for sure. Why don't you come over and smell my ass and then you can tell me?"

A laugh erupted from the small group.

Billy Joe sat off by himself, away from the rest of the Squad. It appeared that they all noticed him at the same time.

"Hey, guys, check out BJ. What's up with him?"

"One of his close friends in the Fourth Platoon was killed today," Doc volunteered.

"He didn't say anything to me about having a friend in the Fourth," Pollack said.

Doc moved closer to the group and reported in more of a subdued voice. "Seems that BJ and this guy went through Basic Training and AIT together, and both ended up here in Alpha Company. They actually both came out to the field on the same re-supply chopper."

"I have a buddy like that too; Bill Sayers is in the Third Platoon. Larry and Sixpack both know him."

"I know that's tough; it's like losing a brother."

"Losing Zeke was like losing a brother and I didn't know him all that long."

"I know what you mean, Pollack, but a lot of these other guys in the Company say that's why they keep to themselves and don't want to know your name or anything about you."

"I've heard the same thing," Scout added.

"These guys will tell you that this allows them to keep their sanity, and if you die then it don't mean nothin' to them."

"Yeah, but you know that's a lot of bullshit, Wild Bill. I'm sure those guys don't have any super powers and have emotions just like the rest of us. So when a fellow grunt is killed, it has to tear them up inside, whether they show it or not."

"Hey, BJ, come on over and join us," Pollack called to his ammo bearer.

The new recruit looked up and waved him off. "I'm okay right here by myself."

"Well then, we'll have to come and join you."

During the next two days, the members of Alpha Company conducted countless patrols and ambushes. There was no contact, which the grunts were thankful for; however, it did not please the Colonel in his desire for body counts.

On the third day, the Company was told to move to a new LZ for an afternoon re-supply. Tomorrow, they would move in a different direction and work through an area they had not seen yet. The thought of having to hump heavy rucks once again did not appeal to many in the Company, but everyone looked forward to the possibility of getting mail. It had been two and a half weeks, and most of the guys would walk ten miles for the chance of getting a letter from home.

That resupply turned out to be one of the best. The Battalion cooks put together enough hot food to feed everyone in the Company twice. The thermos containers were filled with hot roast beef, potatoes, corn, carrots, and ice-cold applesauce and lemonade.

A defensive perimeter was in place around the LZ and Squads rotated through the chow line before returning to their location on the perimeter. The unexpected surprise definitely boosted morale for the Company. In the past, those types of re-supplies only happened on holidays. No one complained and the kind gesture was well received by all.

Once everyone had their fill of a fantastic meal, they were given time to draw out new supplies. All C-Rations were distributed and packed away. The piles of other assorted supplies, including clean uniforms, towels, socks, new canteens, foot powder, bootlaces, razor blades, chewing gum, toothpaste, toothbrushes, and all the cigarettes you could carry, were dwindling fast.

Special Red Cross packages were also distributed and split between the many Squads. These treasures included ink pens, paper, postcards, envelopes, and Christmas cards from children back home.

Pollack opened his card first in curious anticipation of whom it might be from. It was simple, with a picture of a white candle over a green Christmas wreath on the front. A short hand-written note was folded inside:

Dear Soldier,

Our Sunday school gave money so we could send packets to you men who are fighting for our country. I hope they can be of use to you and make your Christmas a little merrier. I'm ten years old and would like to hear from you and where you are stationed.

Wishing you a Merry Christmas and God's blessing,
Phillip Huntley
R.R. #23
Grand Rapids, Michigan, USA

It was only the middle of October, but Pollack was touched by this kid's card. He immediately began to write him a return letter:

Dear Phillip,

Thank you for the Christmas card. My name is John and I am only nine years older than you are. I hope that when you are my age this war will be over and you won't have to go through what I am today. I live in the Detroit area in Michigan and can't wait to get home in nine more months. The weather is very hot here – you probably wouldn't like it. Isn't Halloween right around the corner? I hope you have a good costume picked out. I will not see the leaves change color or snow fall while I am here so I hope you can enjoy the upcoming seasons for me. You can keep writing if you want – a letter from home always makes our day. Thanks again for writing, your new friend, John.

He put the letter into one of the new envelopes, addressed it, and lay it on top of his rucksack. Later, it would be collected and taken to the rear with the rest of the mail.

Suddenly the crowd roared its approval around the perimeter when the Company Clerk approached carrying two large red nylon bags, filled to capacity. The Platoon Sergeants and Squad leaders left their positions and circled around the young clerk. The mail had already been organized by Platoons, thus making it easier to distribute.

Sixpack approached the Squad with a couple of sealed boxes and dozens of letters for his men.

"Mail call! Listen up for your name. Damn, Pollack, this big box and a lot of these letters are for you."

He took the package and nine letters back to his position on the perimeter. He set the package to the side and eagerly tore open the first letter from home. He lay back against his rucksack and started reading the words. When he turned to the second page, a smile slowly developed and then he laughed out loud. Pollack finished and returned the pages to the envelope, tearing open the second one, which was from his girlfriend. While reading, Pollack was so focused on the news from home that he didn't notice the Squad getting restless and whispering among themselves.

Finally, Scout calls out, "Hey, Pollack, what's in the box?"

"I don't know yet. It's from my mother." Pollack opened the third letter and began to read it.

"When are you going to open it?"

"When I finish reading the rest of these letters."

"Come on, man. Some of us didn't get any mail. At least you could open it up and see what's inside."

"Yeah, Pollack, aren't you curious to see what she sent?"

Pollack sensed all eyes on him and he became irritated by the interruption. He stopped reading and looked over toward the rest of Squad. "Will you guys just wait till I'm done with these? We've got lots of time before we leave. Give me about fifteen more minutes."

Hearing the scores of groaning and complaining around him made it difficult to concentrate on the letters. Pollack knew that every time a package arrived from home, the normal protocol was for the recipient to get first pick and then split the bounty with the rest of his Squad. This way, everyone got to share in the celebration and received a piece of the pie. Nobody would be foolish enough to keep everything to himself because it would mean that he'd have to carry around the excess weight.

Pollack felt a pang of guilt and looked up from his reading. His fellow Squad members looked like anxious kids on Christmas morning, trying to be patient while they waited for the signal to begin opening gifts. The sight was truly pitiful.

He set the letters on the ground and reached for the package. "Okay guys, let's see what my mother sent us."

There was a collective cheer and the men moved in closer to watch the ceremonious opening of the package from home.

"You guys know that this is my first goody box from home, so I don't even know what to expect inside."

"We'll love whatever your mom sent."

After the box was unwrapped, and all the crushed paper removed, the treasure lay exposed.

"I'm just going to empty everything on the ground and then we can divvy it up."

Upon lifting a ten-inch diameter metal tin from the box, Pollack opened it to find aluminum foil surrounding dozens of homemade chocolate chip cookies. He took a couple and passed the tin to Scout who was the closest to him.

Ecstatic, everyone began to scarf them down, just like dogs when passed a piece of meat from the dinner table.

After the box was emptied, the group surveyed the selection of gifts on the ground. There were several small cans of Vienna sausages and hot dogs, vacuum packed cans of peanuts, candy, fruit cocktail, a one-pound jar of instant coffee, magazines, and a couple copies of the Detroit News Sunday papers, complete with comics and inserts.

There was also a five-pound canned ham. Although it could not compare to the lunch they had earlier, it would make for a wonderful Squad dinner in a couple of days. They salvaged all the cans of C-Ration pineapple bits that could be found and agreed to take turns carrying the ham until it was time to cook it.

When the bounty was finally divided and packed away, they disposed of the packaging. All the cushion paper, boxes, and various wrappings are burned, and the ashes spread about. That was standard operating procedure when one had to leave behind anything in the bush with names, addresses, or other personal written information. The empty metal tin was filled with stones and dirt and tossed into the closest water-filled bomb crater; it sank easily to the bottom of the twenty-foot deep hole. The protocol existed so that Charlie couldn't salvage anything to be used against the Americans later; either as a booby trap or a psychological weapon.

The anticipation of the upcoming ham dinner made the next two days go by rather quickly. The perfect opportunity for the culinary treat presented itself on the third night. The Squad gathered all the supplies together and converted several empty C-Ration cans into stoves. They punched holes into the sides to provide a flow of oxygen to keep the heat tabs burning.

They had collected ten cans of pineapple bits to use when cooking the ham; all had been opened and set aside. Next, the seven stoves were arranged into a circle large enough to support the can of ham and allow it to cook evenly in its tin container. Once the heat tabs were lit, everything was ready to begin.

Pollack had the privilege of opening the can of ham, accepting it like a communion wafer from Wild Bill, who had carried it through the last leg of the journey.

He pried the small key from the lid, securing it to the small metal tab on the seal of the can. Scout, Frenchie, and BJ crowded around him and watched intently as Pollack turned the key like a wind-up music box. The seal broke with a hiss of air; some juice spilled onto his lap and ran down his pant leg.

"Goddamn! What the fuck is that smell?" Wild Bill and the others quickly backed away, leaving Pollack with a perplexed look upon his face. They fanned the air with their arms in an attempt to dissipate the foul odor.

"It smells like a bunch of dead gooks!" Frenchie pinched his nose closed with his right thumb and forefinger. "It's the fucking ham! The damn thing's spoiled!"

Pollack quickly placed the can onto the ground and moved away from it with the rest of the guys.

"Shit, man, get away from us. You smell just like that ham." Wild Bill gave Pollack a playful shove away from him.

Pollack looked down to see that the juice from the container had spilled along the length of his trousers. He quickly ran to the nearest bomb crater, removed his pants, and jumped into the tepid water. There, he took a handful of mud, covering the length of one of the pant legs, and rubbing it vigorously against the other, using the mud as a scrubbing media. He rinsed the pants thoroughly, took a whiff, and repeated the process once again. It was not until several minutes later that Pollack was satisfied that the stench had been eliminated. He climbed out of the hole, put the wet trousers back on, and returned to the group. Scout was in the process of scolding the rest of the Squad.

"All of us are a bunch of dumbasses. During the last three days, each of us has carried this can of ham, yet none of us took the time to read the label. Here, look at this," he pointed to some large lettering on the side of the can. "Keep refrigerated."

"Pollack, I think you better let your mother know what happened here. There is no refrigeration in the bush. In fact, it had to take at least a couple of weeks for this to get here, and I'm certain it was never chilled again after your mom removed it from the refrigerator."

"I will. I'm sorry, guys, but I was really looking forward to our open range cooking tonight."

"We all were, Pollack, up until ten minutes ago. What a bummer!"

"Yeah, man, thank your mom anyway. Tell her that we were all thrilled and thought that it was really nice of her. Too bad this happened."

"We have to bury this shit so it doesn't attract wild animals. Everyone grab a can of pineapple bits and we'll have a toast to Pollack's mom."

They raised the cans together in the center of the small circle. Wild Bill made the toast, "To Pollack's mom, who is one hell of a fine woman and cookie maker."

"Here - here!"

The next day, the Platoon moved into a highly humid area, rich in vegetation, to set up their NDP for the night. They used machetes and Bowie knives to cut out individual sleep areas and rid the ground of roots.

When the perimeter had been secured and everybody began to cook their C-Ration dinners, Desmond Stumps wandered over and joined some of the members of the First Squad. Desmond had been in country for several months and hailed from Alabama; he was the point man for the Second Squad.

"Hey y'all, this here sure does look like the same place I saw the biggest varmint of mah life while ova here."

"What's a varmint?" Scout asked.

"It's a big critter!"

"Talk English!"

"Okay. Listen up and let me tell the story 'bout the critter then maybe yer will understand."

Those nearby coaxed him on. "Yeah Desi, tell us that story."

"Don't interrupt me then. We found us a place for o'er night jest like this here one. Ah found me a place betweenst some trees and used mah long metal cutting tool to clear out all the stuff growin' there. Whenst I got to the ground, ah had to use mah big bear skinning knife to cut up all those small roots and things that be stickin' up from the ground. Once that were done, ah rolled out mah poncho and liner and had me a bed soft enough for mah granny to sleep in.

"Bout the time ah finished it were time to make mah supper. Ah put mah sack to the side, fetched a can of pork, beans and weenies. Hoo doggy, my mouth is fixin' to start waterin' jest at the thought of them vittles. Yah know they the best vittles over here." This drew moans from the others.

"Ah notice a smooth green and brown log to the side of mah sleepin' area, bout as big as mah leg." He wrapped his hands around the thigh of his right leg for emphasis. "Ah thought maybe some feller had skinned the bark off this here log and used it fer himself to sit on a while back. So I took mah little stove can and vittles o'er to dat log and set down on it whilst mah vittles is heatin' up. Ah wanna tell yah that sumtin' just wan't right wit that log, but ah couldn't put mah finger on it. Ah thought ah felt it movin' and shakin' some an' thought maybe it were concussions from some bombs fallin' someplace, so ah didn't pay it no never mind.

"Just bout dat time, old Arnold come rushin' up, 'OOOWEEEE Desmond – do yer know what yer sittin' on?' he asked me. His eyeballs looked like they were bout to pop out from his head. 'Yer better git up and move o'er here wit me,' he said.

"Well don't yer know that ah was getting de heebie jeebies just a lookin' at his eyeballs and figgering ah better jump up pronto like. Ah moved over by Arnold and looked down at that there log and ah can now see that it was vibrating some. Arnold pokes mah side and points at mah log and ah foller his finger fer bout ten foot away to a tree. Mercy sakes, it took mah breath away when ah noticed dat mah log ran clear cross dat ground from where we was standin' and had climbed up into that there tree. It was bout then that ah noticed a big snake head at the end of mah log up in dat tree - dat rascal's head were bigger 'an mine. It peered to be sleepin' whilst it was hangin' onto the ground. Then we saw that it were all swollen up and maybe four times bigger than the rest of it fer bout three feet or so. Now this here swollen part is layin' on the ground bout a foot away from that there tree. Old Arnold guessed that it must have swallered a wild pig since day all around us and is telling that everytin' be alright because that varmint be filled with vittles and probably would not be movin' for some days. He tells me ah got nuthin' to worry bout and that critter won't bodder any of us o'er night. Some of da otherin were telling that none of 'em were sure but thought it were either a python, a boa constrictor or Ana-sometin' type of a snake. It were too bad that nobody took pictures of that varmint. Ah would be awfully grateful to know what it were." Everyone listened intently, mesmerized by his story and accent.

"Well, you know old Desmond wanted to shoot that varmint in is head, but the otherin wouldn't let me. They say that it would give our position away to them gook fellers and it wood be more dangerous than sleepin' wit that big rascal. That were easy for them to say cause none of 'em are laying anywhere close to that there tree septin' me." Some of the men squirmed as they imagined themselves in that situation.

"Now ah gotta tell ya that this here night were the worstest of mah whole life. Ah built mahself a small fence twenst that critter and me and jest set there on the ground and kept an eyeball open all the nightlong. It were pitch black and them there shadows played wit mah head all da night. And I know to this day that if that fence made any noise at all during that night, ah wood be up and putting some distance betweenst me an that critter.

"But ya know what? In the morning, ah was surprised to find that varmint in the exact same position as it were when it started to git dark the night before. Ah will never ever forget that der night and swear to all y'all that nuthin' in this here bush, even them gook fellers, has ever scared me more than that there snake. I hopes there ain't any round here tonight."

The men laughed and thought it was a funny story, but they could not resist scrutinizing their surroundings and taking a closer look after Desmond had left to return to his Squad.

The monsoon season was beginning in the southern half of Vietnam. It would be hot and sunny most of the day, start raining by seven every evening, and would rain nonstop until eight the following morning. You could set a watch with this pattern.

"At least the gooks won't be out and about in this kind of weather."

Quick to correct BJ, Nung said, "This VC weather. Rain covers all noise of moving and wash out all signs on trails. VC stay one place during day and move nighttime. He know American soldiers not like be wet. They all covered with ponchos at night and no hear or see him. GI also complain loud about wetness and VC hear this. This beaucoup danger time for GI's."

What he had said made the others think hard about the possibilities. Could it really be true? Was it possible for gooks to know where the GI's were bushing and setting up ambushes every night? If so, the monsoon season would be the toughest months of the yearlong tour.

They tried to keep the noise and complaints down to a minimum for as long as possible, but it only lasted a week. The bitching and complaining became progressively louder during the night and increased with the intensity of the hard rain. Rightfully so, there was no protection from the weather in the bush and no way of keeping dry during the night, so trying to sleep soaked to the bone every night soon became a way of life for the troops.

Every morning, the Platoon moved to a new NDP, and because their equipment was always wet, the added weight made it much more difficult to hump. Even their clothes felt heavier. During the moves, the afternoon temperature and high humidity made it unbearable. Everything had dried out in the hot sun, and the grunts sweated profusely. Always too hot or too cold, there was never a happy medium during the rainy season.

The constant rain was also rough on the machine gunners. Their lives and those around them depended upon the weapons in a time of need. A jam or misfire during a firefight could be devastating. Therefore, everyone pitched in to help the gunners with their daily ritual of cleaning and oiling the guns, which would keep them in dependable working order. Any belts of ammo exposed to the environment had to be cleaned with a toothbrush and oiled thoroughly at least twice a day. Dirt particles, sand, and rust on the linkage would cause the weapon to jam. The Platoon would easily go through a gallon of oil each week.

New replacements began to arrive; at least one or two on every re-supply. During a normal rotation, each Squad was expected to go out on recon patrols every other day, but because of the eight guys lost on the LZ, every Squad was now required to go out on daily patrols. The First Platoon should be back up to full strength within the next two weeks, provided they did not lose anyone before then. Everyone counted the days.

Lt. Ramsey developed pneumonia and had to be extracted from the jungle by a Medivac helicopter. He had been so stubborn and did not want to leave his men, but his constant hacking and coughing jeopardized the Platoon. Sixpack had to intercede and ask the Captain to order him out.

With the L-T gone, Sixpack, as the highest-ranking Sergeant, was placed in charge of the First Platoon. He quickly promoted Frenchie to replace him as the First Squad team leader. They wondered how long it would remain that way, as they knew that Second Lieutenants were at a premium in Vietnam. If not wounded or killed, their combat tours in the bush averaged eight months, and then they rotated to a rear job. It just wasn't fair to the enlisted men who sometimes found themselves unable to be pulled from the bush until a few days before being scheduled to go home. It was rare, but it had happened.

During the first night without an officer, a typhoon hit that part of Vietnam. The grunts in the field thought it to be the scariest experience they would ever encounter. The wind blew so strong through the jungle that it carried pieces of trees, rocks, and anything else that could get airborne. Some of the larger trees fell and crashed to the jungle floor. The horizontally blowing rain made it difficult for anyone to see. No safe haven existed for the men to take shelter while riding out the storm.

Sixpack had the soldiers break up into three and four-man teams, and then ordered them to connect their web belts together and secure themselves to larger trees. The wind caused all of the trip wires on both mechanical ambushes and trip flares to disengage, thus causing unexpected detonations and illumination around the perimeter. Mother Nature was at her worst with the terrified men at her mercy.

For once, no one complained about being wet; they were too busy wondering if survival was an option at that point. Each team did everything in their power to stay connected and secured to trees; the heavy wind buffeted them around like ocean buoys during a hurricane. Some of the soldiers who did not bother changing clothes during the last resupply found themselves watching their clothing tear and shred apart. Tabs of material caught in the wind vortex and ripped from their bodies like bandage strips.

Nine hours later, the typhoon wound down and the remaining wind and rain became manageable. It also helped to be early morning as the light of day started breaking through the jungle. Relieved, the teams untied themselves and salvaged what was left of their Night Defensive Position and gear. Doc was already making his rounds and attending to those injured by flying debris during the night. None of the injuries were serious so Doc was able to treat everyone without having to call in a Medivac.

"Thank you, Jesus!" Frenchie crossed himself and surveyed the area. "I have never experienced anything so terrifying in my entire life."

"You and me both. I was so damn scared and prayed all night long. Now when I get home there won't be a pot to piss in. I told the man upstairs that I'd give everything I own to the church if he got me though this storm in one piece."

"Shit, Wild Bill, there isn't much to give is there? After all, don't you just own a bunch of flat land and wild sagebrush in Texas?"

"I did up until now, Frenchie. But you gotta admit, last night might have been the first night in a long time that many of the guys in this Platoon actually prayed."

"I guess you got me there. It's been a while for me, but at least it worked and we all made it through that nightmare."

"Amen!"

"I'll take a firefight anytime next to that storm."

Pollack happened to notice that most of Scout's trousers were missing. "Where the fuck is the rest of your pants, Scout? Your fucking balls are hanging out!"

"This is a new fashion statement."

Sixpack strolled over while they laughed off the experience.

"Hey, Frenchie, get your Squad squared away for Christ's sake. You want to let every gook in the vicinity know where we are?"

"Okay, Sarge. Come on, guys, let's get things cleaned up. We can talk more later."

Several days had passed since the dreadful typhoon. First Platoon was back into the routine of moving every day and pulling ambushes at night.

Alpha Company had been lucky and had no contact with the enemy in quite some time; most of the grunts were thankful. The Colonel, on the other hand, wanted to see more results, so he increased their visibility by having the Companies continuously hump long distances during the day, in hopes of finding the elusive enemy. Noise discipline was deteriorating; complaints continued about the long distances and having to carry sixty to eighty pound rucksacks on tired backs. Some men fell out during the humps, unable to keep up with the pace during the heat and humidity. Unfortunately, some heat stroke victims had to be Medivaced to the hospital. However, waiting for the chopper to arrive gave everyone else a much-needed break.

During the long follow-the-leader marches, many in the column walked along absentmindedly, daydreaming about home, girlfriends, cars, and other things. Then in the evening, they would get together and share those thoughts while eating dinner. They were also so exhausted that many went to sleep even before darkness set in.

Debates took place every evening; some over cars, actresses, musical groups, sports teams, and Vietnam. People were very passionate about these topics and each person believed that his own theory was correct. Sometimes the debates got heated, but all knew when to stop and move on to a different topic. It seemed to be the only way to work off the accumulated adrenaline of the day. Sixpack thought that all the inactivity was causing the Platoon to lose its sharpness.

November was two weeks old and many of the soldiers from the northern states had not yet accepted the fact that the rest of the year would not offer them a snowy season. The winter months would be no different than any other time of the year: hot and muggy.

The Captain tried to convince the Colonel to withdraw the Company and move them to another AO. He told him that they'd already patrolled every acre of the area over the last five weeks and had not seen the enemy or fired one shot. The constant humping wore down his men and some were starting to get sloppy. He warned that even the new Cherries were becoming overconfident and thinking they knew it all.

While the discussion took place, the grunts rested and ate lunch just inside a tree line surrounding a large open clearing. Exhausted, everyone ate their meals quietly, knowing that they would soon be leaving on the next leg of their journey.

The Colonel granted the request and Alpha Company would be airlifted into a new area the following morning. In fact, the Colonel planned to use the same clearing for their pickup point, which would allow the Company to stay where they were until extraction. This was a rare treat and everyone was thankful that there would be no more humping that day.

At night, as usual, the rain started to fall just before seven. Since they had been in the same spot for most of the day, many of the grunts had used their ponchos to build tents or some kind of simple shelter against the nightly rain.

Pollack sat under his plastic canopy, eating a can of fruit cocktail, when he noticed a small brown snake. It was as thick as an average index finger and ten inches long, slithering through puddles of mud in between his legs. "Shit!" he shrieked and propelled himself backward to the edge of his shelter.

Those nearby looked over at Pollack in stunned silence, unsure of what the commotion was all about.

Even while jumping back, Pollack had kept his eye on the snake and saw it moving away from him.

"Hey, guys, watch out! A snake is heading your way!"

"Aw, shit, what kind?" BJ asked in a panic. His eyes wildly scanned the muddy ground between the two positions.

"I don't know. It was small and brown. But he moves pretty fast through the mud."

"Do you see him now?"

"No. You probably scared the shit out of him when you hollered out. He probably turned and went the other way."

"That ain't funny. I'll find the little bastard."

BJ picked up his rifle and used the stock to club the ground all around his position. The noise sounded like a child splashing through rain puddles on the way home from school. He quickly attracted the attention of the other Squad members.

"Beej, what in the fuck are you doing?" Frenchie asked, more annoyed than concerned.

"I'm looking for a snake that Pollack saw crawling toward me a few minutes ago."

"Is it big?"

"No. He said it was as small around like your finger and maybe twice as long."

"I'm sure it wasn't able to survive all that pounding. You probably knocked it silly and it drowned in the mud. Just let it go; you'll be ok."

"I'm really not sure about that."

BJ and Pollack scanned the area between themselves for several more minutes. Confident that the creature was no longer lurking around, they sat back down and continued doing what they were before the intrusion.

Pollack finished the can of fruit, placed the empty can to the side with the rest of the garbage, and then turned to pack the spoon away in his rucksack. He had just lifted the flap on one of the side pouches when he suddenly froze. A terrible stinging sensation buzzed in his left ring finger, and when he looked at it, he saw the rogue snake clamped to his digit.

"Help! I'm bit! Get this motherfucker off me!" Pollack screamed, trying violently to shake the serpent loose. "It won't let go!" The snake held on tight and looked like a small whip cracking in the air.

BJ and Frenchie were already moving toward him, each carrying a knife in his hands; Sixpack and Doc were close behind.

The snake finally released its grip and was immediately flung into the air; it traveled ten feet before landing in a puddle outside of the perimeter.

Pollack bent over and held his finger tightly as if trying to stop a flow of blood. "That fucking snake bit me!"

"Try and find him so we can see if he's poisonous or not," Doc ordered, taking Pollack's hand in his, while BJ, Frenchie, and Sixpack moved to the area where the snake may have possibly landed. Using the knives, they poked along the ground trying to find the illusive creature.

Meanwhile, Doc examined the two puncture wounds in the beam of his small red-lens flashlight. "It doesn't really look all that bad. How do you feel, Pollack?"

"I'm getting real hot and my heart's racing like hell."

"Here, take this," Doc handed him a yellow pill. "It'll help you relax."

Pollack swallowed the pill and puked it right back up, along with everything else he'd eaten that night. He began to shake uncontrollably. The tremors were so bad that two men had to hold him down on the ground.

"Better call in a Medivac, Sixpack. That snake venom is doing a job on him. He's burning up and going into convulsions."

Those nearby consoled Pollack as Sixpack requested an Urgent Medivac, signifying a life and death evacuation. They tore down his canopy and placed him on his own poncho, quickly packing his ruck with his other belongings. One of BJ's ammo bandoliers and his own M-16 were tied to Pollack's ruck; it would now be BJ's responsibility to carry the machine gun in Pollack's absence.

The chopper touched down in the LZ within five minutes of receiving the call. Four men loaded Pollack on board while a fifth tossed in his ruck and weapon.

En route to the hospital, the onboard medic gave Pollack a shot and opened an IV line in his arm. He then moved the convulsing soldier onto a stretcher where he was tied down to control the thrashing.

In five minutes, the Medivac landed at the 93rd Evac Hospital in Long Binh, where doctors already awaited his arrival. He was placed onto a hospital cart and quickly wheeled inside.

First, the doctors stripped him and packed him in ice. Pollack closed his eyes in an attempt to stop the room from spinning and started choking on his own saliva. A nurse reacted quickly, propping his head on some pillows before turning him onto his side.

One of the doctors walked up to the gurney and held a small book in his hand. "Can you understand what's going on?" he asked in a very concerned but professional voice.

Pollack could only nod his head affirmatively.

"Good. While your blood is being analyzed, I'd like you to look at some pictures of snakes. See if you can recognize the one that bit you."

He turned the page and waited for a few seconds before turning to the next one. Each showed a different species. Many of them looked alike, except for some small distinguishing characteristic that made the difference.

"Do any of these look familiar?" The doctor continued to turn the pages.

"No," he mumbled weakly. "It was small and brown, but that could be because it was raining and muddy."

"Take your time. Don't pay too much attention to the colors. Concentrate on the shapes and sizes. Note all the different heads."

When he flipped the page, the sight of the picture made Pollack open his eyes wide in recognition and fear. The doctor noted this reaction.

"Is this the snake?"

"Maybe, but I'm not certain. It was so quick."

"We'll check the blood for this type of venom. So, relax. We can't treat you until we're sure what species bit you. Hang in there, and I'll be back in just a bit."

He returned after what seems like an eternity. "Luck is on your side, my friend. The picture and blood sample helped us to identify the snake." He produced two syringes filled with a yellowish liquid and stuck one of them into each of Pollack's arms.

"Like I was saying, you are very lucky! The snake that bit you is a Banded Krait, and is considered to be the second most poisonous snake in all of Southeast Asia. Their venom attacks the nervous system and will paralyze you, and at that point you'll either die of suffocation or have a heart attack. You'll be all right now. We caught it in time." The doctor gave him a couple of encouraging pats on his leg. "We'll put you in a ward and keep an eye on you for a couple of days. If everything turns out fine, then you'll be discharged and can rejoin your unit."

Pollack was unrestrained, dressed in a hospital gown, and then wheeled through a series of corridors into one of the many wards. An orderly placed him onto an upper bunk and covered him with a blanket. Nurses would soon come in for their routine temperature checks and blood pressure readings.

"You're going to be just fine. Enjoy the rest and air conditioning. If you need me, I'll be at my desk in the middle of the ward. Just call out and I'll come over. Get some sleep and I'll see you in the morning."

Pollack looked down at his nurse, very relieved, and mumbled a quiet 'thank you'.

"You are quite welcome!"

As she walked away, Pollack turned his head and fell asleep.

Chapter Fourteen

Spending the night in an air-conditioned hospital ward in Vietnam wasn't quite what Pollack had expected. He envisioned snuggling up in a nice soft bed, lying on clean sheets, covered with warm blankets. He looked forward to having a very peaceful night's sleep, uninterrupted by either guard duty or pesky insects. In the morning, he would have breakfast in bed, take care of some personal hygiene, and then go back to sleep for as long as he wanted.

"Boy, did I ever have the wrong impression," Pollack thought to himself. Only a portion of what he perceived would actually happen.

To begin with, the nurses, although American and gorgeous, became more of a pest than the insects. They had him wake up during the night every half-hour for a temperature reading or blood pressure check. When breakfast was finally wheeled around in the morning, he was totally exhausted and too tired to eat. Nevertheless, he made a feeble attempt at the powdered eggs and dry toast. After a couple of spoonfuls, he set the tray aside and opted to wash it all down with watery orange juice.

After the breakfast trays had been collected, a nurse ordered him to get out of the bed make it up. There would be no sleeping during the day there. Instead, his option was to either sit up in bed or to walk around the ward. Looking around, he could see many of the other patients already up and making their bunks. With some help, he managed to climb down and make his own.

Afterwards, he pondered over his stay and looked over the ward. He wasn't allowed to walk around yet, but the vantage point from his bunk allowed him to see through more than one-half of the building, which was designed in the shape of a cross. Pollack's section housed patients who were recuperating from illnesses, such as malaria, or, in his case, snakebite. Another section had patients who overdosed on drugs and were either in a coma or restrained to their beds while working through the withdrawals. One soldier, doomed to be a vegetable for the remainder of his life, just lay there with tubes and wires hooked up to him. It was clear that the machines were living for him. He would forever be that way, never changing, until he died.

The illness section of twenty bunks had a TV set in each of the two corners. The American Network in Vietnam played reruns of old favorites from back home. During the afternoon, copies of the Stars and Stripes newspaper were passed among the patients for their reading pleasure.

The nurses' station was positioned in the center of the cross, thus providing them with an overall view of all four sections. Many patients chose to hang out around their station during the day, talking or asking questions.

On the second night, Pollack was given a questionnaire to gather information for his next of kin. They would be notified that he was in the hospital recovering from an injury. A small space at the bottom was available for him to write a personal message if he so desired. He added a short sentence, "I'm okay and doing well. Don't worry! Love, Johnny."

It had become quite boring on this his third day there. Nothing changed and it was the same routine as the day before. On the fourth day, however, there was some excitement as a General from the First Cav made his rounds through the various wards. He stopped and spent a few minutes with each patient, shaking his hand, and sharing some small talk. Before he left to visit with the next man, his aide took a Polaroid picture of them talking and gave it to the patient as a remembrance of the historical visit.

On the fifth day, the hospital released Pollack. The orderly took him to an area where all his gear had been stored while he recovered. His old set of fatigues, rucksack, and rifle were found and pulled from the pile. Each bundle contained a card, with a large red cross imprinted on it, listing the name of the owner. The bottom of the tag read, "93rd Evac".

He signed out and was immediately directed to the 90th Replacement Battalion, located just across the road from the hospital. There, he would be able to hitch a ride back to Cu Chi.

Once there, getting back out to the field would be easy; the First Sergeant would make sure of that.

Pollack learned of his luck when he reached the center; a convoy was scheduled to leave shortly for Cu Chi with some new in-country replacements (Cherries).

The place hadn't changed a bit since Pollack first arrived in Vietnam three and a half months earlier. He headed straight for Alice's restaurant to order a mouth-watering cheeseburger.

Two hours later, Pollack boarded the truck loaded with replacements and became an instant celebrity. His fatigues were filthy, ripped, and smelling; Red Cross cards still attached to his ruck and weapon. Taking a seat in the middle of the truck, he found that twenty 'kids' who weren't even in country for two days surrounded him. They were bewildered, staring at him wide-eyed and mystified. Pollack was also the only one in the back of the truck carrying a weapon. When the convoy started to move out, Pollack decided to have some fun with the guys. He pulled out a magazine from the bandolier of ammo and loaded his M-16. Then he just sat there, watching the passing terrain from the side of the truck.

"Excuse me, sir." One of the closest Cherries was the first to address him.

"I'm not an officer," Pollack responded nonchalantly.

"I'm sorry. Are you in the infantry?" he asked, but more humbly this time.

"Yeah, I'm a grunt."

"Have you been in the hospital?"

"Did you get wounded?"

"No. I was bit by a snake and almost died. I'm heading back to Cu Chi with you guys so I can get back out into the bush."

"How long have you been in Vietnam?"

"Almost four months."

"Is it really as bad as they say out in the bush?"

"It all depends. But personally, I'd rather be out there than in some firebase."

"Why is that?"

"When you get there, you'll see what I mean. Those firebases get hit all the time by rockets and mortars and all you can do is hunker down and pray you don't get hit. You also spend much of your waking hours pulling work details of some kind. No thanks, I'd rather stay out in the field where it feels much safer."

"Did you kill anyone yet?" one of them asked boldly.

"I don't really know because I've never personally had a gook in my sights. When you get caught in an ambush, you never see them and all you hear is shooting. So you point your rifle in their direction and start shooting back at them. If you manage to find any dead gooks lying in the jungle, you'll never know if your bullet is one of the many that hit him or not."

There were no more questions after that. Each of them sat, staring silently into space, thinking about what they'd just heard.

When they arrived at the Cu Chi training center, Pollack jumped from the truck and wished them all good luck, before heading for the Wolfhound Battalion area.

The Company had been re-supplied the day before, forcing Pollack to stay there for the next two days. He was chosen for bunker guard on the first night and then for KP the following night.

On the third day, the re-supply chopper was scheduled to leave around noon, which gave Pollack all morning to get ready. He was able to stock up on supplies and pack up before the bird left.

On the way out to the bush, Pollack felt excited and couldn't wait to see the rest of his friends. When he landed, it felt like a family reunion; they all gathered around to hear about his adventure. When he finished, they updated him on what he had missed during that last week.

The day after the Medivac, the Squad received two new replacements. BJ grabbed the first one off the chopper and made him his assistant gunner. He was quite happy with the M-60 and asked if it is okay for him to keep it. Pollack was quick to agree, thankful that he didn't have to lug the heavy weapon around anymore.

A new Second Lieutenant also came out to take over the First Platoon.

"What's his name?"

"Lt. Stryker, but we call him Rubber Ducky."

"What kind of nickname is that?"

"Just wait until we move out. He's a real clown, and can't lead cows to pasture."

"Sixpack is also back again as our Squad leader," Frenchie added.

"How are you feeling, Pollack?"

"Great, now that I'm back out in the bush."

"Good. How would you feel about being the Squad point man for awhile?"

"What's wrong with Nung and Scout?"

"Nothing. I just want to give them a break for awhile."

Pollack responded without hesitation, "No sweat, Sixpack. I'll give it a try so they can catch a break."

"Good. Here you go," Sixpack handed him a machete and a compass. "We'll be moving on a heading of two-hundred twenty degrees. I want you to follow as close to that course as possible for about two-thousand steps. Just take your time and keep your eyes open. You know the rest of us are depending on you to get us where we're going in one piece."

"I'll get us there. You can count on me."

The entire Company still displayed a cocky mood since there hadn't been any contact with the enemy for well over a month. Stored books and transistor radios found their way out of rucksacks and were being read and played out in the field. The practice had been taboo for as long as anybody could remember.

Pollack found the long hump through the thick jungle the norm every day. The point man had a dual role. First, he had to clear a path for the rest of the column to follow; and, second, he was to always be on guard for the enemy and booby traps. Wild Bill walked a few steps behind Pollack, keeping an eye overhead, as well as on the surrounding area. Pollack hacked and swore at the stubborn growth, finally stumbling into an occasional clearing, only to start anew some thirty feet later. He kept the column headed in the correct direction, but had lost count of his footsteps long ago.

Sensing his dilemma, Wild Bill came up behind Pollack and whispered in his ear, "Don't worry about the footsteps. I've been keeping count. Just focus to your front and in cutting your way through this shit. I've got your back, man!"

The grunts no longer thought of the never-ending jungle as Vietnam. Instead, they imagined themselves in a large box, constantly walking, but never able to reach the other side.

During one of the following days, Rubber Ducky lived true to his name. After choosing a place to bush for the night, the L-T wanted to confirm their location. Being quite certain of the coordinates, the L-T asked Firebase Kien to fire a white phosphorous round so it would explode three-hundred meters away and one-hundred feet into the air, allowing a compass reading to estimate and confirm the distance on the map. Rubber Duckie expected to see the round explode several hundred feet to the right of the perimeter.

When picking out coordinates for a fire mission, it was essential to always know where the firebase was located in relation to your target. The line of trajectory should never be planned to cross over nearby friendly positions in the event of a short charge for the shot. Unlike High Explosive rounds that detonated on the ground and threw shrapnel in every direction, an illumination round, or marking round, exploded in the air. The fifty-pound canister would continue along that line of flight for another two hundred feet before impacting onto the ground. There was no explosion when it touched down. Instead, the canister would hit the ground at two-hundred miles an hour and would continue to bounce and roll across the ground, until it ran into an immovable object or the law of physics allowed it to stop on its own. Nevertheless, if somebody stood in its path, the collision could result in instantaneous death.

The Platoon was already on alert when the phrase "fire in the hole" was passed around the perimeter. All knew of the imminent explosion, but they did not know where it would detonate.

They heard a faraway sound to their east, meaning the 105mm round from Kien was on its way. The White Phosphorus round exploded in the air one-hundred feet away, and, unbeknownst to the men, had the NDP in its trajectory path.

Sixpack yelled loudly, "Take cover! Incoming!" He jumped behind a tree, ensuring some protection between himself and the incoming projectile.

Everyone in the perimeter panicked as they ran for cover. Suddenly they heard a strange noise, like someone blowing air into the top of an empty soda bottle. VROOOM, VROOM, VROOM. It became louder as it closed in on First Platoon's perimeter. The empty canister came tearing through the overhead foliage. The smoking object crashed to the ground and threw up a wave of dirt before continuing along its path. It bounced from the ground and crashed through the surrounding jungle, mowing a path through the foliage.

Screams of pain echoed from the far side of the perimeter. The canister had ricocheted from a tree and then bounded toward the sleeping positions of two new Cherries. Doc and others ran toward them.

A Medivac chopper with a jungle penetrator was requested to withdraw the two injured soldiers. One's leg was almost severed while the other suffered major burns on his face and hands from the heated projectile.

Rubber Ducky defended himself and blamed the firebase for the error. If he had any remorse, he sure wasn't showing it.

Similar errors in judgment continued and the Platoon members wanted him out before anyone else got hurt. Several Squads heard through the grapevine that a bounty had been placed on Lt. Stryker. Many hoped that he would voluntarily leave the field, because if a firefight erupted first, a grunt would most likely take a pot shot at him.

Pollack became comfortable in his new role as point man and found it to be challenging. He did not have to perform it every day, as the position alternated between the four Squads in the Platoon. The best humps were those through light vegetation, where he could focus on his surroundings and not worry about exhausting himself, hacking a path through the jungle.

When First Platoon could finally exit the triple canopy jungle, it found itself in an area saturated with trails. They showed heavy activity, so for the next week, the men set up booby traps and ambushes, but they always came up empty.

The Company would remain in the vicinity for one more week and then Battalion would bring them to Firebase Kien to celebrate Thanksgiving.

It wasn't Cu Chi, but it would be the next best thing, and it would offer the grunts an opportunity to rest up for a couple of days. Sure, Thanksgiving approached, but to the grunts it felt like just another day in Vietnam. Holidays meant nothing there and most of them wouldn't even see a turkey.

Chapter Fifteen

What a big surprise! When the grunts woke on Thanksgiving Day, they found that the open area next to the mess tent had changed during the night.

A large tent had been erected in that area and two-dozen, seven-foot long tables were set up in six rows. Enough wooden chairs existed to feed over a hundred people. An individual place setting sat on the table in front of each chair; the table was set with real plates, silverware and cloth napkins. A menu outlining the dinner had been laid across each plate. The banner, strung across the length of the tent, read "HAPPY THANKSGIVING WOLFHOUNDS – ENJOY!" A dozen cardboard turkey centerpieces had been strategically positioned on many of the tables in order to complete the decorations create some level of ambiance in which to celebrate the occasion.

During the meal, platters of turkey, ham, mashed potatoes, peas, green beans, dressing, turkey gravy, cornbread, muffins and cranberry sauce were brought to the tables and passed between the men. Pitchers of coffee, milk, and soda were in ample supply and dessert consisted of fresh apple and pumpkin pies.

It was a feast fit for a King, but humbly served to the Warriors on the special day. There were no regrets!

The stand down officially came to an end some two hours earlier on the Friday after Thanksgiving, and Alpha Company was once again on the move. This time, instead of flying out in helicopters to their destination, the grunts would hump to a location in the jungle just three clicks west of Kien. Intelligence wanted to confirm rumors of a build up in that area for a possible attack on the firebase.

Alpha and Bravo Company would be the blocking forces; Alpha would line up east to west and Bravo from north to south along the right flank. Charlie Company would sweep south through the area in an attempt to flush out the enemy and push him toward the blocking forces. Potential and expected escape routes would be covered by mechanical ambushes and trip flares.

Four Army snipers were also attached to Alpha Company on the mission. They chose positions behind their ranks that offered the best view of possible approaching enemy soldiers.

Echo Company (Recon) had been flown to the northern part of the jungle earlier in the day in an attempt to locate and maintain surveillance on a potential enemy group.

The grunts itched for a firefight that had been a long time coming. They were more excited this time because, for a change, they could sit and wait for the gooks to walk into their ambush, instead of vice versa.

In two days, Charlie Company completed their sweep through the jungle and joined up with Alpha Company. During that time, they had found absolutely no evidence of any buildup or signs of the enemy within the area. Battalion Loach helicopters had also continuously buzzed overhead at treetop level, in an unsuccessful attempt to draw enemy fire from the jungle below.

The mission was a bust and the blocking forces were ordered to remain in place until the next morning before humping to their next AO.

Only Recon remained active within the area; the four-man stealthy teams stayed behind to watch for things that may have been overlooked during the sweep. The other companies would stay in close proximity in the event they discovered something.

In the morning, Alpha moved to the outskirts of a village within two miles of the firebase. Here, they began the tedious task of searching villagers and checking ID cards once again. Once completed, the Company continued humping west, repeating the process for each village they encountered.

After three days, about six miles from the firebase, the Company found themselves in an area with dozens of small villages. The search would take several more days to complete. First Platoon traveled the farthest and found an excellent location for the NDP. It was inside the jungle, providing excellent concealment. They would stay there for the next week and dispatch daily patrols to check the many villages.

Only two Squads were assigned to the daily patrols; the other half of the Platoon remained within the NDP. OP's were in place outside of the perimeter during the day to provide early warnings if they observed approaching visitors.

The idle days were filled with boredom. Many of the men read and traded paperback books or listened to the American music channel from Saigon on the AM radio. Poncho liners provided a playing surface for gin rummy and poker.

On the second day, Nung returned from a patrol with what many considered a luxury in the bush. When arriving at his sleep station, he unpacked a blue nylon hammock and suspended it from two nearby trees. Next, he snatched his poncho from the ground, attaching it overhead from the same trees to create a roof. It resembled a suspended pup tent which covered the hammock and provided enough head room inside to sit upright. The activity attracted the attention of just about everybody within the NDP and several stood nearby, watching Nung work with deep curiosity. He took four small strips of cloth and secured one to each hammock rope by a knot, letting it hang between the hammock material and the tree. When done, he moved his ruck under the hammock, took hold of his poncho liner, and then maneuvered into the hammock before covering himself. Nung raised the side of the poncho roof and projected a wide, pleased smile.

"Nung, where in the fuck did you find that?"

"Villagers sell for ten dollars, MPC."

"No shit! They have any more?"

"Have many to sell. Hammock is same used by VC. Now Nung will stay dry during nightly rain and sleep much better."

"Why do you have those strips of cloth hanging from the ropes of your hammock?"

"Rope get wet when raining, and without pieces hanging, water move to hammock and Nung get wet. Now water stop at knot and fall to ground."

"When can we get some for ourselves?"

"You give MPC and Nung go to village tomorrow."

Many men made a mad dash back to their sleep areas to dig out their money from the waterproof containers secured to their rucks.

When it was all over, Nung held almost three hundred dollars in MPC notes. Even Rubber Ducky agreed to purchase one.

The next day, Nung returned with a rice sack full of the precious hammocks. After they had been distributed, everyone got busy, trying to mimic Nung's shelter. Several green t-shirts had to be sacrificed as "water stoppers" for each hammock.

The grunts were in their glory and looked forward to the night. Not sleeping on the hard ground and staying dry were luxuries in the bush, especially during the monsoon season.

Most of First Platoon's NDP's were usually located in wooded areas, so it would not be hard for anyone to "tie up" for the night. It would also save time when preparing a sleeping position at the end of the day, as it would not be necessary to remove all the obstacles from the ground. That would allow them an extra hour to read or listen to the radio. The hammocks were so compact and portable that they could be bunched up and stored in your pants pockets.

The immediate area to their west had been pocked with bomb craters. Now that the monsoon season was well underway, they were filled to the top with fresh rainwater. Sixpack designated two of the nearest craters strictly for drinking water, and the next two for bathing. However, each canteen of water still required iodine tablets. At least the grunts no longer had to worry about carrying the excess weight of five canteens or having to ration it for three days until the next re-supply.

Once again, Nung came up with another luxury item for the bush: an unscented bar of lye soap. It was passed from person to person and barely lasted the entire round. Some grunts who had been in country for a while, passed on the opportunity to bathe. They rationalized that the cleanliness would attract more insects and would also be an ironic gesture considering their filthy and torn uniforms.

The only item missing was a portable shitter to bring them closer to civilization.

Over the next several days, members of the First Platoon became businessmen and started trading with the villagers. After each re-supply, they collected and saved many of the unwanted C-Rations, which were normally taken back to the firebase on the return chopper. The meals had incurred nicknames over time. Beans and franks were known as 'beans and baby dicks'; Lima beans and ham were noted as the ever dreadful 'beans and motherfuckers'; and scrambled eggs were simply 'egg chunks,' as the meal was usually solid in the can and had to be broken apart when heating.

Each soldier had to take malaria pills daily, but they caused the unfortunate side effects of gas, stomach cramps and diarrhea. Therefore, eating beans did not appeal to the men, so those types of meals were plentiful.

The daily patrols took these unwanted cans of food into the various villages to trade and barter for items they had, which ranged from ice-cold drinks and rice to live chickens. Villagers were very excited about the food choices and always seemed willing to work out a deal with the grunts. Whenever a patrol was able to bring back a chicken or two to the NDP, Nung took on the role of master chef. He used special herbs and spices and cooked over an open fire before shredding the meat and mixing it into cooked rice. The men considered the meal a real treat, and it was enough food to feed the entire Platoon.

Time had moved quickly and the soldiers realized that Christmas was only two weeks away. Greeting cards were not available, so the grunts got creative and made their own. Rubber Ducky ensured that everyone in the Platoon sent at least one letter or card home to their families for the holidays.

There had been so much time available during the last few weeks for letter writing that most everyone had run out of things to write home about. Some letters simply read: 'Hello, I'm doing OK and everything is fine. Will write more soon. Love, so-and-so.'

The two weeks since leaving Kien had been rather enjoyable. Even Rubber Ducky was content and not bothering anyone. If a new recruit were to have arrived during that time, he would have been appalled. Who back home would actually believe them if the soldiers were to describe the latest activities to them?

But as always, all good things came to an end. First Platoon received word to pack up and get ready to move out later that morning. Not wanting to hump the C-Ration cans through the jungle, the Platoon traded enough for cold sodas and then buried whatever was left.

Alpha Company continued to move in a westerly direction and eventually found themselves having to cut their way through the dense jungle once again. The Platoons still operated separately with their own missions. First Platoon moved to an area just outside of the free-fire zone for the purpose of keeping a medium-sized village under surveillance. The village was suspected of being sympathetic to the VC cause. They hoped that the enemy would expose himself and possibly a cache of weapons or food.

Sixpack organized small three-man patrols and sent them to locations that provided good vantage points of the village from different directions. They were expected to be invisible and to keep a close eye on the occupants during the day. Prior to returning to the NDP's, mechanical ambushes were set to cover possible avenues of travel to or from the village into the jungle.

The routine continued for three days without the soldiers seeing anything strange or out of place.

On the fourth morning, First Platoon was ordered to sweep through the village in force and to search everywhere for tunnels or caches.

When the Americans entered the village just after daylight, they were surprised to find the villagers were expecting them. The first village hut had a large cardboard sign attached to the wall, written in black magic marker that read, 'Alpha Wolfhounds – Go Home'.

"Looks like they have the welcome mat out," Sixpack announced.

"How in the fuck do they know about us?"

"Yeah, this ain't right. It just ain't right!" Scout mumbled.

"They seem to know all about us and we don't know a damn thing about them!"

"They've got intelligence groups too. And if what our brass is suspecting turns out to be true, we could be in a world of hurt."

Rubber Ducky was beside himself and it was evident that the sign shook him up. He paced back and forth in front of the group; unsure as to what should be done next.

Sixpack instructed everyone to split up into three-man teams again and to check out every hut, container, and especially under each bed, for evidence of the enemy. The L-T quickly joined up with Sixpack and stayed close to him.

The villagers were not happy to see the grunts searching through their possessions. Some offered ugly sneers in retaliation to the invasion of privacy; others wore a sinister smirk on their faces as if they mocking the soldiers for their efforts.

Not one villager resisted or spoke, even when prompted by Nung to answer his questions. They appeared defiant but didn't do anything to threaten the soldiers.

The grunts were very cautious and yet very thorough. Many of them had bayonets attached to the end of their M-16's and began using the weapon as a probe, poking into large containers of rice, bales of hay, into the ground under beds, and into the straw walls and roofs of the huts.

It took almost six hours to complete the sweep, and once again, the grunts came up empty handed.

"Shit, they knew we were coming so they must have hid everything."

"Where, Pollack? We looked everywhere."

"I don't know. Maybe the VC came in during the night and carried everything away into the jungle."

"That does make sense, but we won't be able to prove it."

"Wait a minute, Pollack, you may have come upon something," Sixpack stated and called over the L-T. "Pollack thinks the gooks moved everything out of the village during the night. It all makes sense now when you think about it. The gooks knew we were here and most likely the position of our mechanical, so all they had to do was to simply go around them. I think we should leave our NDP for a new one and then set up nightly ambush teams around the village for the next few days."

"I like that plan!" the L-T responded. "However, we've got to get re-supplied before we can pull off something like that."

"Agreed. Run this past the Captain and see if he will sanction it. We can set up for the re-supply right here and then move out, heading back the way we came in, then we can circle back."

The Captain liked the idea but felt it too large of an undertaking for a single Platoon, so he dispatched Second Platoon to join them. Both were to meet after the re-supply, about a mile away, in the jungle and out of sight of the village. There, the two groups would formulate plans for the nightly ambushes and move closer to the village.

Both the first and second nights were quiet. A full moon shone, which helped with their night movements and deployment, but they feared the VC were aware of their plan and were choosing to stay away.

Just after one in the morning on the third night, one of the villagers on a bicycle triggered a mechanical ambush on one of the trails leading away from the village. He was carrying a pouch with papers that warned the nearby VC to stay away until the Americans left the area. It also stated that they knew the Wolfhounds had the village under surveillance and had ambush teams within the vicinity. They would be further notified when it was safe for them to enter.

"How in the fuck do they do this? Why don't we just go in and tear that place apart?" Frenchie asked, terribly upset. "Those cocksuckers are all gook lovers!"

"It won't do us any good. We know there aren't any supplies because of our search, and there surely aren't any gooks around. This message proves it," Sixpack held up the letter as proof.

"I just wish I could get my hands on them. They're all playing us for fools."

"Right on, Frenchie! They're all gooks in my book." Wild Bill pumped his fist into the air to support his brother.

"Look, guys, we are still in a no fire zone, but we were justified in killing this guy because he violated the curfew. We can't just go into that village and rough everyone up. It's wrong and we'll all suffer the consequences sooner or later. You can't cover shit up like that."

"Fuck it, Sixpack! At least it'll get us out of this stinking war. Besides, what can the brass say if we just burn down a couple of the hooches? At least it'll show the villagers that we're pissed."

"The brass may not say anything, but it'll turn the good villagers against us, if there are any there, and make us play right into the gooks' hands. You guys know they preach to the villagers that we're really the aggressors in this country, anxious to burn and pillage their land. Just keep cool. We'll eventually catch them."

"I hate to admit it, but that makes sense."

"I know it does, Frenchie. You learn from your mistakes. Ever heard the saying 'once burned, twice shy'?"

"What kind of mistakes are you talking about, Sixpack?"

"On my last tour, the Company I was with made a mistake. Except for a sniper, it was almost under the same set of circumstances. We jumped to conclusions and burned down most of the friendly village. And the next time we came back into that area, we lost a hell of a lot of our men. The gooks convinced some of the villagers to join them for revenge. They went out of their way to booby trap and ambush us every chance they could."

"What makes you think the same thing will happen again?"

"I don't know, but I've got to spend another eight months in this country and I'm positive we'll be working this area again sooner or later. I'd rather not take that chance."

"Aw, Sarge, I thought you were gung-ho and shit!"

"No, I'm not, but you all ought to take a look at yourselves. Things that you used to just overlook are starting to bug you. Most of you are short and have less than two months to go before going home. I know you've all been through a lot of shit in the last ten months and the lack of action recently is getting to some of you. You guys need to stop being so restless and keep a cool head. Remember what happened to Zeke when he lost his head?"

"Yeah, literally," Scout proclaimed, snickering.

"You're an asshole!" Sixpack's face harbored a scowl and he bit at his lower lip. "You just better keep your shit in order. The first of you motherfuckers that gets out of line, I'll personally kick your ass."

"Oh yeah? Come on, motherfucker!" Scout challenged and moved closer to the Sergeant.

"I don't believe it. Sixpack's turning into a real lifer."

"Frenchie!" Sixpack looked at him with glaring eyes. "I'm no more a lifer than you are. I'm just interested in staying alive and keeping you all alive and in one piece. I may not have anybody back home waiting for me, but I do know that you all have wives and girlfriends waiting. What you do when you get out of the bush, I could give a fuck less. But right now, you do as I say!"

Doc stepped in and stood next to Sixpack, facing the unruly pair. "He's right. Why don't you two guys go and cool off somewhere? If you want to pursue this any further, then come see me and I'll hear you out. Come on now, we're all brothers here and need to keep our shit tight. There is absolutely no reason whatsoever to be talking shit to each other like you are. The enemy's out there!" Doc pointed toward the village.

"Okay, Doc. You've always been straight with us. I'm good with it."

"Thanks, Scout. Now see if you can talk some sense into your buddy, Frenchie."

"No need to. I'm okay for the moment."

BJ and Pollack stood dumbfounded and couldn't understand why they were so upset all of the sudden. They had sat there the entire time listening but too afraid to interfere. They were shocked, as it was the first time that such fallout had occurred within this tight knit Squad and it worried them.

Everyone's mood changed when they were told that Alpha Company would return to Cu Chi and had an excellent chance of seeing the Bob Hope Christmas Show next week. Battalion wanted the Wolfhound Company to patrol through a couple of suspect areas first and then hump to Kien, which should only take a little more than three days. The re-supply that was planned for later that afternoon would be rushed so the Company could get moving and cover the planned three-mile hump before nightfall.

Frenchie and Scout approached Sixpack and Doc during the re-supply and made an awkward attempt to apologize for their behavior. Both admitted that getting short was beginning to affect them. It wasn't the lack of enemy contact during the last month that was upsetting, but instead, it was an uneasy feeling, like a sixth sense, that something bad was going to happen soon. Then again, maybe it was just short-timer's paranoia.

The men made amends and everything was back to normal by the time the Company left the LZ. The total distance to Kien was almost ten miles. It would be tough in some areas, but nobody would complain, as they would get to see the famous comedian and his usual bevy of beautiful American women who usually accompanied him on these USO tours. Most every soldier in the column had seen Bob Hope's Vietnam Christmas Show on TV during the last couple of years, but to actually be in the audience would be an exhilarating experience. Each man already fantasized about the show, thinking of ways to be seen on television. Surely, friends and family would be watching from home, and seeing them on TV would be a wonderful Christmas gift!

The route to the firebase would take the Company through the same area where the large enemy buildup was suspected two weeks earlier.

Their confidence level remained high since there had been no sign of the enemy, either during the sweep or while the recon group stayed behind and hidden for the next four days. The grunts expected a trouble-free hump.

On that first night, each Platoon dispatched a five-man team to ambush different nearby trails. First Squad was spared and gained an extra hour to read or listen to Christmas carols on transistor radios. The songs felt surreal and out of sync, like playing them during the month of July. It was difficult to get in the spirit and it just hadn't sunk in yet that Christmas Day was only five days away.

At 0300, the CP lost contact with Third Platoon's ambush team. Several attempts had been made to reach them, but since there had been no report of weapons firing or exploding mechanicals, they assumed the team encountered radio problems. Not to worry, the answer will be provided upon their return to the NDP in the morning.

Four hours later, all ambush teams had returned except for the team from Third Platoon. The concern for them now grew as word quickly spread throughout the Company.

"Dumb shits probably overslept like our own BJ did a little while back."

"I don't think so, Frenchie. I'll bet you ten bucks they got lost."

"You're on, Wild Bill. I heard that Lt. Carlisle went out on that ambush. He's the best navigator in the Company so the coordinates he sent in last night had to be accurate within ten meters."

"Aw, shit, I didn't know that. Bet's off!"

"No way, bro, you want to pay now or later?"

"Let's see how it shakes out."

First Squad was delegated from the First Platoon to join three other Squads in the search for the missing team. During the briefing, they were shown a map with both their current location and the ambush team's tentative location circled; six hundred meters separated the two red X's. Each search team would target the identical coordinates, but approach from different directions. They would travel light and were expected to reach the destination within forty minutes.

Sixpack's Squad had the most direct route and stopped every two-hundred meters to fire a green handheld flare into the air; the other three teams followed suit. Standard practice was for a lost Squad without communications to respond with a star cluster flare of their own after seeing a green flare. After eight flares, there was still no response from the missing five men.

It took almost an hour for the First Squad to reach the General area of the ambush site. The other teams were also still working their way toward them and were about fifteen minutes out.

Pollack was on point and beginning to feel uneasy. There was a hint of death in the air and it became more pronounced as they advanced. His mind raced, trying to make sense of it all.

He felt a slight tug across his right shin and immediately froze in place. His breathing stopped as he realized what had just happened. A microsecond later, the disengaged trip wire allowed the circuit to complete and sent an electrical charge to the mechanical ambush. When he heard a popping sound, he braced himself for what may have very well been his last second alive. But nothing happened. Pollack turned his head, surprised to find himself standing alone on the trail; the Squad had already sought protective cover. Hearing no explosion, they filtered back onto the trail and approached their point man.

"Pollack don't move!" Sixpack cautioned. "I don't know what you hit, but just stay right where you are."

Too shaken to answer, Pollack remained frozen in place. Sixpack and Wild Bill approached him very slowly, making certain to step in the same footprints that Pollack had originally left on the trail.

"Did you step on something or trip something?" Wild Bill asked. Both he and Sixpack used the knives to probe into the ground beneath Pollack's feet.

"I think I tripped something because I felt it brush against my leg."

Confident that Pollack was not standing on a pressure release mine or booby trap, the two men stood back up and returned the knives to their scabbards.

"Okay, there's nothing under your feet. You can move now," Wild Bill slapped Pollack across the back. Pollack inhaled deeply and took a few unsteady steps to the side of the trail.

"Look around for a trip wire. It had to be attached to something." Sixpack inched his way up the trail, looking over everything with a keen eye.

The rest of the men scoured the two sides of the trail, looking for the thin strand of wire.

Frenchie was ten feet away and standing just off to the right side of the trail. "I found it! everybody on me!"

"Jesus!" Sixpack was surprised to see what Frenchie had discovered. "You guys keep your eyes open. Something is really wrong here."

The two men were looking at a stake in the ground with pieces of metal attached to it with rubber bands. A set of wires led back into the jungle; one was only two feet long, blackened at the end, and lying there on the ground just in front of a Claymore mine. Four other mines were found daisy chained together in the mechanical ambush. The blasting cap had somehow fallen out of the lead claymore and exploded harmlessly when Pollack hit the trip wire. Had the blasting cap been in place, the entire Squad may have perished.

"Pollack, you are one lucky motherfucker. I hope you have nine lives."

"Thanks, Scout, but I don't plan on making shit like this a habit. I'll have to start keeping count of these close encounters."

The men quickly disconnected the mines and gathered everything up to carry back with them to the NDP.

"This is some spooky shit, Sixpack. Gooks didn't put this together; it belonged to the missing team." Frenchie's voice quivered and he looked on edge.

Sixpack paced nervously and replied, "I agree that it belonged to the missing team, but two things are bothering me: why didn't they take it down, and why wasn't the blasting cap secured in the Claymore? Keep your eyes open, guys. Their night ambush position was around here somewhere."

Just then, Fourth Platoon's search team stepped out of the jungle and onto the trail and joined up with the First Squad. Sixpack took a few minutes to brief them before the eight men joined the others in searching through the jungle on both sides of the trail.

Suddenly, one-hundred and fifty feet away from the location of the mechanical, Pollack came upon a sight that took his breath away.

There, just four feet off the trail, laid the missing ambush team. They weren't lost and didn't have radio trouble. Each of them was parallel to the trail and spaced about five feet apart.

"I found the missing Squad!" Pollack shouted. "They're all over here!"

The search parties exited the jungle and jogged up the trail toward Pollack. Sixpack was the first to arrive.

The first man they came upon was lying on his poncho. His throat had been neatly sliced from ear to ear; the deep wound nearly severing his head. The once green camouflage liner still covered the man, but had turned a shade of dark burgundy, almost black. The second, third, and fourth man were all the same way. When they approached the last man, Pollack dropped his rifle to the ground as he recognized the corpse of Bill Sayers. He was not wrapped in his poncho liner like the rest of the team. Instead, he sat on the ground, propped against a tree. His eyes were wide with surprise, and his mouth hung open as if he were trying to call for help. His own Bowie knife had been driven deep into his chest, the handle surrounded by a crust of dried blood.

"No! Not Bill! Please don't let it be!"

Sixpack placed his hands on John's shoulders. "Easy, Pollack. We're too late to help them. There's nothing we can do for Bill and the others."

"Oh my God!"

Sixpack summoned Frenchie and Wild Bill. "Take Pollack off to the side and keep him quiet."

Pollack's mind went blank and he seemed to fall into a semi-comatose state. He sat quietly with the two men while Sgt. Holmes reported their findings back to the Company CP.

During the discovery, the remaining two Squads had emerged from the jungle and converged on the ambush site. The Squad from the Third Platoon had a hard time accepting that their L-T and four other close friends were dead. Tears were shed, prayers offered, and condolences were given all around.

The four Squads formed a defensive perimeter around the ambush sight so choppers could evacuate the dead soldiers. Not much remained besides the bodies as the gooks had taken their weapons, ammo, rucksacks, and radio.

Sixpack walked over to the three soldiers sitting together to the side of the trail. "How's the Pollack doing?"

"He hasn't said a word since we've been sitting here with him."

Sixpack got on a knee and put a hand on Pollack's shoulder. "Pollack, talk to me! You okay?"

He blinked several times in an attempt to hold back tears and then looked into Sixpack's eyes. "I'll be all right."

"Are you sure?"

"Yeah, yeah I'm good. I'm sure it would have been different if I'd heard about his death, but actually being the first to see him did a job on me."

"I know you guys were very close. I am sorry though, but you have to let it go. Bill is not going to be the last friend of yours that is going to die in this war. There will be others so you have to learn how to block out the emotions and live with the hurt, otherwise you'll drive yourself crazy."

Frenchie and Will Bill nodded in agreement.

"Hang tough, Pollack. Be happy you're still alive."

"Anybody figure out what happened to them?"

"The consensus is that a Squad of sappers took them out. This wasn't a coincidence. I bet they were followed and then watched while getting into position and setting the mechanical ambush. Some of us believe the gooks took the blasting cap out and either forgot about it or they were in a rush to get away. They took everything else and we can't figure why they didn't take the Claymore's."

"So they didn't even have a chance to fight back, did they?"

"Doesn't look like it. Looks like Bill was on guard duty and had the radio, so he had to be the first to go. They probably came up from behind to get him out of the way and then killed the others while they were asleep."

"Can somebody really be that quiet?"

"Sappers are the best and are very patient. They've been known to crawl through barbwire, disconnect Claymore's and trip flares, and enter firebases during the middle of the night. Once inside, they remain invisible and usually try to blow up command bunkers. Most of them are good enough to even get out afterwards without being seen."

At that moment, the lead element of the Third Platoon exited the jungle not far from the ambush sight. They wanted to investigate the area and take care of the bodies themselves.

Seeing this, Sixpack stood and turned to go meet with them. Before leaving, he stopped and implored to Pollack, "I promise you this: we will get even for what has happened here. Mark my words." He then moved quickly to join up with the Staff Sergeant who was leading the column of Third Platoon soldiers.

The First Squad approached and gathered around the three men sitting on the ground. Doc was the last to arrive.

"Pollack, you've been through a terrible shock. If you want, I can arrange for you to go back to the rear, and get checked in the hospital. Just say the word."

"That's alright, Doc. I want to stay out here with the rest of my friends and make those gooks pay for what they did to Bill."

"Now hold on. If you start thinking like that, you'll be the next one killed around here."

"You don't have to worry about me. I'm not John Wayne."

"No problem then?"

"No problem, scout's honor." He raised his right hand showing three fingers of the traditional Boy Scout salute.

Since it was so close to Christmas, Pollack wondered if the Army will wait until after the holidays to notify Bill's family. If not, it would certainly be the worst Christmas ever for them, and he hoped they pull through it okay.

He then thought about his own family and how they would take the news of his death. It would probably kill both of his parents, who had already lost much of their families during World War II.

It finally hit him that if the mechanical had been armed earlier when he tripped it, he would have been killed too. John looked up to the sky and made the sign of the cross, thanking God for the extra chance.

Unfortunately, Battalion canceled Alpha's trip into Cu Chi to see Bob Hope. Instead, the men were asked to stay in the bush and find those responsible for the killings. If anyone felt disappointed, he wasn't showing it, as it was indeed a mission they would have all volunteered for anyway.

A countrywide cease-fire was in effect on Christmas Day, and both sides stopped fighting to celebrate the holiday. Alpha Company settled into the jungle next to a large clearing and would remain in place for the next two days.

Two choppers landed during the Company re-supply. The second was loaded with hot food canisters and ice-cold sodas. The Thanksgiving Day feast was repeated, but this time it was served in the jungle without the fancy decorations.

It was a lazy day and most of the men listened to the Bob Hope Christmas Show on their radios. Some sat together in small groups to share in the laughter as Bob joked about the government and politics. Sometimes it was difficult to hear the female guests speak or sing as the cheering and catcalls from the audience drowned them out. Miss America was a big hit; they pictured her in their minds, standing there on the stage in her bathing suit and sash. The afternoon was almost fun and the distractions offered the grunts some piece of mind, even if it was only for one day.

When the cease-fire ended, the grunts got serious again, and all paperback books, radios, and cards were placed back into deep storage. They were ready to avenge the deaths of their brothers.

Chapter Sixteen

The cease-fire came and went without incident. The Stars and Stripes newspapers reported, however, that the gooks had numerous violations throughout the country.

In Alpha Company's AO, the grunts had a premonition that the gooks were well aware that a witch-hunt was underway and remained out of sight. The sensation continued for that entire week after Christmas.

On New Year's Day, 1971, word was received that Delta Company had engaged in heavy fighting and needed help. Alpha was the closest unit and helicopters were already en route to pick up the reinforcements.

Delta Company had been working in a banana plantation for most of the past week, and that morning a patrol member tripped a vicious booby trap going up a hill. The buried 105mm artillery round exploded and sent shrapnel every which way; three soldiers were killed and four critically wounded.

Unaware of a well-camouflaged enemy base camp at the top of the hill, Delta Company remained in position and waited patiently for the Medivac helicopters.

When two of them landed on a plateau, the dead and wounded were carried there and quickly loaded. However, before they had a chance to lift off, the gooks surprised everyone and opened fire on them from the top of the hill. Heavy automatic fire and RPG's were concentrated on the two helicopters. The chopper with the wounded soldiers managed to avoid major damage and was able to escape from the ambush. The second bird also managed to lift off but it was hit several times, forcing it to land and power down just behind a small hillock three-hundred yards away.

The ambush and heavy gunfire scattered many of the Company soldiers who retreated down the hill. Many of them were without their gear and extra ammunition because, in their haste to reach safety, they had to leave those assets behind.

When they finally regrouped at the base of the hill, the Delta Commander requested an artillery fire mission targeting the summit. This afforded him an opportunity to assess the threat and formulate an attack plan.

During the barrage, dozens of soldiers inched their way up the hill in an attempt to retrieve the left behind gear. They managed to reach the area, but then came under intense fire and were forced to turn back a second time. Their efforts secured only half of the gear.

The artillery rounds didn't seem to affect the gooks; their rate of fire was still as treacherous as it had been during the ambush earlier. The Captain terminated the barrage and requested a Squadron of Huey Gunships and Cobras to help relieve the pressure. Knowing the gooks were well dug in, rockets and mini-guns targeted those reinforced areas; a lull in their firing afforded the grunts another opportunity for an assault. This time they were successful and gained a foothold halfway up the hill. There, they returned fire, but were not able to advance any further. The summit was still three hundred feet away, but the gunships had exhausted their armaments and had to leave the battle to re-arm.

While the exchange of gunfire continued between the two infantry groups, several volunteers took it upon themselves to go and look for their wounded brothers and other survivors along the hillside. They located a dozen critically wounded soldiers and dragged them to the bottom of the hill, where the medics could begin treating the men. The fact that only five American soldiers had died so far during the onslaught was unbelievable.

Medivac choppers made repeated attempts to land, only to be driven off by the firing of heavy weapons. Thankfully, the injured were holding up. It would have been suicide to try and carry them through the kill zone to an area where the choppers could land.

The gunships returned after thirty minutes and pounded the hilltop once again. Confident that the protective shield will suffice, Medivacs made another attempt to land near the wounded.

The enemy heavy weapon fire subsided when the Cobra rockets succeeded in destroying some of the reinforced bunkers. It allowed the unarmed medical choppers time to land and collect the wounded. When lifting off, they banked tightly around the hill to get clear of the firing.

When the assault choppers pulled out to refuel a second time, the gooks let loose with mortars, walking the rounds downhill over the hunkered-down men and into the First Aid area. Fortunately, the choppers had successfully extracted all the wounded and the Delta medics had already vacated that area.

Five hundred meters on the opposite side of the hill, Alpha Company troops landed in a small valley clearing, shielded from the besieged hilltop by another larger hill. They relied on the element of surprise and hoped the gooks did not see the choppers or hear them land. The plan was to climb the hill and come up behind the enemy while they were distracted by Delta and the attacking gunships.

Alpha found a good-sized trail leading to the summit, but decided against following it, especially since Delta had already hit a booby trap on the other side.

They moved slowly up the hillside because of the mud and slippery conditions. They finally managed to crawl and pick their way halfway up without having confronted the enemy or his booby traps. Suddenly, gunfire erupted from behind the two lead Squads, which sent everyone diving to the ground. Half of the First Platoon had already passed when two gooks emerged from spider holes to their left flank, opening fire on the advancing file of men. Sixpack cut one of them down and an exploding grenade silenced the other. Three men were hit, including Rubber Ducky, but the injuries were not critical. Rubber Ducky had been shot through the thigh muscle of his right leg; a through and through wound that was lucky to have missed a bone or artery. It was not that bad, but he was so shaken by the event that he went into shock before Doc had a chance to reach him.

After a quick medical evaluation, the three wounded were escorted to the bottom of the hill and the rest of the Company continued the ascent.

Delta Company had fought their way up the hill and finally reached the summit. Only sporadic fire existed as Delta started a cautious sweep across the hilltop.

Meanwhile, Alpha Company was having a difficult time reaching the summit. On the way up, many of the grunts lost their footing and slid down the muddy hillside, taking anybody they fell into along for the ride. They still found spider holes on the hillside and each had to be checked before advancing further. Thankfully, they are vacant; nevertheless, for those that had to uncover the hole, it was a nerve-wracking experience. It took a little over an hour for them to climb the six hundred feet to the summit and link up with Delta Company.

The destroyed enemy base camp was well camouflaged and each bunker on the perimeter had been reinforced with concrete and was inter-connected via a trenching system. Small tunnels were dug into their sides and led to dozens of spider holes on the hillside to the front of the bunkers. Other trenches had been dug from the bunkers to the center of the hill, like spokes on a wheel, where the command bunker and mortar pit were located.

The Cobra assault and artillery barrage had demolished most of the base; huge pieces of timber and concrete were strewn all about. Some of the tunnels now lay exposed, thanks to a well-placed artillery round or rocket. The jungle camouflage was blown to bits; many of the tree stumps still smoldered from the intense heat of the bombardment. The hilltop was now fully exposed from both above and below.

It was surprising that of the thirty-seven gook bodies counted, seventeen were women. It was unclear whether or not they had been visiting or if they were in fact a part of the group of fighters. Evidently, the ladies were active participants in the battle, as all were armed and died with weapons at their sides.

Many of the soldiers had a difficult time accepting the fact that a large group of females had joined in the battle against the Americans. The entire group totaled slightly more than a Platoon in size; yet they were able to hold off two aggressive American Infantry Companies, while submitting to artillery barrages and gunship attacks during the six hours of heavy fighting.

The Wolfhounds received credit for thirty-seven kills. The gooks, on the other hand, had reduced the American's fighting force by twenty-six, ten of them permanently.

The hilltop soon became a high volume traffic center. The Battalion Commander and some of his staff arrived in choppers first.

Subsequent arrivals included intelligence teams, dogs and their handlers, photographers, and representatives of the press. Everyone hoped that air traffic controllers would not arrive on the next inbound chopper.

The Intelligence folks and dog teams searched through the rubble that remained, hungry for any information that could be uncovered. While the brass conducted their investigations, Platoon-sized recon patrols were sent out to scout the surrounding jungle.

First Platoon descended from the enemy base camp, now a popular attraction, and crossed a small valley, before climbing to the top of an adjoining hill. Not as high as the former hill, it was still covered with heavy vegetation and underbrush. When they were able to clear out a window to see through, the other hill was visible at a distance of seven hundred meters. The scarred hilltop still buzzed with activity and choppers could still be seen landing and lifting off.

It was evident that there hadn't been any visitors on this hilltop for quite some time. The men found no trails or areas that had been cleared out. Every step required the swing of a machete to clear a path through the overgrown vegetation. Since finding nothing, the Captain ordered them to follow a ridgeline on the far side of the hill down to the valley floor, which consisted mostly of tall elephant grass and small clumps of vegetation; nothing that should hinder their forward progress in their return to Hill 200.

However, after just moving two hundred meters from the base of the hill, the group of men unknowingly wandered into an area that had been hit some time ago by powdered CS gas. At that time, the explosion spewed the powdered gas everywhere. It was impossible to know how wide of an area had been contaminated; the powder remained unnoticed and had lain dormant on the ground ever since.

Foot traffic activated the powder, causing newly airborne gas. At first, some of the men were startled and wondered why their vision was blurring or their eyes were tearing up. It was comparable to peeling an onion inches from one's face. The powder also made it difficult for the men to breathe. They disrupted the ground more in their confusion, which resulted in more gas being dispersed into the air, worsening everyone's conditions.

Suddenly someone realized it was in fact CS gas.

"We're being gassed. Everyone high tail it out of here as quick as you can."

The thirty-two men tried to vacate the area as quickly as possible. In their haste, they twisted ankles and knees, and some soldiers tripped over one another to get away. Those coming up from behind latched onto the men who were limping or couldn't see and helped them move along.

The mad dash ended after fifty yards when the effects wore off. The men assisted each other in flushing the bothersome powder from their eyes. All continued to cough, some violently, until they were able to discharge the chemical from their throats and lungs. The grunts also discovered that if they weren't careful brushing the powder from their hair and clothes, the chemical would be airborne once again.

When the crises was over, the men began joking and laughing about the experience.

"Did you guys catch the face Pollack was making back there? It was so twisted up, I didn't even recognize him."

"Hell, Frenchie, I didn't see you laughing back there!"

"That's the fastest I moved in awhile. Reminded me of what we went through in boot camp."

"You're full of shit, BJ. We expected it back then. Now tell me that any of you knew this was going to happen."

"That's the first time I've experienced CS gas," Pollack added.

"How is that possible? Nobody gets excused from the gas chamber in Basic."

"Yeah, you're full of shit, Pollack."

"No, it's true. See this long scar on my neck?" He pointed to a four-inch scar across the left side of his neck. "A few days before we were to go to the chamber, four guys broke out of the stockade at Fort Knox and came through our Company Training area to hassle and rob us. Some of us started to fight them, but we didn't know they were hiding box cutter straight razors in their hands. Two of them cornered me between our barracks wall and the hand railing on the slab just outside of the door. One of them swung at my head and I jumped back, thinking that I had cleared his reach. Both then backed away quickly and attacked another nearby recruit. I ran inside and grabbed my folding shovel from my web belt and was on my way back outside when my bunkmate stopped me. He sat me down on the nearest bunk. I remember him telling me that my throat was cut and I was bleeding like a stuffed pig. This was news to me as I wasn't feeling any pain and don't remember getting cut. But when I looked down at my t-shirt and shorts, both were saturated with my blood.

"My buddy removed one of the sterile dressings from the nearest web belt and quickly covered the wound and secured it tightly. Meanwhile, some of the other guys in the barracks are coming over to see what the commotion is all about and notice the emergency. One of them ran to the Orderly Room and informed the Sergeant on duty, who quickly arranged for an ambulance to take me to the hospital.

"They told me I was lucky as the razor had just nicked my jugular vein. Just a millimeter more and I would have bled to death. I needed thirty stitches, both inside and out, to properly seal the wound. Afterwards, I was escorted to the MP headquarters where I was interrogated about the assault. This lasted for most of the night, and I returned to the barracks about four in the morning. The DI and Captain of the training Company let me sleep for the rest of the day and then I was excused from training for the next week and assigned to KP.

"So is that a good enough story for you to believe that I missed the gas chamber in Basic?"

"Damn, Pollack. What happened to the motherfucker that cut you?"

"I heard a couple of days later that they were caught and were going to be prosecuted. I didn't have to testify or do anything else as they had pictures, witnesses, and my story as evidence."

"Did they put you in another training Company?"

"No, we were almost at the end of the program anyway and I was allowed to take the PT tests, which I passed, and then graduated with everyone else."

"Okay, good enough story, Pollack. I stand corrected about you getting excused from the gas chamber. But you guys still have to admit that what just happened to us is still funnier than shit."

They all agreed and started to laugh once again, pointing to one another and making faces.

It was almost five in the afternoon when the First Platoon neared the base of Hill 200. They were instructed to pick an area nearby for their NDP and to get settled in for the night. They were cautioned not to set out any mechanicals as the other patrols were still out and not expected for another hour.

The grunts located a spot where the banana trees provided shade from the low setting sun. The ground had soft, shallow vegetation, which would provide some cushion to their makeshift bed for the night. Pollack and many others chose to lie down and rest for a short period and postpone dinner until later.

Nung climbed one of the banana trees and brought down a bunch of small bananas, passing out the pickle-sized treats to those nearby. Wild Bill walked toward Pollack with a few of the yellow fruits to share.

"Holy shit, Pollack, don't move!" He dropped the bananas to the ground.

"Why? What's wrong?" he asked, startled and concerned, but careful not to move.

"Man, you have got the biggest tarantula I've ever seen crawling up your leg."

Pollack looked to see a softball-sized, furry black creature moving up his leg.

"Get this thing off of me," he pleaded.

"Just lay still and maybe he'll just crawl off you. If you move real sudden-like and scare him, he might bite you."

Pollack thought about how he didn't want to get Medivaced again because he was bitten by another one of the jungle's creatures. He lay absolutely still.

"Hey, guys! Come over and look at this!" Wild Bill called to the rest of the Squad.

"Jesus Christ. That's one big motherfucking spider!" Frenchie had his Bowie knife in hand.

"Where did that come from?"

"BJ, you don't know shit do you? We're in a banana plantation. Tarantulas are banana spiders. They thrive in this shit."

Pollack could feel the presence of the huge arachnid on his leg as it made its way up his body. It continued on its course until it reached his waist.

"Guys, I'm scared shitless here. Please do something to get this thing off me!"

"We can't. If we try to pick it off with a branch or machete, it'll really piss him off. They're real delicate and can feel sensations easily. Let it go, eventually, it'll walk right off."

Pollack felt his heart beating very hard and fast and thought his chest was going to explode. He broke out in a cold sweat as the spider continued its upward trek. When it reached his chest, it paused once again. Pollack was terrified and hoped that his heaving chest didn't scare the thing into biting him.

It had traveled to within inches of his chin, so Pollack clamped his lips together. When one of its legs reached up and brushed the bare skin of his chin, it sent a chill down his spine, causing him to shiver.

"Don't move. He'll be off in a minute," Frenchie cautioned. He and Scout kneeled down and each pinned one of Pollack's shoulders to the ground to restrict his movement.

He could feel each of the eight legs on his face now and closed his eyes tightly until it crossed over. It paused for a third time on his forehead. Pollack dared not open his eyes in fear of what he may see. He felt it begin to move again and slowly maneuver through the strands of his hair. It tickled and he felt an uncontrollable urge to reach up and scratch his head. However, Frenchie and Scout saw him starting to move and quickly secured his arms as well.

Seconds later, when the spider fell off, the men yanked Pollack quickly to his feet before he heard a sharp crack behind him; Wild Bill had smashed the spider with Pollack's steel helmet.

"Relax, Pollack, it's over," Wild Bill took some banana leaves and wiped off the helmet before handing it to him.

"What a fucking relief! I'll bet I aged twenty years during those last ten minutes."

"You handled it well, Pollack. I hope there aren't any more wandering around here tonight."

"Fuck you, Scout. You just had to say something like that, didn't you? I don't ever want to see another spider again as long as I live." They all laughed.

"Come on, let's celebrate. I've got some extra fruit cocktail we can share," Frenchie suggested.

"What's the occasion?"

"Pollack's continued stretch of good luck!"

The following day, Pollack led the way as the First Platoon moved toward their new NDP location; they traveled at a good pace, thanks to the thinning vegetation in the area. The men had humped for over an hour without a break and were complaining loudly. So to keep the peace, Sixpack stopped the column when they reached the far edge of the valley. Pollack moved as far away from the banana trees as possible; he didn't want to relive another confrontation with a tarantula.

After the break, they continued at a relaxed pace until Pollack came upon a trail that was heading in the same direction. There, First and Third Squads switched positions in the file. The new point man and the other three Squads passed Pollack; he fell in behind the last man and First Squad was now bringing up the rear.

Two hours had passed and they found themselves still moving along the side of the same trail. Nung, who was the last man in the long column, passed up word for them to stop. Sixpack immediately broke away from his place in the column and moved back to join up with Nung. Meanwhile, the column of men took a knee and broke out cigarettes, sharing with those who didn't have any. A minute later, a single, light blue cloud of smoke formed, hovering above the men on the trail.

"Sergeant! I think maybe VC follow," he informed Sixpack.

"How many, Nung?"

"Not for sure, maybe only one man."

"Wild Bill, Frenchie, I need you both." They stood up and walked over to where the Sergeant squatted with Nung.

"Nung thinks we're being followed by one or more gooks. So when the Platoon gets up to move out, I want the two of you and Nung to hide out here on the side of the trail and if our watcher comes by, grab his ass!"

"Right on, Sarge. We'll get the little fucker."

"I want him alive, so don't get trigger-happy and waste him." Sixpack then called the Captain on the radio to inform him of their current situation.

The order to move out was passed back and everyone rose to their feet, creating a little more noise than usual to cover up the sounds of the three men sneaking into their hiding places. When the column moved on, the men bringing up the rear, including Sixpack, had to mentally remind themselves not to look back or the trail watcher might get suspicious.

After ten minutes, Sixpack heard Frenchie calling from a distance, "We got the little gook fucker!" The column halted once again.

The four men were moving up the trail towards the rest of the Platoon at a fast pace. Nung had secured the gook; one hand held the bound man's arms tightly behind his back, and the other grasped a crop of the man's hair, pulling on it so he faced upward when walking. Wild Bill carried Nung's M-16 and the gook's AK-47 as he led the way. Frenchie followed slightly to the side of the trio, keeping his rifle trained on the new prisoner's head. When they reached Sixpack, Nung threw the prisoner to the ground at his feet.

"Mr. Victor Charles at your service, just as promised," Wild Bill tossed the AK-47 to Sixpack.

The man's nose was bleeding, and his upper lip and right eye were also red and beginning to swell, yet he exhibited a look of defiance that under different circumstances might have been intimidating.

"Nung, ask him what unit he's from," Sixpack ordered. Nung started jabbering at the man in rapid fire Vietnamese but didn't seem to be getting anywhere.

"He is very stubborn. No want talk."

Without warning, Nung punched the prisoner in the side of the head. The gook staggered and fell to his back; Nung then jumped onto the man, straddling his chest. He yelled viciously at the VC and got in three more punches before Sixpack and Pollack pulled him from the man.

His lip and a gash over his eye were both bleeding along with his nose. The gook looked up to Sixpack, said a few words in Vietnamese, and then started to cry. Nung pulled out his towel, wiped at the blood on the man's face, then pulled him to his feet.

"He say he ready to talk."

"Good. Ask him again what unit he's from."

"He say 274 VC Regiment."

"Where is he going?"

"He say he moving back to area where many men wait to fight. He want make sure that he watch us because we go same way."

Handing Nung his map, Sixpack said, "Have him point out on the map where this staging area is."

Nung unfolded the map, pointing out their current position to the gook. They mumbled back and forth as Nung touched different spots on the map.

"Is here," Nung pointed out the location.

"Ask him how many men are there."

"He say he not know. He just say beaucoup men."

"Okay. Frisk him and make sure he's clean." Sixpack turned to his RTO and said, "Get the Captain on the horn."

Nung offered the prisoner some water from his canteen as they continued jabbering. Captain Fowler wanted to meet up with First Platoon, and asked Sixpack to move up the trail about five-hundred feet so they could meet halfway. The prisoner spilled his guts to Nung, after being assured that he wouldn't be hurt anymore.

The Captain, his CP and Third Platoon met up at the rendezvous with Sixpack's men. Many of the men from the Third Platoon were Cherries and crowded around for a look at the real live gook. Sixpack's men had to step in to keep them all at a safe distance.

"What happened to his face? It looks like he took a beating." Captain Fowler stated when seeing the prisoner for the first time.

"The men had to run him down and when they tackled him, his face fell against a big rock."

"This rock have five fingers attached?"

"No, sir, it was just a simple round, big, gray rock."

The Captain noticed Nung's bloody knuckles. "Did you fall against the same rock, Nung?"

"Yes, Dai Uy (Vietnamese for Captain), both VC and Nung hit beaucoup rock same time."

"Very well, you better go and have that looked at."

"Yes, Dai Uy!" Nung bowed and left the Officer, walking along the column of men to find Doc.

Upon hearing what the young enemy soldier had told the men, the Captain excitedly relayed the information to the Battalion Commander, who immediately dispatched a team from Cu Chi to retrieve the prisoner.

The area and coordinates of the suspected camp were plotted and sent to Firebase Kien for an artillery bombardment.

Captain Fowler asked Sixpack to take the First Platoon and head for that area to sniff around and see what they could find. The Third Platoon would follow on their heels as soon as the prisoner was on his way back to the rear.

It was almost four clicks to the suspected enemy camp and the trail they had been following would get them to within two-hundred meters of their target area. Captain Fowler suggested they follow it and estimated that they could reach the objective in just over an hour.

As the First Platoon made preparations to leave, artillery rounds could be heard landing in the distance as the bombardment began.

Delta Company was patrolling in an area just north of the suspected gook staging area, and had volunteered to assist as needed. They were asked to hurriedly maneuver their people on line in order to block the gook's northern escape route. This was accomplished within twenty-minutes, the blocking force was in place just five-hundred meters away from where the artillery shells were impacting.

First Platoon had made good time toward their objective; artillery rounds continued to whistle overhead and erupt in ground shaking explosions. The noise became louder and more bone jarring the closer they came. When reaching the spot where the Platoon had to step off the trail for the final leg of the journey, Sixpack informed the Captain, who called for an end to the fire mission. The short wait allowed the men an opportunity to catch their breath before entering the jungle.

Suddenly, they heard the sound of gunfire erupting to the north; predominately M-16's with an occasional pop of an AK-47. This lasted only a minute and the firing stopped.

Sixpack wasn't going to move his men until he knew exactly what the firing was all about. They sat tight and kept their eyes open for movement coming their way.

Captain Fowler called to inform Sixpack that the artillery had flushed a group of gooks from the area and straight into the gun sights of Delta Company. They were running full tilt and totally surprised when the ambush was triggered. Many of them died immediately. Some were able to return a few rounds before falling themselves, yet others were seen fleeing to the west. They were currently sweeping the area and had counted twelve bodies so far.

First Platoon was in a precarious position as the prisoner's information had proven to be somewhat true. It was no longer a simple mission to check out a rumor with the expectation of not finding anything. Now, they would have to approach the area very cautiously and do so at a high level of alert. Third Platoon was still some thirty minutes away, and they couldn't afford to wait that long to begin the sweep.

Sixpack split the Platoon into two columns, twenty feet apart, and sent four flankers to the sides. Each of the men sweated profusely as they inched forward, expecting the gooks to open fire on them at any second. They were uncertain if any of those who had stayed behind even survived the shelling; they were pessimistic and prepared for the worst-case scenario.

Pollack was on point, leading the left column. Scout, Frenchie, Nung, Wild Bill, BJ and his assistant gunner, Doc, Sixpack, and the radio operator followed closely behind. Half of the Second Squad followed them and the other half walked twenty feet away on their left flank. A mirrored formation of Pollack's column and flankers kept pace with them twenty feet away on their right.

Sixpack had the artillery group on standby and was waiting for the gunships to arrive - they had been requested before moving off the main trail. Delta Company also remained in position ready to reinforce the sweeping Platoon in a moment's notice. Pollack was the first to step out of the jungle and into the staging area. The gook had not lied; it was definitely there. He passed the first of many destroyed bunkers and used hand signals to those behind him, pointing to other bunkers that needed to be checked. Some were still intact; the logs, dirt and leaf-covered roofs rose up and were only two feet above the ground. Some of the passing grunts tossed in grenades that exploded seconds after shouting out a warning: "fire in the hole." After each explosion, three soldiers shot rounds into the bunker and then walked down the earthen steps and through the narrow entrance to check for bodies inside.

They counted eleven bunkers in total, and because of the camp's overall size, it was highly unlikely that 'beaucoup men' had been staged there. Well camouflaged from above, it encompassed an area no more than one acre.

Traces of blood were seen throughout the area; some blood trails led away from the camp and to the west. As usual, there was not one dead body to be found in or nearby the staging area. They did find food supplies, but no weapons, papers, or anything else of significance.

The Platoon had some C-4 plastic explosive and would use it to destroy the three remaining intact bunkers.

The sweep had continued for one-hundred meters beyond the bunker complex. Blood traces had ended, there were no signs of shallow graves, and nothing other than green jungle vegetation was seen during the search.

Satisfied with the thoroughness of the sweep, Sixpack informed the Captain that the mission was accomplished and that they would hook up with the Third Platoon on the trail. The Officer, in turn, informed Delta Company that First Platoon had completed its mission. The Captain thanked them for their help and wished them well.

Captain Fowler received orders from Battalion to move his Company into the area west of the complex, and look for signs of where the fleeing enemy soldiers may have gone.

They spent the next three days patrolling through the area; the search grid extended four kilometers beyond the complex. It was an exhausting and futile attempt to seek out an enemy, who remained invisible and quiet.

Late in the afternoon of the fourth day, First Platoon was directed to return to the former complex and booby trap the area in the event gooks may try to return and rebuild the camp. They would spend the night nearby and move into the complex during the morning to set up a few mechanical ambushes. Afterwards, they were to join up with the rest of the Company later that day.

In the morning, Third Squad was assigned the task of laying out the mechanical ambushes and the men would leave right after breakfast. The rest of the Platoon would sit tight and wait until they returned. Many of them accepted this potential two-hour pause as an opportunity to write letters, the first such chance in a week. It was very quiet and an appropriate setting to do so.

Pollack addressed an envelope for his first completed letter when the serenity was shattered by the sound of gunfire coming from the base camp. Without a moment's hesitation, the remaining members of the Platoon snatched up web gear, ammunition, and weapons, and moved out quickly to support the eight soldiers fighting in the base camp.

Moments earlier, the Third Squad had walked into the center of the complex before the point man noticed that some of the bunkers were already in a state of repair. He raised his arm to halt those behind him and they all took a knee. While scanning the area, the point man immediately spotted a small campfire not far away; a pot of boiling water and smoking food were visible above the flame.

"Guys, we're not alone here and need to get the fuck out quickly," he whispered to the others and pointed to the campfire.

Slowly, they backed out across the complex the same way they'd come in, hoping not to be spotted during their retreat. Their luck ran out when an enemy soldier exited a bunker near the campfire and was just as surprised to see them, as they were to see him. There was a slight hesitation on both sides, but the gook was first to holler out a warning and fired a burst from his AK-47 at them. Immediately, others joined him, firing their AK-47's from different areas within the complex. There was nowhere to run, and the men know full well that survival would be difficult if they simply dropped to fight from the open ground. All at once, as if receiving an identical mental suggestion, the eight men dove into the nearest bunker and returned fire on their attackers.

Minutes later, when the rest of the Platoon arrived, they found Third Squad pinned down between them and the enemy. Firing upon the gooks from this vantage point would be too much of a risk to the Squad in the bunker. The new arrivals remained unnoticed and all the gook fire continued to be focused on the single bunker with the Americans inside. Sixpack dispatched two Squads through the surrounding underbrush in an attempt to flank the enemy soldiers and stop the siege. The men were almost in place when the gooks caught sight of their movement and opened up on them as well.

The enemy was holed up in four bunkers on the northern side of the complex. The trapped soldiers were aware that reinforcements had arrived and screamed hysterically from within the bunker to ensure the rescuers knew their location.

Sixpack learned that the gunships would not be able to support them yet because of the close proximity to the enemy. They would have to rescue the pinned down Squad and put some distance between them and the base camp before the mini guns and rockets could help them.

In between volleys of fire, Sixpack communicated with the besieged men and coordinated a plan for getting them out. Two of the men in the bunker were wounded, but not seriously, and could walk with some assistance.

The three machine gun teams were able to spread out and get into a defendable position, despite the intense incoming fire. On Sixpack's signal, they opened fire and concentrated on the closest enemy bunker. The Platoon also used their two remaining LAW's on the other bunkers, blowing large holes into them, but failing to silence the guns inside. Now, the rest of the grunts focused on firing through the large holes and into the firing slots, hoping for a ricochet to silence the enemy inside.

The Americans had been firing steadily for over two minutes, yet there was no movement from the Third Squad. They had ignored the signal to exit the bunker and join up with them.

"Don't those fuckers know they're supposed to be coming out during this cover fire? What the fuck's their problem?" Wild Bill called loudly to Pollack, who had already fired four magazines himself during the last few minutes.

"Goddammit, guys, we can't keep this up forever!" he called out. "Un-ass that bunker, come on!"

Still there was no movement from the trapped men and the level of firing continued in hopes they try to rush to safety. Then all of a sudden, Wild Bill rose from behind his tree and ran, zigzagging toward the bunker, and then diving headfirst through the opening.

Firing now intensified as some of the men switched to full automatic and increased the rate of fire at their aggressors. Seconds later, one by one, seven men emerged from the bunker and ran wildly out of the complex and into the concealment of the jungle. Wild Bill then stepped out of the bunker carrying one of the men across his shoulder like a fire fighter. He fired his M-16 at the gook bunkers with one arm as he raced across the thirty feet of open ground. Most of the men who could see him were awed by his bravery and increased their firing even more in an attempt to protect the two trailing men. Once they were all clear, Sixpack tossed a red smoke grenade as close to the four bunkers as possible, then withdrew with the rest of his men to the main trail.

The gunships had an all clear and began their runs on the bunker complex using the red smoke as a beacon. As the rockets and mini-guns fired, the Platoon members retreated to their NDP, where Sixpack requested a Medivac for the two wounded soldiers, and a re-supply of ammo.

Captain Fowler had the rest of the Company already on the move to reinforce and support the First Platoon; he expected to arrive in a little more than an hour.

When the gunships exhausted their ammo and fuel, artillery took over in the interim, pounding at the complex until the gunships returned with a fresh load of ordinance to expend.

The assault on the base camp continued for an hour as the gunships and artillery alternated their firing. Nung was the first to spot the rest of Alpha Company and CP jogging on the trail toward the First Platoon. Once together, the men were allowed an opportunity to catch their breath while a plan was formulated. In twenty-minutes, they moved into position and prepared to sweep through the enemy camp once again.

Many in the First Platoon, especially those in the Third Squad, hoped the enemy had vacated the complex just as before; one close call already was enough for the day.

Before entering the complex, the Captain ordered everyone to fire into the General direction of the bunkers for thirty seconds, and then proceed to check through them once again. It was too cramped in the complex for the entire Company, so several small groups had to be dispatched to provide security outside of the perimeter.

The damage was much more intense than the first time. There was no resistance as before, but the results were much different. This time, they counted sixteen bodies; most found in the destroyed bunkers and four discovered outside of the perimeter, killed during their attempt to flee. The four killed outside of the perimeter wore NVA uniforms, and the remaining corpses sported typical VC black pajamas and Ho Chi Minh sandals. AK-47's were also found within an arm's reach of each body.

The only American casualties were the two men from the Third Squad. The battle was quite a surprise to both sides, but for a change, the men of Alpha Company were victorious and satisfied for the moment.

Chapter Seventeen

By mid-February, major changes had occurred. Most prominently, Frenchie, Wild Bill, and Scout finished their tours and went home in one piece.

Their last night in the bush turned out to be a pleasant experience. Wild Bill had managed to get his hands on some LRRP meals, which were lightweight, dehydrated meals primarily used by the long-range recon patrols. The dry and powdery food mixture came in a vacuum-packed aluminum foil pouch. After tearing off the perforated top, you simply added hot water and stirred. The meals, enough for the entire First Squad to share, provided an entirely new eating experience for the men in the bush. Each meal included beef that was combined with rice, noodles or cubed potatoes, in a rich, creamy sauce. Pollack and the others especially enjoyed the spaghetti and meatballs dinner. The ration packs also included a chocolate bar with a slightly cookie-like texture. It, too, was a special treat and very much appreciated. Cans of pound cake and fruit cocktail had also been saved for the celebration dinner. It turned out to be one hell of a feast considering the circumstances.

After dinner, toasts of hot chocolate were made to celebrate their friendship and for a successful future. Addresses were exchanged and promises made to keep in touch and possibly visit one another back in the world at some future date.

In the morning, as the three of them readied themselves for their final chopper ride out of the jungle, the men hugged and shed some tears. Promises were made to be broken, and it was unfortunate, but this would be the last time any of them heard or saw one other again.

Doc was supposed to leave two weeks earlier than the trio, but instead, extended his tour for six more months so he could get an early discharge from the Army. After what he'd experienced so far in Vietnam, he just didn't want to serve out his remaining year at some stateside post. Although the choice placed him in a more dangerous position, Doc just didn't want to go back to spit shined boots and being ordered around by officers fresh out of ROTC. Most have never been to Vietnam and he didn't want to have to listen to them preach about how to fight a war. His goal was to continue his life in medicine, but he wanted to go about it at his own pace as a civilian.

Wild Bill was awarded the Bronze Star for Valor for his action during the ambush at the enemy base camp. His snap decision to rescue the Third Squad from that bunker had potentially saved many lives. He later said that he only did it so they could all get the hell out of there. He didn't intend for his actions to be heroic; they were mostly triggered by impatience.

Sixpack, Doc, and Pollack were now considered the "old timers" in the Squad and BJ was not far behind; the Cherries now looked to them for guidance and direction. In the last week alone, the Platoon had received four new replacements, one being a Lieutenant. Sergeant Holmes spent most of his spare time with the new L-T and the other three men were assigned to the First Squad.

Lieutenant Alphonso Rodriguez was not a Cherry and had already been in country for five months. He transferred to the Wolfhounds from the First Cavalry, because they started to pull out of Vietnam per Nixon's early withdrawal program to end the war. The L-T preferred to be called Rod unless in the Company of other officers. He was bitter about not going home with the men in his unit, but everyone with less than seven months in country, regardless of rank, remained in Vietnam and were transferred to other units.

Jim Mitchum hailed from Dallas, Texas. A big robust fellow with sandy blond hair, he was a perfect fit for the machine gun team, and was promptly nicknamed Tex by the Squad.

Danny Jigelewski came from Atlantic City, New Jersey; the others quickly dubbed him Ski. He was a former gang member and tried to look very tough in front of everyone. Ski told them, with a heavy New Jersey accent, that prior to coming to the Army, it was common for him to be involved in gang fights at least once a week. Back then, he said, it was always about protecting your turf, similar to what the Americans did now in Vietnam. He was ready to start all over again with this group, his "new gang". Pollack and Doc looked to one other and rolled their eyes. "Let's see how he does under fire," Pollack whispered.

"Yeah, I bet he just can't wait."

Malcolm Jones was a black man from Jackson, Mississippi. His wrists and neck were adorned with several black shoelace braids and crosses. The first person he approached was Doc, also black, but he didn't share any of the so-called "black power" attitudes or rituals. Others with the same skin color would certainly label him an "Uncle Tom". When Malcolm approached him for some dap, he was surprised when Doc offered his hand for a traditional handshake. Dumbfounded and unsure of his next move, he reached out and clasped Doc's hand anyway, shaking it warmly. Back in the rear, Top had already outfitted him with an M-79 and ammo vest.

The First Squad was complete again, but mostly comprised of Cherries. It wasn't the best of all worlds, but at least the extra bodies would help in the sharing of tasks.

On their first four patrols, no contact occurred but it looked like the new Cherries were ready for anything. Their confidence was bolstered with each patrol.

After the next re-supply, the L-T and Sixpack approached Pollack with a piece of paper. He suspected something was up and sat upright in his hammock.

"Congratulations, Pollack! You've been officially promoted to Specialist Fourth Class (Spec 4) as of this past Monday. Here are your orders confirming it." Rod handed the official document to Pollack and then offered his hand to shake.

"Jeez, you're gonna be rich now. What are you going to do with all that power and money?" Sixpack cajoled.

John was surprised by this and quickly scanned the document. His highlighted name stood out from the others on the filled page. Every name listed was from the Wolfhounds, so he'd have to take a closer look at the other fifty names later.

He looked to the men and uttered, "Thanks, guys! This really is a surprise. I can use the extra money every month and I won't let the power go to my head and start abusing the Cherries."

They laughed.

For two weeks, First Platoon patrolled through the Boi Loi Woods. The area once had a reputation of being as treacherous and notorious as the Iron Triangle, but nothing had happened during the period to justify its reputation. They returned to the ritual of never-ending patrols over the same terrain, over and over again.

Ski became Pollack's new slack man whenever he was walking point. Pollack had the job for over four months and felt comfortable, he was also good at his job. During that time, he had personally uncovered several booby traps, thus, saving someone from getting hurt, namely himself. His new slack man had taken to the role in earnest and assured Pollack that he'd always have his back.

Pollack was leading the First Squad down a well-used trail when he suddenly raised his fist in the air to stop the file. He squatted down to examine some fresh Ho Chi Minh sandal prints that crossed the trail. Nung and Sixpack came forward to join Pollack in the evaluation of the footprints in the mud.

Nung was the first to voice his opinion, "Only one VC cross trail not more than maybe one hour before."

"I agree. What do you think, Pollack, want to track him?"

"I don't mind. It looks like the trail he made through the jungle on the other side will be easy enough to follow."

Pollack led the way, looking for broken twigs and leaves that may have fallen to the ground when the gook had passed earlier. A few steps close behind, Ski watched for signs of the enemy to Pollack's front and to their sides. The extra set of eyes was a big help as Pollock primarily focused on the ground. Occasionally, he would come upon another fresh set of footprints on the soft ground. But the further they traveled; the spacing of the footprints became much wider, hinting that the subject had begun to run.

Pollack signaled another stop and awaited Sixpack.

"He's running now. Probably knows we're on his tail."

"You can never tell, Pollack. He may also be setting us up."

"I see a clearing up ahead. Stay here and I'll go up and have a look around."

"Okay, but don't get too far ahead of us. I want you back in no more than five minutes."

"See you in a short." Pollack rose and moved cautiously up the trail toward the clearing. When he reached the edge of it, he noted that a dropped bomb had formed the small clearing. The twenty-foot wide crater was filled to the top with water and sat directly in the center; waist-high swaying grass encircled it and extended out for several feet to the jungle's edge. As he scanned over the area, he was surprised by a sudden and quick movement on the other side of the pond, at roughly the eleven o'clock position from where he stood. Pollack's heart skipped a beat and he froze in place, his eyes locked onto that specific area. Just then, a young VC soldier stood up with a canteen held to his lips. He is taking a long drink of water and had not yet realized that he was being watched.

Pollack hesitated momentarily and then switched his rifle to full automatic, as he brought it up to his shoulder. The gook heard the loud click made by the selector switch on the weapon and quickly dropped into the high grass and out of sight. Pollack fired several short bursts into the area where the man had last been seen. He changed magazines and then increased the arc, extending his bursts to cover as much of the area on the other side of the crater as possible. The rest of the Squad joined him at his side with weapons ready and pointing out into the clearing.

"What's up?"

"I had that gook in my sights on the other side of that bomb crater, but he dropped into the grass before I could get a clean shot off. Now I don't have a clue as to where he may be and don't know if I hit him or not."

The Squad split in two and circled around the bomb crater from both sides, cautiously approaching the spot where the Pollack saw the gook. Pollack was the first to find the gook's canteen lying on the ground and noted that a bullet had traveled through the plastic vessel. Water still seeped from it before being quickly absorbed into the heated earth.

"You may have hit him. Maybe he fell into the water."

"I didn't hear a splash, Malcolm."

Ski called out from ten feet beyond, "I found some blood on the trail that picks back up on this side of the crater."

Fresh blood droplets were visible on leaves at the entrance of the four-foot wide pathway.

"Let's see if we can find him!" Sixpack motioned up the trail with his rifle to the men around him.

Pollack resumed his position at point and continued to see fresh blood spots in the dirt along the trail. After following the splotches for a hundred feet or so, they thinned out and then finally stopped. The men further scrutinized the area to see if the VC had either left the trail or had fallen dead beside it.

Satisfied that he was nowhere around, the Squad turned around and backtracked along the trail to look for any signs that may have been missed earlier, where their elusive gook may have left the trail.

Pollack found a couple of bloody leaves on the ground next to a small pathway leading away from the trail. He had overlooked it earlier as he was only concentrating on the thin trail of blood on the ground. That was what they'd been looking for and he called Sixpack forward.

"Check this out. Looks like he backtracked and ducked up this trail."

"Okay, let's take it slow."

Pollack started up the small pathway but didn't see any more blood after the first dozen steps. He continued forward, his eyes intently searching the ground for any kind of a sign; Ski followed closely behind by only one step. Suddenly, Pollack felt the pull of fishing line across his chest and heard a pinging sound, meaning that he had hit a trip wire.

"Booby trap!" Pollack yelled and then turned and quickly gave Ski a hard shove backwards. He lost his balance after a couple of steps and fell to the ground. Pollack instinctively covered his head with his arms and dove for the ground, away from the "ping" sound, and almost landed on top of Ski. The rest of the Squad members immediately sought cover after hearing Pollack call out the warning.

Pollack felt a burning sensation in his right arm even before hearing the explosion or hitting the ground. As he turned onto his back, he noted that his right arm was bleeding in several spots and the pain felt like somebody was holding lit cigarettes against his skin.

"Doc, I'm hit!" Pollack called out from his prone position.

Seven other men rose from the ground and tried to assess what might have just happened. Sixpack, BJ, and Tex looked through the area and then provided security while Doc checked on his new patient. The medic made a quick diagnosis and started working on the wounds.

"It ain't bad, Pollack. Shit, you'll be back with us before you know it."

Ski stood next to Doc, looking down at Pollack, his facial expression one of concern. The gang member then took a knee next to Doc and held out his hand to Pollack. "Hey, man, I owe you one. You pushed me out of the way before the explosion and probably saved my life."

Doc looked over to Ski. "The Pollack did that?"

"Yeah, he shoved me backwards and yelled 'booby trap' before it went off. I was so surprised that I fell right on my ass."

"Are you hit?"

"Not that I know of. Do you see anything?" Ski stood and turned in a complete circle.

"Nope, don't see a thing."

Ski bent over and grabbed Pollack's good hand, shaking it reverently. "I'm serious, man. Thank you so much."

"I don't even remember doing that. But if it happened, it was only instinct. I'm glad you're not hurt."

Sixpack exited the area where the booby trap had exploded. "Man, that's twice you lucked out. Your elusive friend planted a grenade with a trip wire in a tree."

"What do you mean 'lucked out'? Shit, I'm hit."

"That ain't shit. Fucking scratches is all; a few stitches and your ass will be right back out here with the rest of us."

"It might not look that bad to you, but it sure as hell hurts."

"It looks like he got even with you for shooting him."

"Damn, how far away from the path did he set it? Twenty feet?"

"Shit, no. It should have killed you. He laid it in a tree about chest high right next to the trail. I guess he was expecting you to be watching the ground and set the wire up high where you may not have seen it. When you pulled on the trip wire and the pin came out, the grenade fell behind the tree, which shielded most of the blast. That's why I said you lucked out again."

"Jeez, thanks."

"What do you think, Doc? Will he live?"

"Oh, hell yes. There's a lot of blood but it's not bad at all. He caught three pieces of shrapnel in his right arm. The surgeons will dig out the steel and patch him up as good as new. Go ahead and request a dust off, but make it a routine."

Within minutes, Doc had the injured man's arm bandaged and they all returned to the main trail to wait for the Medivac. The soldiers sat to the side smoking cigarettes, when after thirty minutes, Sixpack received word that a chopper was on its way and should arrive shortly to pick up the wounded warrior.

"Well, Pollack, you got your first Purple Heart. How does it feel?"

"Fuck the Purple Heart. That was one award that I was hoping not to get while here. I am glad though that it wasn't worse."

"You'll heal up fine and after you get the stitches out, we'll probably all meet up together in Cu Chi and drink some beers."

"What do you mean, Sixpack?"

"We're about due to pull an R&R soon, maybe even this week!"

"Really?"

"Yeah, if we get there before you, we'll save a few beers."

"Thanks a lot."

Pollack soon began his second Medivac trip to the 93rd Evac in Long Binh. This time the ride was much more pleasant under the circumstances. He could relax, knowing that his condition wasn't one of life or death.

The burning in his arm had stopped after the imbedded hot steel cooled off. All that remained now was a throbbing reminder of the injury with each heartbeat. He was confident that it would pass once he received a shot of painkiller at the hospital.

When landing at the Evac hospital, the same scenario played out as the last time. A crew waited, but instead of a cart, they had a wheelchair ready. After they removed shrapnel, they closed the wounds with seven stitches. Pollack was resting comfortably in the ward within an hour of his arrival.

The next morning, he was released from the hospital and cleared for his return to Cu Chi. There, the Battalion aid station would change his bandages every morning and make sure the wounds were kept clean.

Alpha Company returned to Cu Chi on Pollack's fourth day at the base camp. Everyone talked excitedly about the entire Company spending a couple of days at an in-country R&R center called Vung Tau. The town was located on the shores of the South China Sea, not too far from Saigon. There, they could forget their fears for two whole days. Pollack was released and able to join the Company on the short vacation. He'd been advised not to get the wounds wet and given a small satchel of ointment and bandages to take along with him.

The first order of business after arriving at Vung Tau was to find a place to sleep and change into a bathing suit to swim in the South China Sea. All the men were issued identical pairs of yellow trunks and a fresh green towel. It was almost surreal to see over one-hundred and fifty soldiers in yellow bathing suits, rushing all at once toward the sea, frolicking through the sand like a group of kids. They kicked sand at one-another, tackled best friends, and then when reaching the water, tried to dunk each other in between the massive rolling waves.

Pollack was one of the last to venture out onto the sand and did not plan to join in the roughhousing with the others. Instead, he found a place and sat in the sand just a few feet beyond the crashing surf. After a short period of time, he entered the sea and tried with great difficulty to walk along the shoreline in shallow water no deeper than his knees.

He found the water refreshing and squatted down to be at a height where the waves wash over him. He remained careful about his arm, keeping it raised in the air to protect it from any wetness. The salty taste of the water surprised Pollack. As a Michigander, many fresh water lakes surrounded him, but he had never swum in any of the oceans.

Pollack wandered along the shoreline and suddenly experienced a sensation that he'd never had before. Even though he was in shallow water, he could feel his feet being pulled away from the beach. He faced away from the beach and dug his heels into the sand, hoping it would stop his skid into deeper water. It proved to be a futile attempt to stop and he found that his feet continued to create shallow trenches on the sandy bottom; and moving into deeper water. The pulling sensation grew stronger. Pollack had always been a strong swimmer, participating in teams during his youth, but he wasn't sure if just letting go was the right thing to do. He started to panic and called out for help.

Two nearby soldiers were just passing when they heard him call out.

"Hey, man, what's up?" one of them asked.

"There's an undertow or something here in the water and it's pulling me away from the beach. I can't make it stop or get away."

"Relax, man, you're caught in a riptide. You have to walk out of it."

"I've been trying to do that!"

"Don't try to walk to the beach, man; stay in the water and walk along the shoreline until you don't feel the pull anymore."

Pollack turned and moved nervously in the direction he'd come earlier. The two soldiers on the beach were only fifteen feet away, but they remained on the sand to watch his progress. After he completed twenty of the hardest steps he'd ever had to take through water, he found the pull suddenly gone and his panic subsided. He turned and exited the sea without any effort.

"Thanks guys, I thought I was a goner."

Both soldiers were familiar with rip tides. "You did luck out, because some riptides will pull a person out to sea a mile from shore. We'll report this to the folks running the beach so they post warning signs for everybody else. Are you okay?"

"I'm okay now. Thanks again!" Pollack walked over to his towel and dropped down onto it. Exhausted, his legs cramped from his muscular tug of war with the sea.

Pollack massaged the muscles of his legs to work out the cramps and watched the others out in the water. The waves were higher than he'd ever seen in his life and many of the men bodysurfed and rode them to the shoreline. Thrilled, they happily jumped back out into the water and swam out to catch the next big wave.

A group of soldiers in waist deep water, with others riding on their shoulders, battled each other in a show of strength and balance. Those knocked over had to move to the side and patiently watch the outcome until only one pair was left standing. Once a winner had been proclaimed, they all mounted up again to start a new match.

The next two days were filled with floorshows, drinking, and whoring around; cash money needed for the latter. The men in the Company had been warned prior to leaving Cu Chi about having sex with the town hookers. They were tested and many carried venereal diseases, which ran rampant in the area. Officers also told them stories about a certain strain of VD called the Black Clap. It had no cure and any GI's who caught the strain would be banished to some God forsaken island out in the ocean, never to be heard from again. That was enough to convince many in the group to abstain from such activities in fear of catching the dreaded disease.

The air-conditioned barracks alone were worth the trip. If you didn't want to go outside, you could remain in the barracks and enjoy the coolness during your stay.

Just like with any vacation, it was over much too fast. The men departed Vung Tau by truck in the early afternoon and arrived in Cu Chi just in time for dinner. The following morning, it would be business as usual with new missions assigned.

Rod approached Pollack that evening. "You know, Pollack, maybe you should consider giving up the point for awhile. I need a good RTO to handle the radio. How would you like to try carrying the radio for a while?"

He stood there with a doubtful look upon his face, but he only had to think it over for less than a minute before deciding to go ahead with it. Carrying the radio would be more work at night, but he wouldn't have to pull night guard or go out on patrols unless the L-T was going. It was basically a no-brainer!

"Okay, I'll give it a try."

"Good. But first you need to get cleared by the medics. Let them check you out and if they say you can return to the bush, then stop by and see Top afterwards. He'll brief you on your new job and will provide you with all the charts, pencils, and supplies you'll need. You'll be my personal RTO, which means that in the field you go everywhere I do. Does that bother you?"

"Hell no! It'll be something different and maybe a little more exciting. At least I'll have an idea what's happening out in the bush instead of guessing about it all the time."

"That's true. Thanks for considering it. I'll see you in the morning."

Battalion medics did not see any problems with Pollack's arm. The stitches had dissolved and the wounds were healing nicely. Therefore, they gave him a clean bill of health and a lifted restriction note to give Top.

After meeting with the First Sergeant and receiving the new supplies, he found it necessary to rearrange his rucksack and pack things differently. The ruck itself had to come off now and would be remounted to a new quick release frame dedicated solely to the radio. If required to move quickly or go out on light patrols, the rucksack could be detached in a snap. The added weight of both the radio and two spare batteries would also increase his normal load by twenty-six pounds.

He was, however, excited with the new toy, and while everyone else was busy socking down that last beer, he sat on a cot, reading over the new material. He wanted to make sure he didn't become a burden in the bush and had to be certain he did everything correctly. He played with the code indicator, making up messages and coding them, then double-checking them for errors before repeating the process.

He turned on the radio and switched to the different frequencies; he had a notepad with every frequency and call sign used in the field. He tuned in on the gunship frequency, Medivac frequency, and then to the various Company frequencies, listening for a few minutes on each channel. The chatter was routine and there didn't appear to be anything interesting going on.

Content that he wouldn't blow it tomorrow; he set everything to the side and waited for morning to arrive.

Chapter Eighteen

Humping with the radio was more difficult than Pollack had imagined; the extra twenty-six pounds felt more like a hundred. The backpack hung heavily from his shoulders; the thinner straps dug deeper into muscle with every step, cutting off the flow of blood and numbing both arms. Only an occasional tingle reminded him that his arms were still there. The extra padding of the towel around his neck did nothing to help cushion the weight.

Originally, Pollack didn't think that carrying the radio would be a big deal because the M-60 machine gun weighed more. However, when carrying the gun, he could switch over to a different shoulder if one started to hurt. The radio sat right in the middle of his back, the combined weight evenly distributed over both shoulders. He would occasionally bounce the backpack upwards and grab onto the straps, pulling them forward and hunching over some so it shifted into a slightly different position, allowing for a brief reprieve to the numbed arms and shoulders.

The frequency must constantly be monitored when the Company moved or bushed for the night. At the start of the hump, Pollack held the handset against his ear at all times. This didn't last long as the constant rubbing, numb arms, and static of the radio made it an almost impossible task. It also prevented him from hearing sounds and noises around him, which made him nervous. During a break, one of the other RTO's suggested that Pollack remove his grenades from the rings on the shoulder harness and attach the handset there. After turning the squelch up to eliminate the white noise and static, he could finally hear conversations on the radio without it being too loud and could also hear the sounds of the jungle around him.

Every RTO carried two different types of antennae with him when out in the field. A small, flexible, thin whip antenna, three feet long, which bent and gave when moving through the heavy bush, was the most frequently used. Sometimes, when signals were strong due to the close proximity of the units, the radio operators folded the whip antennas over and tucked the end into a loop on the utility straps. This was usually the preferred method when on the move, especially in high grass or short underbrush; because everyone was concealed and only the antenna was seen hovering above like a submarine's periscope. The opportunity elated any gook snipers who happened to be out and about. All they had to do was to take a bead on the bouncing antenna, drop a little more than three feet, and fire off a few rounds. Many RTO's had been hit this way, falling dead to the ground before they even heard the shots ring out. Sometimes, the units worked further apart and it became necessary to fully extend the antennae to hear each other. At times like that, many RTO's experienced paranoia.

The other antennae, a long extendable version, was usually used at night or when staying in a position for a long period of time. It consisted of ten two-foot sections of thin walled, three-eighths of an inch diameter steel tubing; a stretchable twine on the inside of the hollow tubes held the pieces together and provided a level of tension similar to an extended rubber band. One end of every tube slightly flared and fit easily over the other end of the next tube. An RTO could hold the base in his hand and let the tubes fall to the ground. With a little shaking and coaxing, the twenty-foot antennae would assemble itself, using the rubber band inside to force them together. It then screwed onto the radio to enable long distance communications.

The most hectic part of the day was when the unit finally stopped and began to set up an NDP. Once the night guard position had been determined, the RTO's followed a routine before they could prepare their sleeping area or eat dinner. His rucksack had to be disconnected from the frame and the radio, and set to the side. He then moved the radio to the central guard position within the perimeter and added the long antenna. Coordinates of the NDP had to be coded and forwarded to the Company CP. In turn, he had to listen for the coded positions of the other platoons and ambush Squads, decipher them, and plot their locations on the map with a grease pencil. When done, he could finally set up a sleep area and cook dinner. The hammock made it much easier if they were in a wooded section. Most everyone already finished eating dinner by the time the RTO began to heat his up. Someone always stepped in to help cover the radio so he could get ready for the night.

Some fringe benefits also came with the job of being an RTO. First, it was no longer necessary to go out on Squad-size patrols or ambushes unless the L-T participated; and second, he was excused from nightly radio watch and guard duty. Therefore, he was usually afforded the luxury of sleeping through the night.

As a result of taking on the radio, Pollack was no longer assigned to a specific Squad. He and the L-T normally rotated every three days and attached themselves to a different Squad after each re-supply. Although his time at night was limited, Pollack tried to join in on the nightly BS sessions. But whenever they joined up with the First Squad, he made it a point to catch up on lost time with his closest friends.

The first two weeks of March had passed very slowly and the Company did little moving around. The higher brass designated Alpha Company as the Battalion reactionary force and wanted them to be on fifteen-minute ready alert. If one of their Sister Companies in the Battalion ran into trouble, Alpha Company would be airlifted to their location as added support. Because of this short lead-time, Captain Fowler had to ensure that they remained within minutes of an LZ at all times.

During those two weeks, Rod and Pollack got to know each other better, as ample time always existed for the two of them to shoot the shit.

"What did you do before joining the service, Rod?"

"My civilian days ended a week after graduating from high school in Hollywood, California."

"Wow, Hollywood? Did you get to see all the movie stars?"

"You'd see some of them occasionally walking along the street, in certain restaurants or driving by in their expensive cars and limos. I only met one star face-to-face, it was during high school when I took my prom date to the Brown Derby Restaurant. John Wayne was sitting at the next table and I was able to introduce myself and shake his hand. He called me a pilgrim, too."

"Wow, that is really cool! Is he as big as they say?"

"Hell yes. He was like a giant next to me."

"He's my favorite actor. I'd love to meet a star just once."

"It isn't that big of a deal. They're ordinary people, just like us."

"That's alright. You used to see them all the time. I'd definitely be in my glory."

"Most of them are kind of uppity though, and don't want to be bothered. They're probably tired of signing autographs or getting their pictures taken. They just want to be normal like the rest of us."

"Yeah, but they forget that these fans are the ones who made them famous. Without them, the stars would just fade away."

"Many of them already have had short careers."

"What did you do after high school?"

"I went straight to West Point."

"West Point? That must have been tough."

"It was, but only during the first couple of years. You could compare it to being twice as hard as Basic Training and lasting four years. My last two years were the best."

"Were the initiations bad?"

"Shit, Pollack. We were slaves to the upper classmen, and were forced to pull their details. They fucked with us every chance they could. One guy would order us to do something, and then another guy would order us to do something different. The first guy would come back and chew us out for not doing what he had requested and then put us on report for extra details. We were always in a state of confusion and getting punished for something or another.

"The first year could be summed up entirely of classes, daily physical training, constant military drills, harassment, intimidation, extra drills and details, and homework, with very little sleep in between all this."

"God, it must have been a real bitch."

"That's not the half of it. I also played football, so I had to put up with the bullshit from the senior players too."

"Didn't you get treated differently because of your sports involvement?"

"Are you kidding? If a cadet couldn't maintain a B average in his studies, then he wasn't allowed to participate in the sports programs. West Point wants to produce the best in everything. If you don't measure up to their high standards, you got booted out."

"I don't think I could have taken all that shit."

"I don't know how I managed either. But it was well worth it. I've had it pretty easy since I joined the Army. I'll have it made when I get back to the states after Nam. With my combat duty and West Point background, I should make full bird by the time I retire."

"So you're gonna stay in the Army?"

"I'd be a fool not to."

"How long do you think you'll be staying out here in the bush?"

"I really don't know. Normally Lieutenants spend six to eight months in a front line unit then get withdrawn to some rear job. Next week, I'll have my six months in. But there's a strong rumor that the 25th Division is going to be pulled out of Nam next month and return to Hawaii. So I don't know what'll really happen."

"No shit? That's the first time I heard that rumor. Why would they go to Hawaii?"

"That's where their stateside home base is."

"Does that mean we'll all go to Hawaii?"

"I really don't know. First, we need to find out what the criteria is going to be. In the Cav, everyone with seven months in country was able to leave with the Division. The rest, like me, were reassigned to other units."

"That means I'll be able to leave with them."

"Now just hold on a minute. I don't even know if it's going to happen, let alone how it'll be done. Just don't go getting your hopes up."

"How can I not? Only having to stay here for one more month is like a dream come true."

"I wouldn't think about it that way if I were you. Just plan to spend your full year here. The military doesn't usually repeat itself and is real creative in making some of their decisions. If the criteria is different than that of the First Cav and you end up not going to Hawaii as you expected, you might go off the deep end and maybe get yourself killed."

"It's okay to hope then, isn't it?"

"Yeah, Pollack, hoping is okay, as long as you aren't disappointed with the results."

Pollack rolled the thoughts around in his head and wanted to feel optimistic about the possibility of making the cut.

"Rod, different subject. Now that you've worked with us for a couple weeks, can you make a comparison to the Cav?"

"There is no comparison really, because there's too much of a difference here. You grunts spend an awful lot of time walking over the same terrain, and end up chasing gooks away. The only time you make contact and get a body count is when you stumble into one of their base camps. The First Cav is air mobile, and we would CA (combat assault) into an area, and hunt down an enemy that had been spotted from the air. We always had running firefights and ambushes to contend with and had dozens of helicopters at our disposal all the time. Sometimes, we'd land and get extracted and moved someplace else after four hours. Down here, there's just too much walking around and chasing an invisible enemy."

The next few days were just as Rod had stated. They humped on endlessly, looking for the evasive enemy. The only casualties were those who suffered heatstroke and heat exhaustion.

The rumor of them leaving Nam grew stronger every day and ranged from a full pullout to a total reassignment.

Beautiful Hawaii suddenly became the main topic of conversations. Every person had their own visions of paradise, but most agreed on various scenarios. Some imagined lying peacefully on a beach and listening to the rolling surf of the ocean crashing upon the sand; others thought of hula dancers with grass skirts. High, tropical waterfalls existed everywhere, along with volcanoes and excellent vantage points. Hundreds of tropical birds cawed in the sweet-smelling jungles. Humping would be a thing of the past, and so would being shot at, eating out of cans, or sleeping on the ground. Pulling stateside duty in a place like that was a dream in itself. Many civilians wished to visit Hawaii, but few could afford the high cost of travel. It would be a rare experience for many of the soldiers in the division, so excitement ran rampant.

Pollack began to feel guilty about not going out on the small recon patrols anymore. Staying behind and monitoring the radio began to get boring, and the excitement just wasn't there anymore.

He pleaded with Rod to allow him to go out on patrols every time they were attached to First Squad. At first, he was reluctant, but seeing Pollack's continued disappointment, Rod approved his request and even monitored the radio in his absence.

The First Squad members were always happy when Pollack joined them on their short patrols; it seemed like old times again. The guys also appreciated his experience in the event they ran into something while out on patrol. It was a great change of pace but short-lived.

After a week, the official word came down from Division and most of the rumors came true. Alpha Company would be recalled to Cu Chi in eleven days to begin out-processing. Those personnel manning the firebases would turn them over to the ARVN and join up in Cu Chi with everyone else. The soldiers were ecstatic as the war would finally come to an end for them.

Chapter Nineteen

The Battalion lifers still wanted one last battle before leaving the country; so running up a body count became their top priority. Some of the pacifists would say that their strategic game of toy soldiers was quickly coming to an end, so it was an opportunity to make the headlines and go home in style.

As it turned out, each Company's final mission was to revisit whichever area had resulted in their highest body counts during the last four months. It was ironic that they didn't take into consideration the fact that these companies also lost a lot of men in the same battles.

Alpha Company would revisit the area where Zeke was killed. The majority of the lower ranking soldiers wouldn't even know they were back in that same area of operations, because all the terrain they patrolled looked the same. It was also important to note that since that earlier battle, sixty percent of Alpha Company had been replaced by new troops, fresh from the states. None of them were aware of the earlier fight or even who Zeke was, and half of them hadn't even been fired upon yet. The old timers were concerned about their chances, especially since Captain Fowler decided for the Company to operate in Platoon sized units during the last week and a half.

During the first three days, Rod and Pollack attached to the First Squad. On the first break together, after moving two clicks up a trail, Pollack moved over and sat next to Sixpack; Rod busied himself with a compass and his map.

"I've seen some familiar sights already, Sixpack, and it's bringing back some bad memories I have about this place."

"Yeah, same thing is happening to me. It does worry me though that we have to come back out here to begin with, and this time there's a lot of Cherries with us. Only you, Doc, and I really know what this AO did to a bunch of good guys."

"I know what you mean. I'm scared shitless. It's unbelievable that we've only got ten more days left in this fucking hellhole and the brass is only concerned about more body counts. Have you seen the activity on the trail? There are gooks out and about! If I was in charge, I'd pull everyone out of the field and let them hole-up somewhere where it's safe."

"I've seen the signs too, but I'm hoping that they stay out of our way so we don't have to lose anybody else."

"Do you remember, Sarge, this is the same area where Larry and I had our Cherry busted and survived our first firefight? I sure don't want it to be the place where I have my last one. I'd be the happiest motherfucker in the world if I never see another gook or have to fire my weapon again."

"I feel the same way," he stopped short, staring into the sky, as if deep in thought.

"Hey, Sixpack!"

"What?" He seemed agitated with Pollack's disturbance.

"Do you think the gooks know we're leaving the country?"

"You can bet your sweet ass they do. If they were smart, they'd stay out of our way for the next week and a few days. I would think that the ARVN would most likely take over this area after we leave. The gooks should get ready for a big shootout with them."

"Ha, that's a joke. You know as well as I do that they very seldom go out into the field and stay put in their base camps."

"I know that too. There's only one thing that bothers me about this area: no other friendly forces have been through here since we left, and the gooks have had plenty of time to rebuild their little camps or even build additional ones. I just hope Rod doesn't walk us right into one of them."

"Why don't you go fill in the L-T about this place? Maybe he'll let us skate and just hunker down someplace for a while."

"I doubt it, but I'll talk to him anyway."

"I'm kinda tight with him. You want me to go with you?"

"Naw, it'll be more official if I go alone."

As soon as Sixpack walked away, Doc slid over. "How you holding up, Pollack?"

"Shit, Doc. Look at me, I'm shaking like a leaf." He held his arm out to show a slight tremor in his hand.

"I don't blame you. I didn't extend my tour to come back to this shitty place. There's something evil in the air. I got a weird feeling that some of us ain't gonna leave this place alive."

"Aw, come on, Doc. Don't start that kind of shit."

"I'm serious. Just look at all them Cherries over there," he pointed to the soldiers sitting alongside the trail. "They don't have a clue about this place and most of them are still Cherries. At least the last time we were here, we had all seasoned vets with us."

"Yeah, and they still kicked our asses."

"Now that's what I'm talking about. What do you think this bunch is going to do under fire?"

"I sure the fuck hope they don't freeze up or turn tail and run."

"Me neither. I wish the L-T would use his head and keep us sitting tight for awhile."

"I mentioned the same thing to Sixpack. He went over to talk to Rod about it. I think it may be a possibility."

"I hope so. Hey, gotta go, I'll catch up with ya later."

"Okay. Stay cool, Doc."

Sixpack returned with a smirk on his face. "He bought into it. We're moving off the trail right here."

Pollack smiled broadly. "All right, Sixpack, way to go!"

"Take a bow yourself. I wasn't thinking about it; you planted the seed and I just ran with it."

It was only three in the afternoon, but Rod sent word down the column to pull off the large trail and set up an NDP. Some of the old timers smiled, sensing a change in plans.

Once they got settled in, four LP teams of two were sent out in different directions, two-hundred feet outside the perimeter to watch and listen to the surrounding jungle.

At 1800 hours, Pollack sent their current coordinates to the CP and informed them that it would be their NDP for the night. The nearest Platoon was three clicks away so there was no risk of bumping into them.

There were no other trails nearby that branched off from the main trail they'd been following, so mechanical ambushes had been placed on the trail to cover the approaches from both directions. The rest of the bush surrounding them was dense and would require a machete to cut a path to the NDP. Several other manually operated Claymore mines and trip flares were placed between the NDP and the main trail itself. All in all, the location appeared to be quite a find and the soldiers couldn't be more pleased with the outcome.

The following day, First Platoon remained in place, rotating the LP's every two hours. Rod had already informed the Captain that patrols were out and the only evidence they'd found so far were signs that the main trail was being used. He was also pleased that they had left mechanical ambushes on the trail. Captain Fowler wished Rod happy hunting and signed off.

The soldiers were well aware that they had a good thing going and maintained strict noise discipline, conducting necessary conversations only in a whisper. They spent idle time cleaning weapons, reading, sleeping, writing letters, or listening to transistor radios with earphones. The NDP is well protected, but the quietness is unsettling. The gooks knew that Americans were in the vicinity; the landing choppers had announced their arrival the day before. Some of the old timers actually believed the gooks knew exactly where they were positioned, but chose not to engage them at this time.

Most of the troops writing letters home expressed their excitement about the Division pulling out of Vietnam and returning to Hawaii. They wrote that many rumors surfaced regarding the pull out, but it was highly unlikely they were all true or false. The grunts hoped for the best and asked that those back home say a few prayers on their behalf.

Hands cramped as the same kind of letter was written to everybody in their address books. If someone ran out of paper or envelopes, there were always extra to share.

That evening, Pollack sent the same coordinates to the CP, and found that the other Platoons were moving throughout the area and staying in different locations at night. They had all been lucky so far and hadn't come into contact with the enemy during the past two days. Perhaps it was true and the gooks really were trying to avoid the Americans.

On the morning of the fourth day, First Platoon packed everything up and left their home for the last three nights to head back to the LZ for resupply. Seeing no movement on the trail during this time, Sixpack and the L-T agreed that it was safe enough for the men to travel on during their return to the LZ. Fourth Squad had the point and everyone in the single file column moved cautiously and maintained a slight distance of ten feet between one other. It was an easy hump as every rucksack and canteen is almost empty.

First Squad brought up the rear of the column; Rod and Pollack positioned themselves between the First and Second Squads. Two large explosions, just seconds apart, occurred when the Squad came within two-hundred feet of the clearing. The ground shook and soldiers instinctively dropped to seek out protective cover. They heard no rifle fire, but did hear cries for help and movement on the trail ahead. Through the settling dust and smoke cloud, soldiers could be seen lying on the ground, writhing in pain, some trying to stand or crawl to the side. The concussions were so loud that those closer to the explosions were temporarily deaf, while those further back had a loud ringing in their ears.

"Medic! Help! We got people hurt up here!"

"Come on, Pollack," the L-T stood and raced to the front of the column.

Slightly dazed, Pollack managed to get to his feet and rushed up to join Rod. Sixpack and Doc stood and followed Pollack.

When they reached the front of the column, Doc jumped into action, assessing each man, and spending only seconds before moving on to the next one. Doc called to Sixpack and others with instructions as to what needed to be done to stabilize the wounded soldiers. If they had no pulse, he would say nothing and move forward. Tourniquets were applied to legs and arms, and bandages applied wherever needed.

"John, get us some Medivacs. We've got six urgent, and four routine," Rod called out.

Pollack quickly informed the CP of what had just occurred and requested that Medivacs be dispatched.

"Sixpack, send out some men and get this fucking LZ secured. Tell them to be careful of booby traps."

Sixpack picked ten men and sent them scurrying across the LZ to secure the tree line on the other side. Then he ordered two men back up the trail to provide rear security. Some of the new Cherries stood around confused, not sure of what to do next; their faces masked in horror.

"You guys!" Rod pointed over to the group. "Get your heads out of your asses and give Doc and the others a hand with the wounded. Get some ponchos for litters, then help move the wounded up to the LZ."

A few jumped quickly toward the wounded, relieved to finally be of some assistance. Others began searching through the rucksacks of the downed soldiers to gather the available ponchos. Pollack remained a step behind Rod wherever he went.

After fifteen minutes, the casualties had all been transported to the LZ. Friends of the wounded knelt beside them, offering consolation, while Doc continuously moved and checked on his patients.

The radio handset came alive and a quivering voice calls out, "Sierra-one, this is Angel-five-zero, on your net, come in." The helicopter pilot's voice sounded like he was slapping at his throat while talking.

"This is Sierra-one, over," Pollack replied into the handset.

"Roger. We're your angels of mercy. Our ETA is three minutes."

"Roger, Angel-five-zero, standing by."

Pollack announced, "Birds will be here in three minutes. Get ready!"

"Sierra-one, Angel-five-zero. What is the extent of your wounded?"

"Sierra-one, we have six on litters for urgent Medivac; two have sucking chest wounds and four are amputations. Four others are routine and are currently stable with upper and lower body wounds. We also have four KIA, over."

"Roger, we'll take your two sucking chest wounds and one of the amputees on this first pick-up. Angel-five-five will touch down behind me and take the other three urgent. We'll return for the others within fifteen minutes. Go ahead and pop smoke."

"Pop smoke, James!" Pollack instructed one of the two men on the LZ who would guide the birds into the zone. James pulled the pin from his canister and tossed it several feet behind him.

"Angel-five-zero, smoke is out."

"Roger, we identify yellow smoke."

"That's affirmative."

"Roger that. We have you in visual. Is the LZ cold?"

"That's affirmative."

"Sierra-one, we'll be coming in from the west. Have those wounded ready so we can get them out as quick as possible."

"Wilco, out."

While Pollack stood at the edge of the tree line watching the two birds on their approach, his radio came to life once again. "Sierra-one, Lightning-six-niner, over."

"This is Sierra-one."

"Roger, Sierra-one, what's the status of your LZ for our angels of mercy?"

He looked up, surprised to see two Cobras circling overhead. "This is Sierra-one. It's cold, over."

"Roger. We'll stay on station until all of your wounded are evacuated. If you need anything, just let us know."

"Wilco. Sierra-one, out."

Ten minutes later, Angel-five-zero called to inform Pollack that he was three minutes out and planning to evacuate the remaining wounded.

Seconds after leaving the LZ, the Medivac called to Pollack, "Sierra-one, this is Angel-five-zero. I'll be leaving your net in a minute. Your wounded have been taken to the 93rd Evac Hospital. A team from Graves Registration will be coming out within the hour to pick up your KIA."

"Roger, Angel-five-zero. Appreciate what you did."

"No problem. Glad we could help. Hope all of your guys make it. Good luck. Angel-five-zero is clear this net."

"Sierra-one, Lightning-six-niner."

"Go ahead, Lightning-six-niner."

"Roger. We'll be leaving the area and heading back to our coop. Is there anything you need before we leave?" Pollack looked to Rod, who shook his head negatively.

"That's a negative. Thanks for hanging around."

"Roger. Take it easy down there. Lightning-six-niner out."

The earlier sensation that many of the old timers had about the gooks knowing their location looked to be accurate. It was clear they didn't want to fight the Americans head to head, so they left a calling card for them instead.

The gooks purposely booby-trapped the trail, knowing full well that the Americans would most likely return to the LZ for either a re-supply or a pick-up. Claymore mines had been used in their booby trap; two of them went off immediately and the third detonated a few seconds later. The entire Fourth Squad, with the exception of their point man and his back up, had been caught in the blast; neither was wounded.

Sixpack approached Rod and Pollack. "Did it dawn on you that neither of the first two guys in the column is hurt?"

"Is it possible that they may have stepped over a trip wire and the third guy in line trip it?" Pollack asked.

"It's highly unlikely for something like that to happen."

"Something just isn't right with this booby trap, Sixpack. We know they used Claymores. Let's organize a search and poke around through the brush on both sides of the trail."

Sixpack took four men and moved into the brush on one side of the trail while the L-T, Pollack, and four others entered the jungle on the other side.

Ski was the first to spot a pair of brown wires running along the ground, not far from the exploded mines heading deeper into the jungle.

"Sixpack, L-T, I've found something," Ski called out, waving for the men to join him.

Sixpack closed in on his position as the L-T and Pollack were crossing the trail and moving toward them.

Without saying another word, the four men began to follow the wires and moved fifty feet deeper into the jungle. They suddenly stopped when reaching a small cleared out area. On the ground lay three empty C-Ration cans, some scraps of paper, and two clackers (devices to detonate the mines) attached to the end of the two pair of wires.

"The mines were manually detonated by who ever was sitting here and waiting patiently for us to come by. He let the first two guys go by and then blew the mines separately, hoping that he might have caught the L-T and RTO in the killing zone."

"Motherfuckers!" Rod angrily kicked at the C-Ration tins. Sixpack interceded and quickly took a hold of the officer. "Easy, Rod, haven't you learned not to kick at things in the bush? They may be booby-trapped!"

Rod hesitated and looked like he'd been slapped across the face. "Aw shit, Sixpack. I'm sorry! Thanks!"

"Little cocksuckers blew the mines and then just slipped away during all the confusion."

Rod suddenly cocked his head as if having a Eureka moment. "Sixpack, we need to stop the re-supply and move someplace else. No telling how many gooks are watching us right now."

"That's a hell of an idea, Rod. I'll gather the troops while you and Pollack find another place and call in the new coordinates."

They knew of a suitable LZ about two clicks to their north, away from the trail and anybody who may have been watching them. All agreed that moving someplace else was the best idea, especially since discovering the clackers. Had they not been found, the re-supply would have taken place as scheduled, and God knows what may have happened next when the chopper landed and everyone was bunched up out in the open. Mortars would have been a solid choice to avoid any physical contact with the Americans. The rest of the Platoon could have been annihilated.

When humping to the new re-supply LZ, First Platoon chose to cut a path through the jungle instead of following one of the wide trails. It was still dangerous choosing this route, as the possibility existed of stumbling into a fortified enemy bunker complex before reaching the LZ. This hump wreaked havoc on everyone's nerves and those walking up front felt extremely paranoid and were overly cautious. It took almost all afternoon to reach the LZ for re-supply.

In regards to what had happened to the First Platoon, Captain Fowler issued a new directive to the Company and changed the SOP (Standard Operating Procedure). He had heard from many others about their sixth senses and feelings of being watched. In an attempt to outsmart the gooks and possibly prevent anyone else from getting injured, he suggested a game of hide and seek. Each Platoon was to set up their NDP and go about their normal practices for that time of the day. They must be convincing in their actions to stay there for the night. Then, about 2200 hours, the Platoons would quietly pack up and move to a new location under the cover of darkness. The new spot would have been scouted out during their daily patrols and should be a minimum of three-hundred meters away.

When everyone settled into their new locations, Kien would fire H&I (Harassment and Intimidation) rounds all around them to keep the enemy off balance.

The next morning, each NDP location was to lay out mechanical ambushes to cover all avenues of approach to their day lager area. Platoons would remain in place for the day and then move out again under the cover of darkness to yet another new location. The H&I firing would continue again later that night.

The game of hide and seek worked well for three days, but then it was time for them to be re-supplied. Everyone worried that when the helicopter touched down, a red beacon would go off in the LZ thus alerting the surrounding gooks as to their location.

Once again, the Captain showed his creativity and scheduled a fly-by re-supply for the Company. He had arranged to use several helicopters for this new scheme. All would be flying at tree top level through the AO; some would feign landings in open fields and return quickly to flying around at treetop level. Each Platoon would be re-supplied from these helicopters without any of them actually touching down. Meals and water would be kicked from the doorways of the moving birds, from just above the trees, and drop onto their positions, or at least close to them. They hoped the charade would be successful and keep the gooks guessing as to everyone's whereabouts.

The Wolfhounds only had four days remaining in the bush before returning to Cu Chi and going home. During that time, small patrols went out during the early morning hours and set up mechanical ambushes on surrounding trails and paths. At last count, First Platoon had managed to leave ten of the powerful booby traps 'live' and abandoned; locations of the departing gifts would be passed on through normal channels to the ARVN.

Alpha Company had been fortunate during the last several days. They did not have to fire a shot and nobody got hurt. Nevertheless, it was an unusually stressful period.

Their last night in the bush was the worst and everyone suffered equally. It was like a nightmare: sitting up in the pitch black darkness, wide awake, sweating profusely, hearing strange noises, minds reeling, and too afraid to move or close your eyes to sleep. The entire group was ready for the nuthouse before the night was even half over. Many of the men chose to lean against trees and watch the surrounding area. The Platoon operated on one-hundred percent alert, yet no one had ordered it.

They heard the explosions of three different mechanicals during the night. This made the men feel even more restless in knowing the gooks were on the prowl. Enemy intelligence was just as good as the Americans', so there was little doubt that the gooks were unaware of the Wolfhounds leaving in the morning. Some speculated that the gooks were moving into ambush positions around the many LZ's and would wait until the choppers landed during the next day to withdraw the troops. Then, the enemy would attempt to kill as many grunts as possible while they were in the open.

None of the grunts wanted to be the final casualty in the field; that night they had grenades within arm's reach and weapons sitting ready on their laps.

When the light of morning finally arrived, each man lay in the same position as the night before. The anxiety suffered by all during that fearful night was evident on their faces. However, it was still too early to celebrate and breathe a sigh of relief.

The soldiers packed and were ready to move out on a moment's notice. Still spooked, not one of them attempted to light heat tabs to warm anything to eat, lest the gooks smell it and come looking for the source. Instead, they sat quietly, glancing at each other and speaking with only their eyes. There was an occasional wink, just to show moral support.

At 0800, First Platoon had been cleared to move out toward their LZ; birds would arrive in thirty minutes. They only had to travel two-hundred meters, but it took the longest time for them to cover this short distance. Overly cautious, like Cherries on their first patrol, they arrived with only five minutes to spare.

Everyone became nervous during the withdrawal and prayed that an ambush didn't erupt at any second. As a precaution, the door gunners fired hundreds of rounds into the tree line on both their approach and when lifting off from the LZ; they didn't stop until the birds were safely away. If the gooks were in fact waiting in the bush, the tactic surely kept their heads down.

A loud cheer erupted from every chopper as they lifted off and headed toward Cu Chi. There was no return fire upon lift off, which was cause for celebration. For many, this was their last flight on a helicopter and Mother Nature gave them a present. The passing terrain had taken on an aura of shimmering, brilliant colors; some sparkled and winked in the glaring early morning sunlight and offered a beautiful, non-threatening vision of what a Pacific island paradise might look like.

That last airlift was uneventful and every soldier in the Company made it back to Cu Chi without injury. When exiting the chopper and clearing the rotor wash, the warriors all stopped and turned for a final look at their chariots. They heaved a deep sigh of relief and then came to attention and saluted the pilots. The grunts held them in high esteem as the pilots were always there for them in a time of need.

It was finally over! No more humping, ambushes, eating C-Rations, and having to carry the weight of another person on your back. Goodbye, Vietnam! Good riddance! And good luck!

However, they would soon discover that the war would not be over for everyone.

Chapter Twenty

In Cu Chi, the grunts found that some of the rumors they'd heard during the last two weeks were true, and others were way out in left field. Yes, it was true that the 25th Division was pulling out of Vietnam and returning to Hawaii, but not everyone would be invited to come along.

The official cutoff time was announced, and only those soldiers who had served nine months or more in country would be allowed to leave with the division. Some of the men would receive early discharges from the service and return home as a civilian; some would be given thirty days leave and transferred to a different stateside post; and the lucky ones would carry the division flags and relocate to Hawaii. Those not meeting the criteria would be transferred to other units within Vietnam, the same destiny Rod suffered when the First Cav went home. New orders were currently being processed and would be issued the following day for those soldiers not leaving Vietnam at this time.

Pollack, Sixpack, BJ, and many of the others in the First Platoon didn't have the necessary time in country and would continue fighting the war someplace else. Weapons, rucksacks, and all other issued military supplies must be accounted for and turned in to the supply depot. New equipment and weapons would be issued to those transferred men when they arrived at their next duty station.

Those men scheduled to leave Vietnam celebrated everywhere within the compound. The base PX had sold out all the beer and liquor, and all the clubs (Enlisted Men's Club, Non-Commissioned Officers Club and the Officer's Club) were packed to capacity. Those remaining in country were not in a partying mood and spent their time within the Battalion area. Most of the First Platoon sat around on cots within their specified quarters.

"This sucks! They wouldn't even let us keep a poncho liner to cover up with tonight."

"It is a bitch, but what are you gonna do, Pollack?"

"It's just like it was when we first arrived in country, Sarge. Only this time, we're not Cherries anymore. We've already danced with the devil and I for one don't really feel comfortable without my rifle."

"Don't lose any sleep over it. I think they're doing this more to protect us from ourselves. Can't you see somebody getting fucked up drunk tonight and because he's not going home, he figures that he has nothing to lose? So this particular person may want to get even with someone or shoot the officers for not letting them leave?"

"You've got a point, Sixpack. I'm not too happy that I have to stay here, but I heard there are some guys that missed the date by only a week and the officers won't let them go home."

"No shit? That is a hard one to swallow. They would probably be the ones to do what Sixpack just mentioned."

"Just keep your chin up, and we'll all find out where we're going to end up tomorrow."

"It would be nice if they kept us together. I've been getting used to you guys."

"Don't count on that happening, Ski. I think we'll all be scattered to the wind. It will be something very special if some of us get assigned to the same outfits. We'll just have to see. You guys do know that we have a formation tomorrow and the Colonel is going to talk to us?"

"Yeah we heard all about it, Sixpack."

"Good. There's also going to be some special parade and presentation. Then afterwards, we'll get our marching orders. This is going to happen very fast, so be prepared!"

After a short parade to ceremoniously retire the Battalion colors and pass on the baton to the ARVN, the Battalion Commander, Colonel Bill Morgan, walked to the podium and a quiet hush fell upon the crowd.

"Gentlemen, I'd like to thank you all personally for a job well done. I am so proud of each and every one of you and would like to take this opportunity to share a few things with you. First, I'd like to say that since March 1, 1968, the Wolfhounds had killed two-thousand one-hundred and sixty-five of the enemy and captured four hundred and eighty-five. Your extreme efforts made it possible to uncover several tons of munitions, firearms, and food staples in many caches throughout the jungle. You have dealt the enemy a terrible blow and severely restricted his attempts to force a Communist regime on the people of South Vietnam. Our campaigns last May and June in Cambodia were highly successful. We destroyed many of the enemy staging and supply areas, eliminated their sanctuaries, lessened their power with the people, and destroyed their morale. If not for these successes, the enemy would have been better supplied and more motivated, and could have been highly effective in missions against us. Unfortunately, we too have suffered high losses during the same period of time, but far fewer than those suffered by our enemy. At this time, I would like to ask for a moment of silence in remembrance of our fallen comrades, who have paid the ultimate price and had given their lives so that others may be free."

Heads bowed, and some men made a sign of the cross before saying a small prayer in their memory. After a brief moment of silence, he continued, "The Wolfhound organization is a proud and fierce fighting machine. I was exceptionally proud to have served with you in the First Battalion. Even though some of you are leaving for other units, remember in your heart that you'll always be a Wolfhound. As a remembrance of this service, I have a small token for each of you. I have here a scroll that is dedicated to all Wolfhounds. It briefly outlines your tour with the First Battalion. Please keep this remembrance and look back at it ten years from now. I guarantee that you'll get cold chills and feel proud all over again. For those of you going back to the states with the Division, brace yourself because stateside duty is nothing like this. You all remember that spit shined stuff, don't you?"

Snickers and war whoops arose from the crowd.

"And to those of you who are unfortunately staying behind, you'll receive your orders for reassignment immediately following this ceremony. Wolfhounds, I offer you all the luck in the world, and God's speed for a safe return home to your families. God bless you all. Gentlemen, I salute you." He raised his arm and held a salute to the men standing in groups before him.

The men quickly came to attention and returned the Colonel's salute. When he dropped his arm, Colonel Morgan turned and left the podium.

The crowd cheered wildly for a couple minutes, and then it was over. Upon leaving the area, clerks handed out the souvenir scrolls to each soldier walking by. Some unrolled the document and stopped to read it; however, most everyone else was in a hurry to return to their Company area to find out where they will be sent to next.

For those leaving with the Division, their orders read to report to their new duty station, Hawaii, after a thirty-day leave. They would begin out-processing tomorrow and leave the country before the end of the week. Those reassigned would start the out-processing immediately and leave for their new units in the morning.

Pollack opened his orders and after a moment of reading, he dropped the document onto his cot. "I'm fucked now!"

"How so, Pollack?"

He retrieved the document, reading it aloud, "It says here that I'm to report to my next duty station in Phu Bai, Republic of South Vietnam, where I will be assigned to the 101st Airborne Division."

"Where the fuck is Phu Bai?"

"My orders say the same thing."

"Me too!"

"Hey I'm going there too."

"Looks like a bunch of us are all going together," Ski confirmed after several other members in the First Platoon called out.

"What's so bad about the 101st?"

"Ski, ever since I've been in Nam, everything I've either heard or read in the military newspapers about the 101st is that they are always getting their asses kicked somewhere up north. It's also very mountainous there and very close to the border with North Vietnam (DMZ)."

"It can't be any worse than what we've been through," BJ added.

"No, guys, I think this is going to be a whole new world up there and the way of fighting is also going to be different."

"You may be a hundred percent correct about what you're saying Pollack, but until I get there and see for myself, I'm not going to get worked up over this. I still got eight months left and it'll just be like joining another new gang."

"I wish that I could look at things the way you do, Ski. It would make it all that much easier for me. But let's look on the bright side, with as many of us going to the same place, there is an excellent chance that some of us will stay together in the new units."

"Hey Malcolm, BJ, where are you guys going?"

"Some place called Chu Lai in the Central Highlands with the Americal Division."

"Me too," hollered Tex. "Where is Chu Lai?"

"In the Central Highlands."

"Where's that?"

"How the fuck do I know? Where's Phu Bai?"

"Up north."

"Up north where?"

"Somebody find a map of this fucking country so we can see where the fuck we're going!"

Sixpack walked into the tent and threw a rolled up map of Vietnam onto his cot. "Here's a map, knock yourselves out."

There was a mad scramble as everyone gathered around for the lesson in geography.

"Who's going up north to the 101st with me?" Sixpack –asked. A dozen hands raised into the air.

"All right! We're leaving for Bien Hoa Airport tomorrow morning at 0800 hours. And for those of you that don't know the date, tomorrow is Tuesday, March twenty-fourth."

"Sixpack, any idea where the L-T is going?"

"Not a clue, Pollack. I haven't seen him since we've arrived here in Cu Chi."

"Neither have I, isn't that strange?"

"Not really. Remember, we're back in the rear and he's probably lying around with the other officers and getting shit-faced with them at the Officer's Club."

"Yeah, you're probably right."

That night, First Platoon had a going-away party to celebrate the time they'd spent together – one last hurrah! Doc was the luckiest in the group as he was very close to being a civilian once again. The military had offered him an early out without having to remain in country any longer or to spend time at a stateside base. He was ecstatic and the men were all very happy for him.

Before things really got started and the beer cans opened, they began exchanging addresses, giving out those from back home. Later when the new in-country addresses were known, a letter could be sent to that home address and the family would forward the information in their next letter to the war zone.

In the morning, most of the men still felt the effects of the late night party. For them, it was difficult to walk, as the sun shone extremely bright and overbearing; some were on the verge of puking and they were about to endure a bumpy truck ride and then a flight in a cargo plane.

There were almost one-hundred soldiers from the Battalion reassigned to the 101st Airborne. Many friends accompanied them to the waiting area. Some of them would be leaving for home or other units themselves later in the day. The transportation, a caravan of four Deuce and a half trucks, turned the corner and stopped next to the group. Last goodbyes were said and hugs given all around before the soldiers climbed aboard the trucks and were soon whisked away.

Pollack opened his duffel bag to retrieve the souvenir scroll that he received from the Colonel and unrolled it. At the very top was the Wolfhound crest; raised gold wolfhound head profiled on a black background. The Latin words, 'Nec Aspera Terrent', roughly translated as, 'And They Fear No Hardship', were printed in gold below the head. A thin gold line framed the black and gold crest.

It read as follows:

KOLCHAK – KING OF ALL WOLFHOUNDS
GREETINGS

To all true Pups, wherever ye may be:
Know ye that from the hazardous environs on Cu Chi, across the Saigon River, from the perimeters of Fire Support Bases Lynch, Kien, Beverly, and Carol, come a staunch and true bearer of the crest, who has washed the jungles of the Ho Bo, the Boi Loi, the Michelin Rubber, the Iron Triangle and Cambodia with the sweat of righteous terror, dared the treacherous crossing of QL 1, bathed in the semi-solid waters of a monsoon-filled bomb crater and had,

through arduous practice, developed the gunship flinch to the satisfaction of his superiors.

Be it further known that since this gallant challenger of Hanoi's agrarian reformers and the Viet Cong local roustabouts has looked unblinkingly into the tunnel mouths of the enemy, known the ecstasy of being a sniper's target and the object of suppressive fires, has been duly initiated into the association of the air-lifted, ambushed, and smoke grenade asphyxiated and accepted into intimacy by the virtuous sisters.

Be it therefore proclaimed that
John Kowalski
Has been found worthy to be admitted to the
OMNIPOTENT ORDER OF KOLCHAK AS A REGAL
BARKER

Be it therefore ordered that all Wolfhound Warriors get all the honor and respect to which he is entitled.

Signed, with a paw print,
Kolchak V
King of all Wolfhounds

Pollack smiled broadly after reading through the scroll and found that he was pleasantly surprised by the contents. He didn't quite understand some words, but he got the General picture.

"Did any of you guys get to read what's in this scroll?" he asked those sitting nearby.

"Yeah, I did," replied a couple of soldiers sitting across from him. "It's pretty cool, isn't it?"

"Hell yes! I can relate to everything written and it's almost like a summary of everything I've done since being here."

Sixpack finished reading Pollack's scroll and handed it back to him. "I couldn't have summed it up any better myself. Nice keepsake."

"This is a treasure!" Pollack reverently returned it to his duffel for safekeeping, and couldn't wait to show his family and friends when he returned home.

Chapter Twenty-One

The replacement center in Phu Bai was on the verge of overcrowding. Soldiers, who unfortunately did not meet the minimum criteria of serving nine months in country and could not go home with their units, arrived from various locations. On top of that, new replacements were still arriving from the states; hundreds of Cherries came in on as many as three flights a day.

"None of this makes sense to me. Why are so many new guys still coming into the country when entire divisions are going home?"

"It's not for us to understand, Pollack. We're only supposed to follow orders and do what the brass and politicians want us to do."

"This is stupid! All those guys in the 25th had lots of experience and were battle hardened. If the politicians want to shorten the war, they should have come up here with us instead of sending in more Cherries."

"Let it go Pollack. It's something you don't need to worry about."

"He's right though, Sixpack. The President is telling the people back home that entire divisions are being withdrawn from Vietnam. I remember seeing the parades and ceremonies on TV back in Cu Chi. The media is showing all these guys leaving on jet planes, but they're not showing all the replacements that are coming in on those same planes."

"All that pacification shit they're talking about is bullshit too."

"There isn't anything that you can do about it. So just focus on staying alive and doing what you're told until it's time for you to go home too."

The entire American concentration of troops operated in the northern most part of the country. Since the First Cav and the 25th Division had pulled out of the war, the responsibility for securing much of the southern half of the country now rested in the hands of the ARVN. Only small units of Americans were actively involved in those areas surrounding Saigon. However, the northern half swarmed with Marines, the 101st Airborne, and the Americal Divisions.

The in-country transfers were only in Phu Bai for a couple of hours when they received new orders. Sixpack, Pollack, and a half dozen former Wolfhounds had been reassigned to the 1st Battalion, 501st Infantry Brigade, and would travel north to Camp Vandergrift in the morning.

The two men returned to the barracks where they had left their duffel bags earlier. Pollack reached in and pulled out a paperback book, then lay back against his duffel to read.

"Goddammit! Fucking sons of bitches!" Sixpack frantically searched through his duffel bag.

"What's wrong?" Pollack asked, concerned about his frustration.

"Some sorry, no good bastard stole my six-pack of brew!"

"Are you sure it's gone?"

"Yes, I'm sure. Somebody rifled through my shit and took it."

"So what's the big deal? Just go to the PX and buy some more."

"Pollack, it's not the same. I brought it over with me from the states. It's been my good luck charm since I've been here."

"Come on, Sarge, you're not superstitious are you?"

"No, I'm not superstitious! But look who's asking? Why in the fuck do you think you have that fifty-caliber bullet hanging from your neck on that chain?"

"Good luck, I guess. But this is different. I wear it all the time and made it back in Kien before going out into the bush on my first mission. I haven't taken it off my neck since. You never took your beer with you in the bush for protection."

"It's a good luck charm too, asshole, but I didn't have to carry it with me. How would you feel if somebody stole your necklace or if you lost it out in the bush?"

Pollack pondered this last question for only a second. "I'd be devastated. I'm sorry, Sixpack, I didn't realize..."

Sixpack interrupted, "Fuck it, don't mean nothin. Just forget about the whole thing."

"Is there anything I can do?"

"I told you to just forget it. I want to be left alone right now. Do you mind?"

"No, I'll go out and take a walk. I'll catch up with you later."

The next morning, forty soldiers left for Camp Vandergrift on a big Chinook helicopter.

Pollack sat near the rear of the bird and saw the surrounding countryside through the opened boarding ramp. The sight was pathetic! The valleys lay scorched and the ground pitted with bomb craters from hundreds of B-52 bombs. Huge mountains, covered with jungle, stretched to the north as far as one could see; they, too, had been scarred by the war. To the east, the South China Sea glistened, the blue-green color extended to the horizon. Their destination, Camp Vandergrift, was located several miles south of the DMZ and would take almost thirty minutes of flying to get there.

Pollack tensed as he suddenly thought that his new experiences were going to be far worse than anything he had ever encountered while fighting in the south.

He leaned to Sixpack and yelled above the loud noise of the vibrating aircraft, "Why do you think they need so many replacements up here?"

"Probably because they get their asses kicked all the time."

"That's not what I was hoping to hear."

"Oh well!"

"Geez thanks."

Pollack couldn't understand why Sixpack was taking out his frustrations on him. He wasn't to blame for the stolen beer and hoped that Sixpack's attitude changed soon.

Vandergrift was a large base camp similar to Cu Chi, but the similarities ended there. Vehicles bounced along muddy chuck-holed dirt roads throughout the camp. Long strips of metal planking, half buried in the mud, served as sidewalks. No beautiful buildings scattered about the base; instead, everything was underground and surrounded by sandbags. No green grass existed with 'Keep Off' signs posted. There were only craters filled with mud everywhere - reminders of the mortar barrages and 122mm rockets that routinely landed inside the compound. Parts of once-filled sandbags and burnt timber littered the muddy ground near bunkers that had been hit. Work crews were feverishly attending to them, filling sandbags and laying new timber so they could be used again. There was no PX, service club, swimming pool, or radio phones to call home in this base camp.

Every person walking around wore a bulletproof vest and carried a bandolier of ammo and a weapon with him. Looking around, Pollack felt that it would be unthinkable for them to lock weapons in the armory overnight. To survive here, they must be with you at all times.

Nothing else could have been more depressing. It was so completely different from how they'd lived or what they'd been accustomed to during the past months in Cu Chi or even the fire support bases. They could have thought they were standing on the moon right now if they didn't know any better.

The group was rushed over to the Battalion area so flak jackets, weapons, and ammo could be issued from supply. There seemed to be a lot of confusion in the area. The XO appeared overwhelmed with his current task, as if assigning replacements to a new Company was something he didn't have time to do right now. So, knowing that bunkers were always in need of repair, he assigned the entire group to this detail until he found the time to determine where they would go next. Sixpack was the highest-ranking NCO (Non-Commissioned Officer) in the group, so the XO quickly placed him in charge of the work detail and pointed to nearby bunkers that would require their attention.

The day went by without any changes or updates, and the mundane task of filling sandbags seemed never-ending.

Later that same night, the enemy fired several rockets into the perimeter during the span of an hour; they landed randomly and in no particular pattern. Everyone inside the bunkers awaited the next explosion and prayed that it didn't land on top of them. Mortar flares were repeatedly fired into the air and ignited above the compound; small attached parachutes allowed the flickering lights to float through the air and illuminate the terrain beyond the perimeter.

Those manning the perimeter were on one-hundred percent alert and watched to their front for enemy movement in the flickering light. Ground attacks were rare against larger bases, but as a precaution, the security around the perimeter had been doubled for the rest of the night.

At 0230 hours Medivac helicopters landed within the perimeter to evacuate the dead and wounded. Two bunkers had sustained direct hits and were completely destroyed; those inside never had a chance. Flying shrapnel also wounded several soldiers; some men got caught out in the open during the explosions or had been hit while inside a bunker and near the entrance.

Fires burned throughout the camp as timber and vehicles smoldered as a result of nearby explosions. Small groups of soldiers fought the fires with pails of water and shovels full of dirt and mud.

Bunker damage that rendered it unsafe was immediately addressed by those inside and neighbors nearby. Other damage that did not impact security or safety could be dealt with in the morning.

At 0500 hours, the gooks started firing mortars into the perimeter, walking them around indiscriminately. Once again, there was a mad dash for the bunkers as everyone dropped what they were doing. Heartbreaking, it left everyone helpless because all they could do is sit and wait for the barrage to end.

The mortar and artillery pits came alive, shooting flares into the sky and sending explosive rounds at suspected sites, where mortar flashes could be seen in the distance. Only they were fortunate enough and able to return fire - everyone else inside the perimeter, had to wait until a target had been acquired for them to shoot.

The barrage lasted over thirty minutes and stopped shortly before daybreak. It was a long, nerve-wracking night for everyone within the camp.

The next day, the entire camp busied itself repairing the damage from the night before. Some were lucky enough to catch up on missing sleep during the night before; others weren't so lucky and had to drag ass all day long.

After breakfast the following morning, Pollack ran into the XO. "Excuse me, sir, but have you got a minute?"
"What can I do for you, Specialist?"

"My nerves have had it, sir. The 25th Division was nothing like this. I've got almost nine months in country. Is there any way of getting a rear job in this division?"

"What's your MOS (Military Occupation Specialty), soldier?"

"11B40, sir."

"That's infantry, troop. Take it from me, you'll be better off in the field."

"If this is some kind of sign of what it's like out there, then I really don't think so."

"I do. Some companies in the boonies haven't been shot at in months. That's the safest place to be. If it was possible for me to be there, I'd leave on the next chopper."

"You're serious?"

"Take my word on it. I've got no reason to lie to you. Matter of fact, I envy you because you're going to the field."

"I believe you, sir. Any idea when we'll get sent to our outfits? My mother doesn't have my new address yet."

"I think most of you transferred guys will be leaving in a couple of days."

"Okay, thanks, sir."

"Anytime, soldier."

Pollack still had his reservations on whether to believe the XO or not and decided to seek out the re-enlistment bunker. After asking half-dozen guys who thought him to be crazy, he eventually found it.

He stepped down into the bunker to find a First Sergeant going over some paperwork at his desk.

"Have a seat. I'll be with you in a minute," he said without looking up.

Pollack sat on a wooden folding chair and waited for his eyes to adjust to the dimness inside. A large crash in the corner caused him to jump up and fumble with his rifle.

"Easy, son. I didn't mean to startle you," the First Sergeant said. "I wasn't thinking when I threw my helmet at the rat."

"Pardon me?"

"The rat. You know what a rat is, don't you?"

"Yeah," he answered, still unsure as to what to do next.

"Well these fucking rats have a tunnel complex under this place. You don't know where they'll turn up next. When you're lucky enough to spot one, you just throw the first thing you can lay your hands on. It's not bad during the day, but it's a real terror at night. They climb in bed with you, looking for food."

"That's odd. I've been here two days and haven't seen one yet."

"You're lucky. You must be in one of the newer bunkers."

"Yeah, I am."

"Well, you'll see them soon enough. Just prepare yourself. Now, what can I do for you?"

"I'd like some information about re-enlisting."

"Okay. What information can I give you?"

"Can I pick any job in the Army when I re-enlist?"

"It all depends if you're qualified or not."

"How about for a clerk typist position? In high school, I had two years of typing and finished the course typing fifty-six words a minute."

"That sure makes you qualified enough, but why in the hell would you want to re-enlist as a clerk typist?"

"Top, I was stationed with the 25th Division down south and got transferred here just this week. I've been in Nam for eight and a half months, but didn't have enough time in country to go home with the division. Since being in country, we've always heard that the 101st was losing a lot of men in all the fighting that takes place up here. I'm really scared and don't want to get killed after all I've been through already. I'll do anything to get out of the field."

"I can't say that your reason isn't justified, but I don't think re-enlistment is the answer. Have you really thought things through?"

"What do you mean?"

"First let me ask you something. Did you originally enlist in the Army, or were you drafted?"

"I was drafted."

"Are you looking forward to getting out of the service when your two years are up?"

"I was."

"You do know that if you re-enlist, you'll have to give up another four years of your life to Uncle Sam."

"I know, but I guess it'll be worth it, just so I don't have to go out in the bush again."

"Now that's the wrong answer, troop. I wouldn't recommend re-enlistment to anyone unless he planned to make a career out of the Army."

"You mean you won't let me?"

"I didn't say that. I just said that I wouldn't recommend it. In your case, I think if you re-enlist, you'll come to regret it. I know there's been a lot of fighting up here and a lot of good men have lost their lives, but it's no different here than it was down south. I think I can help solve your problem. Let me ask you another question. When you first came to Vietnam, were you as frightened as you are now?"

"I don't know. Yeah, I guess so. But it was only because of not knowing what to expect."

"Don't you think you're in that same position now?"

"I'm not sure," he answered after some hesitation.

"Okay. Now just think for a minute. If you would have re-enlisted when you first came into the country, would you have regretted it today?"

"I probably would have. It wasn't all that bad down there. Our base camps were considered the most secure in the country. Companies would come into them for some R&R periodically without having anything to worry about. We never had our bases rocketed and mortared like up here."

"Then why do you want to re-enlist to get a job in a base camp up here?"

"I don't know."

"Look, son. Let me give you some statistics. Almost seventy-five percent of all the casualties up here occur in the rear areas because of the rockets and mortars. There are some ground pounders in the bush that haven't fired a weapon in three months. Would you believe it if I told you that some of the rear echelon troops want to re-up just to get into the infantry and to get away from these base camps? They're just as afraid of dying as you are and will do anything to find a more secure job in this war. So you see, you're better off to stay right where you are."

"You aren't trying to bullshit me are you, Top?"

"I've got no reason to bullshit you. There's nothing in it for me by trying to keep you in the infantry. Now that we've had a chance to talk, I would like you to think about our discussion before you consider re-enlisting. Take all the time you need because it'll be a very important decision that could affect your future. Go out into the field, spend some time there, and see just what it's really like. Then if you still want to re-enlist, I'll be more than happy to accommodate you."

"Okay, Top, that seems fair. You've changed my mind for now. Thanks for your time."

"That's quite all right. Good luck and take care, soldier."

"I'll do my best."

Pollack turned to leave the bunker when Top called out, "Next time you come in here, be sure it's what you really want. I won't try to change your mind then."

"Fair enough, Top, thanks for the break."

"Airborne!" he called out enthusiastically.

"All the way," Pollack said smartly, replying with the correct formal response. Pollack smiled, and finally walked out of the bunker.

Outside, he noticed that many of the soldiers moving about wore jump wing patches on their camouflage jackets. That signified their qualification to jump from airplanes with parachutes; they were a gung-ho bunch. He wondered if they actually jumped from planes up there, since it was an Airborne unit. He looked forward to seeing what the conditions were like out in the field. Would he have to get rid of the hammock?

The new arrivals had finally been assigned to new companies, and as by fate, Pollack and Sixpack stayed together; both assigned to Alpha Company, First Platoon.

After lunch, Pollack, Sixpack, and a dozen other soldiers – two being former Wolfhounds – boarded a Deuce and a Half, and prepared to leave Camp Vandergrift on a rough ride to the Battalion Fire Support Base Carroll. There, they would pull bunker guard until called to leave for the field.

FSB Carroll was roughly five miles northeast of their current location but just the ride out of Vandergrift to the main highway alone was enough to scramble brains. The truck hit every possible pothole in the dirt road, some of the passengers thought it was on purpose. They traveled less than five miles per hour, yet the occupants bounced around the troop transport from one side to the other, bruising their bodies on the side rails and floors. Prior to departing, they were advised to firmly secure their steel helmets onto their heads to prevent injury; it was actually a precaution for not bashing in their skulls. A bystander seeing these soldiers in the back of the truck as it moved by would think that a rugby practice session was taking place on board. It was almost comical and they were lucky nobody got thrown from the vehicle. If they were offered a choice, they would have all opted to walk to the main road instead.

Once the big truck reached the paved two-lane highway, the ride became slightly bumpy but bearable; however, it only lasted a few minutes before they were stopped. Up ahead, a minesweeping team checked the road for mines that may have been placed during the night. It took two and a half hours to reach the firebase.

Fire Support Base Carroll was a small, well-fortified position on the top of a small knoll overlooking the paved highway. Seventeen bunkers were on the perimeter and many more small fighting positions could be seen in between them.

The firebase housed a battery of 105mm artillery guns, two 81mm mortar pits, and a small helipad to accommodate a Loach helicopter. One-hundred defenders supported this firebase, and adding to the total would crowd the positions. The new arrivals were directed to the Commo bunker, which also doubled as the Battalion orderly room, where a First Sergeant was expecting them. He was already standing outside patiently waiting for them to arrive. A large and muscular man with a square jaw and an intimidating look, some might say he looked very much like Sgt. Rock in the comic books.

"Gentlemen, welcome to Alpha Company. I'm First Sergeant Trombley. As you gentlemen are all in-country transfers, I don't really have to tell you what it's like in this country. I do have a small speech to make, however, so bear with me. You are now part of the 101st Airborne Division, the most highly decorated and the fiercest fighting unit in this country. I can see that none of you are Airborne qualified and you may not know how we operate in the bush, so forget everything you did in your former units. Our methods might seem strange at first, but you'll catch onto them in due time. When in the bush, I expect you to perform your duties without hesitation and to conduct yourselves in a manner befitting this unit. We will not tolerate cowards or malingers here. You are now in an Airborne unit and expected to play the role by our rules. Are there any questions?"

"Just one," Pollack said meekly and raised his hand.

"What is it, soldier? Speak up," he scowled.

"When are we going out to the bush?"

"In two days. You'll be issued a ruck and other supplies as soon as I'm done with the orientation. While you are here, you will remain on ready alert at all times."

"What do you mean by ready alert?" someone else asked.

"After you get your supplies, check the bunkers and foxholes around the perimeter. Some are six-man positions and others are four-man. Find a vacancy and move in. Your gear should be ready at all times so you can move out in a moment's notice. Guard duty will be your only responsibility during the next two days. There should be at least two men in each position that are awake and on guard at all times, and that means around the clock. Did that answer your question?"

"It sure did," the unidentified soldier answered.

"Are there any more questions?" He looked them over and gave the impression that would pounce on the next person to open his mouth. There were no further questions.

"In that case, follow me to the supply bunker."

With new supplies in hand, Sixpack and Pollack walked around the perimeter until they found a bunker that appeared empty. They walked in and found three guys huddled in a corner smoking weed. Their entrance didn't surprise the men, and they made no attempt to hide what they were doing.

"Wow, man, check this out," one of the three managed to say. He pointed toward the opening and straining to see through the blue haze, probably thinking Pollack and Sixpack had just materialized from thin air.

"Yeah, far out. Peace, brother," a second man said, then makes a feeble attempt to raise his arm to flash a peace sign.

"What in the fuck are you guys doing?" Sixpack took a step closer to the three men.

"Toking on some weed, man. You want a hit? There's plenty to go around."

"Fuck no, I don't want a hit." Sixpack looked to Pollack, "These fuckers are so far gone they don't even know where they're at."

"Man, who cares?"

"I care. I'm not staying in a bunker full of potheads."

"We're not potheads. We're just peace-loving people."

"Fuck you all!" Sixpack backed up to the bunker entrance. "Come on, Pollack!"

"Pollack? What the fuck is a Pollack?" The three men laughed hard; one lost his balance and fell into onto the other two. All three buckled to the ground together like bowling pins, still laughing.

Pollack stood and watched in disbelief. "These guys are supposed to be on guard duty protecting the camp. They're so stoned that if a ground attack happened right now, they would probably just laugh at the gooks."

"Ground attack? Where do you think we are, man? In Vietnam someplace?" More laughter erupts.

Pollack turned and walked to the doorway. "I'm coming, Sixpack!"

"Shit, dudes, they got beer. Don't go, man!"

"We've got to find a bunker that's far away from these shitheads." They both exited and continued searching for new living quarters. They had walked clear around to the other side of the perimeter before finding another bunker that looked as if it might have some extra room inside.

They poked their heads through the entrance first to see who might be inside before making a move to enter. Four soldiers were inside; two played a game of checkers on a small crate, one was writing letters, and the fourth was cleaning his weapon and looking out at the highway to their front.

"Is there any room in here for two more?" Sixpack asked.

"Why, hell yes, Sarge, come on in. The more, the merrier."

They entered what would become their new home for the next two days and stowed their gear in a corner.

"I'm Larry Holmes, they call me Sixpack. My friend here is John Kowalski, better known as the Pollack." They shook hands all around and the new bunker mates introduced themselves.

The two checker players were Dan and Bill, Peter wrote letters, and Albert was on guard duty. All four were short-timers and were leaving for Phu Bai in three days to process out of the country and go home.

They sat together to shoot the shit for the next few hours. Pollack and Sixpack exchanged stories with the foursome, hoping to learn as much as possible about the conditions out in the field and the type of operations they conducted. The foursome was surprised by all the shit the two new arrivals had been through with the 25th. It was nothing like that up here, and had been very quiet in the bush ever since leaving the A Shau Valley some four months ago. In fact, their weapons were spotless, but the foursome admitted they weren't even sure if the rifles would even fire; it's been that long! They informed the two newcomers that the hardest thing they'd have to endure was the never ending humping up and down the mountains.

During the sharing of information, Pollack's ears perked up when his new hosts talked about a soldier nicknamed Professor. He carried a radio in the Company CP and was also going home in a week. His departure would create a vacancy, one that Pollack very much coveted. He would check into it first thing in the morning.

After breakfast, Pollack walked over to the communications bunker and found the First Sergeant there.

"Excuse me, Top, got a minute?"

"What's on your mind, troop?"

"I heard there's a guy in the Company CP nicknamed Professor, who will be going home in a few days. What's the chance of my taking his place when he comes out of the field?"

"You know how to operate a radio?"

"I do, and think I'm pretty good at it. I carried one in the 25th for two months."

Top thought about it for a few seconds. "I'll tell you what, how about I give you a small test?"

"I don't care, what do you have in mind?"

"Report back here at 1800 hours. I'll let you work one of the radios tonight. If you can convince me that you're as good as you say, then I'll talk to the Captain about it."

"It's a deal. I'll see you later."

He was very excited and anxious to tell Sixpack the good news. His friend was happy for him, but seemed disappointed that they wouldn't be together out in the field.

Pollack stood outside of the communications bunker and smoked a couple cigarettes during the next ten minutes. He wanted to walk into the bunker precisely at 1800 to show Top that he was both dependable and punctual.

Top asked him to monitor the Company frequency on the radio, and warned him that the various groups would be calling in their NDP locations shortly; the coordinates would need to be decoded and then plotted on a hanging wall map. The First Sergeant expected him to handle anything that might come up on the net, emergency or not.

During the night, Pollack had to contact the various units in the field for situation reports every hour. This was going to be a piece of cake as he'd already done it hundreds of times.

The First Sergeant relieved him at 0600. Pollack's eyes were bloodshot and burning from the twelve-hour shift. His relief noted all the unit locations plotted neatly on the wall map, and he was delighted when Pollack handed him a log that he had maintained during the night. It listed every call made, the time of the call, the call sign, and reason for the call. Anything out of the ordinary had been identified with an asterisk.

He also noted that the immediate area on that side of the bunker had been policed. Everything was squared away and the floor had been swept clean of mud and cigarette butts.

Top was impressed with his organizational skills and performance. "You did good, son. You do know that nobody here wants to carry a radio because of the excess weight in the mountains? Are you sure you still want to do this?"

"I am."

"Okay. I won't promise you anything, but I'll talk to the Captain the first chance I get."

"I'd appreciate that, Top."

"That's quite all right. Why don't you go and catch some sleep. You look like the walking dead. I'll come and find you when I've talked to the Captain."

"Thank you, Top." Pollack left and walked to his bunker, which wasn't too far away. In retrospect, it was quite a battle to stay awake during the night with nothing else to do but listen to the radio. The opportunity to clean and organize helped pass the time, and it would be the only chance to show his mettle.

Pollack returned to his bunker and tried to get some sleep. He was overly tired and anxious to hear back from Top about the opportunity. He had a restless morning, tossing and turning, his mind in overdrive and unable to think about anything else except carrying the radio again. He was also worried and wondered what he would to do if the Captain refused to grant his request.

Before nightfall, word was passed to the Alpha Company replacements that the Company would be airlifted into Phu Bai in the morning for three days of R&R. They were to catch a ride on the morning convoy and join up with the Company there. This will be an ideal opportunity for everyone to get to know one another before heading back into the bush on their next mission.

All the new recruits were excited. Phu Bai would be a welcome relief where they would not have to worry about staying up all night and filling sandbags during the day. They would all be able to relax and have an opportunity to fit in as one of the 'new guys' before leaving for the bush.

The convoy arrived four hours before the Company was due to land, and Top greeted them at the R&R center. The new arrivals immediately got to work helping erect tents, readying charcoal in the many barbecues, and filling trashcans with soda and beer. Ice would be added thirty minutes before their arrival. They would also help to barbecue the steaks and pass out ice-cold drinks to the arriving warriors. They had worked very hard and had everything ready for the arrivals.

Pollack got his first look at the Captain when they stood face-to-face in the chow line. The Officer reached in with a paper plate and waited for Pollack to transfer a barbecued steak from the grill. For some reason, Pollack thought his appearance resembled that of a professor. He was much older than expected, his clothes oversized, large rimmed glasses with bifocals hung from a lanyard around his neck, and his green boony hat looked more like something you might wear on a fishing trip. His tightly clamped teeth held a Sherlock Holmes style pipe in place; the puffs of smoke dissipated into the air and smelled of cherry. Standing at six-foot, six-inches tall, he towered over the rest of the troops. With a kind and understanding look upon his face, he appeared more like everyone's father instead of an Army Airborne Captain.

"Thank you, troop," he responded after receiving his steak from Pollack.

"No problem, sir!" The Captain moved ahead to the next serving station. More excited than ever, Pollack looked forward to hearing back from the First Sergeant.

After dinner had been served, the new replacements were allowed to intermingle with the rest of the Company. No stories of firefights or seeing the enemy out in the field were shared. Gripes and bitching about the extremely steep slopes of the mountains they had humped during this last mission was basically the only thing overheard. Some related their personal experiences about seeing a fellow soldier slide or topple down the mountainside, taking all in his path along for a ride. The story evoked laughter from those nearby. Others complained about the length of time it took to go up and down the high mountains - sometimes as long three days each way. As a result, many nights were spent on the steep slopes; nobody could sleep because they fought gravity all night long.

Pollack stood alone, looking for somebody he might know from his earlier days in training. With what he'd heard so far, it seemed that everything the First Sergeant had said about re-enlisting was true. Suddenly, he felt a hand grip his shoulder.

"This is the young man I was telling you about." Pollack turned to see Top and the Captain standing behind him.

"Top tells me you're campaigning to be my new RTO. Is this true?"

"Yes, sir." Pollack had to look up six inches to see into the man's eyes.

"You know this is not an easy job."

"I know that, sir, but I can guarantee you'll be pleased."

"You got your mind made up then?"

"Yes, sir, if you'll have me."

The First Sergeant and the Captain looked to one another and smiled. "Alright, you got the job. What's your name, son?"

He smiled proudly, "Specialist Fourth Class John Kowalski, sir."

"Have you got a nickname?"

"Everybody's been calling me Pollack since Basic Training."

"That's kind of degrading, isn't it?"

"I don't mind it, sir. It sure sounds better than Ski."

"Okay, Pollack it is. Glad to have you aboard." He extended his arm and the two shook hands. "I'm Captain Robertson. I might have some nicknames floating around the Company, but you can just call me Cap."

"Thank you for the opportunity, Cap."

"I'm sure you'll do very well. Top will get you squared away later with a new radio and gear. Then you can meet the rest of the members in the CP. Right now, try to enjoy yourself. I don't know when we'll ever make it back here again. See you soon!"

"Okay, Cap."

He was so excited about the decision that he felt like jumping into the air. He scanned the area looking for Sixpack to tell him the good news. Unable to find him in the large open field, he walked back to the tent area and found the Sergeant was deeply involved conversing with members of his new Squad. He stopped momentarily and stepped away when seeing Pollack approach.

"Sixpack, the Captain accepted me into the CP!"

"That's really great, Pollack. I'm happy for you!"

"You going to the CP?" one of Squad members asked.

"Yep," he replied proudly.

"Man, they're just a bunch of lazy motherfuckers. Why would you want to get in with them?"

"I carried a radio for the Platoon L-T when humping the bush with Sixpack. It was great knowing what was going on around me. Now stepping up into the CP is like being promoted."

"Yeah, we understand. It's a way for you to sit on your ass and not have to go out on patrols with the rest of us."

"Stow it, Joe," Sixpack cautioned. "Pollack has seen his share of shit and probably more than any of you sitting here. He's walked point for months, carried the M-60 machine gun and a radio before our division left for home. There is nobody up here that I'd rather have at my side. He knows his shit and will take good care of us in the CP. So lay off!"

"Thanks, Sixpack," Pollack said, relieved to see his friend so supportive. He snuck a glance at the nearby soldiers; the lecture seemed to appease them and they watched him with some interest.

"That's okay, kid. Keep in touch!"

"Sorry, man," Joe put out his hand. "Welcome to the Screaming Eagles!"

"Yeah, good luck!"

"Keep an eye on them guys and don't let them get over on you. They're a sneaky bunch!"

"Thanks guys! Good luck to you too!" Pollack said and then walked away and out of the tent.

It was no different there than it was down south as each segment of the Company, from Squad size and up, kept to itself. To locate the CP, Pollack peered into each tent as he passed, hoping to spot a group of radios and their handlers. Instead, he bumped into Top, who led him to a bunker near the orderly room.

Once inside, it was clear the group had special privileges in Phu Bai. Each man had a cot, complete with a pillow and mattress, positioned along two of the sandbagged walls, and a thirty-gallon can half-filled with ice-cold pop and beer. It stood sweating just inside the doorway. An oscillating fan in the far corner circulated the stagnant air through the bunker and made it feel somewhat comfortable inside. A worktable and bench had been positioned against the right wall; four radios sat atop and a spotlight overhead provided enough illumination to light the entire living area. Compared to the rest of the Company accommodations, it was a five-star establishment. Four soldiers sat around, all doing something different. Top got their attention as soon as the two men walked through the doorway.

"Gentlemen, let me introduce you to the Professor's replacement. This is John, uhmm, what's your last name?"

"Kowalski."

"Aw, shit. Just call him Pollack," Top said with a smile.

"This here is the Professor." A tall, gangly guy with thick glasses and jet-black hair lay on his cot, deeply involved in a book. He dropped it quickly and reached up to warmly shake hands.

"Sorry I won't be able to go out with you and show you the ropes," Professor said sarcastically. "But I will share everything I know with you during the next couple of days here."

"What more can I ask for? Thanks, Professor. Good to meet you."

"Next, we have Cotton Top." The First Sergeant pointed to a soldier who didn't look a day older than fifteen. He sat on one of the bunks and had been writing letters. His short, nubby haircut and light blond hair must have accounted for his nickname.

"Glad to meet you," he replied in a boyish voice, waving in acknowledgement.

Pollack nodded his head and returned the wave.

"This old bastard is Fuzzy." At the other extreme, that soldier looked to be at least fifty years old. "He is attached to the Company CP, but is an artillery forward observer by trade. Fuzzy is their liaison in the field and coordinates the artillery fire missions and also directs the fast movers when they support us. He doesn't carry a radio but helps out with the monitoring whenever he can."

Fuzzy offered an informal salute and went back to reading his book.

"And last, but not least, we have Stud."

A well-built and muscular soldier got up and strongly shook Pollack's hand.

"One word of caution before I leave," he looked at Pollack with a smirk, "Don't ask Stud why he's called that unless you have a couple of hours to listen."

"Well, since you brought it up."

Top cut him off abruptly. "Never mind, I've heard this story before. I'll leave you guys to get acquainted and see you later." Top strutted out of the bunker leaving the five men to themselves.

The beer flowed nonstop, and with never-ending discussions, the party turned into an all-night affair.

Before the night ended, Pollack knew more about his new partners than he had thought possible, especially Stud. Each of them had at one time carried a radio in one of the rifle Platoons and volunteered for the CP when the openings came up. They were all short-timers with less than four months left in their tour.

The next day, a rumor surfaced that upset most everyone in the Company. They heard that after the stand-down, they would be running patrols through a portion of the A Shau Valley. It had been four months since last humping through the valley, and then, Alpha Company lost almost a third of their men during a month-long period of time. The valley was a notoriously vicious area; Bastogne overlooked it from the east and several other firebases like Birmingham, Currahee, and Blaze, bordered on the west. A Sister Battalion fought a major battle the previous year on a hill that was later nicknamed 'Hamburger Hill'. Many men lost their lives during that battle; it too, was located in the Valley.

Later in the day, the rumor was confirmed true. As the depressing news spread, the partying came to an end as if somebody suddenly flicked off a light switch. Instead, many of the soldiers began to prepare for the upcoming mission, even when they still had an extra day left of R&R.

Alpha Company already drew out supplies for the mission; each man requested additional field dressings for their potential wounds, and without a doubt, extra ammunition that would be needed. One by one, they visited the firing range and test fired their weapons to ensure they were in proper working order.

Each man readied himself mentally and physically for the big fight that they knew approached. It did no good to worry about it; they had to just hope for the best. Pollack knew all too well how they felt; he'd felt the same way before heading into the Iron Triangle and the area where Zeke had been killed. He didn't have first hand knowledge regarding the valley, but had a deep respect for the opinions of those who had been there.

Chapter Twenty-Two

A quiet hush fell amongst the grunts as they boarded the choppers for their ride into the A Shau Valley. Only a handful of soldiers were veterans of the last campaign, they were focused and ready to face the devil. The other soldiers were naïve as to its dangers, but nevertheless, felt extremely nervous, because of all the stories they'd heard in the last day and a half.

It had been two weeks since Pollack and Sixpack had last carried a rucksack. The day before, neither of them had expected the total weight to be any different than what they had been used to carrying down south, so they anticipated an adjustment period of only a day or two after getting a feel for humping in the mountains. Both found their assessment to be way off base, mentally cussing out the brass and everyone they passed walking toward the helipad.

SOP (standard operating procedure) for the Airborne infantry specified that each trooper carry four days of rations instead of three, and six canteens of water instead of two, due to a lack of water in the mountains. Thousands of bomb craters existed in the bush, but without rain, only a thin layer of muddy slime existed on the bottom. The monsoon season was still a few weeks away for the northern part of Vietnam. When it arrived, it would take at least two weeks of heavy rain to fill them, and another week afterwards for the sludge to filter to the bottom. Only then would there be enough water available and fewer canteens needed.

A fifteen-pound flak jacket and steel helmet became part of the new wardrobe and added to the total weight. The metallic lined vest did not cover the entire shoulder and did not provide a suitable cushion for the ruck straps, which made it more difficult to carry. The grunts tried to utilize the little cushion available to support the straps, but when the ruck shifted, the straps fell off and dug into the edges of their shoulders. In the bush, members of the 25th always wore a boony hat in place of the unpopular steel helmet, which caused headaches and stiff necks. In the Airborne, a helmet must be worn and also be strapped tightly under the chin at all times. On top of all that, Pollack had to carry the radio and spare batteries; all combined weighing about eighty pounds. It was difficult enough to just try staying balanced on flat ground, let alone humping on the slope of a mountain. This would be a whole new adventure for the new arrivals!

Each of the four Platoons would be inserted onto different hilltops overlooking the valley, and would then work their way down to link up on the valley floor on the following day. The Company CP would be attached to the Third Platoon for the first three days of the mission.

Pollack hadn't been in the air for more than five minutes but he was already shivering and soaked with sweat. The cool, rushing air battered his sweaty body, causing his muscles to cramp and spasm. He tried hard to clear his mind and to think of something more pleasant that would help control his fear and nervousness. He rubbed at his legs vigorously in an attempt to stop the spasms.

The first sortie for the Third Platoon had successfully inserted half of their troops onto the LZ without incident. They had secured the hilltop, awaiting the rest of the Platoon and the Company CP to land in the next flight. Pollack listened to the radio, keeping the Captain informed of the landings and their reported status. So far, all had been routine with no sign of the enemy.

Looking out of the doorway, Pollack saw the approaching landing zone on the top of a hill. From this distance, it looked like the top of a friar or monk's head, bald in the middle, with thick, bushy hair surrounding it. It was only large enough to accommodate one chopper at a time, but each of the pilots had performed that kind of insertion more times than they could remember. The four choppers flew in a straight line, spaced far apart and stacked at different altitudes. The timing of each landing was executed perfectly; each bird was on the ground for no more than ten seconds to allow the passengers to jump out and move away. Airborne and almost vertical in the lift off, it just cleared the LZ when the next helicopter landed. None of them stopped to hover and wait their turn to land; they continued to maintain the same cruising speed until the final approach. With enough choppers in a flight, the choreographed landing process placed sixty soldiers on the ground in a little over a minute. It was a sight to behold.

Upon landing, the five members of the CP were escorted to a corner of the LZ. Pollack started calling the other Platoons to establish contact with them; Cotton Top got on the Battalion radio to relay information to the officers at Camp Vandergrift; Stud and Fuzzy spoke to the artillery groups at the firebase and sent pre-determined coordinates of reference locations that could be quickly called up when needed. They would refer to them as target A, B, C, and so on.

The plan was to send out small five-man recon teams from each Platoon to check the immediate area and to see if they could locate a safe route down the mountainside. Once that had been established, each Platoon would start their descent until it became necessary to stop for the night.

It was very difficult to determine just how many times the LZ had been used in the past. Beyond the clear landing zone, paths led into the surrounding vegetation from every direction. Small sleeping areas had been hacked out and cleared to the sides of the paths; each had a foxhole dug into the ground just a few feet away.

These areas were filthy and looked like a county municipal park after an all-day picnic. The ground was littered with empty C-Ration cans, cardboard boxes, plastic utensils, and even a few crumpled letters from home. Much of it lay inside the foxholes, but the surrounding bushes also looked like trash-covered Christmas trees with wind-blown debris trapped within the branches and foliage. It was an absolute mess and nobody dared to touch anything for fear of it being booby-trapped.

The sound of gunfire to the west of Third Platoon's location suddenly shattered the serenity. Green tracers ricocheted from the mountainside and rose high into the air. The intensity increased as red tracer rounds joined the green ones in a macabre dance across the skies. A new, deep base staccato sound also erupted from the same location and kept pace with everyone's racing heart beat. Some of the soldiers in the Platoon shifted about nervously and showed cause for alarm.

"Eagle-one, this is Eagle-six, over," Pollack heard from his handset.

"This is Eagle-one, go ahead," he responded.

"Roger. Any idea what's going on? That shooting is awfully close to us."

"That's a negative, Eagle-Six. Ram-four is checking on it now. I'll let you know the minute I hear something."

"Wilco, Eagle-six, out."

Cotton Top was Ram-Four and his ear had been glued to the handset of the Battalion radio ever since the firefight began. He took notes on a pad and collected whatever information he could from the discussions going back and forth between the unit in contact and Battalion HQ. When he knew enough, Cotton Top broke away and provided an update to the others before quickly returning the receiver to his ear.

"Charlie Company ran into a fortified position with a heavy 51-caliber machine gun. They're pinned down and requesting air support. Don't know how many casualties yet but they're calling for Medivacs too."

"Pollack, get on the horn and notify all the Platoons to bring their recon patrols back to base and sit tight," Cap ordered and then moved closer to Cotton Top, listening in on the net with him.

As Pollack relayed the information across the Company net, those nearby stopped their chatter and quieted down so as not to miss out on anything said.

The sound of Charlie Company's firefight continued in the distance, when suddenly, an explosion was heard on the near ridge of the next hill, where the First Platoon had landed earlier.

"Pollack, call the First Platoon and find out what that was," Cap said, concerned and looking anxiously between the two radio operators to take it all in.

"Eagle-niner, this is Eagle-one, over."

"Ah, this is Eagle-niner, go ahead," a nervous voice responded.

"Roger, Eagle-niner, what was that explosion near your position, over?"

"Don't know yet, Eagle-one. I think our recon patrol hit something on the way back in. We're checking it out now. Let you know when we know something, over."

"Roger. Eagle-one, standing by."

There was a lot of fidgeting around on the hilltop. The soldiers had already felt edgy about the nearby firefight, and when it became evident that the explosions were getting closer, they were naturally anxious to know what was going on. When the recon Squad returned to Third Platoon's hilltop, their faces exhibited a deep concern after they were briefed.

"Eagle-one, this is Eagle-niner, over."

"Finally," Pollack grabbed the headset and depressed the squelch button, "Go ahead, Eagle-niner."

"Roger, Eagle-one. Recon patrol hit a booby trap just before they got the word to stop and turn back. We need a Medivac for the wounded, over."

"Wilco, Eagle-niner. How do you classify the wounded?"

"We've got two KIA, one urgent, and one priority."

"Roger. Stand by."

Pollack updated the CP and requested the Medivac. Cotton Top immediately informed Battalion of the situation while Stud and Fuzzy dialed up the Medivac frequency to make the call for help; coordinates and priorities were relayed quickly over the net.

"Inform the First Platoon that birds will be there in about five minutes," Stud called out.

"Eagle-niner, ETA of Medivac is zero-five. Do you copy?"

"Roger. ETA zero-five. Eagle-niner, standing by."

Several explosions and intermittent 'brrrrrr' sounds, lasting for several seconds each, suddenly drowned out Charlie Company's gunfire.

Cobra gunships had joined Charlie Company's fight and were in the process of firing rockets and mini-guns into the enemy's fortified positions. They could be seen in the distance, circling slowly above the pinned-down Americans, and then diving into the fracas like mad hornets. Green tracers rose from the ground and tried to follow the diving aircraft during its attack. White puffs of smoke erupted when the Cobra fired multiple rockets, before a solid line of red materialized from the front of the helicopter, extending to the ground. It stopped as suddenly as it started when the aircraft completed its diving attack. The Cobra climbed back into the sky and would join the other circling gunships until it was their turn for another run at the enemy. From the distance, it looked like the gunships were diving directly into the enemy fire. None appeared to be hit, and it must be assumed that either the gooks fired with their heads down and did not aim, or that the Pilots were doing a hell of a job in avoiding the flying lead.

The effective gunships allowed Charlie Company to withdraw their dead and wounded to an area where they could be Medivaced from the fight.

As Pollack monitored the radio and watched the distant battle, First Platoon's Medivac came onto the Company net and requested that smoke be popped to identify their location. Several seconds later, a thread of green smoke snaked out of the jungle to the side of the hilltop and rose into the air not more than five-hundred meters away. The evacuation was over and the wounded en route to the hospital within a couple of minutes.

"Eagle-one, this is Eagle-niner, over."

"Go ahead, Eagle-niner."

"Dust-off complete. Eagle-niner actual is requesting permission to move to a different location."

"Eagle-one, wait one."

Pollack passed on the request to Cap, who quickly pulled out his map and began to study it. "Tell them that I'll get back to them within a few minutes. Meanwhile, ask them for the nicknames of their casualties and how bad they were hurt."

"Eagle-niner, Eagle-one actual wants the nicknames of your casualties and the extent of their injuries."

"Roger Eagle-one, wait one." Pollack had his pad and pencil ready to record the information. "Eagle-one, this is Eagle-niner, are you ready to copy?

"Affirmative, Eagle-niner, go ahead."

"The two KIA are Baker and Mr. Flowers. Beanpole has upper body wounds with a sucking chest wound, and Sixpack suffered a traumatic amputation of both legs, just below the knees."

Pollack's heart skipped a beat and hoped there was another Sixpack in the First Platoon.

"Eagle-niner, is this Sixpack the same hard striper that just arrived?"

"That's affirmative."

Pollack was stunned and his jaw dropped at the news of his friend. The handset fell to the ground, and he buried his face into his hands. He began to sob and mumble under his breath, "Fucking assholes, why did you have to take his beer?"

He dropped to his knees and started punching at his rucksack, slowly alternating his fists as tears ran down his cheeks.

"Goddamn it! Goddamn it!" he repeated, with each hit on the rucksack. This continued for several more seconds until he was too emotionally drained to continue.

Those nearby were caught by surprise and watched in disbelief as Pollack finished his episode. To them, he looked to be overdosing on drugs or simply going crazy. He sat on his heels, hands with palms down resting on top of each thigh, rocking slowly to the front and rear. "Fucking assholes," he mumbled once more. His eyes were glazed and his look was sodden and distant.

Before anyone else could react, Cap was behind him, holding him tightly in a bear hug.

"Easy, Pollack, easy now. Come on, son, talk to me. What just happened?"

Pollack suddenly stopped as if somebody had just slapped him. He turned his head and looked directly through the eyes of those soldiers staring back at him. When he noticed that the Captain had him in a bear hug, he relaxed and turned his head to the side. "I'll be okay, Cap. Sorry for the outburst."

"Are you sure?"

"Yes, I'm sure."

Cap released Pollack and moved to his right side. Pollack used his shirtsleeve to wipe the wetness from his face.

"Pollack, you just scared the shit out of us. What happened to cause this?"

"Sixpack lost his legs." Pollack took a deep breath. The others, still mesmerized, continued to watch and listen closely.

"Who's Sixpack?"

"He was my close friend." He took a few more deep breaths and regained his composure.

"Pollack, tell me what happened to First Platoon," Cap requested with compassion in his eyes.

"They had a five-man recon patrol down a ways from the hilltop and were about ready to return when they hit a booby trap." He stopped momentarily and took a couple more deep breaths before continuing, "Baker and Mr. Flowers are KIA, Beanpole caught some shrapnel in his upper body and his lung is punctured, and my friend, Sixpack, lost both his legs below the knees."

The expression on Cap's face showed that he too was deeply hurt, but he controlled his emotions better than Pollack.

"Shit!" Cap exclaimed, lowering his head and shaking it from side to side. "What a waste. Did you know Mr. Flowers' wife gave birth to a brand new baby girl last week? It was their first. Now she'll never see her daddy. At least your friend is going to be better off, and will most likely survive. You should be thankful for that."

"He didn't have a life outside of the Army and was planning to make this a career. Now without legs-"

"I'm sorry, Pollack. But we all knew what we were getting into before we came over here. Most everyone here has wondered at one time or another if they will ever make it home alive and in one piece."

"It's just not fair!"

"I know it isn't, but that's the price of war."

"What will happen to my friend now, Cap?"

"They'll most likely send him to Japan to get patched up, and then back to the states for rehabilitation in one of the VA hospitals near his hometown. He'll pull through this okay, you'll see."

"I sure hope so."

"Now tell me what that flare-up about beer was all about."

"Sixpack told me that he had brought a six-pack of beer over with him from the states as a good luck charm. In fact, this is how he got his nickname. It was always locked in the rear supply hut when we were in the 25th. His plan was to drink this beer on the freedom plane in celebration of surviving his tour. But on the first night we got up here to the 101st, somebody rifled his gear and stole the beer from his personal belongings. It broke his heart!"

"I guess I understand now. That was really low! Will you be okay or do you want Fuzzy to take over the radio for awhile?"

"No, I'll be okay. I just need a couple of minutes to get my head back together."

"Yeah, go ahead. Call me if you need me," he said, and then left to rejoin Cotton Top at his radio.

The rest of the perimeter returned to normal. After hearing the whole story, they felt more compassionate and now fully understood why Pollack freaked out by the news. For many of them looking on, scenes like this had already played out countless times. They were well aware that nothing could be done to ease the pain of their brother soldier; one could only offer condolences for their loss and move on. There was a saying in Vietnam gaining popularity, and many soldiers had already added it to their vocabulary: 'Fuck it, don't mean nothing'. It appeared to be the cure all phrase for numbing emotions whenever hearing bad news or seeing a fellow soldier get hurt. Many of the men had it written in magic marker across their helmet covers. It was an excellent façade for hiding how a person actually felt in front of others. However, it was difficult to prove its effectiveness in hiding how they really felt inside.

Thinking about everything, Pollack wondered how many more of his friends would get hurt in the war. He could already see the evil in the place. If the valley lived up to its reputation, then the bloodshed was only beginning and surviving the mission would take a whole lot of luck.

An hour later, the order had been given for each Platoon to begin their descent into the valley. They continued to hack and cut a path down the side of the mountain until it got too dark to continue. It was only late afternoon, but the heavy foliage and tremendous height of the jungle made it appear to be closer to dusk. Cap ordered all movement to cease and for the Platoons to set up an NDP in their current positions.

From past experience as a radio operator, Pollack knew that this part of the day would be his busiest. He dropped in his tracks and immediately began receiving the coded locations from the other three Platoons. While decoding them and plotting the locations on a map, he became puzzled when he noticed everyone digging foxholes into the side of the hill.

"Hey, Cap?"

"What do you need, Pollack?"

"Why is everyone digging foxholes?"

"This is SOP and we do it every night. Matter of fact, you better get busy and start digging yours. The map plotting can wait until after you're done."

Momentarily dumbfounded, Pollack never had to carry the small fold-up shovel in the south. His large Bowie knife was always sufficient to clear away brush or to dig small latrine holes. Pollack had never questioned why it was necessary to carry it up in the mountains. He could only recall twice ever using a shovel in

Vietnam. The first time was when he helped build Firebase Lynch, and the second was a few weeks ago when repairing the bunkers in FSB Vandergrift.

The slope was rather steep; most of the men in the Third Platoon had already tied their rucks to nearby trees to keep them from rolling downhill during the night and hitting trip flares. At least the earth was soft in the spot where Pollack started to dig. Without clay, digging his first foxhole in the brush was quick and easy.

When he finished, he hung the radio on a low tree branch nearby so it could be monitored from the depth of his foxhole.

Awake, the soldiers sat on the steep sloping ground and propped their feet against the trees below them. It was, however, a different story at night. The foxholes were only two to three feet wide, so some of the men sat inside and slept with their backs against one of the walls. Those preferring to lie flat and stretch out on the ground found it difficult to remain in that position. Pollack and others caught themselves during the night and awakened just in time to stop their slide downhill. After having repeated the exercise a few more times during the night, Pollack changed his strategy and moved his sleeping position behind the large tree where his ruck was tied.

Somewhat successful in not waking anymore during the night, Pollack still found himself wrapped sideways around the same tree. Strangely enough, he wasn't the only one to wake up that way.

Later that morning, the Third Platoon continued their descent to the valley floor. On two different occasions, they found their paths ending abruptly in sheer drop offs greater than fifty feet. This caused further delay as the men were forced to navigate around the obstacle and seek out a less dangerous route. Many of them incurred numerous scrapes and bruises on the difficult trek, after having lost their balance and sliding into a boulder or tree. It took the Platoon until late afternoon to complete their downward hump.

Two Platoons from Alpha Company had already reached the valley floor much earlier and had sent out recon patrols to survey the immediate area. Pollack was quite surprised with their findings after they were relayed to him over the radio.

Fourth Platoon was furthest away and due west of the rest of the Company. They had stumbled onto a large well-used trail; deep ruts along its length implied that large, heavily laden carts used the trail to move heavy equipment and supplies. Well-concealed from the air, fishing nets hung from trees overhead, covered with a layer of leaves and brush. This camouflage enabled the gooks to move openly any time during the light of day.

Second Platoon found a stream with four man-made crossings to the other side; stones had been packed tightly on the streambed and came to within one foot of the surface. The stream was three feet deep, the current lazy and slow, and the milky brown colored water covered any sign of the ten-foot wide underwater stone bridges. Not even a small ripple could be seen when the water flowed downstream. The four crossings were evenly spaced along three-hundred feet of the stream, and each had trails that led into the jungle from both sides. Evidence of heavy use was proven as deep tire marks and footprints imbedded in the mud.

Neither of the other two Platoons had an opportunity to send out recon patrols, as their steep descents down the mountains took them most of the day. The following day, the Platoons would all link up and further investigate the two areas of interest.

Darkness closed in quickly on the Third Platoon before they could even locate a decent location for an NDP. So for the second night in a row, they were forced to stop moving, having to quickly set up a small perimeter, dig foxholes, put out trip wires and Claymore mines, eat, and determine guard rotation before being engulfed in total darkness. The ground rose slightly, but nothing as disastrous as the night before; it would be much easier to sleep that night.

At 0300 hours, explosions began to echo loudly through the valley, waking all. Spaced ten seconds apart, one had difficulty pinpointing the origin.

Pollack jumped quickly from under his poncho liner and scampered to where Fuzzy monitored the radios during his turn at watch. They heard a faint whisper on the Company frequency, but it was too garbled to understand. The volume of the radio had been turned up but the transmission remained broken and distorted. Pollack keyed the handset several times, hoping to break contact so he could identify and help the caller. He picked up the radio by its strap and moved it around to different locations in hopes of picking up the weak signal. All the CP radios had the large telescopic antennas installed, which helped with signal strength, but it also made it very difficult to move around in the jungle, as it became tangled in overhead foliage. This continued for thirty seconds without success. Finally, after a slight pause, he heard the word 'Eagle', loud and clear. It was the only word spoken, but they also noticed that the squelch or static had returned. This meant the net was clear and nobody was transmitting any longer. Pollack took this opportunity to call out and try to establish contact with the caller.

"This is Eagle-one. Unit in trouble, please respond and identify, over." He paused for ten seconds and then repeated the call.

After four attempts, the RTO in the First Platoon called, "Eagle-one, this is Eagle-niner. I thought I was able to make out Eagle-seven on that last transmission but it was too weak to be sure."

"Roger, Eagle-niner, thanks."

As the distant explosions continued, Pollack attempted to reach Eagle-seven.

"Cotton Top, call HQ and let them know we've got a unit in trouble and not responding," Cap whispered loudly. Pollack continued his attempts to establish contact with the Second Platoon.

Suddenly the static over the handset was interrupted by a cry for help. "Eagle-one, Eagle-one, we're being mortared."

"Who is being mortared? Please identify yourself!"

"My name is Ralph and I'm in the Second Platoon."

"Ralph, your call sign is Eagle-seven, what is your situation?"

"I don't know. I was asleep when the mortars started to hit. I kept my head down and kept calling out but nobody was answering me. All I can hear around the perimeter is screams for help. I finally got up enough nerve to crawl over to the L-T's foxhole, and found him and the RTO in bad shape. I'm on his radio now but I don't know what to do next. The mortars are still dropping on us. Can you help me?"

"Hold on, Eagle-seven."

The entire CP gathered around Pollack, anxious to hear his report. When he finished telling them about the Second Platoon, Fuzzy asked for the handset so he could talk to Eagle-seven.

"Eagle-seven, this is Tac-one. Are you still there?"

"Yeah, I'm still here!"

"Okay, Eagle-seven, can you hear the tubes firing?"

"Yes, sir."

"This is Tac-one. Which direction are they coming from?"

"Tac-one, I don't have a compass."

"Roger, Eagle-seven. I know where you are, but I just need to know if the firing you hear is coming from the mountain you came down or from a different direction. Listen closely."

"Tac-one, my back is to the mountain and they're shooting from my front."

"Roger, Eagle-seven. I'm going to call in some artillery near your position. The first one is going to be a flare. After it pops, use it as a marker to guide me to the tubes. You're going to have to tell me whether to go right, left, or whatever, and how far. Have you got that?"

"Okay, Tac-one."

"Eagle-seven, I know you're scared, but you're going to have to raise your head up out of that foxhole for just a second for me to be able to help you. Are you okay with that?"

"I have no choice."

"Okay, Eagle-seven, hang in there; it'll only be a couple minutes."

Fuzzy turned on his red lens flashlight and looked over the map. He gave the information to Stud, who quickly passed it along on the artillery frequency.

Only one minute expired when Stud whispered, "Shot out!"

"Eagle-seven, this is Tac-one. The flare is on the way. Watch for it and try to estimate where the tube is compared to where it pops."

"Tac-one, the flare is out to my front, but not far enough. I would say to add about two-hundred feet and then maybe go left about the same amount."

"Eagle-seven, the next one is going to be a high explosive round. You'll hear where it hits. So the same plan. Give me an adjustment afterwards."

"Shot out," Stud informed Fuzzy.

"Eagle-seven, heads up, it's on the way."

"Tac-one, they're close. Maybe add fifty feet and come back to the right a little."

After the next explosion, Eagle-seven called back excitedly, "Tac-one, when that round landed, there was a second explosion. Did you shoot twice?"

"Negative, Eagle-seven. It sounds like a secondary explosion. Perhaps you heard ammo explode. Keep your head down and I'm going to shoot a bunch of rounds in that same area. They'll move around a little, but don't get excited. They won't land near you."

"Thanks, Tac-one. The mortar has already stopped."

"That's okay, Eagle-seven. We're just going to make sure it stays out of commission. Hold tight. Rounds are on the way."

The twelve-round barrage began and sounded like a ferocious thunderstorm had just arrived. The extremely loud claps of thunder were punctuated with bright splashes of light when the rounds exploded in the total darkness.

A new voice called over the Company radio. "Eagle-one, this is Eagle-seven-six, over."

"This is Eagle-one, go ahead."

"Roger. We've got casualties here and need Medivacs ASAP."

"Eagle-seven-six, how many wounded do you have?"

"I don't know. We're still checking foxholes. So far, looks like six KIA and about the same amount wounded. All of them urgent."

"Roger. Will contact dust-offs and get back to you with an ETA. Let me know when you have a final tally."

"Wilco, out."

The survivors in the Second Platoon knew it would be too risky for the Medivacs to pull each wounded man up by cable through the thick valley foliage. It would take extra time that none of them could afford.

The surviving Sergeant in charge got the men to begin dismantling their Claymore mines and using the C-4 plastic explosive to blow away some of the trees. A clear area of at least ninety feet was needed for the birds to maneuver and land safely. A suitable landing zone with several scattered tree stumps had been created in less than twenty minutes.

It took almost an hour to evacuate the wounded and corpses. The final tally was seven killed, eleven wounded, and three missing - almost half the Platoon.

After looking at all the variables, it was surmised that the recon patrol had been spotted earlier in the day by the stream and then followed to their NDP. The shooting had been too accurate to be the result of guesswork. Of the twenty-some rounds that hit, only two landed outside of their small perimeter.

Only twenty-three men survived the barrage, but not all escaped injury. Almost every one of them had minor wounds that required cleaning and bandaging, but none of them serious enough to be evacuated from the field. As a result, they were left to pick up the pieces.

Cap became concerned about their strength, but it was too risky for the Third Platoon to hump over a mile to link up with them. There were too many things that could go wrong in trying to attempt such a rescue. Instead, he asked them to carry whatever they could and return to the mountain the same way they'd used earlier to their NDP. He wanted them to put as much distance as possible between themselves and the area where the mortars fired. At first light, each Platoon would move in that direction and link up with them at the base of their mountain.

Third Platoon was the last to arrive at the Company gathering. Cap didn't even stop to drop his equipment; instead he sought out Ralph, the young man who directed the artillery fire the night before, saving everybody else. He found a very frightened eighteen year-old who had only been in Vietnam for three weeks. Ralph was still shaking and quivering when Cap reached him. Only then did he remove his equipment and take a knee in front of Ralph. When he noticed the Captain, Ralph was embarrassed and quickly jumped to his feet.

"At ease, troop, you don't have to stand up!"

"Sorry, sir, I didn't notice you there."

"Ralph, you don't have to apologize for anything. I am so grateful for what you did last night and had to find you so I could thank you face-to-face. What you did was an unselfish act of bravery. Your courage saved the rest of the Platoon, and possibly some of those who had already been wounded. That was also some good shooting as it seems you knocked out that mortar team after only a couple of fire adjustments."

Ralph was still shaky and seemed to be uncomfortable as the center of attention.

"When we return to the firebase, I'm going to put you in for a Silver Star with a "V" device for Valor. Had you stayed in your foxhole and cowered in fear, we would most likely not be here having this chat. I want to thank you once again, and if you don't mind, it would give me great pleasure to shake your hand."

Cap extended his hand and the two men shook strongly and vigorously. The officer then turned, retrieved his gear, and with Pollack in tow, returned to the CP. Others nearby congratulated Ralph; they were surprised by Cap's announcement and had heard nothing about the act of bravery earlier. Humbled, Ralph just told everyone he only did his job and nothing more.

Captain Robertson was more determined than ever to check out the stream and crossings. He did not like being watched and targeted by the enemy. The Company was split into four separate columns and moved in a route perpendicular to the stream. Their movement would allow the Company to clear a three-hundred feet wide area through the jungle to the stream. En route, they expected to cross through the area where the mortars had fired from the night before. If all went according to plan, the columns would all reach the stream at the same time.

When passing through the area where the artillery barrage had hit, the damage was widespread and devastating. Much of the jungle had been blown apart and the men found it difficult to traverse through the area. Small craters identified where the rounds had hit; the surrounding vegetation had been ripped and shredded. The men did find a larger crater within the area that appeared to have been created by an explosion more powerful than the others. The ground and surrounded area was blackened and bare of vegetation for fifteen feet around. Upon closer investigation, they also found pieces of human flesh clinging to foliage and littering the ground at the far end of the western diameter. They surmised that was where the secondary explosion occurred that annihilated the enemy mortar crew. They only saw the body parts to the west of the crater, so it was clear that the enemy was all close together on the same side of the tube and ammo when the artillery round had hit and exploded their ammunition. There was no sign of the tube itself or its base plate - both perhaps blown across the valley by the explosion.

However, nobody could determine just how many bodies had been ripped apart by the detonation, but it did bring a smile to the faces of the Second Platoon survivors.

When reaching the stream, those members of the Second Platoon who had been there the day before, found that nothing had changed and there was no new evidence of fresh crossings since they were there last.

They searched the immediate area when a distant rumbling noise, further upstream, got their attention and heightened their curiosity. Cap sent the First Platoon on a recon patrol to find the source. They dropped their packs and split into two groups; walking upstream, two Squads on each side of the slowly moving muddy water.

As they moved forward, the rumbling noise grew louder and more pronounced. After moving almost a quarter of a mile, they saw a beautiful waterfall through the trees just a short distance away. The water cascaded over large boulders and then fell thirty or so feet down to the stream. They had finally found the source of the noise. Even from the distance, they felt the cool mist of the waterfall encapsulating them. The vaporized water offered a short, pleasant sensation as it settled onto their bare arms and faces; sending a pleasant chill down their spines.

The ecstasy was cut short when the point man spotted what he thought to be soap bubbles floating in the water. They informed Cap of this observation; he responded that it might be foam created from the falling water. However, he directed them to proceed cautiously and see what else they could find.

The patrol didn't have to move too far before coming upon a pool at the base of the mountain. Almost twenty-five feet in diameter, it sat in a large natural crater; gentle rapids led away in three different directions. The stream they had been following was the furthest away and contained the least amount of water flowing downstream. The surface of the water in the pool was ten feet down from where they stood; walls sloped downward at a forty-five degree angle where large boulders and vegetation littered the water's edge.

Both columns stopped abruptly and dropped to a knee when they heard laughter and loud voices from under the waterfall. The point men moved forward cautiously for a closer look. To their surprise, ten enemy soldiers were near or in the pool. Two uniformed guards were posted near the rim of the crater, but they were paying no attention to the surrounding area. Instead, they cajoled with the other eight naked soldiers bathing in the water.

Both point men returned to their groups and whispered their findings to the waiting men. The Lieutenant called the CP.

"Eagle-one, this is Eagle-niner actual, over."

"This is Eagle-one, go ahead."

"Be advised that we have ten November Victor Alpha (NVA) in the open and will engage in one-mike (minute), over."

Pollack informed Cap who took the handset from him.

"This is Eagle-one actual, talk to me."

"Roger, one actual, we located enemy soldiers in the pond at the base of the waterfall. They're bathing and have posted armed guards on both sides."

"Have you been seen?"

"Negative. They are making so much noise and the guards aren't paying attention. They will be totally surprised."

"Roger, niner actual. Be careful and good hunting. Eagle-one actual, standing by."

Thirty seconds later, a ferocious deluge of gunfire erupted around the crater. The sound started all at once and did not change in tempo; every weapon fired in automatic. After thirty seconds, it tapered off and then stopped altogether.

"Eagle-one actual, this is Eagle-niner actual, over."

"Go ahead, niner actual."

"Roger, engagement successful. No casualties and no survivors."

"Great job! What is your ETA back to my position?"

"Unknown at this time. We're going to search through their packs and toss everything we don't keep into the pond. It seems quite deep and should keep others from stumbling across the supplies. Will let you know when we're done."

"Eagle-one actual, roger, out."

In their search around the waterfall, First Platoon didn't find anything of substance within the stowed gear. They only located two rucksacks packed with soap, towels and clothing; and ten AK-47 rifles and bandoliers of ammo. This concerned the grunts and strongly suggested that either a base camp or an enemy staging area was nearby. They quickly tossed everything into the water, placed a call to the CP, and then moved out to rejoin the Company within five minutes.

The gooks' mistake in using soap had given them away. Had the point men not spotted bubbles flowing in the stream, the Platoon might not have caught the enemy so unprepared.

When moving back downstream, the current carried a continuous ribbon of crimson colored water, keeping pace with the Platoon as they quickly tried to put some distance between themselves and the waterfall.

When Cap received the earlier call from the First Platoon informing him of gooks out in the open, he had gathered the rest of the Company and moved them away from the stream crossings and closer to the waterfall. When the firing erupted, they stopped and waited there in a reactionary mode until the ambushers returned.

Now, everyone could relax and take a break while the L-T briefed Cap about their mission. There were no documents or souvenirs to share, and the fact of only finding soap, towels and clothes within the rucksacks could only mean that First Platoon had stumbled upon an enemy bathing pool. The gooks' high level of confidence and lack of security signaled that their 'home' was very near and the pool might have even been in their back yard.

Cotton Top had been keeping Battalion informed ever since the initial call from the First Platoon. He was also sure to pass on the theory of a nearby base camp or staging area. This piece of information piqued their interest and got the planners working on a mission right away.

When Alpha Company returned to the area where the underwater stone bridges were located, they were quick to note wet ground and muddy footprints leading into the jungle on their side of the stream. A group of people had been in a hurry to get across while the Americans were upstream.

The Platoon leaders quickly dispatched a Squad to recon just inside the jungle on both sides of the stream, while the Officers took a closer look at the area around the crossings.

Pollack looked over to Cap and said, "This is really weird, and it seems like the gooks are all around us."

"I agree. But I believe that this particular group is trying to evade us and keep out of our way; who knows, they might be hustling up some kind of an ambush as we speak."

"Why don't we leave some mechanicals set up here and move away to a different location?"

"What do you mean by mechanicals?"

"You know, booby traps with Claymores."

"I've heard of them, but we've never used them since I've been here. I doubt if anyone even knows how to make one."

"I do."

"You do? How does it work?" Cap asked, intrigued.

"You set up a string of mines to cover a certain area and connect them to each other with detonation cord and blasting caps. Then you set a trip wire somewhere in the middle of them and hook the entire thing to a six-volt battery. When the wire is tripped, the mines explode."

"And you can make these?"

"Yep. I only need the right supplies."

"Okay. Talk to Fuzzy and have him get you what you need. He'll make sure it comes out on our re-supply tomorrow."

This excited Cap. It was something new for him and might even give his Company a slight edge in the valley.

Pollack solicited the help of others while waiting for the re-supply and started to make some of the components for the mechanical ambush. The tops of several C-Ration cans were removed and bent in half, wriggling them back and forth until the lid broke in two. Cotton Top and Fuzzy both helped, using large Bowie knives to cut a small eighth-inch diameter hole into each lid half and plastic knives. Others whittled away at finger thick pieces of wood to sharpen the eighteen-inch long stakes like huge pencils. When done, they had enough supplies to build ten small mechanical ambushes.

After the re-supply, some of the guys in the Third Platoon were anxious to get involved and asked to help in preparing the rest of the equipment. Pollack split up the work and then supervised these volunteers after some instruction. The most dangerous job was to cut detonation cord into twelve-foot long sections and then crimp blasting caps onto each end. It was very important to keep them away from electrical devices, fires, and to handle them gently. The bright and sunny weather would make this process go smoothly. If a storm approached, nobody would want to be near the explosives, as the static alone could detonate a blasting cap. By itself, it's nothing more than a firecracker, but when attached to a detonation cord, there would definitely be an explosion and people would get hurt. For that night, they would only need to prepare six of the sections for the three ambushes.

Some of the men worked with the fishing line, wrapping twenty-five feet around the top of each stake like a fishing reel, and then tying off the end to a plastic knife. To ready it for travel, the knife was secured to the side of the stake and wrapped several times around with a rubber band.

Others worked on the most important part of the device: the actual trigger mechanism. Two of the half moon can lids were used, both orientated so the punched holes were together on the same end and facing upward. The sharpened stick would then be sandwiched between the two pieces of metal and secured near the top with several rubber bands. The intent was to duplicate a device similar to spring loaded clothespins from home; the front of the pieces must touch and the rear with the pierced holes must be apart. Pollack checked the tension of the devices and used the same kind of plastic knife. If the tension was too tight and the knife did not release, the fishing line would snap and the mines would not detonate. If this were to happen, the sudden tug against someone's leg would alert them to a tripping device and a quick search would uncover the ambush, giving the gooks something extra to use against the Americans. On the other hand, if it was set too loose, a strong breeze or twig falling across the wire could dislodge the plastic knife and prematurely detonate the mines. He tried to find a happy medium and made suggestions on how to correct a too-loose or too-tight condition.

Several firing devices for normal Claymore operation also needed to be modified. The fifty-foot long wires were similar to a thin wire extension cord; a blasting cap on one end and a plug that inserted into the detonator clacker on the other. Since the clackers were not used in this ambush device, the plug was cut off and discarded. The two wires must then be separated at the ends and the protective covering stripped back one inch to expose the copper wire; each wire had multiple thin strands. When exposed, they resembled a tiny whiskbroom, and had to be held together and twisted tightly into a thick single strand. Several other wires needed both the plug and blasting cap cut from the ends; the wire stripped back and twisted in the same fashion.

Further along in the assembly process, one of the bare ends of wire with a blasting cap was spliced with one of the wires stripped on both ends. The new, thick, single bare end was then inserted through the hole of one of the metal lids on the trigger assembly and twisted around itself to firmly secure it to the metal lid. The sequence was repeated with the second pair of wires that were then secured to the second metal lid of the trigger. Finally, both the wires with the attached blasting cap and the second pair of stripped wires were spliced together and secured to the same lids.

After Pollack had tested and double-checked everything, he informed Cap that all of the pieces were ready. Cap was anxious to move out and get the ambushes set up. Since the Third Platoon personnel helped with most of the work, he thought it only to be fair that they should have the honor of helping to set them up. The men divided all the fabricated supplies, nine Claymore mines and three six-volt batteries between themselves and prepared to move out. Fuzzy would monitor the Company frequency and keep in contact with the RTO of the Third Platoon: Eagle-five.

At the stream, it only took a few minutes to determine which of the paths offered the best opportunity for a successful ambush.

Pollack and four volunteers moved up one of the paths into the jungle; Cap followed closely behind with a notepad and pencil in hand. When he found a suitable location, Pollack instructed his students where to place the mines, spacing them ten feet apart and back about two feet from the trail. Each Claymore mine contained two ports so they could be daisy-chained and connected together for simultaneous detonation; they would be connected in this fashion for the ambush.

Pollack took two of the detonation cords and walked over to the mine positioned to the far right. He inserted the blasting cap into the well and then walked back to the center mine where he inserted the other end of the cord into the right-side port. He then took the second detonation cord and inserted the blasting cap into the left-side port, carrying the other end over to the left mine to complete the installation.

"Cap, our next step is to position the trip wire. We should place it directly in front of the center mine. This way, if there is more than one person, they'll all be caught in the kill zone."

"If you put it at either end, won't it catch more in the kill zone?" one of the volunteers asked.

"You could, but as I just explained, if we set it in front of the first mine and a group is moving out toward the stream, we'll catch many of them in the kill zone. However, if they are coming into the trail from the stream, maybe only the gook tripping the wire will actually get caught."

"I see your point."

"Let's do them all the same and position the trip wire in front of the center mine," Cap ordered.

"Okay, but first, we need to cover the mines and detonation cord with leaves and twigs so they can't be seen from the trail. But be careful not to disrupt the immediate area and make it look like somebody had been moving around in there; that may tip them off."

The wires were unwrapped from the stake with the trigger device and pushed into the ground just to the side of the center Claymore mine. Pollack removed the rubber band securing the knife on the other stake and held on to it while one of the other men walked to the opposite side of the trail, unwinding the spool of fishing line as he went. Pollack held the knife close to the trigger device and had the other man pull the line taut. At that point, Pollack gave a signal and the soldier drove the stake into the ground, and then camouflaged it before returning to the other side. Pollack separated the lids and inserted the plastic knife. The fishing line had a slight sag in it, but still stretched across the trail a foot above the ground.

Pollack walked through the trip wire in the center of the trail, satisfied with the smooth release of the knife. He reinserted the knife into the trigger mechanism and double-checked everything.

"It's ready, Cap. All we have to do is arm it. Do you want to do it now or arm them all before we leave?"

"No, let's arm this one and move on to set the other two."

The one wire with the attached blasting cap was pulled away from the trigger device and the blasting cap inserted into the remaining port of the far right Claymore.

Pollack then had everyone clear the kill zone and accompany him, while he unrolled the remaining cord and moved behind the ambush approximately fifty feet.

"This is also a dangerous part of arming the ambush. If there is a short in the wires or the knife had fallen from the trigger mechanism, then as soon as I touch these wires to the battery leads, it could explode. To be safe, you should get behind something when doing this."

Pollack moved behind a tree, placed a six-volt battery onto the ground, and then connected one of the bare copper wires to the positive spiral contact on the top of the battery. When he was sure that everyone else had taken cover, he attached the second wire to the remaining battery post. No explosion sounded.

"That's it for this one. She's all set to go," Pollack said with a wide grin. The other volunteers smiled, also pleased.

"Is that all there is to it?"

"That's it."

"Damn, there's nothing to it. Why didn't we ever think of this before? Do you mind if I hook up the next one?"

"Be my guest, Cap."

When setting up the ambush on the next trail, Cap read from his notes and directed the same volunteers in the step-by-step process. This time, the set up went much faster as less explanation was necessary. Cap walked through the shin high trip wire and both Pollack and Cap were pleased with the outcome. Cap unrolled the long length of cord, all five men took cover, and he successfully made the final connection to the battery.

The third mechanical was placed on a trail on the opposite side of the stream. Pollack only supervised the volunteers and allowed them to set up this last ambush by themselves. Later, they would help in the training of others in the Company so that each Platoon could do it successfully.

Third Platoon gathered up on the main trail and then started their mile long hike back to the NDP. Upon their return, there was excitement within the perimeter as they waited for the sound of exploding Claymore mines, which could come at any moment.

They were disappointed when nothing happened during the first night. Doubts were raised during breakfast, questioning the reliability of the ambush and the possibility that the gooks dismantled the booby traps.

The comments swayed Cap and he decided to send out the Third Platoon again after breakfast. They would check on the three ambushes and scout the immediate vicinity for activity.

The sound of a distant explosion took everyone by surprise. Initially, there was a moment of panic before they realized that it was one of the mechanical ambushes detonating. Those around the perimeter smiled and began congratulating each other with high fives. Cap stood up and walked over to where Pollack was still eating breakfast. He was halfway there when a second loud explosion was heard from the same vicinity.

"Goddamn, Pollack, we're tearing them up!" Cap was extremely excited.

"You don't know how good that makes me feel. I was beginning to have my doubts, but now..." a third explosion stopped Pollack in mid-sentence.

Everyone was momentarily stunned that all three ambushes had blown within a five-minute period of time.

"Holy shit! I can't believe it! Has something like this ever happened before, Pollack?"

"Never, Cap. This is the first time for me."

Imploring faces looked toward the CP as men around the perimeter mentally requested permission to check out the ambush results.

"Is it possible that the first ambush could have set off the others?"

"It would be highly unlikely, Cap, unless something was blown into the air and fell exactly onto the trip wire of the other two. You also have to consider animals like wild boars or monkeys that may trip ambushes; I've seen that a few times before."

"Okay then, we need to go and see for ourselves."

Cap contacted the Platoon leaders and informed them that the Third Platoon would be going to check on the ambushes. The others would remain in place and on standby, ready to support them if they got into trouble. They all relished the thought of catching gooks in booby traps for a change, and waited patiently to hear the results.

When the Platoon was within fifty meters of the first blown ambush, the men stopped and Cap ordered a 'mad minute', directed toward the ambush sites on both sides of the stream. Almost forty weapons, M-16's and M-60 machine guns, fired a barrage of flying lead relentlessly through the areas to their front. When the firing stopped, the men split into three separate groups and advanced slowly toward the three ambush sites.

The results were the same at all three. The exploding Claymore mines had destroyed the area surrounding the ambush locations and enemy bodies littered the ground at each of the sites. In total, they counted seventeen dead NVA soldiers in full battle gear. Except for their pith helmets, they were dressed similar to the Americans: wearing fatigues, web gear, canteens, boots, and rucksacks stuffed to capacity. The bodies had been shredded by the blasts as hundreds of steel projectiles ripped through everything in their path. The enemy soldiers lay upon the ground in many different poses; internal organs exposed and many torsos missing limbs. The green and brown foliage on the other side of the trail was spotted with red; human tissue and blood still dripped to the ground. Pieces of white bone were embedded into the bark of some larger trees.

The bodies had to be stripped of equipment and searched before leaving the area.

Billy Ray, one of the Squad leaders, was the first to attempt removing one of the rucksacks and struggled, getting nowhere. "Steven, come over and help me remove this rucksack. It weighs almost twice as much as mine," he said, frustrated.

The point man from New Jersey walked over to help the Sergeant. "Damn, this shit is heavy. What do you suppose is in here, Sarge?" Both men struggled to remove the pack.

"We'll find out if we can ever get this thing off."

Finally, the Squad leader used a Bowie knife to cut through the straps to get it off the corpse; they lifted it to the side and set it down next to the body. Billy Ray untied the straps, lifted open the covered flap, and began withdrawing items, handing them to Steve, who separated them into piles next to him.

Meanwhile, several other soldiers moved toward the other corpses and teamed up to remove those rucksacks, mimicking the actions of Billy Ray and Steve.

"Look at all this shit these little guys carried. We got fish, rice, canned goods, cigarettes, ammunition, a change of uniform, cleaning gear, a wallet, and other personal effects."

"It must be the standard pack for all of them, Steve. This one has the identical stuff inside."

"Yeah, this one does too!" Nate, a black soldier from Brooklyn, added. It turned out that the L-T was correct as all the rucksacks were packed identically.

The odor overwhelmed them; the stench of raw flesh and coppery smelling blood engulfed the air. The sights and smells didn't affect the old timers like Pollack and some of the others. They had either grown accustomed to it or simply didn't care anymore. The Cherries, on the other hand, had all vomited at one time or another, some twice or more, since encountering the carnage.

"Cap, you and the L-T need to see this," the Spanish Sergeant said, leading them back across the stream to the trail on the other side. "Check this shit out!"

The ruins of four bicycles, heavily laden with supplies, lay where they fell. The handlebars were extremely long, extending back to where a seat should have been. That must have made it easier for the porter to stabilize and maneuver the two-wheeled supply vehicle. Every inch of the frame had something tied to it; sacks filled with rice and fish, two mortar tubes and bases, mortar rounds, and extra weapons spilled over the trail.

"Now that's something you don't see in the jungle every day," the L-T said.

"This is the first time for me, Cap. I've never seen anything like this down south."

"This is a major supply route through the country, Pollack; nothing I see here surprises me. Now if we can only determine where they were taking all this stuff."

"You want me to take a patrol up the trail a ways to see what we can find?" the Spanish Sergeant nicknamed Beast asked.

"No!" Cap responded. "These supplies are for more soldiers than we have ourselves right now. Let's be patient and continue leaving mechanicals on these trails to see what develops."

This turned out to be one of the larger finds in the Battalion during the last few months. It took the men almost the entire day to separate and evacuate all the equipment by chopper. Afterwards, three new mechanical ambushes were set up further up the trails before the men packed it up and headed back to the NDP.

Alpha Company spent the next two weeks patrolling through that part of the valley, hoping to find signs of the perceived NVA base camp. They were unsuccessful in locating it, but had much better results with the deployed mechanical ambushes, adding to the body counts and confiscated supplies.

The men had neither fired a shot nor had a casualty during that time, outside of their reconnoitering by fire before checking out blown ambushes. It had to be a new record for Alpha Company in the A Shau Valley.

The other Companies in the Valley weren't as fortunate, as they continued to be mortared, encounter enemy booby traps, and walked into ambushes. At times, wounded soldiers had been evacuated from a Company's area of operations as many as three times in a single day.

Alpha Company heard gunfire and explosions all around them every day, but none were close enough to pose a threat or even worry about.

During the third week in the Valley, Alpha's mechanicals were not being tripped, so patrols had to go out to dismantle them and set them up in a new location; this exercise repeated itself daily as the enemy became scarce.

The Battalion Intelligence Group suspected the gooks may have either redirected their supply routes or stopped them all together in fear of the dreaded American booby traps. When the week ended without having added to the body counts, Alpha Company was ordered back into the mountains to resume patrols there.

The Company started to lose men in the mountains every day, but not as a result of enemy hostilities. Instead, Mother Nature had waged a battle against the grunts. Calls for Medivacs were requested daily as soldiers suffered from heat exhaustion and heatstroke, deep lacerations and sprains that occurred when somebody lost their balance and fell down the uncertain slopes. Back injuries were also on the rise and many soldiers wrenched their backs when the heavy rucksack unexpectedly shifted during a slip or fall. Pollack and the others lost weight rapidly, mostly water, and their thigh and calf muscles burned and screamed from the exertion, only to cramp and tighten up when taking a break. Muscle spasms and charlie horses became part of their nightly ritual.

After two weeks of climbing up and down the mountains without any signs of the enemy, Battalion withdrew Alpha Company from the Valley. Even though it had been a very successful mission, with fifty-two enemy kills credited to the Company, the men were ecstatic to leave the Valley.

Alpha Company's new mission was to become a diversionary force in an area to the west of the main highway between Quang Tri and Camp Carroll. Fire Support Base Barbara was several miles west of the American base; Charlie Company moved into the FSB to reinforce those soldiers already there. Intelligence had received word of a large force massing in the area and were planning an attack on the firebase.

Cap and his warriors were to patrol through the area south of the FSB to see if they could find any signs of the buildup. Intelligence had already cautioned the Company that the force may be Battalion sized or larger, and if engaged by the enemy, the Americans were to withdraw to a more defensible location and wait for reinforcements to arrive.

"What is a diversionary force?" Cotton Top asked.

"You don't know?" Pollack asked.

"No, really, I've never heard the term before."

"It's to divert the gooks' attention elsewhere. In our case, we're going to be the decoys used to flush out the gooks and expose them before they have a chance to hit the firebase."

"That's fucked up, Pollack!"

"On top of that, we won't be able to leave any mechanicals set up and armed during our patrols."

"Why not? Those ambushes are awesome and cover our backs."

"I know they do, but the higher ups are worried that if we run into this large force out there somewhere and have to make a hasty retreat, it could turn deadly for either us or our reinforcements."

"Oh, I didn't think about that."

The short break was over and the men resumed their game of cat and mouse.

During the first day, many sighted recent activity and enemy movement through the area, including the discovery of two recently used staging areas. However, the gooks themselves stayed hidden.

Over the next three days, Alpha continued to send out numerous patrols in every direction, but they always returned without finding any new evidence of the large enemy force. The men began to voice their opinions that they were getting tired of these endless patrols to find an enemy that wasn't there. Most of the men already felt there was no truth to the intelligence information about the build up and attack on the firebase. They soon found out how wrong they were.

The NVA soldiers had been keeping tabs on the decoy Company and had refused to take the bait. Instead, they remained very stealthy, evading the many patrols and slipping around their positions undetected.

Just after midnight on the fourth night, Charlie Company and the protectors of Firebase Barbara were hit by a full-scale assault. Mortars and rockets slammed into the firebase for an hour before the ground assault began.

During this barrage, sappers had already inched their way toward the perimeter and used Bangalore torpedoes to blow holes through the mass of barbed wire. The men in the bunkers kept their heads down and didn't seem to be aware of the activity taking place in the wire around the firebase. Clear pathways leading directly over the berm of the perimeter had been created for the attacking forces yet to come.

The sound of whistles and trumpets blowing from the jungle surrounding the perimeter announced the start of the ground attack. Hoards of enemy soldiers were seen coming at the firebase from three different directions. In a wild frenzy, they screamed insanely as they ascended the hill, firing upward at the firebase on full automatic. Charlie Company defenders did all they could to slow down the onslaught of feverish gooks. Some Claymore mines still worked and quickly blew as the scourge continued pushing forward through the pathways in the wire. The base Mortar Platoon kept the area lit with flares and fired high explosive rounds into the advancing enemy on the hillside.

The 105mm artillery guns had leveled their barrels and waited in the event the perimeter is breached. Beehive rounds were loaded in the chamber; the giant shotguns were ready to shoot thousands of steel darts at point blank range into the advancing gooks.

M-60 machine gunners around the perimeter soon started to misfire as barrels overheated from the constant firing; they were almost out of oil to keep the barrels cool and there were no spare barrels nearby.

As the ammunition began to dwindle, a short pause in the firing enabled some of the enemy to infiltrate into the compound. Some of the men inside the perimeter were surprised and had to resort to hand-to-hand combat to save their own lives. Others weren't even given the opportunity as passing gooks threw satchel charges into the bunkers they passed en route to the Command Bunker in the center of the compound.

Cobra helicopters soon arrived and fired at the enemy running rampant outside the perimeter. Jet fighters came on station, dropping bombs and napalm into the jungle areas surrounding the camp.

After two hours of intense fighting, the raging battle tapered off and enemy soldiers retreated into the surrounding jungle.

Both sides suffered many casualties in this ferocious battle, but the guardians of Fire Support Base Barbara refused to be completely overrun.

While the fight took place, Alpha Company left their NDP and moved into a blocking position, about a mile away from the firebase. A dozen strobe lights were placed onto the ground and pointed into the sky along the line of soldiers. Fuzzy and Stud had already alerted the aircraft circling overhead of the friendly forces blocking the route of retreat. They also informed the birds that the line of strobe lights extended along the length of their ambush. Overhead aircraft commanders assured those on the ground that they were well identified and promised to keep the firing away from them.

Cap was soon informed by one of the Air Commanders that a large group of retreating soldiers was coming their way. Prior to taking the defensive stand, the Company had set up ten mechanical ambushes fifty meters to their front and fifty meters on each flank. They hoped that this first line of defense would stop most of them before the actual shooting started.

Alpha's soldiers had completed their foxholes in record time and wasted no time sliding into them; dirt was packed firmly in front of the hole to ensure a clear line of fire.

While they waited for the aggressors to arrive, the firebase fired artillery and 81mm mortars in the direction of the fleeting enemy, flanking them and funneling them toward Alpha Company's killing zone.

It wasn't a long wait until the first of the beaten and weary enemy forces arrived. They weren't seen yet, but could be heard crashing through the jungle as if being chased by ghosts.

A group of seven NVA tripped one of the mechanicals and fell dead. Those running behind them continued to push forward, thinking that the mortars from the firebase had found them. When a second ambush was detonated, it finally dawned on them that they had entered a minefield. They came to a stop, assessed their options, and then changed the route to follow a path leading across Alpha's front. The grunts had been sitting nervously and waiting for the order to open fire.

Cotton Top gave Battalion a clear picture on the radio of what was taking place to their front. Alpha was directed to hold their fire until the rest of the reactionary force was in position. Bravo and Delta Companies had been airlifted to LZ's a mile away and were currently flanking Alpha's line on both sides; they were only minutes away from being in position.

Artillery was on standby and ready to fire at the enemy soldiers, and Cobra gunships headed back with a fresh and full compliment of armaments. When everybody was in place, the gunships would start their attack and scatter the enemy into the infantry blocking positions.

The Alpha Company men had been watching the enemy closely from their foxholes. Some of them had been counting the shadows as they crossed through their field of fire. One of the Third Platoon members whispered that he had counted eighty-six so far. He may have missed some or even counted others twice; it wasn't important because everyone could plainly see dozens of gooks out there. Pollack kneeled in his foxhole with the handset glued to his ear. He peered over the lip at the shadows to his front in hopes that nobody would get trigger-happy and start shooting before everything was in place.

The gook column suddenly stopped and each person quickly squatted low to the ground at the sound of quickly approaching choppers. It was the middle of the night and they were confident of not being seen; they would sit tight until the birds passed harmlessly overhead.

On a signal from Battalion, the strobe lights were turned back on and the Cobra gunships began their attack on the enemy column with rockets and mini-guns, strafing them to Alpha Company's front and flying from right to left. At the same time, Alpha Company opened fire. They could not physically see the gooks through the smoke and darkness, but nevertheless, fired their weapons from the rim of their foxholes and toward their front. The Americans kept their heads down so as to not make a lucky target for the enemy.

The gooks were so surprised by this action that they became momentarily stunned and unable to return fire. Just then, artillery rounds began to rain down on top of them. After several salvos, the rounds began to move away from Alpha Company's line, impacting further away, in an attempt to block any retreat into that direction, thereby, effectively trapping them.

There was mass confusion within the ranks. Many refrained from firing and sought shelter instead. They took off at a fast run through the raining steel, only to be cut down after just a few meters.

The massacre was over in fifteen minutes when it became evident that no more shadows moved through the area. The Cobras continued surveillance from overhead and looked for a reason to fire again. There were no survivors and Barbara had her revenge.

Alpha Company would remain in the immediate vicinity with the other two companies for another two days to seek out any stragglers and to chase down those that retreated to Laos. Then, as a reward, Alpha troops would be withdrawn and flown to a new base for some R&R.

There was much speculation and discussion between the Alpha Company grunts as to which firebase they might be sent to and how a Company could rest and relax on any of them, especially with all the recent enemy activity around some of them. If given a choice, many of the men would have preferred to remain in the field, where in their opinion, it was much safer in retrospect. However, when considering a place that qualified as an R&R reward, Phu Bai, Da Nang, and China Beach topped the list of probable locations.

The group had worked very hard in the bush during the last five weeks, and welcomed an opportunity to sleep soundly through the night, take showers, and eat normal chow for a couple of days. Now that was an R&R!

Nevertheless, on the day of the scheduled pick up, the men were informed that they would be joining the rest of the Battalion at Camp Brooks near Da Nang. No one in the Company had ever heard of Camp Brooks or patrolled through the area around Da Nang.

Upon their arrival, the grunts learned that Camp Brooks was a soon to be former Marine base camp. The jarheads were going home and vacating their many camps in the area. The 1st Battalion would secure the base during their withdrawal and stay there until the ARVN's took it over.

The grunts soon discovered that the area surrounding Brooks had been friendly and quite secure for some time now. After hearing that, they really looked forward to a well-deserved rest.

Mail finally caught up to the moving soldiers in Camp Brooks. Letters from home were so cherished, that when received, everything else waited. The men were filthy, stunk, wore tattered clothing, and had beards that required shaving. They were hungry, thirsty, and some required medical attention. But that was all secondary, as they held sweet smelling words from loved ones in hand. The top priority was finding a private place in the shade to read them.

Pollack looked through his mail and then remembered that he had not taken the time to send his new address to the parents of his former Wolfhound friends. He assumed the same had happened to everyone else but BJ. Pollack's mother informed him in one of the letters of his new address in the 173rd Infantry, Americal Division. Those addresses were at Phu Bai with his personal gear, and he promised himself that he would make every effort to contact them in the near future.

Chapter Twenty-Three

Camp Brooks was a refreshing change. The area assigned to Alpha Company had all the luxuries of home. The barracks contained beds with sheets and pillows, and electricity allowed them to use dozens of fans and radios left behind by the Marines. The day room had a refrigerated soda pop machine, TV set, and pool table. The latrines were equipped with all the modern conveniences, including hot and cold running water. A mess hall operated by the Battalion cooks also served three hot meals a day.

After two days of R&R, Alpha Company was re-assigned to bunker guard, responsible for securing two and a half miles of the extensive perimeter. Just enough bodies were available within the Company to fulfill this obligation, but the men would have to work on two separate twelve-hour shifts.

The responsibility of the CP would not change much as they would still be monitoring radios and phones that interconnected the bunkers; situation reports still were needed and the results conveyed regularly to Battalion headquarters. The four men in the CP also took on the role of goodwill ambassadors, and every four hours, one of them drove a jeep along Alpha Company's sector of the perimeter to deliver hot coffee, cold pop, and sandwiches to those guys in the bunkers. It was very well received and also gave the grunts an opportunity to get to know those 'lazy' guys in the CP.

Every person in the Company had to work a mandatory twelve-hour shift each day, which resulted in an equal amount of time off to wander through the camp, shoot pool, or just lounge around the barracks to read a book or catch up on sleep.

It was, indeed, a serious change of pace for the grunts who had not had this kind of an opportunity since arriving in country. Compared to what they'd endured so far, it was paradise!

The Battalion lifers were easily bored by the inactivity, so they began to make drastic changes to mirror stateside duty before the end of the week was even over. Company formations now took place every day, both in the morning and in the evening, to accommodate the two bunker guard shifts. Every troop was required to shave daily and get a haircut once a week; boots were to be polished; beds made daily with square corners; barracks cleaned; and a walk through inspection would take place every other day. Non-military issued clothing or jewelry were banned and not to be worn anytime when in the camp; this did not go over too well with the 'Brothers' who continued to wear small items in defiance to the rule.

Since these inspections began, trying to polish muddy worn-out boots, cleaning barracks, and policing the grounds consumed most off-duty time. It was a real hassle and didn't leave much time for sleep or other personal activities anymore. The men began taking advantage of their time on guard duty to sleep and catch up on reading or letter writing. There were always two men in each bunker, so they took turns on watch.

The rules changed again after the second week, which somewhat benefited the young soldiers. When the Marines ran the camp, they had employed young hooch boys and girls from the nearby village to take care of all the cleaning, for as little as five dollars a week. Battalion had now granted the men permission to rehire these young enthusiastic workers; four were assigned to each barracks and worked long hours to please their new employers who lived there. Jungle boots were polished, clothing and linen were washed, and the hooches and grounds remained immaculate. The money spent was well worth it and the men gained back some of the leisure time they had lost a week earlier.

Life on the base soon became boring, as there was absolutely nothing to do outside of bunker guard. The novelty began to wear off.

At the end of the first month, Pollack was on radio watch in the CP when Cap approached with good news. "Pollack, I'd like you to know that I've recommended you for promotion to Sergeant."

"No shit?"

"Yeah, no shit!"

"Thank you, Cap, that's great news. When will I get my stripes?"

"You'll have to earn them. If all goes well, you should be scheduled to stand in front of the review board within a week."

"Review board? What's that all about?"

"Didn't you know that promotion to E-5 and above has to go in front of a review board?"

"No, I didn't. What do they do?"

"They'll ask you questions about military procedures and weapons, judge you on your appearance, and the military manner in which you conduct yourself during the interview."

"You mean I have to go in front of them and answer questions?"

"You sure do."

"Who's on this board?"

"Normally there are five officers from the Battalion who sit on a board like this, and they're normally held about once a month."

"Is that all there is to it? After the interview I get my stripes?"

"I'm afraid it's not that easy. It's really a test. You'll need to know your shit and be able to impress the hell out of them."

"Why is that?"

"Just because you go in front of the board doesn't mean an automatic promotion."

"It doesn't?"

"Hell no! There might be one-hundred soldiers who'll go in front of that board. But Division might only have twenty allocations available for promotion in this Battalion. After the board interviews you, they'll rate you like in the Olympics, and place you in line according to your score. If there's only twenty openings available, then the top twenty will get the stripes."

"How in the hell do I study for something like that?"

"Go see Top. He's got some manuals in his bookcase that might help you."

"Thank you, Cap. I'll go and visit him after my watch is over."

"Okay, let me know if you need something." Cap turned and walked to the doorway, stopping before opening the door. "Hey, Pollack?"

Pollack looked at Cap standing in the doorway; his right hand was closed into a fist and the thumb stuck up in the air. "Good luck," he said and then exited the building.

Later when Pollack arrived at Top's hooch, he knocked on the door and entered when he heard the First Sergeant acknowledge him. Top sat at a desk, holding a couple of books in his outstretched hand.

"Hey, Top, Cap asked me to come and see you about some books."

"They're right here," he nodded toward the two Army manuals in his hand and pushed them toward Pollack.

"How did you know I was here to ask for them?"

"That's part of my job to know everything that goes on around here."

"Shit, you got ESP or something?"

"No, I don't," he replied, chuckling. "Cap was in here a little while ago and asked me if I had any books to help with your exam. When I showed him these, he said he was going to talk to you."

"Will these books give me all the information I need?"

"They should. Ninety percent of the questions and answers you'll need can be found in them."

"Way to go, Top!" Pollack said enthusiastically.

"You know you're the only candidate for E-5 representing Alpha Company, so you take those books and you study 'em real hard. If you need help, then come and see me. I want you to be on top of that promotion list. It'll look good for Alpha Company."

"Why will it look good for the Company?"

"Pollack, it's just like being a parent. The things your kids do always reflect back to you. If your kids are wild and raunchy, then other adults will feel like the parents don't give a shit and aren't raising their kids properly. In our case, if you pass, it'll show Battalion that those of us in Alpha Company are doing our job and training you properly."

"Makes sense. What kind of chance do you think I have?"

"Your chance of making it will be the same as everybody else facing the board. You've got an edge though, as there aren't too many of these manuals floating around. Just study hard. I think you'll make a fine NCO."

"Okay, Top. Thanks for your help."

"No problem, son. It'll be a snap. Now get the fuck out of my hooch. I'm sure you have better things to do than stand here all goo-goo eyed."

Pollack was startled and didn't expect him to react this way. "I'm going, I'm going," he replied and stepped to the door.

"Haven't you forgotten something, troop?"

"No, I already thanked you."

"That's not what I meant, shit for brains. What do you say when you leave the presence of an officer or NCO in this fine division?"

Pollack thought for a minute then answered with a grin when it suddenly came to him: "Airborne, Top!"

"All the way! Now wipe that shit-eating grin off your face and get the fuck out of here."

Pollack rushed through the doorway, and once outside, turned back to look inside. Top shook his head, laughing. He got a big kick out of fucking with people, and Pollack didn't know if he was serious or just toying with him.

The Army manuals were the driest reading material that Pollack had ever read. There was no story to read with a plot; instead, the manuals were just technical information, rules, regulations, strategy, and logical theory. At times, it had taken him almost an hour just to get past one page as he kept nodding off while reading. Pollack soon learned that it was much easier to just scan through the manuals and then spend a few moments in an area that he was unfamiliar with. At the end of the week, he had paged through each book three times and was comfortable with the knowledge he had gained.

When his turn came to face the board, Pollack presented himself smartly and successfully answered every question with little or no hesitation. The manuals had been a great help for the technical and regulatory answers, but aside from them, the other answers only required common sense and good judgment. The last question was asked forty minutes after the interview began. After his last response, the board members congratulated him and wished him well. When he was dismissed, Pollack saluted and executed a precision about face before walking out of the room.

He was very pleased with the interview and felt confident that he would place near the top of the list. All that remained as for the results to be published and his orders to be cut.

Pollack knocked on the door of Top's hooch to return the manuals, but there was no answer. He peered through the screen door to see the hooch vacant. Against his better judgment, he opened the door and quickly placed the manuals in the center of the desk. He then took a blank sheet of paper from the stack next to the typewriter and scrawled a quick note: 'it was a snap! Thanks for all your help - AIRBORNE!' and placed it face-up on top of the books before making a beeline for the door.

The Battalion had been on Brooks for six weeks when another rumor surfaced about their leaving the base camp and returning to the field. It was quite unsettling to hear that a majority of the grunts hoped the rumor came true; they'd had their fill of spit and polish and welcomed the chance to duck bullets and kill gooks again.

During his stay on the hill, Pollack had made numerous observations regarding the men in the Battalion. The 'stoners' and 'peaceniks' were comfortable with life in the camp and would prefer to stay if they had a choice in the matter. On the other end of the spectrum were the boozers, beer and whiskey drinkers who were more aggressive and sometimes appeared to be masochists. Lifers and Cherries fell in between and might favor one direction over the other. The short timers, on the other hand, were a paranoid group, and those with only weeks left before going home hoped they never had to step foot into the field again. Pollack fell into the last category with only six weeks remaining in Vietnam and the current assignment suited him just fine.

All during that next week, small groups of ARVN soldiers arrived daily by trucks and started replacing those Americans in the bunkers around the perimeter. Once again, the rumor started to play itself out as the first of the Battalion's companies left Camp Brooks and returned to the bush. Alpha Company wasn't given the official word yet, but the handwriting was on the wall; only the day and location had yet to be decided.

Alpha Company was informed during the weekend that their life of luxury would end on Monday. The grunts were to begin surrendering all the items they had accumulated during their stay so they could be passed on to the ARVN's; there was no need for any of it in the bush.

Many of the men resented having to leave behind those treasures that helped make their stay more comfortable and civilized.

Of course they followed orders and turned everything over to the supply clerk, but many of the items didn't work as they had been taken apart. Electrical cords from the fans were combined in one large box, while fan blades, motors, and protective covers were separated into several other boxes. Radios were surrendered in the same manner, but because the parts were much smaller, all the tubes fit into a single carton. Unfortunately, some of them broke when tossed into the container.

On Sunday, the last day in the camp, some of the Alpha Company men raided the day room after dinner. The rear cover of the television set had been removed and the plug attached to the picture tube pried off with a broom handle. Even though the power cord was unplugged, there was a bright arcing spark that erupted when the plug was disconnected. At least somebody was smart enough to know that the tube stored electricity and took precautions. The plug was severed from the attached wires and discarded; the rear cover was then reattached.

Next, the men staged a mini-Olympics event and collected all the pool cues and balls, taking them to the perimeter. One redheaded guy from the First Platoon received a gold medal for throwing his javelin (pool stick) the furthest. At first, they thought it would be a little more difficult to determine just how far the pool balls traveled as there was no judge standing out in the wire to note their landing. However, two former high school baseball players in the Third Platoon unanimously awarded the gold when ball number three and ball number eleven traveled the furthest of all thrown.

It wasn't the intent of the men to be spiteful and to purposely destroy everything before leaving the camp, but they did it more for the principal. The ARVN had a reputation, and the Americans were well aware that if anything was left behind and intact, it would be sold on the Black Market within days, rather than allowing the next group to enjoy the items.

Alpha Company was the last Company of grunts to leave Camp Brooks. While they waited on the helicopter pad for their transportation back to the bush, several discussions took place relating to their former treasures. If the Officers were aware of their mischief the night before, they offered no hint or said anything about it.

Not one person in Alpha had any idea of what the other units might have done with their items during their last night in the camp. The men, who had taken all the boxes to supply on that last day, recalled seeing very little stored in the hooch. So they had to assume that the rest of the Battalion had left everything behind for the next group to enjoy. If those items were left in working order, then the ARVN must be celebrating and waiting to take possession of the rest of the bounty after the last Company left the base.

Laughter erupted across the chopper pad as word spread about the perceived expression on the ARVN's faces when opening the cartons of Alpha Company's surrendered treasures. All agreed that it would be priceless and they were sorry they would miss it.

Chapter Twenty-Four

Alpha Company was air lifted to another place with a reputation called Happy Valley. Not too far from Da Nang, the area was expected to be less hostile today than it had been earlier in the war. After landing, they would join up with the rest of the Battalion and set up security for the Marines, who had a firebase on a nearby hilltop overlooking the valley. It had to be fully dismantled before the Marines could vacate the hill and go home.

The Airborne Battalion planned to stay close by for up to a week until the Marines had destroyed every bunker and piece of unnecessary equipment. Nothing was to be left behind for either the gooks or the ARVN. If either of them wanted to move onto the hilltop, they'd have to rebuild from scratch.

Non-stop activity hummed in the firebase and the Marines worked hard and long hours to complete the task at hand. The daily sounds of explosions and overhead Marine helicopters continued to be a distraction to those on the valley floor running patrols around the base of their hills.

From their vantage point, the grunts could not see the actual activity in the firebase. The bunkers that had been visible earlier in the week were gone; every sandbag had been emptied and burned and the dirt used to fill in the holes. Dozens of helicopters had been used every day to move out salvaged lumber, artillery guns, and anything else of value. The rolls of barbed wire, mines, and trip flares on the perimeter were left until the last day.

This was the day when scores of Marines finally spilled over the side of the hill, and it was also the first time those in the valley actually saw the soldiers above. It was like watching an anthill from below; every dark figure moved continuously as scores of men traveled back and forth over the crest of the hilltop. There were some accidents as trip flares ignited, but during the light of day, they hardly noticed.

It was close to mid-afternoon when the last helicopter filled with Marines took off from the hilltop location. The real estate was now up for grabs.

The week had passed without incident and many of the Airborne grunts wondered why the gooks hadn't taken advantage of the situation. Artillery, mortars, and rockets could have been devastating for the Marines, especially if they had waited until later in the week when all protective cover had been destroyed. They were lucky!

After this first week back in the bush, Battalion continued to move the Companies further south each day. Not looking for anything in particular, the exercise was designed to send a message to the enemy that Americans still actively patrolled through the bush. After finding absolutely no signs of the enemy during the next several days, Alpha Company was pulled from the field and flown to the airbase in Da Nang.

Their stay was extremely short. A dozen Deuce and half trucks and several APC's had been waiting for them at the edge of the air field and would leave just as soon as Alpha Company could get on board. The convoy would travel north on the main highway and stop briefly to drop off the Alpha Company grunts at yet another firebase, about thirty miles up the road, before the rest of the Battalion continued to their final destination. Unbeknownst to the grunts, this firebase was located on top of a mountain and they would have to walk up the steep trail to reach it.

When they arrived at their destination, the grunts found a very tall mountain on the side of the highway; a steep ten-foot wide dirt track snaked along and ringed the mountainside all the way up to Firebase Tomahawk on the very top. It angered the grunts when they were told the trucks would not transport them up to the top, and instead, they must make the treacherous journey on foot.

Walking up the trail was so much different than climbing the mountains in the bush. Out there, the going was slow and handholds were in ample supply to help pull you up. Time was not normally an issue, and some hills had taken days to climb. On this ascending dusty trail, however, the pace was much faster and more difficult. The Company expected to reach the summit within an hour and Cap pushed the men upwards. After only fifteen minutes, many of them could not continue. Most couldn't catch their breath and some suffered cramps in their thighs and calves; and just like dominoes, they all fell out to the inside of the trail. Even the Captain was unable to continue and forced to take a break with his men.

This trail had been bulldozed into the side of the mountain, and just beyond the outer edge, the earth fell away in a sheer drop off. The soldiers instinctively stayed to the inside of the lane and now fully understood why they weren't able to ride the trucks to the top. One thing for certain was that nobody risked walking in the loose gravel on the outside of the path, in fear of slipping and falling over the side.

The view was incredible from the trail and became more scenic the higher they climbed. The countryside below was mostly of rice paddies and small villages, so without nearby hills and dense jungles, one could see for several miles.

It took almost an hour and a half for the last man to cross the finish line on the summit. It had been the most difficult climb ever for many of the troops; however, once they arrived on top, they found the surrounding scenery to be breathtaking. From a mile up, there were no signs of war below and the three-hundred and sixty-degree view extended for miles in every direction. To the north, a large mountain range loomed in the distance; the highway they had traveled earlier could be seen snaking through the pass. On the east, the South China Sea glistened like a mirror and reflected the sun in every direction. Small Sampans and fishing boats motored around near shore, and not one military ship could be seen on the horizon. The western and southern most views extended for several miles until the mountains and surrounding jungle took over the landscape. This was truly a magnificent gift from Mother Nature, as she lay exposed in all her absolute beauty; the hilltop took on the appearance of a tourist stop as dozens of cameras captured the vistas in every direction.

Standing only a few miles away from the ocean, you could follow the seascape by eye as far north as you could see. Mountains rising behind smaller hills dwarfed them as they dotted the far horizon and jutted out into the blue-green ocean. Far below, the miles of rice paddies formed a multicolored checkerboard that stretched across the plains until touching the water's edge.

The firebase, on the other hand, offered an entirely different picture. Everything was run down and in a state of disrepair. Huge piles of garbage lay exposed throughout the area, left to rot in the hot sun. There was nowhere to hide from the awful stench as it permeated through everything in the firebase.

During this first night, the new inhabitants were drawn into a different conflict, one that would cause additional nightmares in the days and years to come. A night of uninterrupted sleep and enjoying that restful feeling when you woke up the morning was a thing of the past and would not be an option while in Firebase Tomahawk. All on the hill were forced to participate in the battle, from the highest-ranking Officer to the lowest grade of enlisted man. The rotting garbage dump had provided plenty of nourishment during the past several weeks while the base had been vacant, but now, a new scent lingered in the air that required investigation. Hundreds of curious rats scurried about the hilltop after darkness had set in, and they were determined to find the source of this new smell.

Ongoing screams were heard throughout the night as rats fell from overhead rafters and onto unsuspecting sleeping soldiers. Some were as large as alley cats immediately awakened the soldiers when they landed. The grunts were momentarily in a stupor, and their first thought was to wonder why one of the other men in the bunker would deliberately throw something onto them while asleep. As they became more alert and saw nobody standing nearby, they shifted their attention when they felt the thrown object move across their lap. When the realization hit that a large rat or two shared the cot with them, no two reactions were alike. Those soldiers from the city were more apt to scream out in sheer panic and cower in fear. The country boys were not intimidated by the invasion and immediately fought back with whatever weapon they could lay their hands on. Shots rang out as surprised soldiers began shooting at the extremely fast creatures before realizing that they were putting others in danger with the close quarter firing. Others used machetes, steel helmets, folding shovels, and even boots to disable or kill the invaders.

In the morning, dozens of carcasses lay on the ground outside of bunkers or hung from clotheslines by their tails. Not one person was spared during the night and everybody had a story to share during breakfast.

"Let me tell you 'bout my experience last night. Some screams from the other bunkers woke me up and I sat there for a minute to get a clear head. I thought I was seeing things when I looked over at Cecil. At first, I thought a cat had wandered into the bunker and found a place to rest on Cecil's chest. I thought the cat had a deformation because his tail didn't have any fur on it. Just then, it turned and looked me straight in the eye. That's when I noticed it was a rat instead. I was frozen in place and couldn't do anything but watch. The rat must have picked up a new scent and turned back to face Cecil because its nose and whiskers twitched like crazy. It crept up to Cecil's mouth and started sniffing around his lips. Then suddenly, the rat's tongue came out and started to lick at the corner of the man's mouth, intent on getting to the dried food or something else from earlier in the day." Clarence was interrupted in telling the story while those around him shivered at the thought and made comments.

"Ooooweee, rat tongue lickin' on the motherfucker. God damn!"

"You know I couldn't just sit there and watch. My ass would have been long gone."

"I've been licked by many things in my life, but never a rat. That has got to be a weird sensation!"

"I sure never want to find out."

"Me neither. Go ahead Clarence, what happened next?"

"The nibbling at his lips must have woken him because he opened his eyes and blinked several times to clear his vision. When he glanced down and saw the rat's head only inches away, his eyes opened wide in fear and he screamed like his ass was on fire. It was so shrill and sudden that it scared both the rat and me. Cecil was fast though and I got to give him credit, he snapped his poncho liner and catapulted that rat onto the floor in the center of the bunker. And just that fast, he jumped out of his cot with a Bowie knife and proceeded to stab that creature until it was dead. Needless to say, neither of us could sleep anymore for the rest of the night."

"Hey dig this," another soldier at the table began. "Me and Kevin had to go and piss during the night and headed to the latrine with our flashlight beams leading the way. We both thought we were seeing things because everywhere we looked there were glowing red dots. Then, they started moving around randomly in pairs. Something bumped into my leg and surprised me. When I shined the light around me feet, several rats started to scamper away. That's when it dawned on us that we were surrounded by rats. That scene was so intense that we ran back to our bunker and barricaded the doorway in an attempt to keep out the roving creatures."

Not one soldier at the table laughed at these stories. They were afraid and did not look forward to that next night.

Unfortunately, four men had been bitten during the night and awaited evacuation to the nearest hospital. This news heightened the fear in many but also made them aware of how vigilant they must now be during the night.

In the daylight, only a few rats were seen around the garbage dump. The thousands of others rested and stayed hidden in obscure areas or underground in burrows, waiting for darkness to arrive.

In an attempt to turn things around, Cap came up with an idea that would entice most of the soldiers to get involved and help to clean the hill of the awful creatures. After breakfast, he called the men of the Company together and rolled out his idea.

"We are going to start a contest tomorrow to see who can kill the largest rat on the hill." The men looked to one another with puzzling looks. "We will start tonight and the competition will continue until the day we leave this hill. The only rule is that you use common sense and good judgment. I don't want to see anyone get hurt during this contest, but you are free to use whatever you have at your disposal to win. The deadline every morning will be 0800 hours and your submission has to be tagged and laid out on the ground outside of the Commo Bunker. If you find that there is already one lying there bigger than yours..."

One of the black soldiers in formation called out, "Ain't anybody here got one bigger than mine, this is a complete package," he cupped his hand around his crotch and shook it a few times, "yep, you can just give me the prize right now."

This solicited some laughter and comments from those around him.

"Like I was saying," Cap continued when the chatter stopped, "if there is already a rat tagged and it's bigger than your rat, and then don't bother entering it. Go and dump it in the trash or throw it off the side of the hill. The CP will judge all entries during breakfast and will measure from the tip of its tail to the tip of its nose. I heard that there had been some running through our camp last night that were as big as alley cats, and know that it would make more sense to use weight as a qualifier, however, we don't have a scale so we will judge the length instead."

"What's the winner get?" someone called from the crowd.

"I was getting to that, and I think you'll really like this. The daily winner will be exempt from all details during the day and will be awarded twelve, ice-cold beers to do whatever he'd like with them. If you want to sell them or give them away, that's up to you. Now this is where I think it will be interesting. The names of all the daily winners will be collected and placed into a hat, and I will pick one grand prizewinner on our last day here. Odds of winning will depend on how many days we're going to be here. Nobody knows and if we leave at the end of the week the odds of winning would be better than leaving at the end of the month. The grand prize winner will get a three-day R&R to China Beach and I'll even throw in fifty bucks in MPC to spend as you like."

Jubilation burst in the ranks and the men were excited to hear the news. Plans and strategies were already being shared.

"When does the winner get to go to China Beach?"

"He can leave on the next day if he wants. It'll be his call."

The commotion continued within the formation. The men couldn't believe in their good fortune, and many were anxious to get started.

"There's one last thing I forgot to mention, and this is really important. All entries submitted for the contest must be in one piece from tail to nose. Don't alter the bodies to make them longer, and don't enter anything that is pieced together like a puzzle. Are we clear?"

"Airborne!" the group shouted.

"All the way, men! Good hunting!"

Early the next morning, several carcasses were laid out on the ground before daylight arrived. They were long, but all were eventually replaced by larger examples during the last hour of the daily contest. Six entries were found to be so close, that each had to be measured several times and the lengths confirmed by others. Only one-eighth of an inch separated the winner from second place and measured exactly twenty-nine inches in length.

The winner quickly dispersed the twelve beers between his Squad members and admitted that they supported him during this hunt so they deserved a cold one. But he also made it clear that he was going to China Beach alone. When looking over the dead carcasses on the ground, the thought of creatures that size stalking them at night was mind-blowing and still sent shivers down your spine.

Almost one-thousand rats had been killed and burned in the one-week that Alpha Company had been on Tomahawk. The contest was an excellent motivator for reducing the rat population, however, there were still more than enough left to keep men awake and frightened during night.

It was here, with only three weeks left in country that Pollack found out he'd passed the exam and had been promoted to Sergeant. The posted list of one-hundred and twenty-two names showed John Kowalski's name as the second one on the list; only the top twenty-four candidates were promoted to fill the allotted slots within the Battalion. It was time to celebrate and he quickly returned to the Commo Bunker to inform his fellow CP members.

Cap and Top had been watching Pollack's reaction while he read the newly posted document. They could tell he was excited and energized by the news, and as he read, his movements were somewhat awkward. It looked like he wants to rush away and let others know of the promotion, but his feet were rooted in place to keep him there until he finished reading every last word. He even touched the list a couple of times and rubbed a finger across his name, hoping to confirm that it was really his. When done, his feet didn't move him fast enough to carry him back to the bunker.

The two observers allowed Pollack several moments to celebrate the news of his promotion before heading over to the Commo Bunker on the other side of the compound.

"I am proud of that boy. He did well, considering."

"Yes he did, Top. I knew he had it in himself to do well; otherwise I wouldn't have nominated him for the advance. It's just going to break his heart when I give him the news."

"It probably will, but he'll soon get over it, Cap. There really isn't an alternative available and we have to make decisions that are best for this Company. Seems the boy has a level head and at this point, he's our only option."

The two men stopped momentarily outside of the entrance to the bunker. "You ready for this, Top?"

"Let's do it!"

Cap and Top stepped through the bunker entrance and saw Pollack inside slapping high fives with everyone. A cigarette dangled from his lips and a wide smile made it difficult for him to keep it in place. Fuzzy had drawn a set of yellow Sergeant stripes on a piece of paper, and then using a razor blade, trimmed around the border of both designs before attaching them with straight pins to each arm. Cotton Top and Stud came to attention and repeatedly saluted the new Sergeant in mock military fashion. They were laughing and having fun. Suddenly, Cotton Top noticed the two men standing just inside of the entrance. He stopped quickly, "Um, guys," he whispered, and using his head, cocked it to the side twice and then motioned to the others with his eyes toward the entrance of the bunker.

"Good morning, Cap, First Sergeant," Cotton Top was first to acknowledge.

"Good morning, men! I see that we're late for the promotion ceremony. Care to do it again?"

"No sir, sorry sir."

"We're just giving you a hard time. Congratulations, John!" Both men held out their right hands. "Glad to see you made it. I can't think of anybody more deserving. Well done!"

"Thanks, Cap," Pollack shook his hand warmly. "I couldn't have done it without your recommendation and Top's help." Pollack then reached over to Top and shook his hand.

"Am I supposed to salute you now?" the First Sergeant asked.

This cut the ice and the laughter returned.

"I don't think it's necessary, Top, but thanks anyway."

"We'll let you get back to your celebration in just a few minutes, but we need to discuss something personal with you first. Would you mind taking a break and stepping outside with us?"

"Did I do something wrong?"

"Oh no, it's nothing like that." The three men walked through the doorway and moved off to the side for some privacy.

"I'm sorry to put a damper on your celebration, but I've got some news that might disturb you."

"What is it, Cap?" Pollack's heart skipped a beat and his pulse quickened. He shuffled his feet nervously, waiting for Cap to speak again.

"First off, let me tell you that I see you as a very level-headed and quick-thinking person. You've been a great help to me since joining the CP and have made my job much easier. You're an excellent radio operator and it will be hard to replace you. But I also feel that you're a good leader and I desperately need your help right now."

Hearing the word 'replacement' bothered Pollack, and he sensed bad news on the way. "How can I help you, Cap?"

Without wasting a second, Cap responded, "I'm going to reassign you to the First Platoon as their temporary leader."

Pollack was momentarily stunned and knew that he heard the Captain correctly. "Why do something like that? You know I've only got two and a half weeks left before going home."

"I know that, but I'm afraid I have no choice in the matter. First Platoon has been without an NCO since your friend, Sixpack, got hurt."

"They've gotten by since then, so why now?"

"I've a lot of faith in you, John. You've got more experience in the bush than anyone else that's left in the First Platoon. Their Lieutenant has only been in country for a few weeks and hasn't been out in the field yet. He's fresh out of ROTC and seems quite cocky. I don't want him to be the cause of somebody getting hurt."

"What difference does that make on this hill?"

"If we were staying here, I wouldn't even bother you with this issue, but we're going back out into the bush the day after tomorrow."

"I understand, but the bush has been awfully quiet around these firebases, and not one gook had been spotted anywhere in the last several weeks."

"John, we're going back into the A Shau Valley."

Pollack reacted to the news as if being slapped across the face. "I'm too short for this shit!"

"None of us are happy about it, but orders are orders. I really don't want to have a Cherry Lieutenant leading the First Platoon, especially in the Valley. We'll be working separately in Platoon-sized elements and staying in separate NDP's. I don't want to lose anybody on this mission because of carelessness and inexperience. This is where I feel you can be a great help to me."

"Just what are you expecting of me?"

"You'll be the Lieutenant's right hand man. I'll tell him that he is still in charge of the Platoon, but on this mission, he's going to have to clear everything through you first, and I'll make it clear to him that you have the final say-so."

"What good can I do in only two weeks?"

"I don't know how many weeks we will be in that area, but it would be suicide to let the First Platoon operate in the Valley without a capable and trustworthy leader. The L-T will need guidance and direction. I don't know a better way than on the job training."

"Cap, there's got to be another NCO in the Company who knows the Valley better than I do and can even stay with the First Platoon for the long term. Why not consider them?"

"We have, and without going into the details, you'll just have to accept my word that there is nobody else to choose for the short-term."

"And I'm your best choice?"

"John, we've read your record from the 25th and can see that you were involved in just about every facet of operating in the bush. Christ, you even earned two Bronze Stars because of what you know and what you did. I think the new L-T can learn a great deal from you during those two weeks. Follow your instincts and help save a few more lives before you go home."

"How is the new L-T with this scenario?"

"He doesn't know yet, but won't have a choice in the matter. In fact, only a select few on this hill even know we're leaving in a couple of days."

"Cap, both you and Top have been very good to me since I've come to the Company. I'd like to help you out, but I really don't think I'm qualified to do what you are asking."

"You are more qualified then you know. I have the utmost respect for your judgment and know that you'll be successful."

"I don't have a choice, do I?"

"No son, you don't."

"Okay, Cap, I only hope my luck continues to hold out."

"You'll do fine without luck!"

"When do I go?"

"Why don't you go back to your celebration inside, I'll even send over some cold beer. Take a couple of hours to party and then gather all your gear and come to see me. I'll take you over and introduce you to the L-T and the rest of your new team."

Pollack was not happy with the decision but acknowledged the officer with an affirmative shake of the head.

"Thank you, John!" Both men walked away, leaving Pollack to his own thoughts.

He leaned against the sandbags of the bunker and thought, 'I'm not qualified and too apprehensive to lead a Platoon. Other people must see a different side of me that I don't realize. I am a loner and have had to only worry about saving my own ass. Now I have to worry about the safety and well being of an entire Platoon. Earlier in my tour, I was a know-it-all and unafraid to take chances, often taking more risks than I should have, especially when walking point. Now that I'm short, I feel like a Cherry all over again, experience or not. These are going to be the longest two weeks of my life. I hope I don't get overly cautious or paranoid in the bush. That would be dangerous too, and I might overlook something obvious and cause someone to get hurt. If that happened, it will be hard to live with that on my conscience.'

The bush had, in fact, been very quiet when the Americans were out on patrols; very few units had engaged the enemy and even then, the firefights were very brief. It appeared the gooks only picked on the ARVN's, who were attacked and getting beat up every day. Some of the Americans soldiers had garnered the opinion that the gooks purposely tried to stay out of their way, hoping the lack of contact may send the 101st home sooner.

Of course, nothing ever went according to plan. Some rumors generally came true, but assumptions had never been correct.

When leaving the hill with the First Platoon, Pollack was fully loaded with supplies for four days. He carried a compass around the neck and had two maps stuffed into his trouser pocket. He was pleased that his load felt much lighter and more comfortable overall, without carrying the extra weight of the twenty-six pound radio and spare batteries.

When the birds unloaded First Platoon at their destination, Pollack took readings from his compass to confirm his location. He also looked around to familiarize himself with some of the outstanding landmarks and indicated them on the map for future reference. Once they were away from the LZ, he would take a reading from any two such landmarks to pinpoint his location on the map. However, the method would not work in triple canopy jungles, so he had to depend on marking rounds from a nearby artillery source.

First Platoon's first challenge was to cross the valley and climb to the top of Hill 373. The mountain looked just like any other and was only five-hundred meters away on the map; however, it would take most of the day, as a smaller hill must be traversed first along the way.

Most all hills in the bush were named for their elevation, as indicated in meters, on a map, unless, of course, a firebase stood on top. Other hills, such as Hamburger Hill, were named after a significant battle. That particular fight lasted several days and was referred to as a meat grinder, thus the reason for the moniker. Pork Chop Hill was another example of a hill made infamous during the Korean War.

When First Platoon reached the base of Hill 373, Pollack and the L-T had their first disagreement. Lieutenant Bozolynsky insisted on sending the entire Platoon up the hill at the same time in the event the enemy was dug in on top. Pollack, instead, did not want to risk the entire Platoon and thought it safer for them to only involve one Squad. The most experienced point man, Chris, was in the Third Squad and had a reputation of being an excellent tracker with good instincts. It made perfect sense to send that Squad up and if they saw any signs of danger en route, they could retreat without getting the entire Platoon trapped. The L-T's face was beet red, either from rising blood pressure or embarrassment, and he was unable to provide a clear reason to support his stand. He conceded to Pollack who quickly dispatched the recon team.

The hill had seen much activity over time and many pathways led up and down from the thousand foot high summit. It was not part of a mountain chain, but it did overshadow many other standalone hills in this part of the valley. The slope and rising ridgelines were not as steep as other hills in the area, and therefore, would allow the recon patrol to move swiftly to the top.

Forty minutes later, a lone runner descended and rejoined the balance of the Platoon. They had found nothing unusual on the way to the top, and had secured the summit, awaiting the arrival of their fellow soldiers.

When the Platoon was together on top, Chris appeared anxious while waiting for Pollack and 'Bozo' to join him.

"Sir, I found some enemy signs on the back side of the hill. Can you and the Sergeant follow me so you can have a look for yourselves?"

The two men followed Chris to the opposite side of the hilltop.

"I found these after sending the runner down to get you." He pointed to the dusty ground; several boot imprints headed down a path and away from the summit.

"What's your opinion?" Pollack asked.

"I think somebody was up here and saw us when the Squad first came up and then bugged out when they saw we weren't leaving."

"They do look fresh. What do you think, L-T?"

"They're boot prints and somebody from the Squad must have come to this side of the hill and walked around before you came over here."

"L-T, those are not GI boot prints!" Pollack stepped into the dust just to the side of the other footprints. "See, the design is different, and the feet are much smaller."

'Bozo' took a knee and looked over the prints. "Okay, I see the difference now, but what makes you think these are recent? They look like they've been here a while."

"How about mine, L-T? Does it look old to you too?"

Before 'Bozo' could respond, Chris interrupted. "Sarge, come and take a look at this. It might shed some light and help determine the age of these prints." All three walked another ten feet down the pathway where Chris took a knee and grabbed part of a bush, pulling the branches upward. "What do you think about this?"

Several twigs were broken and the fractures still wet to the touch. Chris dropped the branch and pointed out several more on shrubbery leading downhill.

"This is not a good sign."

"What do you mean, Sergeant?"

"L-T, the breaks are still moist, which means this happened within an hour or so. I'm not sure just how many people were here, but it's certain that they left this hilltop in a hurry after spotting us."

"So that means they're gone, and most likely won't return, because we're up here now. This is good news and should make our job easier."

Chris and Pollack looked to one another and saw the disappointment in each other's eyes. Both were quite aware of trouble brewing, and Chris' opinion would only fall upon the L-T's deaf ears. So it was up to Pollack to convince Bozo that the Platoon was at risk and plans were needed before dark. "L-T, we need to talk. Chris, you can rejoin your Squad and I'll get with everybody else in a few."

Chris walked away. "L-T, take a walk with me." The two men walked over to the path on the side of the hill near the disrupted shrubbery. "Sir, the gooks know we're up here."

"So what's the big deal, Sergeant?"

"L-T, you have to trust in what I'm trying to tell you. The First Platoon is going to be in deep shit if we stay on top of this hill tonight."

"You know our orders, Sergeant. We're supposed to stay on this hill for the next three days and send out patrols."

"We can still do that, but we need to outsmart the gooks so we don't get hurt tonight."

"What is so special about tonight?"

"First, let's review the facts. We find enemy boot prints and evidence of a hasty retreat. So there may have only been a couple of gooks on lookout and watching the valley from up here. That's most likely the reason they didn't fire at our people, and instead, beat a path off the hill. Second, they could also be part of a larger group, and what they'll do next probably depends on what our next move will be."

"What makes you think something will happen?"

"I don't know. It's just a hunch. They had to have seen us land earlier today and now they know we're up here. If we continue downhill after them, they could either booby trap our advance or spring an ambush on us. If we stay up here, then they'll most likely set us up for a mortar barrage tonight."

"We'll just have to dig our foxholes a little deeper and stay put right here."

"L-T, why put the men at risk? The gooks know we're here and most likely know exactly how many of us there are. We have absolutely no idea how many gooks there are or where they're waiting. We need a plan for the night."

"What do you suggest we do, big shot?"

Pollack was taken aback by the comment and could not understand his hostility or his ignorance. He also wondered why the L-T resented him so much.

"I'm pretty sure we're being watched right now, so we should give them every indication that we're staying on the hilltop tonight. We'll dig our foxholes, put out trip flares and Claymores as we normally would when preparing an NDP. Then after it gets dark, we'll take our gear and silently move back down to the base of the hill the way we came up earlier. There, we can set up a small perimeter for the night and also keep an eye on the trails around the hill."

"And just what do you hope to accomplish by doing this?"

"When they mortar us tonight, we'll be in a much better position to direct artillery onto them without having to duck mortar rounds from deep inside of a foxhole. We'll hear the tube firing and will have a much better chance of silencing it. We can pre-plan coordinates with the CP and reference them during the fire mission."

"And what if they don't mortar us tonight? What then?"

"Well shit, sir, we just move back up in the morning. The foxholes will already be dug. We can then dispatch our patrols and stay there tomorrow night. We've got nothing to lose."

"I think it's all a waste of time. I say we stay here tonight."

"Lieutenant, the gooks did us huge favors by letting us know they were up here. Had that not happened, the situation would be much different and I wouldn't be pressing the issue. I thought we could work together, but I'll go over your head if I have to. This is a serious situation and you need to use a little common sense."

Both men rose and stood toe to toe. "You're not calling anyone. I'm in charge of this Platoon, and until you outrank me, you'll do as I say." The Lieutenant's voice grew louder, which attracted the attention of many of the soldiers nearby. Chris had already briefed his Squad and many of the others in the Platoon, so they had an idea of what the argument was about.

Pollack maintained his cool and kept his voice at a normal level. "Look, sir, I do fully understand that you are in charge, but right now you're just a hard-headed asshole that happens to be an officer. I've seen shit like this time and time again during my eleven months here and have learned much more than you were ever taught in ROTC. People survive by instincts and hunches here in the Nam. I've only got a couple of weeks left in this hellhole, and plan to take every necessary precaution to make certain I stay alive along with everybody else on this hilltop. I will not tolerate some college-educated ROTC graduate thinking he knows better."

"Watch your mouth, Sergeant. I could have you busted to Private for talking to me that way."

"You know, I don't really give a fuck, sir. You do what you have to do. Just give me some consideration by letting me do my job."

"Let you do your job? Shit, soldier, you're trying to do mine."

"Call it what you like, sir. All I'm trying to do is to keep every member of this Platoon alive until it's time for me to go home, and I'll do that with or without your help."

He didn't respond. Instead, he kept looking at the ground and shuffling his feet back and forth in the dirt.

"Sir, I'm trying to keep you alive too."

The L-T kicked a stone across the top of the hill and got into Pollack's face with fire in his eyes.

"You know, Sergeant, I don't like you or your attitude. I think you're just a smartass nineteen year-old punk. You think you're hot shit because you've been here so long. Well, I'm not buying it. You kissed the Captain's ass while you were in the CP, and now that you've made Sergeant, he's letting you feel your rank a little before you go home."

"Are you finished yet, sir?" Pollack interrupted.

"No, I'm not."

"Too fucking bad! I don't have time to argue with you anymore. It's getting late and these people need to know the plan."

Pollack turned to leave and the L-T took hold of his arm. "The plan is that we are staying on top tonight!"

The young Sergeant exploded. "You are really a stubborn person. Why don't you get it through your thick skull that I'm trying to help you? I didn't want to be here, but the Captain felt I might be able to teach you something about the jungle. But you don't want to learn. All you give a fuck about is your rank. You want to play your little game of war and make decisions based on what you learned in a book back in college. Well mister, this isn't a fucking game. People get killed out here. Have you ever seen a dead fellow soldier blown to pieces? What are you going to do when somebody in this Platoon gets killed because of one of your dumbass decisions? Are you going to say you're sorry and not make the same dumbass mistake again? Do you think your troops will follow you into battle knowing that you will get them killed? You want to lead men to destruction, then you go right ahead, but count me out."

Pollack walked away, heading toward the RTO to call the Captain. As he passed the Cherries, many of them sat, eyes wide and mouths agape in awe, never before hearing a confrontation like that between an officer and an enlisted man. It was also clear that the soldiers who'd been in country for a while agreed with Pollack and gave him a silent 'thumbs up' signal when making eye contact.

Pollack had the radio receiver in hand and was ready to make the call when the L-T stopped him.

"Hold on, Sergeant. We'll do it your way tonight. But if nothing happens, you'll regret it."

"Regret it? What are you going to do, send me to Vietnam? Don't threaten me, sir. You don't know what I'm capable of doing." Pollack hesitated for just a moment then smiled broadly, looking the Lieutenant straight in the eye. "Thanks for supporting my plan, sir. I'm sure you'll find it much safer this way."

Bozo bit his tongue. "We'll see."

"I'll get everything organized right away. I suggest you inform the Captain on what we've found and what we intend to do tonight."

"Yes, Sergeant," he responded sarcastically.

Pollack just let it slide and gathered the Squad leaders to inform them of their plans for that night. He wanted everyone to be very obvious in their actions to give the perception of staying on the hill that night, feeling carefree. Foxholes were to be dug, sleep positions prepared, and soldiers had to walk around the hilltop, peeking over the crest of the hill whenever they could. Then when darkness descended, he wanted lighters flicked and lit cigarettes waved around in a stealthy sort of way that didn't make it obvious.

After he shared the plan, Pollack studied his map and chose eight reference locations surrounding the hill, assigning each a number. He helped the RTO code the coordinates and then got on the horn with Fuzzy to arrange the preset targets. This would allow for a much faster response from the firebase artillery units when they were called for the fire mission.

After an hour passed, Pollack sat down next to the L-T at his sleep position to go over the plan and preset artillery map coordinates. Surprisingly, Pollack found him to be more receptive and supportive than earlier.

At a little after nine, Pollack was comfortable that it was dark enough for their plan to work and called for the men to move back down to the base of the hill. They stayed low to the ground when moving across the hilltop so as not to create a silhouette against the lighted sky, thus exposing them to whoever might be watching.

The men moved cautiously through the black of night, surprisingly quiet as they moved along the path downhill. Thirty minutes later, they reached the valley floor and silently dispersed into the surrounding foliage on the side of the hill.

The L-T and Pollack stayed awake long after the main group had bedded down for the night. When midnight arrived without incident, he whispered to Pollack.

"So much for your hunch, Sergeant. Is it okay if I go to sleep now or will I miss something?"

"Do what you want, sir."

"Eating crow leaves a bitter taste, doesn't it?"

"Sir, just get off my ass."

"I'm not on it yet."

Pollack saw a smirk on the L-T's face when he turned away to lie down. Pollack was pissed and wanted to avoid any further confrontation with Bozo, so he picked up his equipment and moved next to the RTO about fifteen feet away.

He had heard stories during his tour about men rebelling against their leaders and taking action into their own hands. They called it 'fragging' in Vietnam, which was severe retribution for stupidity and the lack of common sense - the action having resulted in serious injury or death to men following orders. Survival was paramount in war, and repeated action by somebody purposely putting you in harm's way without remorse was dealt with in a permanent manner.

In the bush, firefights and mortar attacks had been the preferred backdrops for many of these deliberate assassinations. It's been said that in the rear, sometimes grenades were tossed into either officer shitters or into their quarters when the opportunity presented itself. Pollack didn't personally know of any such events occurring in the units he'd been with, but his recent dealings with Bozo made him realize why someone would even think about committing such a despicable act in the first place.

During Basic Training and Advanced Infantry Training, those individuals who always got the Platoon in trouble and made them suffer for something he did were given a 'blanket party' as a warning that his fellow Platoon members were unhappy with him and wanted him to straighten up. This message was normally delivered in the wee hours of the night when everyone was supposed to be sleeping. Several individuals would participate in the punishment and would place a bar of soap into a towel, then hold it by the four corners like a sling. It became a homemade swinging persuader. Normally two people were assigned to cover the target with a blanket and to hold him down while the others beat him about the body with the swinging bars of soap. It usually lasted for less than a minute and then everybody quickly retreated to their bunks to feign sleep. When the target pulled the cover off, there was nobody standing around to blame. Sometimes these warnings worked immediately and the message understood. However, some required a second party before it sank in. Drill Sergeants would notice bruises and cuts on a recruit but would never intervene or get involved in this process.

A little after three in the morning, the two guys on radio watch shook Pollack awake. "Sarge, Sarge, wake up!"

Pollack sat up quickly and tried to focus his eyes in the darkness. "What is it?"

"We just heard tubes firing to our front."

The hilltop above suddenly erupted as mortar rounds began to land; one exploded every ten seconds. The grunts were wide awake after the first round detonated, and continued to watch the light show above.

- 396 -

Pollack unfolded his map, covered himself with his poncho liner, and then turned on his red lens flashlight to review his preset locations. He took a compass reading and saw that he was very close to preset six.

"How far away do you guys place those tubes?" he asked from underneath the blanket.

"I'd guess about three hundred meters," responded one of the two men.

Pollack uncovered and saw the L-T already moving toward them on his knees.

"Better call in for the big guns to silence those tubes. Tell Fuzzy to use preset six and add one-hundred and left one-hundred. You can adjust the fire after the first rounds hit."

Pollack could see a look of disbelief on the L-T's face in the flash of each explosion and couldn't believe he actually smiled when reaching for the radio handset. The L-T called in the mission to Stud, who was already in contact with the artillery unit on the nearby firebase. Three artillery rounds landed in the expected location, but the mortar tubes continued to fire. The L-T added another fifty and left fifty. Seconds later the next barrage came in and the mortars stopped. Two more fine adjustments were made and another three rounds sent on their way; the sequence is repeated twice more before the fire mission was terminated.

"I just wanted to make sure we got them," the L-T said meekly after the end of the fire mission.

"Good shooting, sir!" Several men offered up whispered congratulations.

He was all smiles now and scooted up close to Pollack so that no one else could hear their conversation. "Sergeant, I'm sorry. You were right."

"No need to apologize. Just help me do my job."

"You got it."

Pollack felt good about what had just happened. Twelve mortar rounds exploded on the hilltop; not one person was hurt, and it looked like the Lieutenant had finally seen the light. It was turning out to be a great day.

The two men got along just fine from then on. No more bickering or threats to each other, and the L-T showed more trust and respect for Pollack's suggestions. They finally worked together as a team.

It was like that for the next two weeks. First Platoon moved from mountain to mountain, changing tactics and direction from every hilltop.

Unfortunately, they set a clear and predictable pattern to their movements that neither of them realized. Re-supply had occurred three times since arriving in the valley, thus exposing their position each time. Their location and daily route of travel was monitored by those gooks hiding out in the hills and jungles; it would not take much thought to predict where the next re-supply would take place.

The Platoon had been very lucky so far, and had managed to kill eight NVA soldiers with mechanical ambushes during the last two weeks. They had yet to encounter a booby trap or fire their weapons, and because of that, no casualties occurred.

Pollack was nervous during his last re-supply in the field, as the war would officially be over for him in two days. He hoped the lucky streak continued, but knew it was only wishful thinking.

After the re-supply was complete, First Platoon crossed the hilltop and followed a ridge leading to the valley floor. They were only thirty minutes into their hump when the lead Squad triggered a booby trap. They were very fortunate when the tripwire pulled the grenade into a tree before it exploded, thus shielding the men and absorbing most of the explosion and shrapnel. Two of the men suffered minor wounds; they were quickly attended to and the file of men continued their decent. The point man became hyper vigilant and soon came upon a second trip wire several minutes later.

Upon investigation, they found another grenade attached to a second trip wire. They cut the wire and continued forward, but shifted their line of travel to a higher portion of the ridge.

They moved less than one-hundred steps when a third trip wire was discovered, once again attached to a grenade.

The L-T and Pollack felt this to be too much of a coincidence and felt very apprehensive now about continuing along the same route. They decided against venturing any further and returned to the hilltop.

Only two options remained at that time: first, spend the night in the current location where the re-supply had taken place; or secondly, move downhill the way they came up earlier in the day and then set up an NDP in the valley.

They found the hilltop didn't meet their needs. The ground was very hard and rocky; it would take forever to dig foxholes there.

Ample time remained for them to leave by the trail they made coming up. So after a short break, they moved off the hilltop for a second time.

Movement had been halted after descending one-hundred and fifty feet, when the point man spotted yet another booby-trap. But this time, it was on the same trail they created earlier when climbing to the top. It dawned on the men that the gooks were watching them and that they were trapped on the God-forsaken hilltop.

After discussing the situation with Cap over the radio, he suggested that the First Platoon remain on the hill until morning when choppers would be able to evacuate them from their prison. All except Pollack would be moved to a different hilltop nearby. The Sergeant would remain on board and would fly to the rear to out-process and go home.

There was no doubt in anyone's mind that they would be in plenty of trouble after it grew dark. Pollack and the L-T repeated the exercise from the first night together and chose preset targets for artillery, calling them in to Fuzzy. Meanwhile, everybody else tried desperately to dig a hole in the rock hard ground. Their only rewards were a small oval hole no more than a foot deep, and blisters that broke and bled. Unlike the other hilltops, that one had particularly higher brush and thicker foliage around the crest of the hill and downward which made it impossible for anyone to see the activity on the hilltop from below. One or two of the men had given up and had already scouted out the conditions fifty feet down the side of the hill.

"Sir, Mikey and I scooted down the hill a bit and found the ground much softer and easier to dig. We should consider moving off the hilltop and ring the hill down where we found it softer."

"How far down?"

"Fifty feet!"

"You know, L-T, they make a good point. We can sneak down, dig foxholes, and set up some Claymores and trip flares all around the perimeter. We've enough bodies to set up a ring of foxholes about every twenty feet or so."

"What about the booby traps that had been left for us?"

"The men will have to probe the ground as they are moving downward and inform anybody if something is found."

"Isn't that dangerous?"

"Being on this very hilltop without any protection will be more dangerous."

"Sarge," Mikey interrupted, "it'll be perfect down below because there are some outcroppings of rocks and we can set up under them and have some kind of overhead protection when the mortars start dropping on the hill."

"Are you willing to take the risk with all the booby traps we've found so far?"

"L-T, we've already gone there and back and haven't seen anything that could hurt us."

"Let me get the Squad leaders together and see if we have their support. Mikey, I already know your decision. I'll be back in a short."

Pollack gathered the men around and explained the option. There was no discussion and everybody thought it to be an excellent idea, even if it meant being alone all night long with your closest neighbor twenty feet away.

Maintaining a low profile, each man crawled down the hillside to his assigned location. It was true; the earth was much softer and easier to dig in. Not everyone had been fortunate enough to find rock outcroppings close by, but nevertheless, dug their foxholes deep enough to protect them during the one sleepless night. Dead tree limbs, large rocks, and anything else that would help fortify their position was collected and used. Trip flares and Claymores were set out only ten feet to their front, dangerously close, but it was as far as anyone cared to venture in the thick vegetation.

When nightfall arrived, the men felt confident that they had been stealthy enough in setting up their NDP. The thick shrubbery and high vegetation provided sufficient concealment for all their activity and movement. Of course, since they would not be able to communicate with each other above a whisper, they would be on one-hundred percent alert and tasked with protecting their portion of the wide perimeter. Signals would be sent around the perimeter once an hour to ensure everybody was awake and okay. They did not consider a ground attack as the heavy vegetation made one highly unlikely. Instead, they were more concerned about the expected mortars and rockets that would be raining down upon them very soon.

Pollack felt exceptionally anxious at having to spend his last day in the bush in that kind of a situation. He was scared, and much more so than his very first night in the bush. The Sergeant had prayed to God, asking Him to watch over him on this, his final night in the field. He didn't want it to end here, especially after everything he'd been through so far.

He thought of Zeke, Bill Sayers, Junior, and Sixpack, and how their lives had impacted his. He also thought about those fellow Wolfhounds who had been transferred to other units and wondered how they were coming along. They were all his friends and brothers and he hoped to see them again sometime during his lifetime.

At midnight, the sound of mortar tubes firing from the jungle below interrupted his thoughts. Everyone on the side of the hilltop knew they had several seconds to prepare themselves for the worst; all cringed in fear when the rounds began exploding on the hilltop above. Some of the men had pulled their rucksacks into the foxhole with them and used them as cover while they curled up in the bottom. No screams of pain erupted from the men around the perimeter; instead, some of the newer Cherries called out for their mothers. The barrage lasted ten minutes and had been centered on the top of the hill. They were very lucky and not one person was hurt.

The L-T had been directing artillery and using the preset positions which he and Pollack had plotted earlier. They weren't sure if the mortar team had been silenced by artillery or not; however, if they weren't hit, the rounds were close enough to scare them away for now.

An hour later, a second barrage started. Most assumed it a response to not seeing Medivac choppers arrive to evacuate the wounded, and they tried once again, but from a different firing location. This time, the gooks moved the rounds across the hilltop and over the sides near their foxholes. First Platoon responded with an artillery barrage of its own and the tube stopped firing after two salvos. The Americans had been spared a second time and nobody was hurt.

At 0230, the enemy's third attempt to inflict damage upon the Americans failed once again. This time, the mortars were directed more to the side of the hill, moving them down toward the valley. Some secondary explosions occurred as some of the booby traps exploded harmlessly below.

The L-T had reacted each time the tube fired and continued to fine-tune his return fire, moving the rounds around in an attempt to find the mortars. All in all, the gooks had fired over thirty rounds during their three barrages, and the Americans had fired twice that many artillery shells back at them. Both sides were unsuccessful in finding one-another, so their luck continued to hold.

Daybreak was only a few hours away and Pollack counted the hours left in the field. Quiet once again, it was anybody's guess what would happen next. All hoped the mortar crew had given up for the night and wouldn't pursue their attempts to find the dug in Platoon. They needed to remain vigilant, as sufficient time still remained for the gooks to come up and find them.

A whisper was heard from Pollack's neighbor to the left, "Sarge, you okay?"

"I'm good!"

"L-T wants a sit-rep from the perimeter. He also says to stay on your toes and watch downhill for movement. Pass it on."

"Got it!" Pollack communicated with his other neighbor and also found him to be in good health. The message was received and then relayed to the next hole, and so on, until it came back to the L-T who had originated it.

A sudden and loud noise in the valley instantly drew the attention of those in the First Platoon, dug in on that particular side of the hill. It sounded like a rush of air, almost like the sound a bottle rocket makes after you light the fuse, but much louder. After a few seconds, another such loud 'swooshing' sound was heard from the same area. "Rockets! I saw two pair firing away from us," whispered Pollack's neighbor. "The L-T also saw them launch and will engage with artillery."

Pollack looked out from his foxhole, quite concerned about the rockets, as they were a first for him. He'd neither witnessed a launch nor seen the effects afterwards.

The sound of two back-to-back explosions, mere seconds apart, erupted on a hilltop about a mile away from the First Platoon's location. The detonations sounded much louder than artillery, even at that distance. A light flickered on the horizon, and the bright glow on that hilltop grew as the seconds ticked away. The quietness was interrupted as the first of several artillery rounds landed in the valley near the suspected rocket launchers some six-hundred meters away. There were no secondary explosions heard and the fire mission was called after three salvos into that area.

A loud whisper startled Pollack, "Sergeant, the L-T wants you to meet him on top of the hill."

Pollack's curiosity was aroused and wondered why the L-T would even want to meet on the hilltop with all the rockets and mortars firing through the valley. He put on his ammo harness, took his flashlight, map, and weapon, and started to ascend the fifty feet to the summit along the pathway he'd created earlier. The L-T waited for him. "Sergeant, let's go back to the foxhole that I'm sharing with the RTO. We can talk there."

The two men scurried down the pathway and moved as quickly and quietly as possible through the pitch-blackness of night.

"L-T, is that you?" a voice challenged from below.

"Yes, Spencer, Sergeant Kowalski is with me."

They reached the two-man hole and joined the RTO who sat on the back ledge of his foxhole and let his feet dangle into the blackness of the hole. Spencer had the handset glued to his ear.

"Anything change, Spencer?"

"No, sir, still the same."

"Sergeant, something's not quite right. Earlier when I tried to contact the Battalion FO in the CP to coordinate the fire mission against the rocket launchers, I couldn't reach Fuzzy and had to call the firebase directly."

"Did you try contacting the Captain?"

"Yeah, there's no answer there either."

"I've been able to speak with Second and Third Platoons, but haven't had any luck contacting the Fourth or the CP," Spencer volunteered.

"Who was on the hill that just got rocketed?"

"Nobody knows."

"Spencer, switch to the Battalion net and see if there's any traffic there."

The RTO dialed in the frequency and listened intently. "Sounds like Fourth Platoon is talking to Battalion."

"Let me have the handset, Spencer."

Somebody from the Fourth Platoon spoke directly to the Colonel, but Pollack didn't recognize the voice. Then when he heard the call sign, he knew it was the Platoon Sergeant. Four rockets had landed on the hilltop; there were many injured and dead. Only the one radio was available so he tried to coordinate everything at the same time. The Colonel responded that he would direct all support units to use that frequency so it would be easier for the Sergeant and everyone else.

Flares started to pop over the glowing hilltop and hang in the air, providing much needed light to those below. A number of gunships came on station and began circling overhead; only their running lights were on and the red beacons moved about like fireflies. There was no need for them to fire yet, but their presence allowed the pilots of the Medivac helicopters to feel more comfortable during the evacuations. In fact, several red flashing lights were aligned in the sky and moving toward the hilltop at that very moment. One by one, they dropped out of sight as they landed, only to reappear in the sky seconds later, executing tight turns and heading back the way they came.

"Looks like the Medivacs are extracting the wounded. Is there any word on the casualties or the CP?"

"Not yet, L-T. The Sergeant has his hands full coordinating the artillery, gunships, and Medivac pilots during all this chaos. Even the Colonel is keeping quiet."

The men continued watching the activity to their front and saw the string of flashing red lights of the Medivac Choppers heading back to the hilltop fifteen minutes later. Meanwhile, the L-T passed on the message that Fourth Platoon was hit by the rockets and were on the hill with all the activity taking place. His neighbor to the right acknowledged and passed it on to the next foxhole. Pollack wondered what would happen when the message got to his vacant hole. Somehow, two minutes later, the message completed the circuit.

"I'm really concerned about what's happening on that hilltop. Wasn't the CP supposed to be attached to the Fourth Platoon tonight?"

"I believe you're right, Sergeant. Perhaps that's why we can't reach them on any of the frequencies. Maybe the radios are just damaged."

"Hopefully, you're correct. But it does bother me to see so many Medivac choppers landing. A shitload of people got hurt on that hilltop, L-T!"

Pollack handed the receiver back to Spencer. "Let us know when the Platoon Sergeant starts to brief the Colonel about what has happened."

"No problem!"

Pollack was anxious to find out about Cotton Top, Stud, Fuzzy, and Cap. From what he'd heard so far, it didn't look good. Even if the radios had been damaged, one of them would have been communicating with the Colonel instead of the Platoon Sergeant.

At five in the morning, the sky to the east began to lighten, signaling the approaching dawn of a new day.

"L-T, the Colonel's on the horn with the Sergeant."

This time the L-T took the handset.

"Four 122mm rockets hit the hilltop. The first one landed in the midst of the CP, killing everyone and destroying the radios. Nine killed, thirty-one wounded; Platoon strength is less than twenty. Some of them have minor wounds and are still with the Platoon. Survivors will be pulled from the hill at first light and brought back to the rear area-"

"L-T, if it's okay with you, I want to head back to my foxhole. We've still got another hour before daylight and we still need to keep our guard up until we're pulled off this hill."

He nodded his head in agreement, so Pollack returned uphill and then back down to his own foxhole. Once there, he dropped into the hole and informed his neighbors of his return.

Pollack was devastated. The CP took a direct hit and they were all dead. He thought back to that last day they spent together. It was the day of his promotion and Pollack remembered the mock ceremony and homemade paper stripes. The smiling faces of Cotton Top, Stud, Fuzzy and even the Captain burned fresh in his memory.

Was it fate that put him in the First Platoon? Perhaps the man upstairs had other plans for him, either later that day, or maybe twenty years in the future. He shuddered to think that if he hadn't received the promotion, he would most likely have been on that hilltop and had his life snuffed out along with the other members of the CP. He was sorry for their losses, but thankful that he survived.

Pollack tried to shake the vision from his head and knew that he must put it aside for the time being to focus on their own situation. He wasn't out of the woods yet and still has to survive until his airplane left for home.

In the morning, a flight of choppers picked up the First Platoon and transported them to another hilltop on the outskirts of the A Shau. As the men jumped off the chopper, Pollack thanked them and wished them luck. He remained on board and waved to the men as they deployed around the hilltop to secure the new perimeter. He would never forget the looks on their faces as he left the bush for the last time and returned to Phu Bai.

By eleven-thirty in the morning, Pollack had turned in all his supplies and weapon, received his travel orders, and said his final goodbyes; a sincere and deep hug was shared with the First Sergeant before boarding a truck in a convoy headed for Cam Rahn Bay.

At eight-thirty in the evening, on August 4, 1971, two-hundred twenty soldiers boarded a Pan American jet bound for the United States. Chronologically, they were all very young and most would not be able to buy beer when getting home. However, every one of them looked twenty years older. The pain, suffering, and horror they'd experienced during this past year were evident, especially in their eyes, which appeared distant and hollow. Faces were also drawn tight from stress and fear; lines were hardened and stern looking. Some of the men who boarded had eyes wide in disbelief; unable to comprehend that the war was finally over for them. They followed those in front of them like mindless zombies.

It was very quiet onboard as the jet taxied to the far side of the airfield and then turned onto the main runway. The turbines whined loudly, pushing everyone back into their seats when the plane accelerated. All on board held their breath and waited for the mortars and rockets to land. As soon as the wheels of the aircraft left the ground, there was one huge cheer. Everyone clapped. Many smiled, while others sat silently, crying.

Pollack sat back in his seat, thankful that he had somehow survived this war; it was truly a miracle after all he'd been through.

Zeke had called it 'luck' and a person either had it or he didn't. He thought about it and agreed that he had his share of luck during his tour of duty. He should have died or been seriously injured on several occasions, but luck allowed him to make it. He clasped his hands behind his head and looked up at the ceiling above him. He noticed a tiny inscription written next to one of the air nozzles. He had to get out of his seat to read it: 'When I die, I'm going straight to Heaven – because I've served my time in Hell.'

He sat back down and smiled broadly, knowing that he would never experience anything like this ever again. The rest of his life would be charmed.

Epilogue

The return flight took them across the northern route over Japan and Alaska to a final destination in Ft. Lewis, Washington.

There, they were shepherded off the plane and moved across the landing field to a large building. On the way, many signs greeted them. Some said the country was proud of them. Some offered thanks. Others simply read: 'Welcome Home'.

Once inside the building, everyone stripped, showered, endured another physical examination, and then requisitioned new uniforms, much smaller than what they wore a year ago. Pollack was surprised with how much he had changed physically, rarely paying any attention to it in Vietnam. He remembered that upon his leaving for war, he weighed one-hundred ninety-six pounds and had a thirty-six inch waist. That day, he weighed one-hundred fifty-five pounds and had a twenty-nine inch waist.

When they were all fully dressed with the appropriate ribbons and campaign medals in place, the soldiers were escorted to yet another building where they were served a steak dinner.

There were no speeches or parades. When they finished eating, they were driven by bus to the airport and had to make their own connections to get home.

The whole process had been repeated thousands of times and just happened too fast for many of the returning veterans. One night you're getting shot at and looking at the bodies of your dead friends, and then two days later, you're sitting on your front porch, watching the kids play in the street and the cars drive by. There was no transition period to unwind.

Pollack did not regret anything he did during his time in Vietnam, but found it difficult upon his return. He was the only person from his graduating class and group of friends that went to Vietnam, so nobody could share his experiences or even have the faintest idea of what he'd gone through.

Friends and family tried to understand but they weren't quite able to comprehend what he told them. He was only able to get so far before they lost interest or rolled their eyes. In their minds it was just a bunch of war stories that he was blowing out of proportion. After all, it was impossible for somebody to go through all that.

Most of these conversations usually ended with Pollack saying, "I guess you had to be there to really understand."

Pollack never heard from any of his former friends in Vietnam and does not know whether or not they even survived. Trying to find them after the war would prove to be futile as only first names and nicknames were used during the war. Even though he may know the city, state and first name of "Scout" for instance, he'd have a most difficult time ever finding his friends again.

###

Thank you for taking the time to read my book, Cherries - I hope you have enjoyed it. A blog site is available with more posts and information relating to this book. You can also view a slide show and physically see some of the items referenced in the book. Please visit http://cherrieswriter.wordpress.com/ and leave your comments and questions about my story. I promise to respond to every posting.

About the author:

John Podlaski served in Vietnam during 1970 and 1971 as an infantryman with both the Wolfhounds of the 25th Division and the 501st Infantry Brigade of the 101st Airborne Division. He was awarded the Combat Infantry Badge, Bronze Star, two Air Medals, and a Vietnamese Cross of Gallantry. He has spent the years since Vietnam working in various management positions within the automotive industry, and he recently received his Bachelor of Science degree in Business Administration. John is a member of the Vietnam Veterans of America Chapter 154 and lives with his wife, Janice, in Sterling Heights, Michigan. This is his first novel.

LaVergne, TN USA
26 July 2010
190867LV00002B/105/P